FAMILY CONFESSIONS OMNIBUS

ANGEL LAWSON

A.K. ROSE

Hunted by my Stepbrothers

Foreword

Readers,

A few things before we dive into Hunted!

First, this work originally came out on Kindle Vella in serialized format. If you read it there, it's the same here—just bundled up! The series is currently on-going and if you're impatient for the next bundle, feel free to check it out on the Vella platform.

Second, friends and family looking to be supportive: please turn back. This isn't the series for you, not if you want to make eye contact over civilized meals in the future. Thank you.

Third, **trigger and content warnings**: this book is for real a dark romance about psycho stepbrothers, their two friends and their mission to hunt and kill. Their favorite prey? Their stepsister. In this book you can expect: non-con, dub-con, graphic murder, the disposal of bodies, bondage, kidnapping, mental and emotional gaslighting and I feel like ten other things that I should remember and can't. Just BE AWARE.

Thanks,

Angel & AK

Make sure you follow Angel on her Facebook Group, Angel's Antics to connect with authors, readers and all the good stuff: And for more about AK Rose

Website
TikTok
Instagram
Facebook

ONE

Kate

____

*T*HUMP.

They're at it again. The noise. The walking. The muffled goddamn voices above my room. I thought by now they'd be better at hiding what they do. They don't care. Of course they don't care. I mean, why would they? It's not like they give a shit about me, laying underneath their bedroom.

If the Davenport brothers have proven anything, it's that they don't give a shit about me.

I shift and turn, the house humid from the afternoon storm, hating the way my top sticks to my skin.

God, I didn't want to be back here, in this house... in this family. Four years away at school and it's like nothing has changed. A family of strangers, except for mom. Mom, who always does whatever Montie, my stepfather, wants.

Thump.

I flinch at the sound. I can't sleep, not with them on the floor above or the damn southern sweltering heat. *Bang.* The shutter smacks against the window, making me flinch. Jesus, this house. I never know what's causing the creaks and groans.

Is it the hundred-and-fifty-year-old rafters or the ancient oak tree out front, draped in ghostly Spanish moss? The house has been in Monte's family for generations and no matter how clean my mother or the housekeepers keep it, the scent of musty air clings to everything that resides inside.

I forgot how sticky the night breeze feels, nothing like the cooler weather up north. There, the heat of summer is still a few weeks away. Lightning flashes in the distance, the soft white lighting up my bedroom before it flickers and fades away. Thunder follows with a low creeping rumble.

No, not thunder. My senses sharpen at the sound. I lift my head from the pillow, listening. A car. *Their car.* The deep sound of the engine echoing off the trees. I rise from the bed, sliding my feet from under the sheets. The sounds are followed by the slam of a car door. One, two... only two tonight. For now, at least. They tend to roam in a pack, or at least they used to.

At the window, I adjust the curtain and lift my gaze, searching for the lick of cool air as headlights flare on the street far below my window.

I skim my hand against my breast. My fingers brushing my nipples, tight, puckered, aching with my impending period. The flimsy negligee is more lace than satin. Pink with matching panties. It's all I can stand to wear at night in this heat. The family is rich, *filthy* rich, so why the hell don't they have AC?

"It would detract from the historical preservation of Davenport Manor if we added air conditioning," I can hear Monte explain. God forbid we offend the preservation society for a little bit of comfort and sanity.

Down on the driveway, the car pulls out, headlights lighting the way until they are gone.

I breathe a sigh of relief knowing they're gone. I wouldn't be here now if it wasn't for the interview at the Gazette in the morning. I should've known better than to get a degree in a dying field–print journalism. But it's my passion. To my dismay, Monte pulled a few strings and got me the interview with one of his friends. Nepotism isn't the way I want to make it in the business–but my mother never would've let me live it down if I'd declined such a kind gesture from my stepfather. So here I am, back in Davenport Manor, sticky with sweat and listening to my stepbrothers bang around upstairs all night.

Some things never change.

I hate being here while they're home, especially when mom and Monte are gone. They'd already scheduled their trip when I announced I was coming back home to look for a job. I got home two days ago and have managed to avoid the boys the whole time.

Boys.

They're men, now. Twenty-five and twenty-four.

Thump.

I flinch and look at the ceiling. Lightning flickers again, this time brighter, bolder, carrying with it the faint scent of ozone on the thick air. I swallow more than suck, taking in that bitter scent and licking my lips, tasting salt and sweat.

Thump.

It's followed by another sound this time. Low and deep. A groan.

My heart thumps, muffling the sound as I swallow and glance at the window, searching the place where the car was parked. Still gone. Still empty... but that sound.

Moan...

"What the fuck?" I whisper, again staring at the ceiling.

The sounds were always the same; the thud of footsteps. The creak of the old hardwood floors. They did it on purpose; I was sure of it, just to piss me off. They were always the same, *my stepbrothers*. Moody. Brooding. Secretive.

Oliver and Jack Davenport.

Stay the fuck out of our way.

The words resound in my head. It was the first interaction we ever had. Sure made a lasting impression. The only one that counted, really. After that was a long succession of doors being slammed in my face and hostile glares from Jack, mostly. He's the oldest–the scariest. The main asshole who didn't care about getting a new little sister when our parents married. Oliver wasn't much better, although, sometimes, when we were alone, he'd talk to me, making me feel special. But then, just as fast, Jack would appear and whatever kindness he showed me would vanish quick as a whisper.

Mom would say they were just dealing with their own emotions about losing their mother. They were just hormonal teenage boys. Well, I was fourteen, with raging hormones of my own.

"*Help...*"

The voice is louder, stronger, and I stumble back, slamming my hand against my chest. I wait a beat, then walk to the door, cracking it open. Listening, certain I'd heard wrong, I—

"*Help... someone help me...*"

I yank the door shut; the latch echoing in the quiet house, and press my back against the wood.

Fuck. This is my fault. I'd always had nightmares here. Always had the wildest imagination.

"Please..."

The word hit me like ice in my veins. I stop, panic roaring inside me as I muster up the courage to open the door again. "I heard wrong. I heard wrong. I heard—" I tell myself, but I know that I didn't hear anything wrong. I'm not crazy, I promise myself as I push the door open wider, glancing along the balustrade to the stairs. I step into the dark hallway. Dark and silent and old. My bare feet creak on the hardwoods as I near the stairs. "Mom?"

Silence answers, wind whistles through the cracks in the downstairs windows. I step out further, gripping the banister and move to the first step. "Mont?"

There was nothing. Nothing. My mind was playing tricks. I knew I shouldn't have had that last glass of wine—

"Anyone... please..."

I jerk, wrenching my gaze up to the stairs. The voice came from the third floor.

The one place I was forbidden to go in the house. A place where bad things happen. But that was years ago, and before I heard someone crying for help. I move without thinking, rounding the landing, and climb.

Stay the fuck out of our way.

"Stay the fuck out," I repeat, climbing the first stair and then the next. The house is hulking and mammoth. Character, that's what mom called it. The damn thing just creeped me out.

When mom and I moved into this house, it was my fourteenth birthday. Even then I was scared, weirded out by the size and musty smell. But all mom saw was a future. One where we weren't poor, and she was no longer a widow and single mother.

I try not to think about that as I climb the stairs. The third floor was off limits to everyone, including the housekeeper. I ignore the rules put in place all those years ago. I'm no longer a scrawny teenager intimidated by my stepbrothers and their friends.

"Help..."

Christ, the voice is louder the higher I go. "Hello?" I call out, inching to the top of the stairs. I scan the landing and squint, searching for the murky outline of the bedroom doors. My heart pounds remembering the only time I came this far into their territory. I'd paid for the violation. I clear my throat. "Jack? Oliver?"

My voice trails into a whisper as I quietly make my way to the first door.

Creak.

My pulse jumps with sound. Heart hammers, I jerk my gaze over my shoulder. But there's no one there. Just this house. "This creepy fucking house. I swear I'm gonna die of a goddamn heart attack in this place." I say it out loud, like I can force myself to reason. I turn back, moving to the doorway and grip the handle.

My nightie sticks against my thighs, pulling taut as I turn and ease open the door, inch-by-inch. "If this is some kind of twisted joke, I swear I'll scream so loud the entire neighborhood will hear." My voice betrays me. It's nothing but a croak.

I can't hear a thing over the booming of my heart. Still, I force myself to move, stepping inside the bedroom. The scent of something dark and sultry hit me. I recognize the scent, the man it belongs to, and inhale deep...

Only that's a mistake. Under the seductive scent of something erotic and manly, a sickening, copper smell hits my nostrils... *blood.*

I reach out, my fingers smacking against the doorframe, before I reach along the wall, searching. *Click.* I hit the switch, and the room floods with a dull, yellow light, leaving me to turn my head. I freeze.

"Help me." The voice comes from a man and for a second I don't understand what I'm seeing...

No.

God...

It doesn't just smell like blood, it's there. Everywhere. The guy lies on his side on the ground. His hands tied behind his back, curled up, with his ankles strapped together by tape. A chair turned over behind him. There's blood *everywhere,* weeping from his head, dripping into his eyes. He looks up at me.

"Jesus." I glance around, trying to absorb what has become of Jack's bedroom. There's a bench along the wall. Spread across the surface are dozens of knives. Several coated in the sticky residue of blood. "What is this? Who are you?"

"Untie me." The guy pleads and closes his eyes. "Please, just untie me and let me go."

"I'm c-calling the cops," I stutter, moving back to the safety of the hallway.

"No." He shakes his head, his voice slurring. "Just let me go. I promise not to say anything. I promise you'll never hear from me again. *I just need to get out of here before they come back.*"

I step forward, glancing at those knives once more, and then kneel down. But I don't touch him. He's filthy, muddy, and God, bloody. I glance at the tape wrapped tight around his jeans and then drift my gaze up to his arms cinched around his back.

"The key." He urges, holding my eye. "You need to find the key."

"Key?"

"For the handcuffs."

Oh, shit. I nod. "Okay. Okay, I can do this," I say, more to myself than him. I rise and scan the bedroom, trying to figure out where they'd put the key. I spot a messy desk, although it was more than that, more like one of those investigation rooms the cops use on Murderers Most Wanted. A large map hangs over the desk, string zig-zags between photographs and hand-written notes. "Oh fuck, oh fuck," I chant to myself. This is bad. So fucking bad.

I search the desk, fumbling through drawers and under stacks of paper, but there's no key. I turn, spotting a duffle bag splayed open on his bed. I stumble forward and hesitate, not wanting to touch the damn thing.

"Hurry," the guy bleeding out on my stepbrother's bedroom floor whispers. *His anxiety is contagious.*

"I'm trying," I snap, then take a deep breath. It's just a normal day, right? Just a goddamn normal day in this hellhole.

I yank open the bag and rifle through the contents. Black masks. Black tape. Two rolls of it, because of course, I mean why wouldn't you have plenty, right? I yank through the stuff, touching cold steel before tearing my hand away.

I can't do this.

I can't...

Get your shit together, Katie! He's right. They'll be back soon.

Desperation kicks hard. I step forward, grabbing the handle of the bag and upend the contents on the bed. Metal glints underneath the mess. I shove rolls of plastic bags aside and grab the set of two tiny keys.

"Yes! That's it!" the guy shouts, as I turn and hurry toward him.

"I'm going to get you out of here." I kneel, filled with purpose, and reach for his hands. "And then we'll call the police."

He rolls onto me, his breath warm against my thigh. I should be more aware of how high my nightie rides, and how exposed I am, but I push that aside. This isn't the time to be self-conscious. Not when I'm saving someone's life.

My fingers tremble as I shove the key into the lock.

Creak.

The house shifts, only this time I don't care. I *can't* care. The lock gives a *click,* and the cuffs release, allowing his hands to fall. He rips the tape off from around his ankles, and I exhale in relief.

"I left my phone in my room, just let me go—" my words are cut short when I feel the tight grip of his fingers around my throat.

"Stupid bitch." He snarls, squeezing tighter. He isn't the helpless victim anymore. The glint in his eye, the curl of his lip, it says everything. He's not the prey, he's a predator.

Panic roars, and a scream is trapped by his fingers as he grips tight.

"Aren't you a doll?" he laughs. "Coming up here to save me like a good little bitch. It's going to be fun to cut you up." His breath is rancid and hot. "Right after I rip that pretty nightie off and stuff it in your mouth so no one will hear your screams while I fuck your last breath out of you."

His anger and rage are palpable. It tremors through his blood slicked fingertips. I see a flash of my future, my stepbrothers returning to find me exactly how he described. Would they laugh at stupid Kate for getting herself into such a mess?

His gaze jerks over my shoulder, and he stills.

The flash of silver glints beside me as a knife carves through the air and buries into the center of his throat. Then, with one savage jerk, his throat tears open. Blood shoots out, splashing my chest just like the warm, sultry night air. A scream rips free, shrill, *terrifying*, before something clamps across my mouth, cutting off the sound.

Warm leather flattens against my lips. A heavy breath near my ear. I'm hauled to my feet, pushed backwards and slammed against the wall. My head cracks with the impact, detonating white stars behind my eyes as I stare into the chilling eyes of a murderer.

"Shouldn't have come up here, little sister." Jack sucks in a hard breath and glances over his shoulder. The man chokes and sputters. His hands flap wildly against the floor as he bleeds out. Then my stepbrother turns that depraved glare my way. "Should've stayed the hell out of our way, like I told you to."

My heart booms. Terror screaming inside me as he lowers his gaze to the blood that drips down my breasts, adhering the thin fabric of my top against my chest. "The question is, Katie. What the fuck do we do with you now?"

TWO

Kate

"I know you've been gone for a while, sweet Katie, but surely you remember the first rule of living in Davenport Manor?" Jack says, his eyes dragging from my chest to meet mine. I only hold them for a moment, intimidated by the darkness lurking inside. I know they're gray, but in the shadowy light, they look black and soulless.

"Stay out of your way?" I say, inevitably looking over at the lifeless body on the floor. Moments before I'd untied him, tried to save him, then he turned on me. Right? Isn't that what happened? I'm no longer sure.

"So you do remember." His gloved fingers graze down my cheek to pinch my chin. "Too bad you didn't listen." He lifts an eyebrow. "Again."

"I-I heard him calling out. He was begging for help." I suck in air. "I thought it may be one of you."

"Nice try," he says. "He should've been dead, right, Ollie?"

My other stepbrother, Oliver, emerges from the corner. I'm not sure how long he's been standing there, watching us. Like his brother, bigger than the last time I saw him. His shoulders are broader and his features more defined. He's the yang to his brother's darker yin, but even with the lighter hair and eyes, it's clear they're related.

"He didn't have a pulse when we left," Oliver says, treating me as if I'm invisible. I wish his brother did the same, but his eyes haven't looked away from me since he pinned me to the wall. "Must've just been weak."

"Yeah well, that little mistake made things really fucking complicated." Sweat beads on Jack's forehead and he lifts his hand to wipe it off. It's then that I see he's still holding onto the knife, blood dripping off the end. A drop lands on my chest, still warm as it slides between my breasts. "Jesus, you're filthy."

"That's what you're worried about?" I ask. "Me being filthy?"

"I'm worried about evidence getting dragged all over the house," he replies. "Strip."

"What? You're *deranged*! I'm not–"

My argument falters when he tips the blade of the knife against my skin. Slowly, he drags it upward. The sting is faint but effective. He could plunge it into my throat so easily and be done with me in a heartbeat.

Just like he slaughtered the man on the floor.

My chest rises and falls, the point of the blade pressing into me with every breath. He carves it under my collarbone, slipping the tip beneath the thin strap of my nightie, and jerks upward, slicing it in two.

"That makes it twice you haven't followed my rules tonight, little sister. Want to go for three?" His grin is wicked. Daring. I slam my hand out, knocking the knife from his hand. He starts, eyes widening in surprise, but before either of us can react,

Oliver charges over, lunging for the knife and pointing it at the two of us.

"You," he says to Jack. "Now isn't the time for games. We have a fucking mess to clean up." He swings to me. "And you?" He narrows that gaze to mine and my heart twists in my chest. His eyes hold mine for the first time. His voice grows stony and cold. "Follow directions for once in your fucking life, especially if you want to keep it. I haven't decided what the hell we're doing with you, but if you think I won't toss you in the landfill next to this asshole just because your mother fucks our father, you're wrong."

He would. I know he would. There's no bluffing with the men I'm supposed to call family.

I learned that lesson the hard way.

Jack straightens, annoyance flickering across his features, but he doesn't argue. He holds out his hand. "Nightie."

I push off the remaining strap and let it fall to the floor. Covering my breasts with one arm, I bend and pick up the soiled lace and hand it over.

"Panties, too," he adds, looking down at the thin satin covering my crotch.

"They're not–"

He gives me a hard, calculated look and I remember Oliver's threat. I'd always suspected these guys were up to no good, but before tonight I had no idea they were actual... well, what are they? Kidnappers? Murderers? Serial killers? I had no freaking clue what I was dealing with here, but if I wanted to survive the night, I was going to have to adapt. Dropping my arm, I hook my thumbs in my panties and drag them over my hips.

"I see you like the natural look," Jack says, staring between my legs. "Nice."

Oliver snorts and adds. "Just means she isn't getting laid at that fancy college Dad paid for."

I wince. *Jesus.*

I've lived with all female roommates for years and barely had one boyfriend during that time. Grooming... down there just wasn't a necessity. Oliver looks over and takes me in and the warm, familiar, heat of humiliation trembles over my body. I pick up the panties and hand them over. They're wet. I know that and it only heightens the lick of desire slowly sliding between my legs when he rubs his thumb over the damp crotch.

"Good girl." He jerks his head to a door across the room. "Go stand in the shower and wait."

I shiver in the balmy night air and do as he says, hating how they make me feel. Why the hell did I have to come up here? Why couldn't I just stay away?

I skirt the edge of the room, making sure not to step in any of the dead man's blood. It's a relief when I push open the door and flip on the light, revealing the large bathroom.

I take a breath of clean, bloodless, air. It's as dark as the other room, but it's been fully renovated, walls and floors covered in a rich slate gray tile. The counter is made of black marble and the accents in brushed gold. Across the space is a second door, slightly open, and I see the second bedroom. Oliver's.

A tremor runs up my spine. I refuse to slip into the memory of what happened in there.

Bang. I flinch at the sound from the other room and jump into the shower, standing on the cool tiles.

Jack enters the room a minute later, stripped down to a pair of black boxer briefs.

Jesus Christ.

He was in good shape when I left, constantly working out, jogging, and lifting weights. He's transformed into something different—manly. Deadly. His abdomen ripples with lean, hard muscle. His chest smooth other than dark curls of hair scattered between his pecs. Tattoos circle his biceps, as well as across his ribs. I haven't seen him undressed before, not totally anyway, and I consume it all. Heat licks at the base of my neck as I sweep my eyes over the fine trail of hair beneath his navel, and between the hard lines of his hips. My mouth dries, and my nipples tighten. I avoid looking low, at the weapon I know he packs under those black briefs. I glance away as memories rise. Memories I don't want to relive.

Not here.

If he's aware of my struggle, he doesn't reveal it. He doesn't speak as he steps into the shower, spinning the faucet handle. The water gurgles then shoots out in a hard spray. I step out of the way, yelping at the cold water. He grabs the nozzle and lifts it off the hook, pointing it in the direction of my belly and chest.

"Grab the soap," he directs me, nodding at the bar on the shelf. I pick it up and catch that scent from earlier. Masculine and musky, and it hits me between my thighs. *God.* How can someone so evil smell so good? "Scrub down, head to toe. You need to get every speck of blood off your body." Our eyes meet and he winks. "Happy to help out in those hard-to-reach places if you need it."

I run my hands under the water and lather up, turning away from my stepbrother's imposing stare. The water turns hot and scalding, but I accept it. Anything to burn off the blood and grime. Pity it can't burn away the disgrace. I close my eyes and soap up my hair, feeling Jack step closer to hold the stream over my head. I let the heat roll over me. Under the stream of water, I gather the courage to ask, "Who was that man?"

Instead of an answer, I hear the squeak of the knob turn, the water ceasing. I open my eyes, and he's standing in front of me, droplets of water running down his defined chest. My long hair snakes down my neck, thick with water. "Why did you kill him?"

"It's what we do, little sister." He meets my stare. "We're hunters."

Hunters. Stupid images of rifles and forests rise in my head. That isn't what he means and I know it. My first thought is of mom and Montie. *Do they know?*

Of course, they don't know.

My mom may be under the spell of her husband but she's not the kind to aid and abed murderers. And in an instant, it hits me. All the creaks and the groans from above my bedroom. That's what they'd been doing all this time.

Hunting.

I rock forward, thrusting my hand out to brace against the tiles. "I'm going to be sick."

"Over the drain, so I can wash it down."

A bark of laughter breaks free from my throat. He doesn't miss a beat. Doesn't even flinch. So calm. So controlled.

But not always.

I try to steady my breaths, attempting to keep from passing out. No, he wasn't always so controlled. But I'm not going to think about that night, remember? I'm going to pretend that didn't happen. Mom and Montie are gone. No specific date of when they're coming back. It's one of the reasons mom wants me here. To keep an eye on things.

'*The boys are hardly here. You won't even see them.*" Her words sprout like the lies.

"Sure I won't," I whisper, realizing with chilling clarity my stepbrothers can do whatever they want to me and no one would know.

"Won't what?" Jack steps away, grabbing a towel and tossing it to me. His gaze lingers a little too long on my body, on my taut nipples and fluttering stomach. For a second, I think he's going to touch me.

But he just turns away and leaves the room.

"FORGET EVERYTHING YOU SAW TONIGHT. *Everything you heard. It never happened. Understand?"*

Those were the last words Jack said to me before sending me back to my room wrapped in a towel. I'd spent the rest of the night staring at the ceiling, listening for the sounds of my stepbrothers as they cleaned up and disposed of the evidence of what they'd done.

No, what we'd done?

Am I part of this?

No. That man was supposed to be dead before I went upstairs.

I toss and turn, running through the whole event repeatedly. The cry for help. The scent of blood. The realization he was going to kill me. The sound of the blade ripping through his throat. The feel of Jack pressing the tip of the knife against my chest.

Oh God.

As dawn breaks, the sound of footsteps, heavy and loud on the stairs, propels me up and out of my bed. I rush to the door and press my ear against the wood. Their footsteps pause, hovering on the landing. I almost wish they'd killed me last night—finished me off so I didn't have to wait.

Because they *will* kill me.

Time stands still as they linger in the hall. I swallow back the bitter bile rising in the back of my throat and clamp a hand over my mouth. I'm so focused on not puking, that I barely register the sound of their feet as they continue to the first floor. I'm still standing there when the car doors open and close outside, echoing against the early morning.

I exhale, breathing out the tension of the night. But I can't hide here forever and now I can't take back what I know.

All I can do is try to take control of my life until they decide to snatch it away with the savage jerk of their knife anyway.

I have an interview today down at the Gazette. If I get the job, I'll earn a paycheck, and then I can get out of here. Away from this house. *Away from them.* I can put what they did behind me. Just pretend like nothing happened. I've done it before...so I can do it again. *Right?*

THREE

Jack

"Get the bleach," Ollie mutters as he drops his shoulder.

Thud.

The wrapped body hits the floor of the trunk. I'm going to have to scrub harder, make sure I get every fiber out of the lining. I've told him before about placing it, not just dropping it like that. How many times do I have to explain myself?

My mind races, tracing every touch, every drop of blood from the moment we took him. There was no way they'd track this scumbag back to us. Although, you can never be too careful.

Especially when you had bodies in the backyard. Literally.

Ollie doesn't bother to look my way, just yanks the asshole's feet around and stuffs him in, knees up in the space. I work on autopilot, so used to the movements. Track, hunt, capture, kill. Then dig a nice big hole and come back to clean.

It's here where most killers come undone. They don't take the time. They rush it. They don't plan. They aren't organized. I place the three bottles of cleaner into the gaps between his feet, tucking one under his arm in a sickening embrace and straighten.

"Nice." Ollie casts me a look.

I smile and that makes him stiffen, then shake his head.

"What?" I ask.

My little brother doesn't answer, peeling his gloves free and turning them inside out before tossing them on top of the body. He walks around the car and climbs into the passenger's seat. I follow, sliding in behind the wheel of the Audi A8 and start the engine.

I drive, taking the quiet residential streets nice and slow until I make my way to the freeway, then we travel the hour to the turn off to Glenwood Forest. We have a cabin out there, it's isolated and quiet, and a nice big barn equipped with barrels of sulphuric acid. Enough to get rid of a body...*or five.*

Adrenaline courses through me as I press the gas a little harder than I should, earning a side-ways glance from my brother. But he bites back a remark. I know it's not my driving he wants to talk about it's her.

Our little stepsister.

It was a shock seeing her back in the house, her scent, and quiet movements. Dad mentioned her returning home as they were leaving the house for their trip. I didn't pay much attention. I never do, focused on my mission and nothing else. But now that she's back things feel strangely... right. Like finding a missing piece of a puzzle. She'd left so abruptly. We'd never been able to finalize what'd happened that night. No reconciliation. But now... now we can finish this for good.

So yeah, Oliver wants to talk about her. I don't. I just want to think about her standing there drenched in blood. How I wanted to fuck her, right there in the mess. Or when she was lathered and wet in the shower. I should've pressed her against the dark tile, spreading her thighs and made her scream. I lick my lips and glance in the rearview mirror, spotting a pair of headlights half a mile back. She shouldn't have come upstairs. It was her own stupid fault. Whatever happened now—that was on her.

Would she betray us again? My pulse speeds. Balls ache. Fingers twitch to touch her pale, slender neck.

We spend the remainder of the drive in silence. But instead of comfort it's strained. There was no music to muffle the thoughts in my head, just the hum of the Audi's tires on the road. Until...

"She shouldn't have come back."

That's all he said. Just that...*she shouldn't have come back.*

He's right. She shouldn't have returned to Davenport Manor–to the Davenport men. Not after the last time. Maybe our little Katie had forgotten the lesson we taught her? Maybe it was time to remind her exactly the kind of *brothers* we were? My cock twitches, growing harder as I finally catch sight of our turnoff. I hit the turn signal and tap the brakes.

Red lights flare at the rear of the sedan. I watch the mirror, the other car turned off at the last exit. We turn around the sweeping bend, leaving the freeway behind, making sure no one followed. We'd left her alive. She could have called the police.

Nothing but darkness surrounds us. I slow when rocks kick up, peppering the underbelly of the car, taking the terrain a little slower. We drive until the familiar turn-off. I nose the Audi onto the dirt drive, making my way to the small cabin, and around to the large empty stables. I pull up, waiting as Ollie climbs out and opens the gate, leaving me to drive through as he hits the lights.

We work quietly, removing the bleach and other items the asshole had with him when we interrupted his plans. The cheap black bag hits the concrete floor with a thud. I stare at the thing, fighting the urge to look at his other instruments. But there's no time for that. Instead, I move to the door at the end of the stables and press my finger to the scanner, waiting for the locks to release.

The room is padded. Silent. The saw sits at the end, gleaming and waiting. We haul the body out of the car and slam the padded room closed. The whirring screech is muffled outside. We'd tested things a hundred times. Sounds, smells, and everything else we use. Making sure nothing can be traced back to us. Then we start work dismembering the body on the cloth tarp, starting with the fingers. We spread across the body, using a wrench to remove the teeth before grinding them to dust, then to the eyes, on to the skin.

By the time we load the parts in containers and cart them to the forest, I've worked up a sweat. Ollie hasn't said anything after his remark in the car. I busy myself doing my fair share of the digging. We prepare for this too, working out in the basement of the house, lifting weights and adding cardio. We have to be in top shape to pull off every step of this. My muscles strain until they burn. *Whack. Slop. Whack. Slop.* Over and over and I'm lost in the movements... thinking about the reason we do this.

What bad men do to innocent females.

We bury the bins, then return to the cabin, lighting the fire in the barrel just outside the backdoor. Ollie works the buttons of his shirt, peeling it free before dropping it into the fire, standing there naked as I do the same. A few minutes and the clothes are nothing more than embers.

"We need to let Davis know," Ollie says, staring at the flames before meeting my gaze. "And Paul. If we decide to remove her from the equation, they'll need to be on board."

I nod carefully. "I agree."

"This is a goddamn mess," he mutters.

He's right, but it's also more than that. This is a *problem.* Not one that can be sawed into tiny pieces and destroyed.

As I stare at the embers and the glistening plastic button as it burns, I realize one important factor. "She doesn't tick the boxes."

Ollie flinches with the words. Anger burns in his eyes. Anger for me and for her. But mostly anger for himself. It was his fault the asshole was still alive. It was his fault she went up there in the first place. His fault we're having this conversation at all. But no matter how much blame I want to shovel onto my brother it always comes back to the same argument. It might've been his actions that caused this. But the blame for all of this rested on one man. A faceless man we hunt in our dreams.

He's the reason why we hardly sleep. Why are hands are bloody, and why we can't let Katie fuck things up.

Ollie turns and makes for the cabin, and I follow. Inside he heads to the kitchen while I go to the bathroom. I twist the taps, listening to the squeal of the old pipes and step under the cold spray. Remnants of blood wash away as I grab the soap and scrub.

Katie...

I close my eyes and slide the soap over my chest before moving lower.

All that blood.

All that mess.

Those innocent brown eyes wide with fear. *Jesus.* I reach down and grab myself. I'm already hardening, even with the cold spray. I fist my length and close my eyes, imaging her hand wrapped around my cock. Soft, small, firm.

Jack...please don't do this.

Her voice resurrects as I slide my hand back, hitting the hilt, and then pump all the way to the thick head. That rush moves through me. "Goddamn, Katie." Her name on my lips is pure poison. She hates it when I call her by the nickname. Her nose wrinkles every time. A correction lingers on those plump pink lips. Fucking with her, is an addiction I haven't tasted in many years, but now that she's back, it's a bitter taste I can't seem to deny.

The vein along my length pulses. My balls twitch and my lower body seizes. I come hard. Slick, creamy, spurting on my fingers. I open my eyes and look at my cum and the memories return. Memories before she ran, before the little bitch betrayed us.

I open my hand, watching as the remnant of desire washes away before I turn and twist the taps, ending the spray. If I was hoping for relief, it doesn't come. I dry and dress before gathering our things and turning to the car. We're back in the car within the next hour, the car scrubbed and cleaned, removing every spec the two-bit rapist left behind.

Headlights splash against the asphalt as we take the freeway back to the city. But we don't go home. Not yet. They say murderers always go back to the scene of the crime, and that's mostly true. For us, it's more than reliving that rush.

We live in the scene of the crime. From the first one to the very last. That way we don't forget.

I drive past the seedy nightclubs and closing bars. It was morning and in a few hours, the sun will rise, shedding new light on the mess we'd found ourselves in. But it's not darkened alleyways and depraved brothels where we find ourselves.

We drive past the quiet low-income residential streets pulling up outside a small, bare, plain house. The windows were darkened, the occupants fast asleep... *and safe*. Tonight could've ended very differently, indeed.

The cheap ass go-bag was still in my boot, the tape, and the ties along with the knives. The scumbag even thought to add a box of condoms, you know, to cover his tracks.

A twenty-four pack too... he was expecting to stay for a while.

Too bad his time was cut short, cut by my goddamn knife.

"He deserved it," Ollie says. His words draw me away from the memory of how I was the one waiting for him when the sick asshole broke into her house, planning on waiting for when she came home.

"He ticked our boxes," I answer.

"Yes, brother. That he did."

I turn my head to look at him, but it isn't the hard planes and the careful, stony eyes of the man I see. At this moment it's the wide, terrified eyes of my little brother. The one I held, huddled close together, with my hand across his mouth to smother his screams.

Run, Jack! Mom's desperate whisper came back to me. *Take your brother and hide.*

We did run and hide that night when violence came for our mom. The same kind of violence that almost came for the woman who lived inside the house in front of us. The same kind of violence we protected her from.

We may not be able to escape our nightmare, but we make sure we take out as many sick bastards we can while we're living it.

FOUR

Kate

———

The Gazette office is tucked in the middle of a long row of ancient buildings on Main Street, the words Established in 1874 embellished in gold over the front door. The offices are on the top floor, and after climbing three flights of stairs, I find myself sitting across from the editor, Henry Parks, as he flips through my portfolio. I majored in journalism–my primary interest in investigative reporting. From the crease on his forehead, I get the sense he knows what sparked my interest.

I spent four years living in the house with a ghost and the victims of her unsolved death left behind. So, you could say, yeah, I have a personal investment.

"Your stepfather and I go way back." Henry's hair is bushy, standing on end and his eyes redder than my own. I glance at the almost empty bottle of whiskey on the shelf behind him, then shift my focus back. "He says you had excellent grades and graduated top of your class."

"Yes, sir, I did."

He looks down at my resume and raises a hairy eyebrow. "You wrote a six-part series about the Cross Bridge murders for the school paper?"

"For my senior project, yes." The Cross Bridge murders are one of the most well-known unsolved cases in the state. Real-life crime has always fascinated me, but maybe not so much now. "As you know, no one could figure out who killed those two women. I didn't either, but my investigation renewed my interest and dug up a few promising new leads. Many of the locals were reluctant to talk to me about it, but I had a feeling there were secrets to uncover." I lean forward, nodding my head to the folder in his hand. "The case was reopened by the police because of my hard work."

"So you're determined."

"Yes, sir. *Very.*"

He nods. "You've got grit. I like that."

I thought I did too, but after what I witnessed last night, my enthusiasm for digging into the underbelly of unsolved crimes has dampened. I swallow hard, driving away the stench of hot blood that still clings to my nose.

It's one thing to investigate a crime. But it's another to be that up close to it. Even if I was an unwilling participant and the murderers live a floor above me. I was a witness. A risk. The fear that overwhelmed me last night? I can't it wash off.

Not that Jack didn't try.

Just leaving my bedroom had taken a feat of strength that morning. I had to push past every single fear I had as I stood outside my bedroom, head craned, listening for movement. I made sure that Jack and Oliver had truly left the house and there weren't any other victims lurking around every dark corner of the house.

That house...

That creepy, godforsaken nightmare of a house.

The strong scent of bleach wafted down the stairs, following me until I stepped outside. But, now that I'm here, I try my best to pretend none of that happened. Henry is my only option. The only job interview I'd managed to secure and that's only because of his connection to my stepfather. If I can just get this job, save a little money, and build my resume, I can get the hell out of this town and away from Jack and Oliver for good.

He chews on the tip of his pencil; I suspect trying to decide how to reject me in a way that doesn't destroy his relationship with my stepfather. I glance around, looking for anything to further the conversation. The desk is a mess. Stacks of coffee cups from the diner, a jar of broken pencils, old newspapers. I catch sight of the top one and my heart skips a beat.

I lean forward and point at the black and white photo. "Who is that?"

He frowns down at it. "Just a missing person." He looks up at me, then back down at the paper, then back at me again. I can see the wheels turning. "There's a series of them. White males, primarily ages forty to sixty. One day they're living normal lives, the next they vanish."

I quell the tremble in my voice. "Sounds like they got antsy and took off. That's not unusual."

"That's what the police say too, but... I don't know," he scratches his head, "something about it bugs me." He holds up the paper, giving me a better look at the image. The copper scent of blood tickles my nostrils. "This guy, Charles Miller, has a family, a wife and two kids, coached soccer, has a steady job, no girlfriend or mistress that anyone has heard of. No financial issues. He left his job one evening and hasn't been seen for three days."

And he'll be missing forever, I want to say, but don't. Can't.

He drops the paper in the pile. "I could use someone to run this down. Shake the weeds a little and see if there's anything there. The families, they're getting frustrated with the police. There's no urgency to find these men."

My heart thuds in warning, telling me to stay away from anything to do with these men, but I find myself nodding, shaking his hand, and accepting the position when he offers it.

"It won't be easy," he says, directing me to the secretary for paperwork, "but maybe you can make progress like you did the Cross Bridge case."

I thank him and I don't truly exhale until I'm back in the shadowy stairwell.

Jesus Christ, what have I done?

There's no doubt the missing man in the paper is the same man that tried to rape and kill me at Davenport Manor last night. The eyes and ugly set of his jaw are the same. It's the same man Jack murdered before he got the chance. And I just agreed to look further into the story?

I blame trauma and the lack of sleep for such a stupid decision. Taking another deep breath, I steady my hand on the railing as a new, *sane*, plan formulates. I'll go home, call Henry, and tell him that this isn't going to work. I'll just explain that while I was at the interview, I received a job in another town, and I'll just get the fuck out of here while I still can.

"I don't remember your tits being so big." A low whistle follows and my heart jumps into my throat. "I shouldn't be surprised. You always were a sexy little thing."

I turn and see a figure emerge from the darkened corner. One minute he's shrouded, the next he's in the light, blocking me from the staircase. The man is tall and imposing and once my heart dislodges from my throat, I get a better look at his profile. Underneath the sharp cheekbones and thick layer of stubble, I recognize a vaguely familiar face. The memory strikes hard and fast; the four of them standing over me, their jaws tight, eyes mean.

Fuck.

Davis Higgins, best friend to my vile stepbrothers was there that night. I should be shocked, but it tracks. Honestly, I'm surprised it took him this long to find me. My eyes flick down to the badge attached to his belt. Detective Davis Higgins, Wilmington PD.

"It's been a long time, Kate." His eyes travel up and down my body. "How have you been?"

"What do you want?" I ask because Davis is the kind of man that wants, or takes. He never *asks* for anything. He's handsome, he always has been. There's a twinkle in his hazel eye, one that implies mischievousness, while his smile is lazy and disarming. In one weekend he'd score the winning touchdown for the Wilmington football team and talk as many girls out of their virginity as he could. He's the kind of devil that you don't realize is there until it's too late. Until you've already let him in.

And he's got me cornered.

"I heard someone saw little Kate back in town, and I needed to see it with my own eyes."

There's no doubt that someone is Jackson Davenport–Davis' best friend and co-conspirator. "Well, here I am. You've seen it for yourself." I gesture for him to move. "Are we done?"

"Unfortunately," he says, grimacing and rubbing his chin, "no. Now that I've confirmed it for myself, I've got to make a decision."

"W-what kind of decision?" I hate the stammer in my voice.

His hand reaches out, fingers grazing along my cheek. "If it's better for me to make you 'disappear' or keep you around." The pads of his fingertips linger near my mouth. I fight the shudder running down my spine. "Do we *use* you, or *dispose* of you?"

A million terrifying scenarios run through my mind. What sticks out is that he knows about last night. Knows what I've seen and how I can expose my brothers. "You're just as crazy as they are," I force out. "You're all monsters."

"I happen to know that you have a thing for *us* 'monsters'." The grin he gives me is the kind of nightmares and I push past him, but only because he lets me. I stumble down the steps, wrenching my ankle in the process. Forcing myself not to look over my shoulder.

I make it to the bottom floor, pushing open the door to the outside, warm heat slapping me in the face. I limp to the car, locking the door once I'm inside, and the rush of tears I've been holding back all night finally releases.

I let it all out while I'm alone, knowing that I can't make decisions while I'm emotional like this–that I can't let them see me cry. I know for a fact any sign of weakness only makes them meaner.

I crank the car and roam the streets of Wilmington. It's been years since I've been back here, but it all looks the same. The weathered sign is still up at high school and further down the road is the county library where I spent most of my afternoons, nose deep in a book, so I didn't have to go home.

There's the public swimming pool and the diner, but there are new things too. Upscale apartments overlooking the river. New subdivisions and an outdoor shopping mall. I loop around the streets, settling my nerves. I stop at the stoplight in front of the police station and feel the hairs rise on the back of my neck. I get the sense I'm being followed–watched–and turn toward the station.

Sitting in the parking lot, in a black and white Wilmington Police marked SUV is Davis Higgins. Our eyes meet and I sense more than see the smile on his face. I want to run and hide. I want to tell the world who this man, this protector, really is.

But look how well that turned out for me last time? Idiot. Why the hell did you agree to come back here in the first place?

Because you wanted to see them.

Shame fills me, burning a hole right through my soul.

I could drive around for hours, wasting gas, or I can accept it and go back to Davenport Manor. Make them see they don't scare me. Force them to acknowledge that it's my home too, right? Except, I never had control there and never felt safe. Delusion is such a snarky bitch.

I grind my jaw and turn the car back to the rambling house. There's no use running, they'll just follow me. *We're hunters,* Jack's words fill my mind. My mind shifts to the stack of newspapers and the list of missing men.

Hunters.

That chill creeps along my spine. I know what they are now. *What they truly are.*

There's no reason to hide–they'll find me. My stepbrother's cars are gone when I get back to the house, but I'm still quiet as I walk in the kitchen door. I only stop to grab a knife from the butcher block on the counter, before tiptoeing up the stairs and locking myself in my room.

I look up at the ceiling, waiting, listening, planning.

It's obvious to me now that the only thing I can do is try to try to take them down. That's the real opportunity Henry is giving me at the Gazette: Access.

And I plan on using it.

FIVE

Oliver

I CROSS MY LEGS AND LIFT A HAND, MOTIONING TO THE waitress to the back corner of the bar. Unfortunately, she's not the only one that notices, and Sophie Pressler thinks I'm waving to her. I give her a tight grin, hoping it'll appease her, but she slides from her seat among the pack of women she's sitting with, leaning forward and whispering something that prompts six nearly identical heads to turn toward me.

Whatever she's saying, I really don't want to know.

Fuck, I think, watching her make a beeline for me. I scan the entrance for any sight of my brother. He's not here.

"Ollie!" Sophie calls in her high-pitched whine.

I fight the twitch at the corner of my lips, feigning a smile instead. "Sophie. How have you been?"

"Still waiting for your call," she says with a wink while sliding into the seat opposite of mine.

I open my mouth to tell her now's not a good time, but that would just be speaking to the wind. She doesn't ask if I want company. Women like Sophie never do. Never have. She's been following me around since tenth grade, and it's never clicked that this isn't going to happen. I guess that's part of being the kind of woman that gets what she wants when she wants it. She's made it very clear over the years that what she wants is me.

The problem is that she doesn't know me and if she did? Well, she'd go running.

They don't even try with Jack. He's got his mysterious, alpha thing going on, but women sense the darkness in him. A few have tried to penetrate it but come out licking their wounds.

Me? I'm more accessible. Less psychopath, more friendly. I don't do what I do because of a twisted need to hurt and maim. That's my brother. He's broken, deep down, all the way to the core. With him, there's no coming back.

That's not me. I do this because it's the right thing. The moral thing. I never want another woman, another family, to go through what ours did.

Sophie brushes her fingers against mine. The move is gentle, quick. She has no idea what these hands have done, how much blood they've been covered in. It would repulse her. But women like her never want to dig under the surface. It's almost an insistence, a fantasy really, of pretending that I'm a worthy catch. All they see is my handsome face, the fit body, and the money. God, they definitely see the Davenport money.

I glance over to the table across the bar. It's obvious the group of women believe that I'm one flirty conversation away from finding the love of my life Sophie.

"I've been so busy," she starts, fussing with the stack of gold bracelets on her arm, "with the charity ball I'm organizing. It takes up *so* much of my time. You just have no idea the kind of work that's involved."

"I can imagine," I mutter, looking toward the door for any sign of Jack.

"But I love it. It gives me purpose. I can feel that sense of pride by giving back to the community." She tugs at the straps of her sundress, lifting her tits casually, in an attempt to draw my attention. And all I can think of is Jack slicing the straps on Kate's blood-drenched nightie the night before.

Seeing her in the middle of it all was like a wet dream. One I'd gladly sit here and replay over and over if Sophie would just shut the fuck up. All her presence is doing is making me feel something else, like giving her a nice short stab wound between the ribs.

But that won't happen.

Because she doesn't tick any of the boxes.

It's our rule.

"Anyway, how have you been?" she asks regarding me with a coy smile while resting her hand on my forearm. Trust me, Sophie, you don't want to know.

"Just working a lot," I say, "like you, trying to make the community better–"

"I heard your sister's back in town," she interrupts. "Bless her heart, I know she had a hard go of it last time she lived here." She regards her nails. "Bridget said she saw her going in the Gazette. Is she interviewing?"

She pauses for a beat, clearly wanting me to answer. "I don't keep track of my stepsister's appointments." I flash her an apologetic grin. "Sorry."

"It always happens, you know. People run off to bigger and better places, but they still end up back here." She gives me a tight smile. "It's a small paper, but it'll probably be a good fit for someone without experience."

The longer she talks about Kate the colder I get. The sensation plunges deep inside me at the mere mention of her name. The mask of pretense slides from my face. My smile falters, and I plunge headfirst into those icy waters of rage. I think about reaching across the table between us and taking her by the throat, feeling her pulse beneath my fingertips as it wanes. The urge is so strong, so intense, that my nails dig painfully into my palm.

"Sophie."

My eyes flick up to the indifferent tone. Once again, my brother saves me from getting into trouble.

He strides forward, then stares down at her in that intimidating way Jack Davenport is known for. The mere presence of Jack is enough to make people like Sophie Pressler scurry back to the shadows, like a cockroach, and run away. Far, far away. "You're in my seat."

"Jack," she says, eyes wide. What little color she has under inch-thick makeup vanishes. I see that tremor of fear in her eyes. See it *bloom* like the blowback of a syringe. She rises from the seat in a hurry but instead of stepping toward him the way she inserted herself in my presence, she backs away. "Of course, I was just leaving."

They react differently to my brother. Always have. It's like, on some level, they know exactly what he is, what he's capable of.

He's what you call a natural born killer.

Cold. Unreadable. Those dark eyes pinning his victim in place.

I watched the reaction with just a hint of amusement. It was like plucking the wings of a fly watching her flail and stumble, casting a pathetic fake smile my way as though she was almost embarrassed. "I'll catch you later, Ollie."

"Sure," I answer, fighting that tight curl in the corner of my lips.

Jack takes his seat and adjusts his jacket, regarding me with a rising brow. "Can't leave you alone for an hour, can I? Always attracting flies like honey."

"Then you shouldn't be late," I state, watching Sophie flutter her hands my way as she nears her rumor-mongering bunch of bitches. I stare at them, cataloging every face. "They're already talking about Kate."

My brother stiffens. I glance at his cock. *Quite literally*. It's the only topic of conversation that does.

He thinks I don't see the way she affects him, but I do. The way he reacted last night. Pinning our little sister against the wall... the bloody blade sliding along her skin. He's affected by her. *Christ, aren't we all?*

I lick my lips as that heavy thump in my chest hits harder.

"That's a problem," Jack says carefully.

I stare at my brother, uneasy about the whole thing. Kate finding Charles Miller tied up and in our rooms wasn't in the plans. Neither was the bloody mess. The whole thing went off the rails and I don't sense that it'll straighten any time soon. Not as long as she's here.

"We can't react rashly," I tell him, spotting another figure walking in the front door. "We'll figure something out."

My brother grunts and I watch Davis walk in, all smiles and nods. He's a typical public servant. He worked his way up from a rookie beat cop, through the ranks until he made detective. The people of Wilmington town trust him. They know he carries a badge and is out there doing 'good work.' It never crosses their minds that something more nefarious could be happening under the surface.

He waves at Rich, the bartender, then heads over to a table where a group of older men congregates every afternoon. He stops and shakes the hand of every person at the table.

I watch him with the same regard as I watch my brother. Two very different men... two very different killers. Davis works the room. Shaking. Smiling. He's the man everyone loves. The hardworking detective keeps everyone safe.

From everyone but us.

He chuckles, slaps one of the men on the shoulder, and tears himself away, making a slow beeline for us. He takes a seat next to my brother, glancing away as the waitress nears carrying four glasses of neat scotch and places them on the pub table in front of us.

"Thanks, sweetheart," Davis says, giving her an easy smile. She blushes in return, flattered by his charm. When she turns, the mask he wears slips away, along with the false smile.

"I saw our girl," Davis says, keeping his tone casual. "You didn't tell me how much she's grown."

Jack and I glance at one another. Katie was a cute girl when she left. Now she's drop-dead gorgeous. Her hair is longer now, although still blonde. Her eyes are the same vibrant blue. Somehow her lips are plumper—and I definitely noticed that her tits are round and full. After Jack cut off her nightie, my gaze had lingered over the curve of her hips, meatier now, and the valley between her thighs.

Shit. The crotch of my pants grows tight just thinking about her, and I shift, seeking a more comfortable position.

"I can see why you didn't kill her last night," he adds, smirking at my brother. "You want to play with her first."

"And you don't?" Jack snaps. "Because I don't see any blood on your hands."

Davis shoots us both a dark look. "Which is exactly why we have a problem. She needs to be taken care of, immediately."

"We were saying that exact thing," I say.

"Gentlemen." The voice comes from behind, and our friend, our fourth, Paul Sanders takes the last empty seat and the glass the waitress left for him. He sniffs the liquor before taking a small, measured sip.

"Doc," Davis says, cutting him a glance. "We were just talking about the complication Jack and Oliver ran into last night."

"Katherine." He says her name with reverence. "How did seeing her make you feel? I'm sure it brought up a range of emotions."

Jack grunts and swallows his drink. I shake my head. "We didn't feel anything, Doc. She almost fucked the whole thing up and got herself killed in the process. She's a liability, like always."

"That's it? You only view her as a liability?" He's skeptical. "No emotion or other feelings associated with seeing her again?"

Jack slams down this glass. "You know how I feel when you do this! We're not your patients, Paul. We're here to solve a problem, not analyze our goddamn feelings."

Davis glances around, grimacing at the noise. "You two save the therapy for later." He lowers his voice further. "You said she saw the prey in your house? Watched you kill him?"

"She tried to save him," I say. "Good thing we showed up when we did."

"There's no way she can keep that to herself," Davis says, "call it a cop's instinct."

"Then it's simple, isn't it?" Jack says. "She has to go."

Just like that. No weighing up the options. No finding another way. Everything in my brother's world exists in black and white.

"You're talking about family," Paul says, watching us carefully. Being with Paul is like being trapped under a microscope. "Eliminating her brings about a host of other problems. Montie will have questions. Her mother will be devastated."

"We'll say she left," Davis says. "It wouldn't be the first time Kate ran from Wilmington."

"Last time it was with their help," Paul says, adding, "*after* she squealed. Like it or not, she relies on them. It's why she came back here. Vanishing without a trace will always lead back here, to Davenport House."

There's an unspoken statement hovering between us. Kate didn't tell on all of us. She told on me.

Even so. "She doesn't tick the boxes," I say. "We set rules for a reason."

Paul nods. More than anyone he understands the importance of boundaries and rules. It's what allows him to sleep at night–to continue practicing psychiatry despite his dark hobby.

"Then maybe it's time we add another?" Davis says. "Just a small one, one we can bury six feet deep, in a little Kate-sized box."

Jesus...

I glance at Jack to see his reaction. But there isn't one. Just a whole lot of nothing. But I know better. His silence speaks louder than words.

"Fuck," Davis says realizing it too.

Ready to change the subject, I nod to Davis and ask, "Do you have any new information on the Binder?"

The goddamn raping murderer we'd been hunting for the last two years and hadn't been able to catch. This piece of shit is different from the others. Sneaky, clever. Smart. His movements and actions are calculated and controlled. His weakness? Black hair. Pretty. Vulnerable.

He takes them at knifepoint. Snatching them after a late night at the bar. He binds them with zip ties and duct tape, then uses them, over and over, until there are only shards of the woman left behind. For years he operated like clockwork, and then, suddenly, he hasn't committed a single act of violence in over two months.

He's toying with us.

"No," Davis says. "The police are at as much of a dead-end as we are."

"He's not finished," my brother snarls. "He could strike any moment. He *will* strike any moment; he's just waiting for the perfect victim to cross his path."

Jack would know.

It takes a monster to know one.

And Jack is a monster to his core.

Davis shifts in his seat. Paul swirls the liquor in his glass. The moments are subtle, but I can tell. We're all getting antsy. Add our sister showing back up and fucking with our system and this feels like a ticking time bomb. I glance at Sophie Pressler, catching her looking my way.

They're already talking.

Already gossiping.

How the hell can we get rid of her now? And how the hell can we find the asshole defiling the women in this town when he's in hiding?

I drink as the urgency hums in my veins. Silence ebbs between us. But it's not an awkward silence. It's a scheming silence. A moment where we all weigh up the pros and the cons. The waitress nears carefully, and I shake my head and drain my glass.

"She has to go," Davis presses, unwilling to let it go.

"Then she has to go," Jack acknowledges. "It's as simple as that."

"You'll take care of it?" Paul asks.

Jack holds each of our eyes. "Consider it done."

SIX

Kate

___

GET ON YOUR KNEES, KATIE.

Crying won't make us go easier on you.

Open your pretty mouth, that's it. Wide enough for all of it.

That's it, swallow it up.

I jolt awake, the hyper-realism of the nightmare shocking me from sleep. My breath comes in shudders, my T-shirt soaked through with sweat. That dream–nightmare–God, I haven't had it in years. I shouldn't be surprised it came back now that I'm here, back where it all happened.

Where *they* happened.

My pulse pounds with the sound of anxiety. But that's not the only place I feel that consuming throb. I swallow hard and close my eyes. Torment wells between my legs. The want. The *ache*.

Revulsion follows. I hated what they did to me that night, but I hate how it changed me even more. I'd never been so scared, the kind of terror that lingers. That night changed me, taught me to

49

crave something dark and desperate. Like a drug I haven't been able to kick.

I slide my hand down the front of my panties. I feel the slick heat and press the warm pad of my finger against my clit. I shudder and exhale, still thick in the feelings of my dream. Still, I can't help myself, it always makes me feel like this, so horny— so fucking hungry.

Dropping my legs to the side, I keep my eyes closed, conjuring up the wisps of the memory. They'd stood over me, leering and evil. Each one taking a turn, drowning me.

Open your mouth, Katie.

Even now my mouth opens on command.

Now swallow.

My breath is a hard lump in the back of my throat.

I loathe how these men make me feel. Lost and desperate. When I left Wilmington, I tried to live a normal life. Meet normal men and make normal friends, but the four years I lived in this house left me scarred. Normal men couldn't give me what I wanted. What my new friends needed from me, a close confidant, I couldn't give them.

How could I explain to people what it was like living in this house—with these boys? All the secrets and lies. The terror and how traumatic... and utterly addictive.

My breath catches and outside my periphery, I hear a rustle. Jesus. This fucking house, with its creaks and tremors. My brain understands this, but my heart doesn't, and it rattles against my ribcage. My hand stills and I open my eyes, blinking as they adjust to the gloom. Slowly a shape appears, just as I feel something hard and sharp, dragging up my belly. It carves an arc between my breasts to my throat.

"Hello, Katie." Jack's voice cuts through the night. "Don't stop touching yourself on my account."

"Jack," I whisper, easing my hand out from between my legs.

"You were whimpering. Nightmare?"

I swallow, but it just pushes the knifepoint into my skin. "Just a dream."

There's a long moment of silence between us, one where he looks down at me, seemingly able to recognize that I'm trying to get my heart and throbbing want under control.

"I've spent the day trying to decide what to do with you." His cheekbones catch the light, hard and cut from marble. He's devastatingly handsome even as he guides the knife back down to my breasts, circling them methodically. I barely breathe, terrified of moving too quickly. "Davis thinks we should get rid of you–quick and simple–toss you in with the bastard from last night."

Toss me in where? A pit? A fire? The marsh? The alligators would dispose of me in hours.

He shifts the blade to my nipples, tracing them carefully, eliciting a spine-rattling shiver. He smiles when they peak and harden, pressing against the thin cotton of the shirt I found in the dresser. "So sensitive," he murmurs, then tweaks one, pinching hard. It sends a shock of pain through my body. "Paul is overanalyzing this whole thing. You know how he is."

Paul Sanders. My mother had proudly told me that he's now a doctor. A psychiatrist. Quite the catch. The thought that he has any kind of influence is terrifying.

"Oliver is," he pauses, "predictably, unsure. He's always had a soft spot for you, Katie. Ever since that night. It makes sense. You *are* the one that made him a man, after all."

Heat flares between my legs with the words. Even here with the curled edge of the blade pressing against my flesh, he knows exactly what to say to make me wet.

My heart pounds as he speaks, tormenting me with the knife and his little speech. He wants me to think there's a way out of this, but I know better. This is just part of the game for him. I have no choice but to play.

"What about you?" I ask, knowing he wants me to. "What do you think you should do about me?"

He sits suddenly, the bed creaking under his weight. I feel his hip pressed into my outer thigh. His legs are spread enough that I see the hard bulge tenting the front of his pants. He tilts his head and looks down at me, carving the blade down my belly. He could gut me right here. Take my life before I inhale another breath. Both of us know that. The pale light spills in from the open window, catching the hard muscle in the back of his jaw tic before it's consumed by the dark pits of nothingness as he stares at me. I can see now that he was never planning on letting me leave. Not alive, or without consequences.

"I know what I should do," he says in that dead-lost voice. "We've been so careful for so long, diligently working our way through the list, and then you show up. *Always* sneaking around. Going places you shouldn't. Disrupting things. You're a liability, sweet Katie. A risk we definitely can't afford. You know too much."

"I don't know anything," I promise. "I was exhausted from traveling and never left my room."

His smile resembles a wolf, gleaming in the dark. "Nice try."

"Then just let me go," I whisper. "I'll pack up and go. Drive away and never come back. You never have to see me again."

His expression shifts into something harder, indiscernible. But for a second... a split, *terrifying* second I see something else. Something akin to regret. But that is a lie, a monster like my stepbrother regrets nothing, especially when it comes to me.

"That won't do," he says carefully. "Because you went traipsing around town today, applying for the job at the Gazette. It'll be suspicious if you don't show up as planned. Mr. Parks will call my father, who will start asking me questions." He drags the knife down the front of my panties, stopping to press the flat edge against my clit beneath the fabric. I gasp at the rush of unwanted desire spreading through me. "Questions, I don't want to answer."

I don't move an inch as he toys with my body, igniting a dangerous fire deep in my belly. It's foreign yet familiar. Disturbing yet delicious. There's a long beat between us as he considers the situation until his eyes flick to mine and back down to the knife. His next movement is so quick. A sharp yank on the blade. It slices through the thin fabric of my panties and his fingers push roughly between my legs.

The invasion is merciless and perverted.

"Jesus, your pussy is wet." He laughs darkly. "Fucking drenched."

"Stop." I protest, squirming away, but in his other hand, he brandishes the knife. Steel catches the moonlight; fear pins me in place. "Jack, please."

"Please what, stepsister?" he asks, licking his lips, sliding deep inside, stroking, igniting. "You want more?"

No.

Yes...

I open my mouth to tell him, no, but he slides a second thick finger inside me, pushing them in deep. The sensation shocks me to finally speak. "No! I don't want–" His fingers fuck in and out, his thumb rubbing my clit. I bite down on a groan.

He drops the knife and climbs over me, straddling me with knees on both sides. With his free hand, he unbuttons his pants and pulls out his cock. It's large and thick and he strokes downward, the lean muscle in his forearm taut. "Tell me to stop," he says, continuing to violate me with his fingers. "Tell me you don't want it."

"I d-d-don't wa-a…" but the words are lost as the heat spreads from my core across my body. I'm on the tip of a very different knife, the blade of want and desire. Both hurtling toward one another after years of dissatisfaction.

He isn't kind.

He isn't gentle.

He's rough, angry, and filled with deep rage.

He's also the man I can't stop dreaming of, thinking about.

I cry out when the orgasm hits me, every muscle inside me clenched tight. Jack positions himself over me and says, "Do you remember what I told you would happen if you came back to Wilmington?" I can barely nod, body loose from release. He withdraws his fingers and slowly slips them into his mouth. His lips part, his tongue darts out, sliding between his fingers. He takes my juices into his mouth, sucking hard, before gripping my face with the same hand. Forcing me to look at his dark, wicked face, he says, "Do you?"

"Yes."

"What did I tell you?"

I hear the words ringing in my ears. I've heard them every day since I left. And every minute on my drive back to Wilmington, the bells of self-preservation rang in my ears. *"If you come back here, Katie, I will fill every hole in your body with so much cum, you'll explode."*

I repeat it to him now. And in those endless dark pits where no soul lingers, I see excitement. He drags his teeth over his lower lip, and I've never wanted to kiss someone so badly in my life. To feel them consume me. He lowers his hand, sliding between us. I don't have to look down to know what he's doing... I've seen this all before.

He strokes himself, short, sharp. It doesn't take him long, and he lurches forward, ejaculating all over my lower belly. The muscles in his neck strain as he milks his cock, draining every drop of his seed into a thick, sticky pool. He stares at it for a second, as though he's taking it all in. Him, me... before he slides his finger through the mess, then lifts his fingers to my lips. Bitter saltiness hits my tongue as he pushes in. I have no choice but to open.

I know what he wants.

That's it, swallow it up.

He watches me carefully as I slide my tongue out, consuming every drop, and swallow. The salty taste of him lingers in my mouth. It's a taste I both loathe and crave.

"Are you going to kill me now," I whisper, watching him tuck himself back in his pants. The blade of the knife glints beside me on the bed, but I'm still pinned in by his body.

"I should," he admits, bending over and wrapping his hands around my throat. "I should choke the life out of you and get it over with right now." Jekyll and Hyde have nothing on Jackson

Davenport. He's everyone's worst nightmare and my own personal hell. "But I have a better idea."

The way he says it is chilling, how he looks down at me with a depraved shimmer in his eye. It's not his conscious, or even his sexual depravity. No. It's darker and more evil than that.

"The boys and I have hit a dead end. We've been running in circles for months." He rises and picks up the knife, tucking it safely in his boot. "But I see now that there may be a way for you to redeem yourself."

"What the hell are you talking about?" I ask, confused.

"We're trying to catch a monster," he says, looking me up and down, "And you're going to be the bait."

SEVEN

Kate

Bait?

What did he mean, bait?

Jack straightens, towering over me like some debased God, and looks down at the filth he made on my stomach. "Get up."

My heart hammers. "Why? To use me as bait? What does that mean?"

"Get up because I told you to." He presses the steel blade against my arm, in warning. "For once in your goddamn life, Katie, just follow directions."

I wait for the slice of pain, for him to finally snap. Fear propels me from the bed to keep him from hurting me. My shirt falls until it catches on the sticky remnant on my belly. I wipe it with the fabric.

"What are you going to make me do?" I ask, watching him unlock the door and push it open. I don't know how he got in here, but the invasion of my privacy is nothing compared to what he did to my body.

My bare feet slap against the hardwoods as he drags me at knifepoint down the hall. All of a sudden it hits me. He's taking me upstairs.

I know one truth: Bad things happen upstairs.

"No." Fear kicks inside me. I yank my arm, not caring if the knife cuts me. "I'm not going up there."

I'll take the cut. I'll give the blood. I'll hedge my bets at surviving, *anything,* as long as I'm not taken to their rooms. I know what they can do, what they will do with the wall of knives and tools. He clenches his cruel grip around my wrist and forces me up the stairs.

I buck and dig my feet in until they slip and squeal, but I'm no match for his strength. Adrenaline, fight or flight, surges through me and I heave my head toward his, slamming the hard bone of our foreheads together. Pain rattles me, but he grunts, "Son of a bitch."

The reaction is swift and furious, his hand whipping out and slapping me hard against the face. My neck snaps to the side, ears ringing. He stares at me for a moment, like he's waiting for me to respond but I just blink away the tears.

He's too big, too strong and he easily drags me toward their room. He kicks the door with a loud bang. "Open up."

The door swings open and I sense the darkness waiting for me inside. Darkness in the outline of powerful, dangerous men.

"Took you long enough," Davis growls, eyes narrowed in suspicion. He's standing in front of the 'murder board.' Tacked up newspaper articles, shadowy photographs, post-it notes, and string interconnecting them all. When I'd been up here the night before, things were too chaotic for me to get a good look, but this time I try to absorb what I can.

It isn't random, all information seems to be methodically curated. There are dozens of men's faces, most connected with the missing men Henry Parks wants me to investigate. Other words jump out at me: Rape, Murder, Bound, Gagged.

Through the fear and panic in my brain, some of this starts to click together like pieces of a puzzle.

"We're hunters."

They're vigilantes, looking for a specific kind of killer. One like the man that stole Jack and Oliver's mother away from them. A man that has never been caught.

A throat clears, drawing my attention from the board to where Paul sits in a chair, legs crossed, eyes quietly observing. The scrutiny makes me feel anxious. Inconsequential.

Jack tosses me inside, and I land hard on the floor. I scramble to my knees. In an instant, I'm back to that night when all four of them cornered me. A mixture of emotions war in my blood. Fear, terror, repulsion, want.

This is the room where I was transformed from one person to another.

Click. The door shuts behind me and locks.

"Kate, Kate, Kate..." Davis clucks, his arms crossed over his chest. His eyes travel down to where the hem of my shirt barely covers my bare pussy and ass. I tug it down, grabbing the wet sticky spot that hangs just below my belly.

"Just let me go," I beg, my voice barely a whisper. "I won't tell anyone about what you guys are doing."

Jack stands at the door, barring any escape. "I already told you, Katie, we have a job for you."

"Otherwise, you're worthless," Davis adds, but then adds darkly, grabbing the front of his pants. "Well, maybe not *entirely* worthless."

That emotionless tone hits me hard. They view me as nothing but an object–a vehicle to abuse and use at their whim. Coming back to Wilmington, to this house, was a terrible, stupid, mistake. More than ever, I realize that the only thing I can do now is try to stay alive.

"Oliver," Jack calls, eyes focused across the room.

I jerk my gaze to the bathroom door. Oliver leans against the doorjamb, apparently lurking there the whole time.

"Don't be scared," Paul says, offering me his hand. I stare at it for a moment–at this small kindness–but I know better and refuse to take it.

"You and Oliver get her ready. Make sure she understands the assignment."

"It'll be easier for all of us, Katherine, if you don't fight," Paul says. My full name rolls off his tongue, gentle but firm. He jerks his chin toward, Jack and Davis, in some silent command. The two leave the room. "Hopefully that'll make you feel better. Those two can be impulsive. Rash."

"And you want me to believe you two aren't?" I look at Oliver. "I watched you slit a man's throat! You're just as bad as your brother."

"Jack isn't bad," he says. "He's determined. Focused, and unfortunately, you came up here last night and stepped right into trouble." Oliver walks toward me, taller and with much broader shoulders than when I saw him last. His features are less harsh than his brother's, his eyebrows eased and his lips soft. I try not to flinch when he brushes a strand of hair from my face, but it's instinctive. When our eyes meet, the dark glint is terrifying. "You know too much now, little sister. Too much to let you go, but if you're smart, you'll do what you're told."

"Or what?" I ask.

"We won't have to figure out where to hide your body."

Images flash through my mind; I'm on the ground, blood gushing from my neck, the four of them standing over me for the last time.

I have no doubt it's a premonition if I don't do exactly what they want.

"What if I don't want to be used? What if I'd rather you kill me?"

Oliver looks down, eyes dilating as they fix on the spot where my T-shirt barely covers my exposed bottom. "When did it ever matter what you wanted?"

Paul clears his throat. "I think we should get started on the... uh, transformation." He nods at my shirt. "Take it off."

I push down at the hem, my words a lump in the back of my throat. "Paul, please don't do this. You're a doctor. A psychiatrist. You have to know this is crazy."

"What I know, Katherine, is that you're testing my patience." He grabs the hem of my shirt and yanks it upwards, exposing my pussy. "Either you take it off, or I do... the choice is yours."

My knuckles ache as I clench my fists and glance at the bright lights of the bathroom. Oliver's bedroom is darkened, but there's a door there and for a second, I think about taking my chances. Until reality slaps me hard.

I'd never make it.

Not even out of the bathroom.

They'd be on top of me in an instant.

Menacing and predatory.

Then there'd be no stopping them.

I turn my head, holding Oliver's gaze. He jerks his chin. "You heard, Doc. Take it off."

I swallow hard and grasp the shirt from where Paul still has it in his grip and drag it over my head. My nipples pucker, and I know it has nothing to do with the gentle caress of air and everything to do with their stares.

"Good girl," Paul says with a small, smug grin. "See? That wasn't so hard. Now we can see what we're working with."

He pushes me in front of the long mirror, and the harsh light against the black tile makes me feel even more exposed. I fight the instinct to cover myself, waiting as Paul and Oliver scrutinize my body like a specimen under a microscope. Oliver runs a washcloth under the faucet and bends, wiping the remains of Jack's semen off my lower belly.

"Her tits are perfect," Paul says, standing behind me. He reaches around and cups my breasts in his hands. "Big, but not too big. Natural." He teases a nipple, forcing it to harden. "No need for a bra."

Oliver nods in agreement, while Paul's hands ghost over my ribs, fingers splaying across my hips. His thumbs rub tiny circles into my skin. "She's slim but not too thin. He likes a little flesh on his girls." He palms my ass, fingers grazing the divide between my cheeks. "Yes, this is good. Perfect, actually. I can't believe we didn't think of it before."

"Obviously we have to change her hair," Oliver says, opening the vanity drawer and pulling out two boxes of hair dye and setting them on the white, porcelain sink.

"What the fuck is happening?" I ask, unnerved at them discussing me as if I'm not standing right here.

"He prefers brunettes," Paul says with causal authority. "Eight out of his nine known victims have had dark brown to black hair. The other woman's hair was wet at the time of the abduction, making it a shade darker."

All I can think is that this is actually happening. They are truly going to use me as bait for one of the men taped to their wall.

I jerk my gaze to the box of dye and whisper, "You're insane."

Behind me, Oliver steps close and lifts his hand, picking up a strand. "We're hunting men the police can't catch. No one can stop these men. No one has what it takes to do what we will to rid Wilmington of the worthless pieces of shit that terrorize our community."

That terrorized his mother, is what I want to say because it's clear that is what all of this is truly about. Vengeance for their mother. One rapist and murderer at a time.

"Plus," he adds, coiling the hair around his finger and giving it a sharp tug. "I always wanted to fuck a raven-haired beauty."

My stomach clenches at the admission.

"You'll need to remove all your body hair," Paul adds. "Arms, legs, pussy. It's clear that he has a fetish. If you don't do it, he'll do it for you."

Bile rises to the back of my throat, unbelievably, this man sounds more terrifying than they do.

"Don't forget to dye your eyebrows." Oliver opens the box of dye. When I don't move, he adds, "Get started."

My hand trembles as I grab the box, pulling out the bottle and instructions.

Oliver takes one of my hands and inspects my nails. "These are in bad shape, but there's no time for a manicure. Just keep your hands low. Maybe he won't notice."

"He'll notice. Make sure you wear the gloves." He gestures to the gloves that come with the dye. "We don't want to stain those pretty fingers of yours."

I remove the gloves out of the packet and slip them on. I go through the motions, checking and rechecking the directions. My eyes meet Paul's in the mirror and he nods encouragingly as I pour a glob into my hand and rub it into my hair. Having always liked my hair, it's the first time I've done this, and it hurts to think about my honey blonde hair smothered under the blue-black dye. It feels like they're smothering me, making me into nothing more than a plaything.

Or worse. Unrecognizable bait.

They're stripping away the old Kate and replacing her with someone new or someone unidentifiable. If one of these men kill me would anyone even know it's me? My hands shake and the dye slips down my forehead like a sin-stained tear.

Once I've used one bottle, Oliver opens the next box.

Paul clears his throat. "I want you to pay close attention to what I'm about to tell you. The man we're looking for is single, a loner. He's not going to approach you, not directly, but he's going to give you cues that he's interested. Innocently bumping into you, standing beside you to order a drink."

I wipe an inky stain dripping down my forehead with a wad of paper.

Paul glares. "Are you listening to me?"

"Yes." I swallow. "Who is this man? Who are you trying to catch?"

The guys exchange a look and Paul says, "The Binder."

Oliver hands me the next bottle. I take it, but my heart punches against my chest at the sound of the name... the name that's been plastered across the headlines of every paper in the region. Cold plunges through me.

"No," I whisper and shake my head, stumbling backward. "No. No fucking way."

"Yes, fucking way," Oliver says, pushing me back toward the counter. There's something terrifying and gleeful in his tone. "We need something to lure this guy out, to draw him right into our trap. We needed bait, little sister, and The Binder is our elusive fish."

"You won't be alone," Paul says in a reassuring voice. "We'll be there, making sure that you're safe. Our goal isn't for you to get hurt, it's to finally catch him."

But I know they don't care if I do get hurt, that's the truth of the matter. These men care about nothing and no one but one another and their perverse mission.

"Tick, tock." Oliver points to his watch, then motions to the other box of dye. I grab it and open the contents. Again I make sure all the strands are covered before I peel the gloves from my hands, and drop them into the sink.

"While that sets, we can deal with the rest of your body. There's a razor and gel in the shower." Paul nods to the large, tiled shower. "Do you need assistance?"

I snap my gaze to his, but there's only a sinister smirk on his lips.

"No." Shame fills me when I slowly step toward the shower. They make no move toward me, just watch as I turn the unfamiliar taps and step into my stepbrother's shower.

"Make sure you're thorough. I want you smooth."

I make sure to keep my hair out of the spray and pick up the razor. Soap lathers against my skin and I run the blade along my legs, then underarms before I stop, knowing where they want me to go next.

"Get good and soapy," Oliver says with his arms crossed, eyes skimming my body. "You don't want to get a rash."

There's no reason for me to shave between my legs. There was no way in hell I was planning on letting it get that far with The Binder. I narrow my eyes at the two men. "The only reason you want me to shave is for your own sick pleasure," I say, lifting my gaze, daring the two of them to deny it.

Paul studies me for a moment, and then says to Oliver, "Will you go lay out the outfit I selected for tonight?"

"Sure." Oliver gives me one last look before leaving us alone.

I shiver even though the water is still warm.

"It's not about what we want, Katherine," Paul says, eyes riveted to my pussy. "It's about stepping into this role, understanding who and what you're up against. You have to become the kind of woman he wants to hurt. Otherwise, all of this is for nothing."

Still wearing his shoes, he turns off the water and steps into the shower. He motions for me to sit on the teak wood bench in the corner. He bends until we're eye level. "I know this is difficult for you. It's scary and overwhelming. We're asking a lot from you and, well, your brothers didn't get us off to a good start. Watching a man bleed to death is a jarring experience. Although, I think we can both agree that the alternative–him raping and killing you, would have been worse." His tone is kind. Calm, and he gives me a small smile. It makes it hard to find my balance. To know what's real or not. "I know you don't want any more women harmed, do you?"

I shake my head and give the only answer I can. "No."

"Then help us take down The Binder for good."

He says it like I have a choice, but he picks up the bottle of shower gel and pours a thick, creamy dollop into his hand. Rubbing his hands together he builds up a soapy lather and looks between my legs, raising his eyebrow. "Spread apart like a good girl, Katherine."

I feel like crying. I'm overwhelmed like he said, confused by his words. My legs fall to the side, and he hums happily, reaching out for the thatch of hair covering my pussy and coating it with the thick, foamy lather. Despite my fear, his movements feel good, relaxing, so much kinder than the forceful way Jack had fingered me before. I lean back against the wall and allow him to take the razor from me. He makes a long stroke over my mound, removing tufts of hair with skill and precision. Deep down I know that with every swipe, with every piece that gets swept into the drain, I'm losing a part of myself.

"Lift your leg," he murmurs. "We want to make sure we get everything."

We.

The way he says it implies comradery. Cooperation.

I clench my jaw not even caring that the dye runs black over my shoulders. Hard breaths consume me before I lift my leg for him. My slit is exposed and his gaze drops, taking me in. "Such a pretty pussy. That's why they keep coming back for more, you know that, right?" I shiver when his fingers spread soap over my clit, sending a flare of heat to my core. It takes every ounce of willpower not to succumb to the urge to rock into his touch.

"That's it," he says when he gets every last piece. He rocks back on his heels and eyes his work. "Beautiful and sexy."

Embarrassed at the way my body reacted to his attention, at the way my heart pounds in my chest, I hurry. Turn back to the shower, I massage my scalp, rinsing my hair until the water runs clear, and then step out.

Paul waits for me, holding up a fresh towel wide. I snatch it from him, wrapping it around my body as if he didn't just study and touch my most intimate parts.

"You need to be very careful, Katherine." He steps closer and rubs another towel over my wet hair. "This man is not to be played with, and you're every bit his type."

"Thanks to you and your little makeover."

Always stoic, always calm, the doctor ignores the bite in my tone. "There's something else I need to tell you about The Binder."

I raise an eyebrow, clenching the towel tighter around my body.

"He may have a disfigurement of some kind, a scar or an old injury. Something that will make him appear vulnerable. Perhaps inferior." He catches a droplet of water from my neck with his finger. "But that couldn't be further from the truth. As you know, sometimes the most dangerous men are the most unexpected."

"Are you talking about The Binder or yourself?"

He shrugs, but the grin playing on his lips says everything.

"So, I'm just supposed to trust a bunch of murdering psychopaths to protect me from a rapist serial killer?"

"Sweet Katherine," he says, holding my eye, "if there's any confusion at this point, let me make it perfectly clear; you don't have any other choice."

EIGHT

Kate

I step out of my car, contemplating climbing back in and just hauling ass out of this town for good. I don't have to return to the house for my things. Don't have any real obligations, other than getting myself as far away from the raving murderers I found myself living with. I glance back at my car, the urge to flee overwhelming.

Drive, you idiot. Just drive. A tiny whisper follows. *Help them. Help his next victim and then you can run.*

It's pointless anyway. They'd allowed me to drive to the bar alone, only to keep up the facade that I'm a single woman looking for fun. But I'm not alone, following close behind me the whole way was the familiar throbbing growl of a four-wheel drive. Now that I'm here, neon white headlights blind me against the deep black of the underlit parking lot. A predator's playground.

Paul exits his Range Rover, never glancing my way, just waking directly to the front door of the rowdy bar. It's late, almost midnight. All I want is to be back home in bed, and not smoothing down this absurdly tight dress that barely covers the black lace thong and my freshly shorn pussy.

I take a deep sigh and head into the seven levels of hell.

Thud. A car door slams behind me, followed by heavy footsteps. I know that slow, lazy gait anywhere. Jack.

I hate walking in front of him, knowing he could pounce at any moment. I know he's judging me, assessing the outfit Paul had laid out on Oliver's bed. Short, tight, and low cut. No bra. Scraps of lace for a thong. The shoes are new—expensive—all of it purchased from a boutique downtown. Paul stood beside me while I dressed, explaining every piece, and how it was specifically picked out with The Binder in mind. He has a type and I've been dyed, plucked, and dressed to fit it.

"Damn." His voice is low, impatient, barely audible over the loud music drifting from the bar. I wince at the implication and catch my reflection in the front window. The woman in the glass is a stranger. The black dress isn't my style, asymmetrical and hangs low off one shoulder. The dark hair makes me look older—more mature. Foreign.

This isn't me. That's all I think about as I step inside. I'm a shell of my former self. A woman who witnessed a murder. A woman whose stepbrother violated her hours before. A woman who has been molded into a prey.

Unexpectedly, Jack doesn't follow me inside, instead, parking himself near the door. I don't know if that makes me feel better or worse.

Heads turn toward me as I walk through the room. Why wouldn't they? I'm shiny and new, dressed to seek attention. I ignore the other customers and head deeper into the moody bar. The corners are dark, filled with black steel and the warm amber tones of lacquered wood. It's masculine and powerful.

The kind of bar I normally wouldn't be caught dead in, but apparently the perfect hunting ground for The Binder.

I don't party or really drink apart from the occasional glass of red wine to relax. But, God, I need a drink now—maybe two. I work my way through the crowd to the bar, stepping around a guy who slides out of his seat and directly into my path.

He hits me, jerking his gaze to mine. Brown eyes shine as he smiles. "Oh shit, sorry about that."

I smile. "No problem," and we play that little game where we dart back and forth, blocking each other's way. It's not until I pass that I realize that it could be him. Any of these men could be The Binder. I glance back, searching for a scar or disfigurement, but only catch sight of the back of his head as he walks away.

"Good job, Kate," I mutter and face the bar. They can dress me up as bait, but I'm not sure how successful I'll be. I look back again, and this time my pulse thunders as I catch the guy staring at me. The vibe isn't creepy or rapey. More like he's disappointed in himself for fucking up his chance at talking to me.

I've had limited experience in dealing with guys approaching me. Coming from an all-girls' school, the only thing I had to guard was my collection of bobby pins. But I'm not worried about that. I'm more concerned that I just screwed up an opportunity at catching him, and exactly how angry Jack will be when he realizes I screwed it up.

I force myself to keep going, turning sideways to squeeze between the guys sitting at the bar and the ones who spill out into the gap between the stools and the tables.

Spying someone vacating a stool further along the bar, I head toward it, passing Paul as he sits at the bar nursing a drink. His eyes meet mine and I'm so panicked that I'm going to fuck this up again, that they're going to decide I'm useless, that I stumble over someone's shoe, that the stool is taken by the time I get there.

Jesus. I am so fucking bad at this.

"Excuse me," I say to the man occupying the stool. "I was just about to sit on that."

"Were you?" he replies, dismissively. I push my hair over my shoulder, and he gives me a second look. He pats his knee.

"You saw me walking toward it."

"Sorry about that, Princess, I didn't see anything past the way your tits look in that dress." His eyes glue to my chest. "But I'm happy to share. There's more than enough room for the two of us."

Heat races to my cheeks as I scowl. "You're disgusting."

"And you're wasting my time." He waves to the bartender. "You can sit on my lap, sweetheart or you can go find your own damn seat."

"Here." A guy slides off his two stools away. "You can take mine."

He shoots the asshole a disappointed stare, then pushes his glasses up his nose with a finger.

"Gonna eyeball me, mutherfucker?" The seat-stealing swine chimes up, his voice rising over the music. "Come on, I'm right here."

A hand lands on the asshole's shoulder, and I see Paul's head tilted toward his.

"Let me buy you a drink," Paul says, drawing the man's attention. "That girl's not worth your attention. Dressed like that? She'll obviously fuck anything with a cock between their legs."

The man grunts and a moment later they click their glasses together.

My savior seems relieved that the asshole is distracted and motions with his hand to the seat. I look him over. Geeky in a cute, take him home to me momma kind of way. I don't forget my mission and check him over for scars. None there. A safe spot to get my bearings.

"That's so sweet of you, thank you. Nice to know gentlemen still exist in this godforsaken town."

He just gave a slow shake of his head and a low chuckle. "It's my pleasure, you're actually saving me, this is definitely not my scene."

I laugh. "Me either."

"You can't tell," he says, eyes dropping down to my outfit. "You fit right in."

"Well, every girl has that little black dress in the closet for the right occasion." I reach out and pick a piece of lint off his V-neck sweater. "I think you look nice."

"Can I get you a drink?"

"House red," I say, thankful for some liquid courage. Neither of us speaks while the bartender fills my glass. Once I've had three sips, I spin my stool toward his and say, "I'm Kate, by the way."

"Ryan." I get a better look at his eyes. One is bluer than the other. "I'd ask you if you come here often, but we've already done that."

"I actually just moved back to town," I say, feeling more comfortable. "Just trying to get my bearings again."

"Oh, did you grow up here?"

"Sort of. We moved to Wilmington when I was fourteen and then I moved out a few years later for college."

Ryan and I talk while the buzz of the bar surrounds us. I keep my eyes on him, ignoring the feel of the eyes I know are tracking my every move. I learn he's a computer programmer, lives down by the bay, and has cats.

"I need to get out of here soon," he says as he drains his glass. "One sad, lonely drink is more than enough. The cats will think I've abandoned them."

Something in my chest gave a flutter. "How many are there?"

He holds up four fingers. "They turn into fluffy but terrifying monsters if they've not had their eighteenth meal for the day and I'm afraid, I'm only up to seventeen."

I give a chuckle, forgetting the reason I'm here. For a second this almost feels... nice. Until he breaks the spell, smiles awkwardly once more, and says, "Good night, Kate. It was really nice to meet you."

"Wait," I start to call out, but my voice is drowned out by the jukebox kicking in. My gaze meet's Paul's, where he's sitting down the bar, and I remember my mission. Ryan clearly isn't The Binder. I mean, he has four cats and nerd glasses. I return to my still-warm seat.

I want to do this even less than I wanted to a second before. The sweet cat-guy makes me yearn for something real, something honest. Something *I* could convince myself I need. Not this. Not the nightmare I'm currently living in.

"Another drink?" the bartender asks, leaning close.

"God yes." I push the empty glass back over.

He opens the bottle and the dark red splashes against the curve of the glass and the pinprick of hairs rise off the back of my neck. Blood. All I can see is blood. Blood hitting my chest. Blood sliding between my breasts. The way Jack looked sitting on the edge of my bed. The way he came all over my belly.

A tiny pulse throbs between my legs. I hate it. Hate how they control me, how they turn me into... *Jesus*. Like they're the locks and I'm the key, designed to fit in their darkness.

I spin away from the red liquid and watch Mr. Nice, seat-giving guy walk away, without asking for my number or even my last name. Before I can decide what to do next, I hear the sound of a scuffle starting down the bar.

Not a scuffle. A fight.

"Hey!" the bartender barks, jumping over the bar. A glass smashes against the floor and a woman screams as a shard punctures her leg. The chaos only grows in intensity, and at the sight of real blood, something inside me snaps.

Get out of here...get the fuck out of here now.

It's that image of the lock inside my head that drives me from the seat. I'm not their key... and they aren't my fucking locks. They're my tormentors–they have been for years–and I've allowed myself to get caught back up in their insanity.

As the sound of fists smashing into one another consumes the bar, I slide out of my seat and look for the exit. I duck through the crowd as two others joined in the fight. A bar stool crashes over the bar, slamming into bottles of liquor. The sound of glass rains down on the floor.

I do what I do best—run.

The hallway that leads to the back exit is only a few feet away. I exhale when I reach it, taking one last look back over my shoulder to make sure Paul hasn't noticed my escape.

"Hey baby, where you running off to?" The asshole who stole my seat cuts off my path. "You scared? Want a big guy like me to protect you?"

"Not if you were the last ugly fucker on earth."

"Jesus you're a mouthy bitch." His eyes widen, looking at something over my head, I turn just in time to see another stool hurtling through the air. I duck in time, but the asshole doesn't, getting slammed in the face.

For once in my damned life, it feels like someone, or something is looking out for me. I step over him, spying the back door. I rush forward, using the screams and chaos behind me to hide my escape. Hopefully, Jack's also distracted by the fight. I have to move fast.

I hurry, my heels clattering on the tile floor as I rush along the hall, passing the women's bathroom, and then the men's. A howl of triumph roars in my head as I catch the crisp night as it wafts from the cracked open door at the rear of the building.

I can't go back to my car. Maybe if I'm quick enough, I can catch Mr. Four Hungry Cats and beg him for a ride. I grind my jaw and yank open the door. Getting out of here and away from them is the only thing driving me. I enter the alley and hurry around to the side of the bar.

In the distance, I catch sight of Mr. Nice Guy as he steps down from the sidewalk and crosses the mouth of the alley.

My heart hammers in my chest, and I barrel forward, lifting my hand to call out, *Hey!* But the words lodge in the back of my throat, caught when a shadow steps behind me.

A hand clamps around my mouth, stifling my scream, and a strong arm wraps around my middle. In the panic blur of fear, I watch Mr. Nice Guy as he, and my hope for escaping strides away. I'm torn backwards into the dark of the alley, away from hope and escape.

The voice against my ear is a hot whisper, "Gotcha."

NINE

Davis

SHE FIGHTS. SHE *ALWAYS* FIGHTS. EVEN WHEN IT'S FUTILE. It's one of the reasons I never stopped thinking about her, even after she left. The fire in her eyes. The way she draws back her shoulders defiantly, pushing her tits out. She's feisty, and there's nothing I want more than to break her apart.

That fight in her is definitely the reason my cock is rock hard and growing bigger with every squirm of ass.

"I should kill you," I say, wedging one forearm under her throat while the other wraps around her waist, pulling her against me. "Just blow your fucking brains out and save us the hassle."

I sense the moment she recognizes my voice, by the way her body stiffens. Yeah, this bitch would rather be in the hands of The Binder than Davis Higgins. Katie is impulsively foolish sometimes, but she's not dumb.

"The fight in the bar got crazy. People were throwing things," she says, chest rising and falling. "I got scared."

"You don't get the opportunity to be scared, you stupid little cunt." I spin her around, releasing her and simultaneously shoving her against the brick wall. I yank the gun out of my waistband and press it against her temple. "This isn't a game. It's a mission. One that, somehow, your step-brothers have decided to make you part of."

"Fuck you, Davis," she says. "Either use that gun or shove it up your ass."

Hot rage explodes in my veins. "What did you say, slut?"

"You heard me. I did exactly what I was told to do. I let Paul and Oliver dye my hair and groom me. I let them dress me up and bait me on the hook. I sat at the bar, flirted with a few guys." The glint in her eye is a dare–like she wants me to pull the trigger and put her out of her misery. It's tempting but no. Not yet. "So yeah, I tried to run, because you four are a bunch of fucking serial killer hunting psychos."

It's the fight that makes her say things like that. Any other female would've fucking given up already, gone to the cops, killed themselves, or broken down in a whimpering mess. But there's something in her that's unquenchable. I know the feeling, the darkness twisting around my soul. It propels me, motivates me.

"Oh, Kate, you dumb little whore." I run the nose of the gun down her cheek. "Your mouth is so pretty, but you say such stupid things. I'd get off cramming this in your mouth and pulling the trigger." I laugh. "But then you wouldn't be able to suck cock anymore and that's one of your best features." Her jaw opens to say something back–something smart I'm sure–but self-preservation kicks in and she clamps it shut.

"Good slut," I tell her. "You're learning." I drag the tip of the gun down her throat, pressing it hard against her chest, over her heart. Her breathing stills, the first real sign of fear she's shown since coming out here. I laugh, and run it over the swell of her tit, watching the nipple pebble on contact. "Fear makes you horny, doesn't it?"

"You wish," she replies, but it's barely a whisper, "you psychotic asshole.

I don't let her insult stop me, continuing to move the gun lower, down her belly to the hem of her skirt. I nudge the fabric up, until the barrel of the gun is between her legs. "It's like you want me to hurt you."

"If you're going to kill me, then kill me," she says. "Just get it the fuck over with."

"Sweetheart, if I could do that you'd already be in the ground, but your brothers can't stop thinking with their cocks and their cocks are focused on you." The instant the tip of the gun hits the crux of her body, she shudders in actual fear. "But to be honest, I kind of understand the appeal of keeping you around. It's fun yanking your strings like a sexy little puppet. Pushing you to your edge."

With my free hand I reach under her skirt and twist my fingers in the thin scrap of lace covering her pussy. I raise my eyebrows at the wet heat and laugh. "I knew you liked it rough. Do you always get wet when someone shoves a weapon up your cunt?"

"No." Her tone is defiant, but there's no mistaking the juices flowing between her legs. "You repulse me. Just being near you makes me sick."

"Oh, if that were only true." I grin. "But here we are, alone in this alley, your pussy gushing, and you need to be taught a lesson."

"Y-y-you're," she stutters as I run my finger over her clit, "deranged."

"We know that already, Katie, yet you keep pushing me." I lean in and lick the lobe of her ear. "Spread your legs, it'll go easier that way. I'd hate for the gun to go off by accident."

She doesn't—*always fighting*—so I nudge her knees apart roughly with my own. I spread her folds with my fingers and place the nozzle at her core. There's resistance, but not as much as there should be, and I inch the gun inside. Her knees tremble, and I circle my hand around her hip, holding her up against the wall.

"Don't do this," she says, wincing as I push the gun in a little further. "I won't disobey again."

I don't stop, fucking the gun in and out of her pussy. She takes it, knowing that one false move could end her life. A bead of sweat trickles down her neck and I bend, darting my tongue out to lick it. She tastes like salt, smells like fear. My cock is so hard, like the gun, locked and loaded, ready to explode. I swallow back the burning desire. This isn't about me. It's about making her understand her place.

"Say you want this," I tell her. She shakes her head and I push the gun in further. "Say it."

She swallows, eyes brimming with angry tears. "I want it."

"Say you're a filthy whore." I brush my thumb against her clit and her whole body quivers.

She cries out. "I'm a f-f-ilthy whore."

Her sob is interrupted by the sound of footsteps crunching on the gravel, echoing off the brick walls. I slap my hand over her mouth. Fucking hell. The last thing I need is to get caught back here by some goody-goody citizen. I spend a lot of time managing my public persona with the community so that no one suspects a thing about my true mission.

"Shhh." I still my hand, the gun lodged deep in her pussy, and look whisper, "Don't make a fucking sound."

Looking back over my shoulder all I see is the outline of a figure at the mouth of the alley. Huddle close to Kate, blocking her with my body. No one can see me with her.

"Over here," he calls, and two more shadowy figures emerge. The tallest one walks forward. As they get closer my shoulders relax. It's just the guys.

"This one tried to escape." I pull away from her, giving them a glimpse of Kate's face. "You caught me in the middle of administering punishment."

The guys huddle around, and Jack reaches out, lifting her skirt to reveal where I've got the gun. I pull it out a little and she emits a soft cry.

Her eyes dart from one guy to the next, looking for sympathy. "Please make him stop. I promise I won't try to run again."

Jack grins, eyes flicking to Kate's. He runs a finger down her cheek. "You like it, don't you?"

"No," she grinds out, breath hitching. The next words she says come as a desperate plea. "Please." But she sinks back down on her own, filling herself with the barrel. Her hand reaches out to grip Jack's bicep, steadying herself.

"Jesus Christ," Oliver says. "She's begging for it."

I grin. "Such a dirty, dirty, little slut."

Feeling bolder with the guys backing me up, I focus on fucking the woman in front of me. Jack tucks his arm around her waist, holding her up, while Oliver lifts her skirt and Paul shines the flashlight of his phone between her legs so we can all watch. I glide the gun in and out, fucking her with the barrel. Slick pussy juice coats the steel. With each push and pull she cries out, begging for more, for me to go deeper, for me to give her what she wants.

There's a point, when her head drops to Jack's shoulder and her shoulders tremble that I'm not sure what Katie wants more, death or an orgasm.

The only thing I can give her right now is the climax, and when it comes, it rushes over her like a tidal wave. Her pussy clenches, I feel the resistance as her muscles grip the black metal.

"Fuck me," one of the guys mutters, my heart is pounding too hard for me to discern who. They're horny as fuck, *we're* horny as fuck, but now isn't the time or place. This is about her understanding her place. Understanding that we own her, body, and soul. Life to death.

I pull out the gun and wipe the sticky residue from her pussy off with the hem of my shirt. I nod at Oliver. "Go check the parking lot and see if the fight cleared out or if I need to go handle things."

He walks back down the alley and I take a deep breath, needing a minute to get my body under control. I glance over at Kate, watching as Jack holds onto her shaky frame. Big brother's got a hold on her.

Paul pulls out a handkerchief and wipes between her legs, adjusting her panties over her swollen pussy. "We'll ice that back home," he says, lowering her skirt. It should bother me that he wants to dote on her like this, but it's his way. How we react to this female, how we treat her, use her, has always been different.

Down the alley, Oliver waves to me.

"Get her home," I say. "Even if The Binder is still here, she's not in the condition to deal with him."

"Got it," Jack says, getting her to her feet. He and Paul start the other way, circling around the building to get to the car. I wait until they're out of sight to meet up with Oliver.

We all have different roles. Mine is to maintain order and control. And although it may seem like I lost control back there, I didn't. I gave Katie exactly what she needed.

Jack and Paul will make sure she gets home and is taken care of, because we didn't catch The Binder tonight, and we're going to need to use her again.

TEN

Kate

I can't move. Even an inch and my pussy throbs, raw and tender. The ache reminds me of exactly what happened last night. I lift my gaze to the rear-view mirror and catch sight of the stranger looking back at me—as if I'd forget.

He fucked me... with a gun.

My pulse speeds at the memory. Disgust. Terror... and *heat* rolls through me. I hadn't come that hard in a long time. My body still clenches with the memory, desperate to feel the steel. Paul took me home, carried me upstairs, and tucked me into bed with an ice pack between my legs. I moaned when he inspected my body, his fingers sliding in where the gun had been. *No trauma,* he said. *Just a bruise. You'll be better in a day or two.*

I woke terrified, listening for creaks in the rooms upstairs. It took me thirty minutes to gather the courage to use the bathroom. But the moment I stepped outside my room the house felt too still. I showered, pressed my towel against my swollen pussy, and then dressed, applying makeup before I grabbed my things and left.

I pull out of the driveway and see the Audi on the street. Jack sits inside, waiting, watching. Paranoia makes me check the rear-view mirror as I make my way into the city, but if he's there I don't see him. I know that doesn't mean anything. There are four sets of eyes on me at all times. Last night taught me that.

I go through the motions, finding a parking place. Gathering my things. I take a final look in the mirror, before focusing on the building in front of me. The Gazette is one place I need to be, and yet right now I'm terrified of walking to the door.

Thoughts of me running are cast aside as fast as they come. If I run now, I'm as good as dead. Davis made sure I understood that I'm a trigger pull away from disappearing for good. My only hope to survive is to be useful, more useful than last night.

My body aches with every movement, but I finally get out of the car and quickly walk to the Gazette. I force a smile as I step through the doors and cross the foyer, taking the elevator this time to my new office.

"Kate," Henry barks when I walk in, barely lifting his gaze from a stack of folders spread out on the desk in front of him.

I hurry into his office, the words *sorry I'm late* on the top of my tongue, but he's already giving orders.

"I need you on this." He rises from his desk, gathers the files, and motions me to follow him. He stops abruptly, and turns, assessing me. I catch concern, then a flicker of annoyance. "Your hair. It's different."

My pulse skips. Heat races to my cheeks. "New job, new hair," I say, forcing a laugh.

"Hmmph." He turns and continues toward the wall of missing men. "I want you looking into these guys, picking them apart. The police haven't found a connection yet, and I want *us* to be the one who finds it first. This is everything we have so far. It's not a lot, plenty of blank spaces for you to fill in."

"Sure." I take the files. None are particularly thick. I sense a lot of work ahead.

"Your desk is in the corner. The computer password is on a sticky note on the screen." I try not to laugh at the old-school setup of the office. It's like stepping back twenty years. "If you need anything else, Delores can help you."

I glance over at the secretary across the room. She's made no effort to greet or speak to me. "I think I should be fine."

I step up to the board and look at the men, taking care to avoid the one I'd watched get brutally murdered in the top floor of my house. Did my stepbrothers and their friends really hunt and kill all these men? And if they made it on their list, why? What had they done to get on their radar, because, although I'm not here to make justifications for their psychopathic ways, there does seem to be a method to their madness?

If my experience with the man I'd watched Jack kill in his bedroom was telling, they hunt, and kill, bad men.

But it's not just the missing men on my radar now. I scan the walls, not finding the information I'm looking for. "The Binder. Who's on that case?"

"Me." Henry settles those critical eyes on me. "Why?"

I give a careful shrug. "Just wanted to see if you needed another set of eyes."

He shakes his head. "I wouldn't bother, there hasn't been any new activity on that in weeks. You'll have your hands full anyway." He moves toward his office. "I expect good things from you, Kate. Don't let me down."

"I won't, Sir."

He pauses. "Oh, and by the way. The new kid does the grunt work. We get lunch from Stevie's down the street at one. Don't be late. You don't want to work with us when we're hangry."

"Got it."

My desk is ancient, with scratches on the top, the chair squealing on the hardwood floors. I wince at the sound and sit tenderly. Before anything, I down two painkillers and get to work, punching in the log-in details.

Thankfully, the system is modern, similar to the kind we used in my journalism program. I open a new folder and a giddy feeling blooms in my chest. There's nothing more exhilarating than a blank document. Like I can fill it with anything I want. I can craft a story from a few facts and a lot of digging. This job really came down to how much work you were prepared to put in, with some elbow grease and hard work, and I know I can unearth the darkest secrets about those around me.

This is what I came back to Wilmington for.

Gotcha.

Davis' voice fills my mind, shocking me back to reality. I open the top folder and splay out the documents before I get to work transferring details into my own format. Name, address, date of birth and employment history come up easily, but I know there's more. Something connects these men other than my brothers.

Hours pass, a true distraction for the first time in weeks, and when I finally look at the time, I see that it's close to one. Lunch. My fingers ache, but it's a good ache, a comforting ache. This ache I understand. This ache will get me the things I need.

The Binder slips into my mind as I stride out of the building and cross the street. Running last night was stupid, for more than the obvious reason of pissing Davis off. The reporter in me wants to find him, to feel that rush of coming face to face with a man like that. I can be the one to lure him out, to call the cops on his ass and watch as he's handcuffed and taken to jail.

Solving The Binder can be the thing that gets me out of this hellhole for good.

I walk down the street, moving slower than I'd like, but the soreness between my legs won't allow me to go further. Thankfully, Stevie's Diner is nearby. A small, blackboard sign sits outside a cobblestone courtyard.

It's quiet inside. A few people sit in booths toward the door where there is light from the windows, and a mix of guys in business suits and work uniforms sit at the counter.

"Help you?"

I turn at the voice, catching the barman wiping his hands on a cloth, heading my way.

"I'm here to pick up the lunch for the Gazette?"

"Oh, yeah, you're the new girl." He smiles, giving me the once over. "Henry and the crew have a standing order. You want to add something to that?"

"What's your special?"

"Crab and coleslaw baguette, with a side order of fries."

"Sure. I'll take that."

He nods, giving me a wink that seems friendly, but after the last few days everything creeps me out. I move to the other side of the bar and crash into something hard.

Something that gives a grunt.

"Oh shit!" Panic surges through me but it eases when I jerk my gaze to the guy I just walked into. For once, it's not one of my stepbrothers or their friends. "Sorry!"

"No." The guy lifts his head and gives me a soft smile. "That's totally my fault. Too busy on my phone."

I stare at him. "Wait... I know you."

A slow grin tugs at his mouth as he tilts his head. "Right. From the bar from last night, right?"

"Mr. Nice Guy," I reply, and instantly regret it.

He laughs. "Wow, I've been called a lot of things but that's a first."

"Sorry, sometimes I speak before I think."

"It's fine. I can think of worse nicknames." He looks me over. "I see you made it out of the bar unscathed."

For a second, I think he knows what happened in the alley, and the burn in my cheeks returns. "I, uh," I stumble over my words. "Barely."

"That fight started right after I left," he says, unaware that I'm struggling. "I tried to get back inside to make sure you were okay, but they'd blocked the doors."

"Yeah, that was crazy. I ran out the backdoor." And straight into trouble.

"Good idea." He grins. "So, you work around here?"

I jerk my head toward the door. "Just started today at the Gazette."

"The Gazette?" His brow rises. "Well done, small paper, but a good reputation." He glances over my shoulder, and I follow his eyes to a table of a woman and two other men. "Well, I should go finish my lunch. Breaks almost over."

"Oh, sure." A flicker of disappointment moves through me. It's refreshing to talk to someone normal. "Sorry again."

"Hey, no worries. It was good walking into you again."

I give a chuckle, lifting my hand in a wave, but he's already squeezed back in the booth, talking to his coworkers. I wander to the back of the diner and slide into an empty booth. I've settled in when there's movement in the corner of my eye.

"Got room for your big brother?"

The movement is so fast and seamless I'm stunned for a second, then that panic rushes to the surface. "Oliver."

He turns his head and levels me with a stare. "Just checking to see how your first day of work is going."

"I thought stalking me was Jack's job."

He shrugs. "He had business to attend to, but don't worry, one of us is always watching".

I swallowed hard, forcing the flutter in my chest back down. Hoping to get this over with, I say, "Work is fine."

He shifts his body toward me, his eyes moving down my body until they stop between my thighs. His palm lands on my upper thigh. "Good. I'm glad to see you were feeling well enough to go in today. I'd hate for you to make a bad impression so early."

I shift, clamping my things together. "I'm sore, but you and I both know that if I didn't show up Henry would call Montie and we'd all be screwed."

"That's why I've always liked you, Katie. You're smart." He looks across the diner where Mr. Nice Guy is paying for his lunch. "Except when it comes to men. You have terrible taste."

There's a hard glint in his eye and fear surges up my throat. "Don't hurt him. He's just a normal guy. He's got four cats, for god's sake."

"You don't get to play with normal guys, Katie. You have us." He licks his lips, his eyes glinting. "And only us."

"I know," I answer quietly. "He's nothing to me and therefore should be nothing to you."

"It's not that easy. Our mission is dangerous. We can't have any loose ends." He reaches out and tucks a piece of hair over my ear as if making a point. "Remember that if you get the urge to make new friends with 'normal' people. It won't end well for anyone." The threat isn't lost. Talk to anyone else about their disturbing secrets and I'm dead. They're dead. Silence and cooperation are the only way to stay alive.

"I understand," I whisper.

"Good." He shifts next to me and drapes his arm over my shoulder. "Now, I'd love nothing more than to finger you under the table, while Mr. Nice Guy over there watches, but even I understand your pussy needs a break."

I look over at Mr. Nice Guy—Ryan. He's laughing at something one of his co-workers said. What would I do if he came back over here? I blink away, not wanting to make eye contact and find out.

Oliver's hand grabs mine and he places it on his belt. Our eyes meet and he nods. "Undo my belt."

Shock hits me. "What? Here?"

"Undo. My. Belt, Katie." He searches my eyes, drinking in every flicker of humiliation. "I've had a raging boner since last night and since we've got a little time," he flattens my fingers over his hard bulge, "why not?"

My breath races as I try to think. But he's boxing me in, forcing me to... Jesus.

"Can't we go somewhere else? The bathroom?"

He shakes his head, a small smile twitching on his lips. "Sorry, sweetheart, you know how I like it."

The flash of that night comes roaring back. What he did to me. How they watched. I glance at Ryan, then back at Oliver. Even though there's no one directly around us, we're very exposed. "I need to get back to work."

"Then you better fucking get started."

And that's that. He never once looks away as I slide my hand along the slick leather and tug, sliding the buckle free.

"The button."

I swallow hard, fingers move to the button.

"Keep going."

His voice is so slow and hypnotic that I find myself doing exactly what he wants, sliding the zipper low.

"Your hand, Kate."

I do as I'm told, sliding my hands under the fabric and wrapping my fingers around his cock. He's thick and hard. I can't stop my body from responding, growing warmer, softer, clenching as my fingers curl around him. My pulse races when the sounds from the kitchen invade.

"Concentrate," he commands, his arm sliding along the top of the seat, pulling me closer.

The way he's sitting obscures the view of what I'm doing. But we're out here, *exposed*.

"Jack's had a taste, so has Davis. But you don't come to me. You don't *come* for me." His voice sinks into my mind and in this second, I know that this is the most dangerous thing that they can do to me.

My body will heal.

My innocence is already in tatters.

But my mind. God, my mind will forever replay this moment. My mind will forever replay the intoxicating thrill of playing these dangerous games.

"Look down."

My head lowers with barely more than a *push* of his desire. My fingers curl around his shaft. The thick veins pulse under my fingers. My mouth waters at the sight and I know that this is wrong. This is so very fucking wrong, but all I can see is that night. Him, me... *all of them.*

He reaches over, slides his thumb along my lips as I work his cock, sliding all the way up, and then down, fisting him.

He doesn't say a word, but I can feel him hot under my hand, that thick head blushing bright as I fist him harder. He doesn't growl, barely breathes, even when I feel him come close.

"Napkin," he finally grunts, jaw tight, cheeks red.

I use my free hand to snatch one from the middle of the table and then discretely continue stroking his cock. I'm fixed on the movement, where the tiny slit beads with a tiny clear drop. My fist tightens, gripping him hard as his body kicks.

I'm fast with the napkin, catching the cum as it shoots, then slides down the hot skin. I wipe him, tending to him.

I'm wet and aching. Sore or not, I'd let him fuck me just to soothe the desire, and the shame of that hits hard. I don't know why I'm gentle when I slide him back inside his pants. But he takes over, tugging up his zipper and buttoning his pants.

"Kate!" A voice rings out across the diner. I look up and see the guy behind the counter holding up my order.

I nod, body shaking, and call out, "Coming."

"Well, one of us did," Oliver says, slipping his belt back in place. "I'm glad you understand this arrangement." He eases out of the booth, shoulders ease, demeanor calm like I didn't just jerk him off in a restaurant full of customers. I feel small with him standing over me but alive as my body is consumed by fire. "I'll make sure to let the others know. I hope you enjoy your first day at your new job. Oh," he reaches out and touches my chin, "don't forget, Katie, someone is always watching."

I don't move until he's exited the diner, and I pretend my hands aren't shaking as I grab the order off the counter. I keep my eyes forward on the street. I don't need to look for them to know they're there.

Up in the office, I hand out the food, stopping last at Henry's desk. He takes the stack with one hand and gestures for me to wait with the other.

"I'd set up a meeting with an expert before you started," he says, opening his carton of food. Inside is a greasy hamburger and fries. "If anyone understands the psyche of who is behind the mystery of these missing men it'll be him." With greasy fingers, he hands me a post-it note. "Here's the name and address."

I look down and what little appetite I had instantly vanishes. Yeah, Henry's right. This guy definitely knows the ins and outs of this case.

Dr. Paul Sanders
3 PM

Fuck.

ELEVEN

Paul

"And how long have you been feeling this way?" I ask, posing my pen over the paper while looking at my client expectantly.

"Since childhood, if I'm honest with myself."

"Mmhm. And these urges. They're frequent?"

The man sitting on the black leather chair picks imaginary lint off his pants. It's a tell. He does this whenever he's considering his answer, if he's going to tell the truth or fudge a little. "Once or twice a week," he finally answers, keeping his eyes down.

"Do you abstain or give in?"

His wedding band gleams on his left hand, vanishing as he rakes it through his dark hair. "I try to fight it off, but when it gets too much, I lock myself in my office and get on the forums or online groups."

"But that's all. Nothing in person? No sex workers? No meet-ups?"

He shakes his head. "No. My wife... I love her. I love my family. I don't want to screw this up."

"You just want to fulfill your cravings."

His eyes meet mine. They're filled with urgency. Desperation. "Yes, and I can meet that on the video calls."

My client is a submissive. He wants to be controlled and dominated. Unfortunately, his wife of fifteen years is a sweet little thing who works in a preschool and volunteers down at the nursing home once a week. In the bed, these two are an uneven match. I tap my pen on the notebook.

"What do you think would happen if she walked in on you like that? Or stumbled onto the bills."

A bead of sweat appears on his temple. "She'll leave me. My life will be over."

"Do you think the lies would hurt worse or the truth?"

He considers. "The lies."

I nod. "Then maybe we need to consider bringing her into this conversation. She may be more open minded than you think, but at the same time, you're risking everything by keeping secrets."

"I don't know if I'm ready," he admits.

"I understand, and I'm not here to pressure you. I just want us to talk over all of the options available to you." I make a show of checking my watch and then giving him a small smile. "Our time is up, but I think we made great progress this week." We both stand and I rest a reassuring hand on his shoulder. "We'll get through this complicated situation. I promise."

He pulls a handkerchief out of his pocket and wipes his wide brow. "Thank you, doc."

"Of course, that's what I'm here for."

He exits and I sit at my desk, scribbling a few notes. Mitchell Wasserman had initially been a person of interest, but the more he reveals himself, I realize he doesn't fit the profile at all. I cross him off the list for good and slide his file into the cabinet, then press the intercom button on my phone and say, "Paige, you can send her in."

My pulse quickens when Katherine walks through the door. She looks gorgeous–even though I miss her natural hair color. The dark tone does highlight the pink of her plump lips, sending a zing of electricity through me. Her skin is flushed– she's anxious–although she keeps her shoulders pushed back, in an attempt to look controlled and professional. Underneath the bravado, I see the hesitancy in her gate. Her core aches from Davis' brutality. I wondered if she'd actually show today, but I know not to underestimate this woman. She's stronger than she looks.

"Close the door," I direct. It clicks shut, sealing us in. "And take a seat."

My office is located in a converted carriage house back behind my home, a bungalow nestled in the heart of the historic district. I wanted a place my clients can feel safe, but more, a place I can control. The walls are soundproof, the furniture comfortable– pricy but unassuming. The whole office is carefully curated to create a sense of assurance while also establishing my authority as a professional.

"How are you feeling?" I ask as she gingerly lowers herself down on the loveseat. "Do you need any pain medication before we start? I have prescription samples in the cabinet."

"I'm fine," she says, smoothing out her skirt. I spot a stain on the gray fabric. Spill? She notices my attention to it and covers it with her hand. Hmm… guilt. "Since I'm here for the Gazette, I'd like to keep our conversation focused."

"Of course, I'm at your service."

Her eyes narrow, but she flips open the cover of a notebook. "Let's start with your qualifications."

I smile. "I have a MD in psychiatry, did my residency at Emory University, and have taken several courses at the FBI with the behavioral unit, that allows me to establish myself as an expert in human behavior."

Katherine writes all this down in loopy girlish letters. I allow my gaze to linger over her long legs and the red toes peeking from the cutout in her shoes.

"That's all very impressive," she says. "I'd always known you were smart, but that's quite a resume for someone your age."

"I was very motivated." I rest my hands on the arms of my chair. "As you are aware, I was rocked by the sudden and violent death of a person I was close to. It influenced the direction of my studies and ultimately my career."

I'm speaking of Jack and Oliver's mother, of course. She'd been raped and tortured, then brutally murdered when they were young. When they'd finally come out of hiding, Jack found her lifeless body in the kitchen, laid out on the butcher block countertop like a hunk of discarded meat. Even now, I can still hear Jack's screams. We all changed that day–watching her body being carried out the back door in a zipped-up black bag. We'd made a pact that very day. Find who killed their mother and serve justice.

Katherine thinks she knows us, but she has no idea what we are truly capable of. We are methodical–Davis and I working in careers that keep us close to our mission, allowing us to cover up details, finding the men to hunt. Jack and Oliver provide the means and the opportunity to fulfill our promise. The house, the tools, the brutal strength.

From her seat, she watches me closely, like she'd peel me apart like an onion if she could. Too bad she can't. I won't allow that. "The Gazette is digging into the series of missing men from the Wilmington area. There is a lot of speculation, that they ran off, possibly with a mistress, or that they have financial troubles. Others swear they wouldn't leave their families, that there is no evidence of affairs or debts." She leans forwards slightly, giving me a view into the V of her blouse. "What do you think happened to these men?"

"It could be any of the things you mentioned. Some people are very good at keeping secrets from the people in their lives."

"But so many? Nearly a dozen men have gone missing in a similar way, and we're supposed to believe that's a coincidence?"

"I don't believe in coincidences," I admit. "It's possible something bigger is at play here. They got mixed up in the wrong things." I raise an eyebrow. "You see nothing connective in their pasts?"

"Nothing anyone has noticed."

"What do you notice, Katherine?"

She holds my eye for a long moment before reaching into her bag and pulling out a thick folder. She flips it open, finger skimming down the reports. Her luscious lips move as she reads quietly to herself, and I feel her energy change when she finds it.

"They've all been charged with a domestic incident," she says, looking back up at me with wide eyes. "Some are old—years, but they're all in the file. Assault, battery, terroristic threats." She closes the folder. "All directed at women."

I grin. "See? Not everyone is as shiny and clean as they look on paper. You should know that."

"There's something else," she says, shifting slightly in her seat. Nose wrinkling at the pain. "They were all assigned to court-mandated counseling."

There it is. The connection. These men went through the system, landed on Davis' caseload, he testified in court, encouraged the judge to consider an alternative to jail time. Two weeks later their probation office makes an appointment with the best therapist in town.

Me.

"This is how you find them," she says, voice barely a whisper. "The men you hunt."

"To be fair, they put themselves in our path."

Her skin turns pale, her hands shake. We are now at a crossroads, and she knows it. I lean back in my seat. "You're a smart girl, Katherine. I'm not surprised you figured it out, but what you need to remember is that you're part of this now. Your hands are bloody."

"You want me to bury it."

"I want you to use your influence, just like I use mine, to make Wilmington a better, safer place." I stand and cross the short distance, sitting next to her on the loveseat. "These are bad men. The things they revealed to me in this very room—you'd be horrified and repulsed."

"There are better ways," she says quietly. "Legal ways."

"Are there? Is that how you'd feel if it was you they assaulted, or a friend, or child or *mother*?"

I rest my hand on her thigh, pushing the hem of the skirt up. "What are you doing?" she asks.

"While you decide how you want to handle this assignment, I'm going to check how you're healing."

She tugs at her skirt. "It's fine. Just a little sore."

I give her a sympathetic smile. "You don't have to act brave for me, Katherine. I know you're in pain. I see it on your face every time you move. Lie back, let me check you out." Her fingers loosen their grip on the fabric, but I see her eyes dart to the door. "No one can come in. The door is locked. We have absolute privacy."

She exhales and adjusts her body, leaning against the arm of the love seat. Carefully, I remove her shoes, then push her skirt up, revealing the soft pink of her panties. I ease them down her thighs, over her knees and feet. There's a spot of something dried on the fabric and I lift it to my nose. It smells of sex. My cock swells.

"Did you get horny today?" I ask. "Who?"

Her cheeks turn pink. "Oliver visited me at lunch."

"Ah," I say, well aware of Oliver's exhibitionist predilection. "He left you wanting."

It's not a question, but she bites down on her bottom lip and nods.

"For a full examination, I'm going to need you to spread your legs," I tell her, allowing one leg to drop to the floor, while the other rests against the back of the sofa. My cock strains between my legs, making it difficult for me to sit, but I ignore it, focusing on Katherine and her sweet, precious, pussy.

I reach for her folds, spreading them gently apart. Still, she hisses. "Too much?" I ask, continuing to probe a finger along her entrance. "I see the bruising." I sigh. "Davis can be such a sadist."

"He hates me," she says, looking at the ceiling. "He'd kill me if he could."

I chuckle. "True. Brutality is his first reaction, but once he sees how resilient you are–how useful–he'll settle down." I brush my finger over her clit and watch as her body trembles. "Does that feel good?"

"No," she lies, still looking anywhere but at me. "Can I go?"

"Not until I'm sure that everything down here is in working order." I press my thumb against the hot little nub and the muscles in her thighs tense. A bead of wet heat builds at her entrance, and I spread it around. "Not many women could have taken Davis' abuse last night and carried on today like nothing happened."

"I didn't have much of a choice, did I?"

"Understanding the reality of your situation isn't a flaw, Katherine." I push my finger into her pussy. "Relax. Breathe. Let me examine you."

Her hand clenches on her belly, tightening and releasing as she struggles to breathe. Her nose wrinkles when I get to the bruise, I feel the heat of the inflammation against my knuckle. Keeping my thumb on her clit, I continue to toy with the nub, watching it swell under my ministrations.

I remove my finger from her pussy. "You still need time to heal properly, but you're wet and craving. Do you want me to meet those needs?"

Her body squirms, hips rising to force the thumb still on her clit to press harder. "This is wrong." She starts to push down her skirt again. I capture her hand in mine, forcing her to stop.

"My office is an area of sacred trust and confidence." A shudder rolls through her. "Anything that happens in here, is said in here, will never leave these walls." Her eyes meet mine, they're glazed with want and desire, but I need to hear her say it. "People come here to tell me their secrets, their wants, urges, and desires. Tell me what you need, sweetheart."

She takes two short breaths and I think she's going to refuse my assistance, but then the final exhalation comes out ragged. "I need to c-come."

I smile, pleased that she's being truthful. "Good girl. Tell me how."

Her hand runs down her pubic bone, fingers connecting with mine. "Touch my tits."

"Of course." I reach for her blouse, unbuttoning the pearl buttons and exposing the pale pink bra that matches the panties. Her nipples are hard, peaked, pushing at the lace. I push the fabric aside and pinch the hard pebble between my fingers.

She cries out. "God yes."

"What else, Katherine?" I dip my head and lick the peak, sucking until she mewls. I look up at her. "Tell me what else you need." This time, the words are caught in her throat, her cheeks red with embarrassment. This is a woman that is feisty and determined but no one has ever asked her what she wants. It's common with the women that come into my office. A skill to learn. "How about I explore, and you let me know if it suits your desires."

I kiss down her belly, feeling the muscles tense and tighten under my attention. I lick her skin, and suck on the flesh just above her smooth mound. She doesn't stop me, so I continue, traveling to the slit between her legs, licking the swollen, pulsing clitoris. Her legs tense, clamping around my head. I hear her shudder an exhale. She tastes delicious—sweet—as delightful as I'd hoped. I flick my tongue over the bruised area near her entrance and she moans.

"Too much?" I ask, licking her juice off my bottom lip.

"N-no." Her hips rise to meet my mouth. "God no. The pain..."

"What about it?" I perk up.

"It hurts but... it also feels really good."

That little revelation is worth its weight in gold. I bend back down and dart my tongue in and out of her pussy, only stopping to ask, "Is this what you need?"

Her fingers curl into my hair, pulling my face forward. I laugh, breathing hot air on her sensitive nerves. *I guess so.*

Her body falls into a steady rhythm, and I do my best to keep up. She's desperately horny, the boys have been greedy little bastards. Oliver and Jack worried more about their needs than anyone else's. And Davis... well, I watched her get off with his gun buried in her pussy, but that was about him, not her. Katherine has been a good girl the past few days. She deserves to be taken care of.

Her body tenses before she comes, her thighs, her belly, her fingers in my hair. My cock engorges and I will it down—this is about Katherine and not me. For now, at least. There's nothing more that I enjoy than laying the seeds, tending the garden, and then reaping the fruit. When I finally have my way with this precious thing, it'll be worth the patience. She can fear the others, but one of us, she needs to trust.

"Oh god," she moans, hips rising and falling frantically. "I'm c-coming."

I lick her through her orgasm, letting her ride my face as she falls into oblivion. I don't stop until her fingers loosen, and her thighs fall to the side. I lift my face, slick with *her*, and meet her eye. "Do you feel better?"

"I do." Her cheeks start to burn again. "That was... um," she sits up and tugs down her skirt, "I should go."

"Of course." I stand, pulling a handkerchief out of my pocket and wiping my mouth. "There's a bathroom just outside the door if you need to freshen up before going back to the office."

"Right." She slips on her shoes, holding onto the arm of the loveseat for balance. Her knees are wobbly. "Thank you for... speaking to me today."

"Any time, Katherine," I say, moving to sit behind the desk. My boner is painful and in need of relief. I'll tend to it the instant she's gone. "Remember, you need to decide where you fit in with all of this because revealing the truth about what happened to those men isn't an option." I give her a tight smile. "Not if you want to stay alive."

She nods, brain still rattled by the orgasm, but I'm sure the message was delivered. She leaves without another word, the door snapping shut behind her. I sigh, leaning back and unzipping my pants, releasing the monster trapped inside.

When I first heard Katherine was back in town, I agreed with Davis. She should be taken care of quickly and efficiently, but now I understand the reasons to keep her close. There are so many different ways to use her for our purposes, I think, closing my eyes and fisting my cock, while I think of her wet, slick pussy. And there's no way she's getting out of here until we've all left our mark.

TWELVE

Kate

The house in front of me is in complete darkness. I sit in my car and try to slow the pounding of my heart. I don't want to be home this late, but after meeting with Paul, Henry had me running down a dozen other leads for the Gazette. I don't want to climb out of this car and enter the lion's den. But of course, what I want and what I have to do are very different things.

It's not like there isn't a damn serial rapist loose in the city. I lift my gaze to the darkened windows of my stepbrother's rooms. A rapist isn't the only monster I have to worry about. Getting home late means less time for me to lock myself in my room before they return.

I inhale, gather my nerves and exit the car. With any hope, I can be showered, in my pajamas, and barricaded in my room before my stepbrothers get home.

I grip my keys between my fingers like a weapon and race for the porch. Locks and cupboards barricaded against my bedroom door didn't seem to protect me before, so how did I think anything else short of my own demise would now?

Nothing stops them from coming after me. Not even being exposed to others during the day.

Still I have to try.

I insert my key into the lock and turn. I'm inside in a heartbeat, making my way through the house in darkness.

"You're late."

I freeze at the chilling tone and a quick movement comes from my right. I spin, my heart slamming against my chest as out of the darkness, evil lurks. Jack's dark eyes glint like shards of broken glass as he strides toward me.

I spin and stumble backward, hitting the hard banister of the stairs. "I... had to work late. Henry made me–"

"I don't give a shit what Henry made you do."

A scream echoes down the staircase. Or I think it's a scream, I barely hear it... still, the hair rising on the back of my neck confirms that it's real. I know because that's the entire reason Jack is here, grabbing my arm and yanking me against his hard body. I look down as I slam against him, terrified there's a weapon in his hand. But there isn't. There's just him. His muscular, intimidating, body. His scent... dark and tormenting, fetid and raw, with undertones of woodsy pine.

"We've been waiting."

"Waiting?" I barely force a whisper.

"Yes, Katie... waiting." He looks up the stairs. "Since you were late, Oliver had to draw it out."

He drags me up the stairs, and I cry out at the sudden movement. My core still aches from Davis' assault. I grab the railing, not just to stop myself from falling but because I realize what's happening.

"No." I jerk my arm, trying desperately to escape from his cruel hold. "I'm not going in there."

His fingers dig in, bruising as he pulls me after him. He's so much stronger and I have no choice but to stumble after him. Otherwise, I'm sure he'd have no problem dragging me to the top. When we get to the landing, I think he's going to drag me into his bedroom. But he doesn't. Instead, he goes to Oliver's.

Another groan spills out once more, sending chills up my spine. "Stop," I hiss. "Don't make me go in there... *don't—*"

Jack spins, striking like a serpent to cover my mouth with his hand. My back presses against his chest, my shirt sticky from sweat.

"You're the one digging around, desperate to know what we're doing." His words are a hot growl against my ear. "Isn't that right, little sister?"

He's right. I did, but now that we're here, I don't want to know. Not anymore.

"I'll show you exactly what happens up here to the men we hunt."

He drags me into Oliver's room and closes the door behind us. The room is dark, the only light spills from under the connecting door to the bathroom.

"Shh," Jack whispers as he steers me into the adjoining bathroom. "Don't say a fucking word."

We're both silent as he forces me across the dark gray tile. From here, I can hear the murmur of voices on the other side. I don't want to do this. Like, I *really* don't want to. I'd rather walk barefoot across broken glass.

"What happened to Sara when you took her home from the bar?" Oliver's voice spills under the door connecting to Jack's room.

I shove my hand out, grabbing the cold hand basin as Jack's hand clamps over my mouth again. "You want to know, then fucking know."

Oliver continues, "What? Cat got your tongue? Well, maybe I can fill it in for you." A loud slam echoes through the room and I jump against Jack's body. "You took her home from the bar, then the next day she files a police report saying you not only drugged her, but you raped her... *violently.*"

The laughter that follows stops me cold. I no longer fight against Jack's hold against the basin. I still, listening to the man's sick amusement and stare at the door that stands between me and this bastard my brothers caught in their snare.

I twist until I can see the shadowy outline of Jack's face. "Is that The Binder?"

His reply is low, barely a whisper. "The Binder doesn't leave witnesses, Katie. You know that."

"Drugged her?" the guy in the adjacent room blurts, then laughs again. "She fucking wanted it."

"And yet toxicology came back with GHB in her system," Oliver says, voice eerily calm. "You want to try again?"

"I'm telling you the truth!" he shouts. "That bitch was all over my cock at the bar. She wanted every inch of it when I shoved it inside."

"So she's a liar, then." I hear the pace of footsteps on the hardwoods until Oliver's voice is just on the other side of the door. "She just made up the fact that she woke up with a killer headache, no memory, tied to your bed, and your cum stuck between her legs? Is she the liar, or are you?"

I flinch at the roar in Oliver's voice and despite myself, curl against Jack. My pulse is nothing more than a rush in my ears. I know Jack is a monster, but in this moment the heat of his hold is comforting and unlike the man being interrogated in the other room, he's the monster I know.

"You got the wrong idea." That sick piece of shit argues in the next room. "I love women, man. Like really, fucking love them. I don't need to drug them to be with me. You know how bitches are. One minute they're all into it, the next they're crying rape. It's bullshit."

In a blur, Jack reaches around me, twists the door handle, and propels me forward. I stumble wildly into my brother's room, jerking my gaze to the man sitting bound on the chair in front of me.

The room is dark, lit only by a small lamp, but it's enough to reveal the cuffed man's blood-soaked shirt. The knees of his jeans are torn and his tongue darts out to lick the puffy split in his lip. I'd call him the victim, but that's not true.

There were no victims in this room—except for me.

"How's it going, baby brother?" Jack asks, stepping over a smear of blood.

"Just showing Michael here how we're kindred spirits," Oliver says. His knuckles are red and raw. "I see you brought us something to play with."

"Yep, pretty little thing, right?" Jack says, drawing a knife out from behind his back. He tilts his head toward me while speaking to the man, Michael, in the chair. "I mean, considering how much we all *fucking love women*."

"Jack." I stumble back, jerking my gaze to Oliver and then to the man on the seat. "Whatever the fuck game you're playing, I want out."

The man's eyes are wide, that same sick excitement he probably gets when he assaults women. Jack lunges, grabbing me around the throat, hard enough to consume me with panic, but not hard enough to cut off my air.

"We want to show Michael how much fun we can have together. After all, we're the same, right?" Jack clenches his hold, moving me backwards, throwing me on the bed. He's on top of me in an instant, cinching his fingers tighter around my throat, straddling me. Those thick, muscular, thighs clamp tight, trapping me in place. He lifts the knife in his hand. "We just want to know what you did to her. How you did it. I'm impressed, honestly."

"Yeah?" Michael says, eyebrows lifting.

"Sure. Tell us what you did to her, Michael. Tell us and we'll let you go." He cocks his head toward the man and grins. "And you can have *her*."

All I see is that blade. The tip pointing down at me.

"I..." Michael starts, licking his bottom lip. "I didn't rape that girl."

Jack's lips curl. My stepbrother lets out a savage snarl and plunges the knife down, driving it into the mattress. The blade stings, grazing my ear. I scream, but his hand comes down over my mouth, smothering it.

"The thing is," Jack says coldly above me. He never shifts his focus, those inhuman eyes fixed on mine. "I don't think you love women at all, do you?"

"I told you–

"You lie in wait, dosing them with GHB when they're not looking, drugging them into oblivion. Then you take them home, tie them down, and fuck them until you've had your fill."

I jerk my gaze to the asshole and shake my head. If he admits what he did they'll give me to him. Knowing my brothers, they'll just sit back and watch, just to torture me, *then* kill him.

But he says nothing, that sick desire making him smile. Jack pulls the knife free and rises from my body, grabbing my arm as he moves. With one powerful yank, he turns me over, shoving my face into the bedding.

"Tell us," Jack demands as steel touches my lower back.

I freeze with sensation, my shirt ripping. Cold air kisses my skin as my clothes are destroyed. The blade nicks my shoulder. I whimper with the sting and close my eyes. This is it. This is the moment they kill me for their own demented enjoyment.

I ready myself for the end, for this torment to be over.

There is no more fighting now, no more pleading. It never did any good anyway.

Not with them.

"I did it."

Jack stills above me.

"I did it, okay?"

Jack's warm hand lands on my side. I tremble at the contact.

"I met her at the bar and offered to buy her a drink. She said no. She *laughed* in my face. So yeah, I fucking drugged her and took her home. She was so fucking out of it, didn't even scream when I took what I wanted."

The sting on my shoulder trickles. I know its blood, sliding down the curve of my shoulder blade. But there's nothing I can do, just lay there shivering while this fucking monster strapped to the chair talks, telling us he destroyed a woman's life in a single night.

He gloats... entitled prick.

"So there. I told you what you wanted to know. Untie me," he says. "Untie me and we can have a little fun tonight." He grins at me. "I'll show you some of my favorite tricks."

My insides clench tight. He's imagining doing all those things to me, to my body and my mind.

"Yes," Oliver says, "it's definitely time to have a little fun. Brother?"

The weight of Jack's body lifts from my body and the mattress rises as he leaves me. My fingers clench, fisting the comforter. I can't help but open my eyes and turn my head as my stepbrother's stalk toward him.

But the way they move—I just know this is going to be bad. It's predatory, ruthless.

"Jack," Oliver says, giving his brother the go-ahead.

My stepbrother is an animal, a *beast*, as he lunges, driving that knife down and into the rapist's throat. Steel carves through flesh. Part of my mind knows this is what they wanted all along. That part screams in triumph as does my brother. Jack unleashes a roar, yanking the knife free to plunge again.

Over and over and over.

Blood arcs, cascading over the room. Part of me is wielding the knife with him and I know I'm fracturing. Tiny splinters of my mind are breaking away, leaving the terrified and sickened side of me behind. I'm two different versions of myself.

One who screams for justice.

And one who cries for vengeance.

When my stepbrother is finished, he straightens. Blood drips from the knife in his hand as he turns to me. "Now do you see, Kate? Now do you *really* see what we do?"

I don't want to.

So help me God, I don't.

But it's all there, painted red.

And I admit the truth, "Yes."

THIRTEEN

Kate

"Are you any good?"

I turn to the smooth voice and point to myself. "Are you talking to me?"

"Yeah," the good-looking guy laughs. His hair is blond, eyes a bright green. He gestures to the pool table. "You've been watching that game for a while now; thought maybe you were interested in a match."

"Ah," I reply in understanding, cheeks heating up at getting caught. He's right I'd been watching the pool table intently. Embarrassingly. I flip the tables. "If you noticed all that, you must've been watching me."

Crack!

The balls smack together, drawing my eyes back to the table, to the man behind the cue. My eyes skim the way his broad shoulders pull the black cotton of his T-shirt taut and the confident way he holds the stick. His free hand casually touches the woman's lower back, and he can't keep his eyes off her cleavage as she bends over to take her shot.

"Busted," the man next to me says, grinning wide. "The truth is that while I was looking for someone to play a game of pool with me, I noticed the most beautiful woman sitting all alone." He offers his hand. "I'm Christopher."

"Kate." I clasp his hand and note that his grip is firm, but not harsh. After the last few days, any sort of tenderness feels alien.

"So, Kate," his eyes drop to my lips and back up again, "are you up for a game?"

Again, I look over at the pool table and the man sinking the final ball into a corner pocket. His partner pouts, having lost, but she's not really upset. She throws her arms around him in congratulations and then presses her tits against his side. He draws his gaze away from the table and our eyes meet, causing every hair on my body to stand on end.

Jack.

It's been two days since I watched him murder a man on the third floor of the house. Shockingly, for the most part, since then they'd left me alone. I'd gone to work, waiting for the news to come across my desk at the Gazette that there was another missing man. It didn't arrive until this afternoon. Michael Holland. Age thirty-six. Divorced. Left work, hasn't been seen since. Unfortunately, when I got home, ready for a meal, a long shower and bed, I'd been told to change into the black dress and get to the bar.

"Kate?"

I blink at the man next to me. "Sure, yes. That sounds fun, but fair warning. I've never played."

"Don't worry. I can show you." Christopher leads us to the pool table where Jack collects the balls, dropping them into the triangle. "Up for a game?" he asks Jack. "Two on two?"

"Yes!" The girl smiles. "We're going to kick your asses!"

My stepbrother doesn't acknowledge me, just jerks his chin in agreement. Christopher grabs two sticks off the rack and hands one to me while he introduces himself to Jack and then Christopher looks over at me.

"I'm Kate," I add, gripping the pool stick like a support.

"Brandi," the girl says, waving at the two of us with jewel tipped nails. Up close I realize how young she is. Probably barely out of high school. Her lips are painted a bright red, her eyes heavily made up. Her fingers catch a loose strand of hair, and she tucks it behind her ear. It's a shade lighter than my dye job but pulled up in a tight ponytail. Through the thin, pale-yellow fabric of her top it's obvious she's not wearing a bra. The round areolas of her nipples distractingly visible through the fabric. She's young, but she doesn't seem immature, carrying herself with a confidence I can't even pretend to have–especially around Jack. I mean, who wouldn't with tits like that?

"Nice to meet you, Brandi," Christopher says, giving her a warm grin and somehow managing not to look at her chest. This guy oozes charm the way Jack simmers with rage; low and under the surface.

"Flip for it?" Jack says, pulling out a quarter.

"Heads," Christopher claims as he tosses the coin in the air. Jack lets it land on the table spinning around the green felt. It falls to one side.

Jack grins and winks at me. "Getting tail always brings me luck." He rolls the balls to the center of the table and removes the triangle holding them in place. He bends, giving a nice view of his ass. Jack and Oliver have a workout room in the basement of Davenport Manor. It's obvious to everyone in the bar that he works out.

Little do they know; he needs the muscle mass to carry dead bodies out of the house in one trip.

Crack! The white ball slams into the triangle, snapping my gaze away from his ass. I tuck my hair behind my ear as the guys figure out how many balls went into the pockets and who gets solids or stripes.

"Oh, stripes!" Brandi cheers, pushing up on her tip-toes to kiss Jack on the cheek. "Good job, baby."

My eyebrow raises at the term of affection. Is this girl more to him than just a simple mark? Sure, she fits The Binder's profile, but is there something else going on?

"Katie, your turn."

I lift my eyes to Jack's, who smirks at me as he takes a pull from his beer. A warm hand rests on my shoulder. "Her name is Kate, right?"

I nod, feeling grateful to be heard for once. "Right."

My stepbrother's eyes crease at the sides, the slightest hint of annoyance. "Ah, right. *Kate,* it's your turn."

I step forward, flustered by his intimidating presence, stressed that one of them is going to catch on that we know one another. I find an angle and line the white ball up with the solid green ball across the table.

"You got it?" Christopher asks, easing up next to me.

"I think so." I focus on the angle I need to make the shot. Across the table, in my peripheral vision I see Jack's hand wind around Brand's hip, thumb dipping under her low-rise jeans.

The stick wobbles and I feel movement behind me. "Here, let me help." Christopher's body swoops in behind me, his knee sliding between my legs and nudging them apart. "You've got to keep your knees and shoulders even," he says, "Then while bending over, take a step forward," he accentuates this by tapping my hip with his fingers. "And make sure you keep your chest level with the ground."

With the weight of him behind me, I feel calmer, more in control. Just knowing there's someone between me and Jack makes me feel better. I pull the stick back, aiming at the white ball and *smack!* I make contact, sending the white ball into green and ultimately into the corner pocket.

"I did it!" I jump up. "I got one in!"

"You sure did," Christopher says, smiling. "You get to go again."

He doesn't help me this time, well, not as much. When I bend over, making sure to keep my chest level, he rests his hand on my lower back, sending a warm heat up my spine. I think I have the shot lined up, when he brushes my backside with his hips, jolting me forward in surprise. I scratch, the cue hitting the felt. I feel Jack's hard gaze on me, and when I look up, he's not looking at my face but down the front of my dress.

"Shit," I say to myself, covering up.

"Fucking hell," Jack mutters, pushing his fingers through his thick hair. "Anyone else need a drink, or just me?"

"Let me get it," Christopher says, already walking toward the bar. He points at Jack and Brandi. "Two beers?" Then to me. "Another martini?"

"Yes, please."

"Sweetheart," Jack says, slapping Brandi on the ass, "why don't you go help him with the drinks."

"Good idea," she says, tapping him on his nose. "Don't miss me too much."

He grunts, eyes glued to her ass as she sashays off. He waits until they're both at the bar to ask, "What the fuck are you doing?"

My eyes snap to his. "What you told me to do. Come to the bar, get a drink, flirt with a few suspects."

He snorts. "That guy doesn't meet the criteria."

"And Brandi does?"

"She's a brunette, sexy, young—she fits the profile as much as you do, unlike Prince Charming over there." He licks his bottom lip. "I'm here on a mission. You're basically letting him dry hump you against the table."

I blink. "You did not just say that."

"If you'd bent over a little bit more, he could shove his cock right up your pussy."

Rage licks my spine. "Shut up," I tell him. "I'm only here because I'm forced to be here by you and your deranged friends."

His lip curls into a snarl. "Look at you, acting all ballsy out in public," he steps close, "when two nights ago you were begging for mercy. Do you think he'd want you if he knew who you really are? How you get wet when I run a blade down your soft skin and how much you want your stepbrother's cock buried inside of you?"

I drag my eyes up from his mouth and whisper, "I doubt your little girlfriend would stick around long if she knew that you're a psychotic murderer with delusions of grandeur. You do realize that not every woman thinks you're God's gift, right?"

"I don't know, Kat*ie*," he accentuates the nickname, "I'm pretty sure every woman I've been with would admit that my cock is pretty fucking grand. I'm sure, if I gave her the chance, Brandi would agree."

My heart thunders, pounding wildly against my ribcage. Jack isn't just a murderer, he's a narcissistic asshole. He does the things he does because he thinks he's owed it, entitled to it. I know that it fucking kills him that he can't catch The Binder because it makes him look weak. I also know that if I'm not careful he'll take all that rage and sadism out on me.

"Sorry that took so long," Christopher says, drawing me away from Jack's cold blue eyes. "A martini for the beautiful Kate."

I swallow and give him a small smile, taking the drink and then immediately resting it on the edge of the pool table. "I, um, I think I need to use the restroom. I'll be right back."

I hurry away from the pool table, pushing through the crowd of people toward the back hall. A woman steps out of the bathroom, and I step in, breathing in the cooler air away from the bar.

My hands shake as I turn on the water, splashing a little on my face. Pushing Jack like that... it was stupid. So fucking stupid.

A woman steps out of the stall and moves to the sink. I catalog her: red hair, freckled skin, green eyes. Not The Binder's type. Lucky girl.

She catches my eye in the mirror. "You okay?"

"Yeah. Just got a little hot out there, you know?"

"It's packed." She grins. "But it's ladies' night. The wolves are on the prowl."

"That's the truth." I turn back to the mirror and hear the door swing open. In the reflection I see a wall of black: T-shirt, hair, jeans.

Jack.

"Get out," he tells the redhead.

Her eyebrows raise and she opens her mouth to speak. I shake my head. "It's fine."

She exits and he slams the door behind her, flipping the lock.

"What do you want, big brother?" I ask, playing calm, but my nerves start buzzing the second that door is locked. "Brandi not holding you attention?"

"I want you to shut your mouth for five goddam seconds, Katie." He steps forward, hips pressing against my backside, pinning me against the counter. His cock is already hard and demanding. "I want you to remember who you're talking to. *Who* I am, and *what* I can do if you're not careful." His hand splays across my stomach and our eyes meet in the reflection. "But the thing is, I think you do know, and I think you like testing me."

Do I? I wonder. Because I can't seem to stop myself even though I know every interaction with him will end the same, with me in pain, begging for mercy. Yet here I am, anyway.

His hand drops down to the hem of my skirt. He lifts it, revealing my backside. He palms my ass. "I've been thinking about your ass for two days," he says quietly. "Ever since I flipped you over on that bed." He rocks against me, the denim rough against my bare skin. "I should've taken you right there, made that pervert watch as I defiled you, but," his fingers twist in the black lace thong, tearing it off, "he didn't deserve to watch." He nudges my legs apart. "This is between me and you."

The hand on my belly wanders, sliding up my torso until he reaches the low V in my neckline.

"You were out there teasing me with these," he says, pupils dilating. He yanks aside the dress, revealing my tits. No bra for me either, Paul made it clear I should go without. My nipples peak at the rush of air and his hand cups underneath, kneading roughly. "Teasing and taunting me all the time."

He pinches my nipple and I drop my head back, crying at the pain. His teeth graze the side of my neck, nipping and biting at the flesh. Each pinpoint of pain jolts through me, electrifying my body, the currents zinging down my body until it pools into something hot and molten at my core.

He bends me forward, both our faces level in the mirror. His fingers sweep between my legs. He grunts. "Fucking slippery wet."

I squirm against the friction, wanting more. He wastes no more time, unbuckling his belt and pulling out his cock. I can see it in the mirror, skin blistering red and taut with engorgement. My knees quiver, because this time there's something different passing between us, something raw and feral. There's no out this time. I can see it on his face. It's the face of a hunter that's finally cornered his prey.

"I've waited a long time for this," he says, pressing the tip of his cock against my entrance. "I've wanted to fuck you since the day my daddy brought your mama into our house. I dream about you. Watch you. Fantasized about you while you were away, but now that you're back, I'm not letting the opportunity pass by again, and," his eyes narrow, "I'm not letting another man's cock inside of you before I get a chance."

With that he punches in, driving in the length of his erection. He isn't slow, or tentative, no, he goes in hard, and before I have the chance to adjust to the size of him, he pulls back and slams in again. My breath knocks out of me, lost in the relentlessness. His hand grips my hip, fingers digging into my flesh as he holds on tight. My eyes flutter shut as he fucks me, the sound of our skin slapping a harsh echo in the tiled room, but tight fingers on my chin force them back open.

"Watch me as I claim you, Katie. I need you to see it."

He pins our gaze together, and I ignore everything else. The way the edge of the counter digs into my lower belly. The sound of our ragged breathing. The shouts from the bar outside and the loud banging on the door as someone tries to come in. I push all of that aside, consumed with the fact Jack Davenport—*my stepbrother*—has me bent over the counter in a shitty bar bathroom and is fucking what little bit of sense I had, right out of me.

I watch him in the mirror, cheeks red, jaw clenched, the picture of perfect restraint. But I feel him inside of me, feel the thickening of his cock pressing against my walls. He's close, seconds away from shattering inside of me. He may be asserting his claim over me, but one thing is clear, my pussy lives rent-free in my stepbrother's pretty head.

"You going to come for me," he commands, bending so his mouth is close to my ear. "You're going to clench those walls around me and milk me until I have nothing left."

I want to say no, but the weight of him behind me, the hard way he plucks at my nipples and bites my flesh, builds my own unrelenting desire. My skin grows hot. My knees buckle. The first sparks of an orgasm lick at my spine and suddenly there's no will anymore, there's just want—just release—and the waves crash over me, shudder through me, spinning me out of control.

"There it is," Jack grunts, continuing to pound into me. "Milk me. Suck me dry." He comes in an eruption, deep and guttural. His cock pulsing against my walls. We push and pull against one another until there's nothing left but the sweat and breath between us.

"Jesus fucking Christ," he says, holding me up with an arm around the waist. "That was eight fucking years in the making."

Eight years. That's how long he's been wanting to get inside of me.

He pulls out, taking his heat and weight with him, and lean my elbows on the counter, feeling his cum drip down my leg. He bends, dragging his finger through the sticky mess, and pushes it back inside. "Don't you fucking dare clean up," he says, tucking himself back in his pants. "I want you sitting in that—*me*—for the rest of the night. If Prince Charming wants in your pants, he's going to have to wade through my cum to get there."

Realizing I'm not going to get a moment of privacy, I swallow and stand, taking a minute to straighten my panties and dress. My hair is a mess and I have a red welt on my neck from where he sucked a hickey into my skin. I do what I can, but anyone out in that bar will know I just got fucked good and hard in the bathroom. Which, according to the smirk on Jack Davenport's face, is exactly the point.

We exit the bathroom, accosted by the sound of music and loud talking. For the first time, I wonder what Christopher thinks of me disappearing for so long and Jack vanishing with me. The pool table is now occupied by two new players. My drink is long gone. I skim the room for Brandi or Christopher, but I don't see a sign of them anywhere. How long were we back there?

Jack shifts next to me, and I hear the deep vibration of his phone. He pulls it out and looks at the screen, jaw tensing as he reads.

"What?" I ask.

"It's Davis," he says, shoulders straightening. "Someone saw a woman forced into a car outside the bar thirty minutes ago. They reported it to the police. He caught the call."

"Here? Who?" I ask, looking around the room, trying to place all the people I'd seen before we went in the bathroom, but all I can think about is Jack and the way he looked minutes before when he was pumping me full of his cum.

"Here," he repeats, walking toward the door. He catches my hand and pulls me with him. "We've got to go."

"Where?" I ask, stumbling behind him.

His dark eyes meet mine. "The girl forced in the car? She matches Brandi's description."

Jack

Red and blue lights flash as I grip Katie's arm and lead her out of the bar.

"I'm just so shocked." A bystander whimpers, her arms wrapped tight around her middle as she talks to the two officers. "It happened so fast. One minute she was screaming with his hand over her mouth, then the next they were driving off."

I keep my gaze on Kate's car parked at the edge of the lot, catching movement as one of the cops turns to watch me. *Don't be a punk,* I mentally warn him... *keep your fucking focus on her.* He shifts his attention back to the woman who starts sobbing. I expect a little sense of relief, but there is none.

The bastard was right here... *right fucking here,* and I just let him get away.

"Jack?"

I snap my gaze to Kate as she stumbles in her heels. I'm moving fast now, hunting for *him.* "What?"

She flinches with the tone, but steadies herself like a good girl and tries again. "The description of the guy," she whispers. "Did Davis give you one?"

The marks on her throat are darker in the wash of cop lights. Marks I left behind when I took her in the bathroom and my pulse ignites. She'd felt so good under me, *around* me. Rage moves through me, seething, writhing, moving deeper than it's ever been before. I don't want to think about the reason why—not yet. "He's sending it now."

Beep.

I stop in the middle of the parking lot, scan the message.

> Six foot, sandy blond hair, wearing jeans and a
> blue button down.

I hold out the phone. "Look like someone familiar."

"Oh my god," she says, brushing my arm as she leans in and reads the message.

"Yep. Sounds like your Prince Charming to me."

This woman barges into my world, daring me with every fucking smile she gives to someone else. Tonight, I reached the tipping point and it cost us.

I rake my fingers through my hair in frustration, as she whispers, "There has to be a mistake."

"There's no mistake," I snap at her, then swallow my rage.

"He doesn't fit. None of this fits."

"Jesus Christ, Katie. What the fuck are you talking about?"

She flinches at my tone, then takes a step backward, but it's not my anger that has her stumbling away from me. It's excitement. Her dark eyes glint as she turns toward the bar. "If he paid by credit card, they'll have his name." I want to tell her to wait, to get in her goddamn car and get far away from here. But she's fucking quick, shifting gears from being railed in the seedy bathroom one minute to an investigator the next. "Wait for me." She lifts her hand, risking a glance to the cops. "Just wait for one minute."

She runs and I track her, fighting the fear of letting her out of my sight, that need to hunt.

My cell vibrates and it's my brother. "Ollie." On the other end of the phone is silent. He knows my mood in an instant. Even he is careful when he speaks, which says volumes. "Are you okay?"

"Do I sound okay? He was right there, and I fucking missed him!"

"No. Is Kate..." *Is Kate what?* I want to snap, but my tone would be criminal. *Dead?* Does he think I killed her? "Is Kate, what, brother?"

"The report said it was a brunette..."

It clicks. He's asking if Katie is the one in the report.

"It wasn't her," I say, both relieved and angry. Why am I relieved? This was the plan, to use her as the bait and lure out The Binder. It worked too; except I was too busy fucking her in the bathroom. "We were, uh, distracted and he snatched the bitch right out from under our noses."

I glance to the window. Inside the empty bar, she leans against the countertop talking to the bartender. That sexy black dress rises up the backs of her thighs, legs probably still slick from my cum. My cock twitches in my pants. Eight fucking years and I had to be balls deep inside her when The Binder decided to make his move.

"Jesus, Jack. How the fuck did you go off mission? It's not like you to get distracted."

"It doesn't matter," I tell him. "At least he's out in the open again. We can start to track him."

Of course that doesn't help Brandi who will be lucky if he makes it quick. I hang up. One second longer and he'll sniff out the truth. That I lost control tonight. I fucked up majorly, all because I wanted to get my dick wet. A figure moves in the doorway of the bar, I know the instant she steps out that she has no information. I could've—tried—to tell her. We're not just dealing with any two-bit fucking idiot here. He's smart, calculated, a worthy adversary. Until I catch him anyway.

"You need to go home." I jerk my head to her car. I try to keep my words in check and meet her gaze. "Now. Oliver's waiting on you."

She shakes her head and takes a step closer. I force myself not to watch how her body moves under her dress. A body I was eight inches deep inside of minutes ago—and I already want again. I clench my jaw as she touches my arm. "He wanted me," she says, guilt spreading across her features. "We can lure him again."

My gut clenches with the words and not in a good way. Something alien shifts under my skin, and I'm torn with the need to cut it out or fucking kiss her. Instead, I look down to where her hand rests on my arm, then lift my gaze. "Get in the fucking car, Katie, and go home."

My words are ice, and she flinches, yanking her hand away, nails scratching my forearm.

I move fast, taking a long stride forward. Her heels catch as she stumbles backward into the dark where the cop's lights no longer reach. "You fucking touch me again, sister, and I'll make you regret it."

Her breath catches and her eyes widen, and we're back on this collision course once more. Where she's scared of me and all I want is to hurt her.

This time I'm the one who grabs her. I want her throat, but I keep myself in check and clench my fingers around her arm instead, feeling her tremble. "You're the reason he got away tonight. *You're* the reason I let him escape. You and your—" I lower my gaze to her body and suck in the cold night air. "You're lucky I don't drag you someplace no one will ever find you and leave you there. Get the fuck in the car, Katie, and get your ass home before I do something I'll regret."

She knows me well enough to know that I'm not joking. Her hands shake as she stabs the button on her keys, yanks open the door and slips behind the wheel of the piece of crap. The *thud* of the car door is like a gunshot in the night. I know the cops will be watching as she starts her engine and shifts in reverse.

Brake lights flare red as she leaves, hitting the asphalt before driving away. I keep my eyes down and make for my car across the lot. I was barely out of my car when I drew Brandi's gaze earlier tonight. She'd been waving off a group of friends as I strode past. She looked at me like I was her ticket to somewhere, and I recognized her like she was the exact kind of sexy bait The Binder craves.

Only it wasn't the goddamn Binder I captured. It was this fucking festering *thing* inside my chest. I glance along the street, knowing Katie would be running with her tail between her legs all the way home. But that isn't what I want between her legs. I hate knowing that. I yank open my door and slide inside the Audi before starting the engine and pulling away from the bar.

Beep.

I glance at my cell, keeping under the speed limit as another cop car races past.

Davis' message is short and clear:

> No further information. He's gone. I'll be at the house soon.

He's gone. Slipped through my fingers.

Those words don't sit well with me, nothing about this whole night sits well with me. Did I really miss the signs that Christopher was The Binder or was I too focused on Katie to care? The way she flirted with him drove me insane and I snapped, wanting to mark and claim her. Instead, I fucked everything up.

I prowl through the streets, taking the long way home. For some reason, I don't want to go back there right now. I don't want to know she's in the room underneath mine or see the disappointed look in my brother's eyes.

Prostitutes stand on the corner, watching me in earnest. But that dead thing in my chest shrinks with the thought. On a normal night, I'd be up to the distraction, but nothing about tonight is normal. Nothing has been normal since she came back to town.

I should find someone else. Someone different. Someone to fuck and fuck and fuck until I get my stepsister out of my system. Until my thoughts stop automatically drifting to her over and over again.

I *need* a lot of things. But none of those are what I *want*.

I want her... and that scares the fuck out of me.

My headlights splash against familiar houses and familiar streets.

I lift my gaze finding her car in the driveway. I give her time to scurry up the stairs and barricade her door. Not that it would enough to save her. I have my ways in and out of every room in that house.

I pull up behind Ollie's Mercedes and kill the engine. The lights are on inside the house, and the smell of cooking, butter, bacon and chocolate assaults me the second I enter the kitchen.

"I can do that, Ollie," Katie says. I force myself not to react to the sound of her voice. "All you need to do is sit."

Adrenaline courses through me as I make my way through the foyer and turn to the kitchen. She's there, standing over the stove with my brother right behind her.

"I have a special method," Ollie tells her. He presses her against the stainless steel edge, his cock nestled at her ass. "You let them get good and crispy on one side, then you flip it." He curls his fingers and then drags along her arm. "Just like that."

She doesn't notice me in the doorway, but my brother does. Grinning as he turns his head. He gets a thrill out of me watching as he slides his finger under the strap of her dress and tugs it aside and kisses the smooth skin. I knew he visited her today at lunch. I watched from my car. He looked satisfied when he left, but that desire is always bubbling under the surface for all of us. We're hunters, it's never enough.

I place my phone and keys on the counter, watching as my brother fondles her as she cooks pancakes on the griddle. Late night food, the kind you get after a night at the bar. Although not exactly the kind of food you make when you hear that a serial killer has struck again. Or maybe it is? Maybe that's why this woman is so hard to resist.

"That's the way," he says, Her hand shakes, the spatula tapping against the bottom of the skillet as he reaches around to cup her from behind. The door opens and Paul steps in. His eyebrows raise as he sees the two of them at the kitchen counter. We watch my brother as he slides his hand to her hips and draws her dress higher.

"This is a change of attitude," I say, interrupting the scene. "Going domestic?"

She jolts when she hears my voice, ears turning red. She smooths down her skirt and faces me. "I thought you may be hungry after everything that happened tonight." She glances at the griddle. "I'm making pancakes."

"Pancakes," I repeat, trying to follow the scene. I shrug. "I can eat."

"Good. You guys take a seat at the table. I'll bring everything out."

I enter the dining room. It's a formal room, all china and crystal gleaming behind glass cabinet doors. I take the chair at the head of the table. My father's seat. Oliver sits at the other end, frown on his face.

"What's your problem?" I ask.

"You just had to interrupt. I was about to–"

"Fuck her?"

Our eyes swing to the door when Paul enters. He looks tired, probably spent the last hour talking to the police. "Is that what we're doing now?"

"Jack fucked her at the bar," my brother says, calling me out, "getting so distracted that he let the Binder get away!"

Paul turns and glances my way.

I was the first to crack.

The first to come inside her.

The first to taste what we all wanted.

"Did she tell you that?" I ask, temper rising.

"She didn't have to, big brother. Even if I hadn't heard it in your voice on the phone it was obvious the instant she walked in the door." He leans across the table and hisses, "You're getting sloppy."

"Fuck you. I am not."

"You're distracted and obsessed," Oliver says.

Paul looks me over. "When was the last time you slept?"

"Jesus Christ," I run my fingers through my hair. "This guy, this Christopher guy, he didn't match the description. Handsome, charming, no scars, no social unawareness. He didn't check a single box." I glare at Paul. "Your profile is shit."

Paul's lips twist into a frown and his eyes narrow. "Impossible."

"I talked to him. Played pool with him and Katie flirted with him. He didn't tick."

Paul taps his fingers on the table, eyes glazing deep in thought. "He must have changed something? He took that time off, went underground, maybe he changed his appearance? Pushed through his social awkwardness?"

Oliver sits up. "What do you mean Katie flirted with him?"

I roll my eyes. "I was there the whole time. I had it under control."

They both snort.

Fair enough.

The sound of heels click on the floors, and Katie emerges like a domestic goddess carrying a big plate of pancakes and a pitcher of syrup. "Luckily mom had a new bottle," she says, placing the pitcher on the table. She exits the room, all three of our eyes following her ass as it vanishes back in the kitchen. The scent of pancakes fills the air and my stomach rolls over with hunger. She returns, this time with a platter of crispy bacon and a bowl of cut fruit. "Grab those plates off the buffet and we can eat."

Oliver grabs the plates passing them around. I've lifted the plate of pancakes in the air when Davis enters the kitchen.

"Jesus it smells amazing in here," he says, following the scent. He observes the four of us, all seated at the formal table with a wary eye. "What's going on?"

"I made breakfast," Katie says, giving him a small smile. "Grab a plate and a stack."

He glances at me, but I'm focused on the food, already piling six pancakes on my plate. He shrugs off his jacket and takes a seat across from Paul. We may be monsters, but we still have to eat.

Once the food has been passed around and everyone is mid-feast, Katie exhales. "I have a plan." Eight eyes lift to stare at her. Davis doesn't stop chewing. "Tonight was a mistake. Jack and I were on the mission, we were focused and then... well, we got distracted. I feel awful about it. Brandi may not have been the sharpest tool, but she doesn't deserve whatever is happening to her right now."

Oliver snaps a piece of bacon in half.

"What's your point, Katherine?" Paul asks.

"If you guys will fill me in on what's really going on here, I think I can use my job to help find this bastard. It's not my case but I have access to the database and all of the files–"

"So do Davis and Paul."

She nods. "True, but it feels like you're missing something. Maybe I can take a look. A fresh eye."

"No," I say, going back to my food. "You don't need to be nosing around in our stuff."

"It's none of your business," Oliver adds, stabbing his fork into a piece of pancake. "We agreed to use you for bait. That's it."

"But it is my business. Literally. I investigate crimes exactly like this. You have me out there, flirting with these guys, acting like a piece of meat." She looks at each of us. "I can do that, but god forbid I use my brain?"

"We didn't keep you around for your brain, sweetheart." Davis laughs and leans back in his chair. "You stick to the bedroom and kitchen. We'll do the rest."

She frowns, but I see that same spark of determination in her eye now that she had at the bar when she went back looking for clues. She feels guilty. Enough to make this worthwhile?

"Maybe she has a point," I say. "She has access down at the Gazette. Maybe we're giving her access to the murder board upstairs and see if we're missing something?"

Davis glares at me over the implication that maybe he missed something. But we did. Christopher didn't fit the profile.

Oliver's eyes meet mine across the table and I raise an eyebrow. We've sat in these same positions a million times before, the two of us plotting. Scheming. Tonight is no different.

He nods and licks his fingertips getting off the syrup. "I'm okay with it as long as... well, you give us something in return."

"What?" she asks. "I don't have much. My car. A few hundred dollars in the bank." She takes a deep breath. "But I get paid next week..."

Oliver lifts his chin. "That's not enough."

Her forehead creases. "Oh, I um..."

"We don't need your shitty car or your pathetic bank account," Paul says, catching on. "What else do you have to give us, Katherine? Something of value."

Realization spreads slowly across her features, first in her eyes and then the wrinkle of her nose. Finally, she says, "You want me."

"We do," Paul says. "At our whim. No fighting."

"Well," Davis laughs, "maybe a little fighting."

She considers it. She doesn't run. She doesn't yell. She considers it. "I do this, and you'll give me full access?" She looks at me when she asks. "*Everything* about the case."

"Yes."

"Okay. I'll do it. Whatever you want. I don't want another girl to get hurt."

So instead, she'll sacrifice herself.

"Good girl," Paul says, giving her a warm, encouraging smile.

She smiles back, half-hearted, but it vanishes just as quickly when Oliver pushes his plate aside and says, "Let's get started."

"Now?"

"Get on the table," he replies, patting the surface in front of him. "Now."

She doesn't look at any of us for help, which is good because it's not going to come. Standing, she squeezes between Oliver's knees and the table. He runs his hands under her skirt, cupping her ass, and lifting her on the table.

Paul stills beside me. It's been years since it's been like this—me, Oliver, Paul and Davis... all of us surrounding Katie, all of us hard and horny.

My brother doesn't waste any time, lifting the dress over her head and tossing it on the floor. She's naked, other than the bare slip of lace covering her pussy. The light from the chandelier catches the red mark around her throat from my fingertips.

"Here," Davis says, grabbing a knife off the table and holding it up to the light. A heartbeat later, he stops in front of her. She shudders, nipples pebbling as he presses the knife against her hip. He cuts the thin lace of her panties off her hips, letting it fall away. He looks at Oliver. "That better?"

"So much." He takes the knife and presses the flat edge of the blade against the inside of her thigh. "Open for me."

She has no alternative but to do what he wants. I see it in her eyes, that spark I saw in the parking lot still burning bright. So fucking eager. She wants in by any means necessary, and so do we. All the fucking way.

She spreads her legs apart, her cheeks blushing red as Ollie parts her pussy. He wants us to watch as he plays with her, taunts her. She reaches out, grabs the edge of the table as he bends down and sniffs.

Her brows furrow, nipples tighten, she's a picture of tormented restraint as he slides in deeper and murmurs, "You smell like my brother." His eyes flick to mine. "How did he take you?"

"F-from behind." She pants, her knuckles buckling as he dips two fingers into her cunt. She comes so easy with us, like a good little whore. "We shouldn't have done it." I see it clearly. She blames herself. She should. She's the one that flirted with that asshole to make me jealous. She's the one that flaunted her tits, her lips, her everything.

Next to me Paul shifts, hand running down the erection in his pants. My cock is hard, throbbing beneath the denim. It's barely been two hours since I fucked her, and I want it again.

"Was he good?" Oliver asks. "Did he make it good for you or did he just fuck you hard and dump his cum inside?"

Her eyes dart to mine seeking approval to discuss what transpired between us. There are no secrets between me and my brothers. I nod. "I c-came for him," she says, stuttering when Oliver drops down and licks her clit.

His movements, his actions, they're like talons inside my chest, tearing me apart.

She shudders, falling back on the table, splayed out like the best kind of dessert. Paul stands, cock in his fist, and reaches out to pluck at her nipple. She yelps, but it's followed by a low hum. Davis takes the knife and runs the tip up and down her body, spreading a chill across her overheated skin.

Me? I watch them enjoy her. Torment her. Terrorize her. And I watch as she takes it because she negotiated this. She wants the information we have about The Binder more than anything—her self-worth, her safety, even her life. Her long dark hair spills across the table, shiny and soft looking in the overhead light.

"Come for us, Katie," Ollie demands, thrusting his fingers in deeper, harder. "Or would you rather come on my cock?"

Before she can answer I push back my chair, the legs scraping on the hardwoods. Katie's eyes meet mine as I stand. This girl... she's given up everything for information and I can't help but wonder exactly what kind of deal we've made.

"Joining in?" Oliver asks, grinning up at me.

"Not tonight," I say, exiting the room. "I already got mine, you guys have fun."

I take the steps two at a time until I reach the top of the stairs and head to my room. Before I reach the door, the sound of her orgasm carries up the stairs, a deep all-consuming moan that hits me straight in the balls.

Fuck!

FUCK!

I enter my room and go straight to the bathroom, the door flying backward as it slams against the wall. I lean my palms on the countertop and look into the mirror. Feral dark eyes reflect back. I was reckless with her tonight. Too fucking reckless. In the bar. Downstairs. And I know she's only going to want to do more.

I'm in dangerous territory now, I know that. No, *she's* in dangerous territory. Because for the first time in my life, I have no idea what I'll do if I lose control.

FIFTEEN

Kate

"Cream? Sugar?" I ask.

"Black is fine."

Last night, I made pancakes.

Then I got finger-banged on the dining room table by my stepbrother.

This morning I made coffee and now I'm sitting across from another man, a doctor for God's sake, who jerked off while I had that soul-shattering orgasm in the next room over.

My life is fucked up. It's surreal. And I'm fully entrenched.

"Has there been any word about Brandi?" I ask.

He shakes his head. "Davis says she didn't return home last night. Neither did Christopher. Both are missing."

"Maybe that means she's still alive," I say hopefully.

He gives me a sympathetic smile. "It's always good to stay positive, Katherine, but The Binder doesn't keep his victims alive for more than twelve hours. He tends to play with them hard before growing tired and disposing of them."

He's so aloof about it–the torture, rape, and murder of an innocent young woman. How did he get this way? When did he lose any softness toward others?

"Maybe this time it'll be different," I say, because I can't accept that Brandi is gone. "Maybe we can make a difference."

"You mean by telling you what you want to know about The Binder?"

"Yes, exactly. The more I know, the more I can try to help find him."

With his eyes never leaving mine, Paul takes a sip of his coffee. "What makes you think you can provide fresh eyes to this? Davis is a detective, after all?"

"Because I'm not mired by the traps of working for the government. I'm a journalist, trained to see things through a different lens, just like you are." I add in a bit more cream and stir it in. "Besides, one important difference is, that I'm a woman. I know how a woman thinks, I know how to get them to open up. People will talk to me in a way they may not talk to the police. It's already well known the community thinks they've screwed up this case and are upset about the lack of progress with the missing men. But I can get in and out of places with less notice and if The Binder does notice... well, it's a good thing I'm his type."

"And this access to our insight and notes, it's worth being at the whim of the four of us?"

My pulse picks up and I panic that sweat pools under my arms. That's the real question–the real reason Paul is here. To suss me out. To *profile* me.

"I wouldn't be the first journalist to compromise for the sake of a story. Is it any different than going undercover? Immersing yourself in a world to reach the very truth?"

"You sound very noble for someone that got fucked by her stepbrother in a bar bathroom last night while another woman was snatched off the streets."

My cheeks burn. "That was a mistake."

"That, was years of pent-up sexual frustration finally coming to a head." He watches me closely, "The question is was it his frustration or yours?"

Both, I almost say but swallow it back. Not that Paul hasn't figured it out. "How did it feel being surrounded by the four of us again? Did it bring back memories?"

"No." I lie. I felt the shame and humiliation, although this time it was different. I have a goal now. A purpose. I knew what I was getting into. Not like then, when I was young, innocent, and pure.

Paul's expression is infuriatingly impassive. "I would've thought it may trigger some latent emotions you may have buried."

"Is that why you took the opportunity to jerk off while I was on the table?" I snap, my calm slipping. "Were you trying to trigger me?"

He shrugs. "Seeing you like that... I admit it. I lost a little bit of control. That was a failure on my part." He pushes his blond hair off his forehead. "You're a beautiful woman, Katherine. You always have been. Seeing you flat on your back, knees bent, while Oliver fingered your wet and quivering pussy to orgasm... absolutely breathtaking. Your strength and sensuality are exhilarating." He smiles gently. "I did clean you up afterward, didn't I? Make sure you were okay?"

He'd done exactly that. Wiping up the cum he'd spent all over my mother's dining room table. Inspecting my vagina for further bruising. He'd given me a cold compress and sent me to my room with instructions on how to clean and prepare myself.

He shifts in his seat, aroused again and I steady my breathing. Paul always speaks like this–little compliments, mixed with soul-crushing belittlement. He wants me to react, to get embarrassed and humiliated. I know it, but still, when he looks at me with those aquamarine eyes, I lose a little grip on reality.

"I felt nothing but release," I tell him, unwilling to admit anything else. "It's just another part of the compromise I'm willing to make to help find this bastard." I swallow. "The situation with Jack at the bar. Nothing like that will happen again. I won't allow myself to get distracted again."

"It's less about your distraction, Katherine, and more about how very good The Binder is. He's always out there, always watching, and now that you're part of this, there's an expectation you'll do both your job and be available to the needs of the men in this house." He tilts his head. "Are you truly prepared for this?"

For depravity and desperation? For pain and orgasms? For humiliation and ecstasy?

I do my best to keep the tremor out of my hand as I answer, "Yes. I'm ready."

THE CAR SMELLS of leather soap and the strong scent of spicy cologne. The dash is filled with electronics–a small computer, radio system, GPS. It's a muscle car–a Mustang– royal blue. Davis Higgins sits behind the wheel in tight black jeans and a black button-down. My eyes keep going back to the gun holstered on his hip. It's the same one he raped me with days before and the memory of the fear I had while the weapon was inside of me licks the back of my spine.

I'm with a man sworn to protect and serve and I've never felt less safe.

"From a police perspective, can you tell me a little more about why The Binder has been so elusive?"

He drives with one hand, cruising down a suburban street. His other hand is on his thigh, inches from the gun. "Once the girls are in his vehicle he's gone. Just vanishes. Like the other night with Brandi. Someone saw him put the girl in the car. Called the police, but then he just disappeared. Totally off the grid. He has some kind of holding area we haven't been able to locate."

"And Jack and Oliver... they haven't found it either?"

His eyes cut to me. "No."

"What about the guy from the bar? Christopher?" I think about his handsome face and easy smile. Jack kept calling him Prince Charming. It fit.

"That's where we're going again. To check his house." He flips on his blinker and turns into a nice neighborhood. "I finally got an ID on him. Christopher Watkins. Thirty-two, single, an accountant with a firm downtown."

"Does he tick the boxes?" I ask, using the words I've heard him, and the guys toss around.

"Not all of them. Not yet, at least."

He pulls up to a modest home. It's a newer build, unlike the historic area that Davenport Manor is located. Not inexpensive though. A cop stands at the front door, acting as a guard. "Is he waiting for you?"

"Yeah, they cleared the house, but since I'm lead detective, I get the first run-through."

I grab my bag and follow him out of the car. The cop gives me a wary look, but Davis nods him off. It's a testament of his authority. No one questions him. Well, except me.

"What are the boxes?" I ask as we enter Christopher Watkin's home. "The criteria?"

His eyes scan the living room, cataloging each photograph, knickknack, book, and piece of electronics. "Male, obviously. Over the age of thirty. Long-term resident of Wilmington." He enters the kitchen and picks up a few pieces of mail, flipping through them. "He'll present as a functional member of the community. He'll have a good job, although possibly a problem with absences. He'll volunteer." He opens a pantry door. The inside is bare other than protein bars and a loaf of bread. "His record with women will be spotty. No real long-term relationships, obsessive behavior. On the outside, he'll look like a catch but on the inside," he nods to the empty pantry, "he's barely holding it together."

I follow him out of the kitchen and down the hall. The first room is a small bathroom. I catch the scent of Christopher's cologne from the night at the bar. The next room is his bedroom. It's neat, but depersonalized. I walk over to a dresser and open the top drawer. Inside are socks. I push them aside and see a piece of paper flat against the bottom. It's a photograph of two boys standing next to a stream, their skinny arms wrapped around one another's shoulders. On the back, someone wrote, 'Clearwater Creek.'

I look up and around the room, realizing that there aren't any other photographs in the house. On an instinct, I tuck the photo into my bag while Davis investigates the closet.

"Find anything?" I ask, shutting the drawer.

"Nope. Guy lives pretty basic."

"That's weird in and of itself, right?"

"Maybe," he says, pushing past me. We look around the rest of the house, but nothing stands out. Davis walks out the front door and stops by the cop. "Fingerprint the whole place and get a DNA profile. Make sure you send me the report."

"Yes, sir," the cop says, tipping his hat at me as I follow Davis back to the Mustang.

A few minutes later we're back on the road. The photograph burns an imaginary hole against my leg, taunting. Where is Clearwater Creek? Who are the two boys? If I find the other one, will it lead me back to Christopher? I'm mulling all of this over when the car shifts into a higher gear and Davis speeds down a long stretch of road.

"Where are we going?" I ask, trying to catch a landmark.

"I thought we'd take a ride out to his office building, do a little stakeout," he says, giving me a wink, before grabbing my hand and pressing it against his cock. "If I take the long way it'll take ten minutes to get there. Can you work that fast?"

I know the only answer is yes. This is what I asked for. Inside information in exchange for whatever they want.

"Here?" I look out the windows and see the trees flash by.

"Two birds, one stone, Katie. Why waste a good car ride when you can suck my cock on the way." He touches my chin. "Don't pretend to be a shy little slut. After that little scene on the dining room table last night, I know exactly how far you're willing to go."

He's right. He's also carrying a gun that I know he's willing to use. I shift in my seat, getting closer, and unbuckle his pants. He leans back, giving me space, and I pull him out. He's long and thick—hard—the skin soft as velvet. I run my thumb over the tip, spreading the perfect drop of precum around.

"That's right," he says with a shudder. He lifts his hips. "Use that dirty little mouth for something more useful than asking questions."

I bend, positioning myself between his body and the steering wheel. The engine thunders, traveling fast down the road. I take a tentative lick, tasting the salty tip. His hand lands on top of my head and presses down, pushing his cock deep into my throat. I gag, and his fingers wrap around throat, massaging. "Don't you dare fucking gag. You hear me?"

I brace myself, willing the reflex aside. It passes and I grip the base, stroking him up and down. "Show me your tits," he says, and I pause, rising to unbutton my blouse and expose my black bra. It's lacy and see-through. "That's a good girl. Pull 'em out. Let me see those perky brown nipples."

I tug down my bra and my breasts spill out. He reaches out and tweaks one, sending a jolt down my body that settles in my core. Satisfied, he nods back at his cock, and I lower my head like the dirty slut he wants and resume sucking him off.

"God yes," he says, applying pressure to my head. I take him in deep, then pull out again, spending time on the tip, flattening my tongue until I suck enough to feel that throbbing pulse in my mouth. "You do that good. As good as a goddam pro."

With each pass his foot presses harder on the gas, the hum of the Mustang getting louder on the road. His hips rock to meet me, his cock plunging in and out of my mouth. The harder he gets the more heat builds between my legs, soaking my panties.

"Son of a..." he mutters, breathing erratic, and twice his foot slips off the gas, lurching us back before he regains control. "Come on, sweetheart," he says, hand leaving my head and returning to the wheel. The speed, his breath, the punch of his hips. He's close and I find myself falling into a rhythm, drawing that ragged breath out of him, making his fingers curl on the steering wheel as he tries to stay the course. I like it. A little too much. This tiny flicker of power makes me so very wet.

"You better be ready to swallow." It's all the warning I get before he groans, car swerving on the road. Fear and adrenaline pump through me, both hot and horny, fearful, and exhilarated. I grip the base of his cock with one hand and his thigh with the other. He comes hard, hot spurts of cum shoot in the back of my throat. I swallow it down, more eager than I'd like to admit. I like the way he tastes, how he makes me feel, dirty and sexy at the same time.

I pull myself up, wiping my mouth. His thumb touches my lip, swiping at a drop of cum, and pushes it back on my tongue. "Greedy little bitch," he says, chuckling. "God, you love cum, don't you?"

"If I do," I say, straightening my bra and shirt, "it's because you taught me to."

He hesitates, and I blink, shocked that I said it. I never mention that night–especially to them. I don't want them to know how it affected me. Paul asked all those questions about triggers, and fuck yes, I'm triggered, just being in that house, being near them, feeling their hands on me, and especially now, tasting Davis's cum in the back of my throat, a reminder of what they did.

A reminder of how much I've spent every day since, craving it.

He drives the rest of the way back to town, chest rising and falling as he catches his breath. His gaze moving to the puckered peaks of my nipples. I shift in my seat, the wet heat sticky between my legs.

"Horny, huh?" he asks, glancing over.

"I'm fine."

"Don't tell me you didn't get fucking dripping doing that. I know sucking cock makes you hot." He snorts. "I know tasting cock makes you even hotter."

"I should get back to the office. Henry likes me to pick up lunch at one."

He glances at the clock. It's twelve-forty-five. A dark grin twists on his mouth. "You get yourself off in the next ten minutes I'll drop you off at the diner. If not, I'll drop you off here and you can walk."

I've fallen right into Davis' trap. Get in trouble at work for not being on time, humiliate myself, again, for his pleasure. If the throb between my legs wasn't so bad, and the taste of him wasn't still on my lips, I'd probably tell him to fuck off. But he's got me this car, the smell of sex still in the air. I slide my hand down the front my skirt and reach underneath.

"All the way, Katie. I want to see your pussy."

I hike it up and push my panties aside. I think he's going to keep cruising around, but he pulls up to a stoplight at the edge of town. "You're kidding," I say, fingers pausing. "Someone will see."

"Not if you're quick." He holds my eye. As much as I want to fight back, my fingers move on their own finding the slick heat and I rub my swollen clit. "That's right. Spread it around."

"This is ridiculous," I say, cheeks burning.

"Show me more."

I place a foot on the dash and lift my hips, tilting myself into a better position. He licks his bottom lip and presses the gas continuing to drive through Wilmington. He moves at an unnervingly slow speed.

"Fuck yourself, Katie," he directs. I push in a finger, then another. His eyes dilate and I stifle a moan. "How do you like it? Hard? Fast? Slow? Deliberate?"

"A-all of those," I say, truthfully. I know these men well enough that they each have their own way. It's what I think about at night in my bed. Being dominated by Jack. Humiliated by Davis. Exposed by Oliver and doted on by Paul. They'd each push me to my limit, making me beg for more even when I know it's depraved and wrong. I continue to finger myself, feeling the first flickers of an orgasm. My eyes dart to the clock. I don't have time to draw this out if I'm going to get back to the office on time.

Davis watches me, moving his hand to my inner thigh, spreading me further so he can see. "God, how I want to ruin that pussy," he whispers. "Just fill you up with my cock, pound you so hard you won't be able to walk for a week." He stops at another stop sign. His fingers stretch out to brush against my clit. I shudder against the shock it sends up my body, drawing me one step closer to my release. I need him inside me, his calloused fingers, his hard, harsh, degrading fucking tongue. His cock... God I need his cock. I bite my lip at the thought, and I watch as his gaze is fixed on that. Teeth. Lips. I slide my tongue over the tender flesh, the taste of him still salty in my mouth.

He continues to drive, and I work myself to the edge, sparks shooting through my limbs, the walls of my pussy quivering around my fingers. I refuse to look outside the window, at the people walking the street. I focus on myself. On chasing that orgasm, on the sound of my breath and the scent of sex filling the car.

"Jesus Christ," he mutters as I thrust my hips, little cries falling off my tongue. "You're the filthiest little bitch I've ever seen." His eyes narrow. "Say it, Katie. Tell me you're a filthy bitch and come for me."

"I-I'm a f-filthy bitch," I grind out, body buckling as the rush of release washes over me. Warmth coats my fingers, slippery and sweet. "God, I'm disgusting. I can't help it. I can't stop." I buck against my hand, body clenching with wracking waves. "I can't stop."

"Then don't."

My eyes meet his, and there's something familiar and dark in the way he looks at me.

"Why can't I stop?" I ask, struggling for breath. "I came out with you today to get information for work. I sucked you off and I just... oh my god. What's wrong with me?"

"The same thing that's always been wrong with you, Katie." He reaches out and tucks a piece of hair behind my ear. "You're one of us."

SIXTEEN

Kate

I MAKE IT BACK TO THE OFFICE CATCHING A SCOWL FROM Henry as I stumble into the office and dump the lunch order on the nearest desk.

"You're late," he mutters as I near his office with his food in my hands.

"Sorry, I got caught up doing research."

He looks me up and down. "You look a damn mess, what did you do, wrestle a damn tiger?"

I place his sandwich down on the desk, my hand skimming over the flyaway strands, still feeling Davis' hand on the back of my head. But Henry doesn't wait for an answer, just grabs his food, casting me a sideways glance that says, beat it.

I hurry out, grab my own meatball on rye and make for my desk. The photograph crinkles as I sit, making me scan the office before I carefully reach in and pull the image out. My pulse races at the sight. It was more than lifting evidence in a crime scene. No, that rush was exhilaration. I was doing it. I was the one who'd found the information I needed to uncover the

Binder. I'd deliver him to the cops—the *real* cops, along with my psychotic stepbrothers and their deranged best friends.

I only hoped Brandi was still alive. I grab half of my sandwich, take a bite, and turn the photograph over. *Clearwater Creek.* I punch the details into the search bar and stare at the pretty creek that ran through what looked to be a campground just outside the city.

I search for any other details I could find, but there are none.

It could be nothing... I glance at the photograph—the only personal memento I found in Christopher's place—or it could be something. I take another bite, tearing into the sandwich as I start to rise and log out of the computer.

"Got something?" Henry calls out as I gather my things from the desk—sandwich included.

I give him a shrug. I'm getting better at hiding things now. Maybe too good. "Not sure yet. It's probably nothing." Even as the words slipped free, I know they're a lie.

There's a nagging feeling in the pit of my stomach. Instinct, I guess. Whatever it is, I can't ignore it. I hurry down the stairs of the Gazette and head to my car, tossing my stuff on the passenger seat, and enter the location on my phone. I take the roads east out of the city toward Clearwater Creek. I feel a smile of satisfaction tug at the corners of my mouth, at least until my cell rings.

Jack.

The name flashes across my screen, sending my pulse fluttering. Why the hell is he calling? My body clenches. *At their beck and call, remember?* I hit the button sending it to voicemail, then glance back to the road, the fleeting feeling of success slipping away.

He has to ruin my moment, doesn't he?

I focus on the road, that nagging feeling in my stomach now heavy like dread. It isn't the drive that has me clenching my hands around the wheel, it's him... my fucking stepbrother. Always there to remind me that I shouldn't have come back here.

Should've told mom I was heading somewhere else to start my life. I wanted to. I had plans.

Liar.

I swallow hard, knowing that it's always going to come down to this—them, and me. This... *clash* that's been brewing since the night all those years ago, like a storm in the making. I can feel the electricity in the air, the impending thunder and lightning. But maybe if I can solve The Binder case, I can get out of here for good.

I glance down at the photograph edging out of my bag. Clearwater Creek must mean something to Christopher, or he wouldn't have kept the picture. Guys like this, serial killers, they tend to cling to nostalgia, things that bring back a sense of safety and belonging. If my hunch is right, it may be the answer to all of this.

Excitement burns as I thought about what Davis said, *on the outside, he'll look like a catch but on the inside...*

"On the inside he'll be rotten to the core. A rapist and murderer, won't he?" I whisper. Soulless. Depraved. A quick look at the moving red dot on my GPS tells me I'm close.

The sign is old and faded, but the name is still clear: *Clearwater Creek Campgrounds.*

I hit the turn signal, slowing the car.

My stomach churns as I take in the setting. Trees close in, tall and thick. There's not a car in sight as I drive down the rocky road. A sign for the campgrounds, urging me to turn with the point of an arrow. But I don't. That adrenaline is silent until I pass the sign, then it comes to life like burning vengeance.

It's close... I'm close. I can feel it. Movement in the rear-view mirror draws my eyes behind me. For a terrifying moment, I think it must be him, Christopher, waiting, watching. It's just the wind in the trees, but then... I blink, almost missing it. I turn completely not trusting what I see in the mirror but it's there. It's real.

A rusted, old mailbox, that points to a dirt road in the middle of nowhere, a peeling faded name on the side, *Watkins*.

The scream in my stomach punches a fist in the air. *I got him!*

Holy shit. I've got him.

My hands are so slippery I can barely turn the wheel. But I manage, letting the tires skid until they hit a rut. Rocks kick up, peppering the underbelly of the car. I slow as the road narrows, branches reaching out, clawing the sides of the vehicle as I wedge myself in the drive. My skin itches and my brain screams at me to go back, call the police, call Henry, *Jesus*, call Jack. But maybe all of this is just my imagination gone wild again. Too many days in that house, too many nights being toyed with and tortured by my stepbrothers and their bastard friends.

I'm trying to figure out how to get out of here, to turn back, when I catch sight of a small cabin at the end of the drive.

I scan the grounds, searching for a car, my pulse frantic. This is it. I know it. But when I pull up, I don't get out. Not yet.

I wait for that tiny voice inside my head to tell me again how stupid this is, but it's strangely silent. Leaving me to look around one more time, then kill the engine and climb out of the car.

Birds chirp in the trees above. The place is quiet and serene. It's a perfect hideout, especially if you've got something to hide.

Jack, Oliver, Davis, and Paul burrow into my mind as I close the door carefully behind me. They'd be furious if they knew I got here first, ruining their deranged little game of cat and mouse. I don't give a shit about them. I'm here for Brandi, for all the other women this asshole tortured and killed. That's what propels me past my fear and toward the cabin.

The windows are dark and filthy. The grime is so thick I can hardly see anything inside. I cup my hand against the glass and search for movement, but there's none. Maybe this was a dead end and a total waste of my time?

Instinct tells me otherwise.

I head for the corner of the square building, scanning the trees, and then carefully walk to the front of the cabin. Between the sharp, piercing calls of Jaybirds, the bubbling rush of water fills the air. The creek must be just through those trees. If I go down there, I bet I'd find the exact spot where the photo was taken.

But the moment I turn the corner to the front of the cabin, I stop. The front door is ajar, almost like someone was expecting me. From this distance, all I can see is shadowy darkness waiting for me inside.

A surge of adrenaline courses through me as I jerk my gaze over my shoulder and search the trees. Hard breaths drive through my chest as I turn back to the doorway and take a step onto the porch landing. Floorboards creak under my weight, old and worn.

Part of me doesn't want to get close. Part of me doesn't want to step inside. But there's a bigger part that pushes to the surface and takes control. That part of me forces me to keep moving. I ignore the way my hand shakes when I reach out and grab the dented round handle, pushing the door wider.

Hello? The word surfaces in my head, but I bite the insides of my mouth, scan the darkness and then step inside. There's a faint scent that catches my attention, faint, flowery... and very, *very* feminine for such a dusty room.

The cabin is no more than a room. The walls are slats of wood, the floor cement. Rusty bunk beds are lined up against one wall. A small bathroom is attached to the back. There's an old metal table in the middle of the room, piled with supplies. A lantern, rope, chains, tape, and a variety of sharp instruments–weapons. My gaze skips over these to the shackles screwed into the wall. Four. One for each wrist and ankle. A square gray tarp is taped to the floor underneath. My pulse screams at the drops of red on the tarp, I don't need to get any closer to know it's blood. Under the flowery scent is the coppery tang of blood–a smell I've become all too familiar with lately.

I turn back to the bunk beds and see something yellow shoved back in the corner. I step closer. It's cotton—pale yellow. I move deeper, that terror a siren as I stop, and even though I shouldn't– it's evidence–I pick it up.

It's a shirt.

Her shirt

Memories of what she was wearing that night at the bar rushes back to me. Low-rise jeans, figure-hugging yellow shirt, nipples pressed into the thin fabric. I can still see Jack's hands all over her. I lift the shirt to my nose and inhale the lingering scent of her perfume.

Brandi had been here. How long ago? Where is she now? The barest sound of a creak on the porch floorboards carries across the room. The hairs on the back of my neck rise and I realize how fucking foolish I'd been coming here alone.

"You really are testing me, little sister, aren't you?"

My heart lunges into my throat when I hear him, and I spin.

Jack stands there, just inside the door, bathed in shadows pressing the point of his blade into his gloved finger. In the faint light, his cheekbones appear cut from marble, his eyes dark and haunted. "Davis said you were asking questions, being... how did he put it? '*A more nosy bitch than normal.*'"

He strides forward, gripping the handle of the knife. Not once does he look at the shirt in my hand, or the shackles embedded in the wall.

Those dark eyes glint like the edge of a blade, focused on me.

I stumble backward until I hit the wall. "I had a lead," I tell him. "I wanted to be sure before I got you guys involved."

"You shouldn't be here, Katie, but of course, you couldn't just leave well enough alone."

"This is his place," I say, gesturing to the shirt. "This is Brandi's. We're close. Maybe we can still save her."

He shakes his head. "You and I both know it's too late for that." He speaks so definitively. "What it's not too late for, is for me to do what I should have the day you came back to Wilmington." He lifts his hand, and swings, burying the blade into the wall near my head as he snarls. "I'm going to teach you a goddamn lesson."

I duck, pushing away from him. Agony flares as I catch my leg on the steel screw of the shackle. I swallow the pain, well aware that all the bargains and agreements and negotiations we'd come to were now null. I'd betrayed him. Kept secrets. And now, he's pissed.

I lunge for the door, terror driving me to escape into the woods. Behind me, I can hear the brutal thud of his footsteps as he follows me down the porch.

Jack is no longer hunting The Binder.

He's hunting me.

SEVENTEEN

Jack

I GIVE HER A HEAD START.

After all, the thrill is in the hunt.

I knew something was going on with her–the turnaround was too quick, too seamless. One minute I was fucking her in the bar, forcing my way inside of her, the next she was making pancakes and spread across the dining room table letting the vultures get a taste.

But it was the story Davis told me about her sucking his cock in the car and getting off afterward that sealed it for me. Katie didn't want to help. She wanted access. She gave my brother and my friends exactly what they wanted so they'd leave her to her investigation. She's looking to make a career off this story–a ticket out of town–while we're focused on one thing; revenge.

There's no fucking way I'm letting her take that sweet victory away from us after so much hard work. And there's no way in hell she's turning us in after the years we've spent cleaning up the garbage in this town.

"Little sister," I call, letting my voice carry through the woods. "Run, run, as fast as you can..."

I can't see her, but I can hear her, stomping through the dense woods. The creek is close, the water bubbling and gurgling nearby. I follow her tracks, knowing they'll end up by the water. Good, all the easier to clean up the blood.

"I knew you were up to something, Katie," I say, spotting a bent branch. "You were too compliant. Too willing to do whatever we wanted. That's not how you operate." I catch sight of her dark hair vanishing behind a tree. The sound of a stick snapping. Her frantic footsteps. "There are a few things I know about you. Things I know for sure. You're a fighter. You don't follow rules, especially our rules. You're looking for a way out of Wilmington, but most of all you hate looking vulnerable in front of us. Sucking Davis' cock in the car is one thing, but fingering yourself while he watched... that's something my little sister would never do." I climb up on a felled tree. "Unless you were trying to throw him off course."

Other than the sound of my voice echoing off the trees, the forest has grown still. She's out there, silent, waiting, listening. Most likely, trying to get a sense of direction. It's hopeless. I know these woods, spent time at this camp myself as a kid. Soon she'll be lost, walking in circles, falling right into my trap.

"Not that he minded," I say, sidestepping a thick root, "Davis is a sucker for road head. Do you know how many women he's forced to do that when he pulled them over for speeding?" I laugh. "All those greedy, desperate mouths. But I have no doubt yours was the best he'd had."

I keep my eyes alert, looking for footprints, broken branches, disturbed foliage. I find all of these, pausing to use the tip of my knife to pluck a pink thread from her blouse where she snagged it on tree bark. I continue in the direction of the creek, aware of the setting sun. Soon it'll get dark. She'll be cold, and I'll strike.

"I'm not going to lie," I continue, not sure if she can hear me or not, "I didn't expect you to ever come back home. Seeing you in the house like that after all those years... it brought back memories." Some good, some bad, all formative. "I remember the day my father brought you and your mother home. You had a rainbow on your shirt, tiny white shorts. No bra, but your tits were just starting to form. So innocent and pure. A lamb walking into a den of lions."

Snap!

I still, eyes darting down a small incline. I take a step, my boots sinking into the soft dirt. "Did you know that we agreed to leave you alone as long as you stayed in your place? As long as you didn't get in our way? That was the deal. You were too close to home, too much potential for trouble. That's why we made it crystal clear you weren't to come upstairs." I look down and see the imprint of a shoe. I keep going. "But did you listen? No, you just had to go put your goddamn nose in our business. You made that happen, Katie. You forced us to do that to you that night, just like you're forcing me to do this to you now."

A massive tree stands at the edge of the creek. Hundreds of years old. The perfect hiding spot. I can't see her, but I can hear her short, quick, breaths punching through the trees. I inhale, drawing in her scent. Carefully, I pick up a rock and toss it to one side of the tree, while circling around to the other. The ruse works, flushing her in my direction. She darts out from her hiding spot, right into my arms.

Her body slams into mine. I spin, pinning her against the tree, my hand around her throat. I feel the hum of her flesh, the life beating under my palm. One little twist is all it would take. Her fight is nothing compared to my strength. I grin down as she runs out of steam. Those wide, terrified eyes stare at me.

Here is the real Katie. The one who seethed and plotted under the surface. The one who'd do anything but willingly give in to us.

"Gotcha, little sister," I say, pushing a piece of hair off her cheek with the point of my knife. "There's no escape this time. It's just me and you out here." I push against her, whispering. "When I'm done with you, I'm walking out of here alone."

"Jack," she says, breath hitching in a way that makes her tits rise and fall, "it doesn't have to be this way."

I laugh. "Yeah, Katie, I think it does."

"So what? You'll just kill me here? Dump me in the creek? Hope no one will ever find me?" Always fighting. Always bargaining. "They'll know it's you."

"Actually," I say, running the blade down her throat. "I have a better idea."

She swallows. "What's that?"

"I'm going to pin this one on The Binder."

IT'S dark when I get her back to the cabin, the sound of nightfall coming from the forest. Everything looks the same as when we left, the door ajar, the table filled with instruments–the shackles on the wall. I turn on the camping lantern hanging by the door, filling the space with light.

"Strip," I tell her, sitting on the single, metal chair by the table.

"Jack seriously. This is insane, even for you."

I point the knife at her. "The Binder's victims are all found naked."

"They're also found…" she can't bring herself to say it. Bound. Tortured. Raped brutally. "You're really doing this?"

"You gave me no choice." I lean back and drop my hand to my cock, massaging the already erect muscle. "We're on a mission, Katie, one that isn't going to get derailed by your convenient sense of morality and desire to win a Pulitzer."

"Look," she says, taking a small step forward, "I know this is about what happened to your mother and all the trauma you experienced. I unde–"

My hand stills, my erection thick under my palm. I stand, chair falling behind me from the force. I reach out and grab her. "Don't you fucking dare tell me you 'understand' my trauma. My best friend is a shrink. I don't need your psychobabble."

Her eyes widen, filled with terror and pain. Good. Feel it. "You want revenge," she continues, "I don't blame you, but this isn't how you get it."

"He started this you know," I say, her face so close I can feel her breath on my mouth. "Paul tumbled down the rabbit hole of psychology, looking for a way for me and Oliver to soothe our rage to feel 'in control.'" My hands grip her upper arms tighter. "We tried a dozen outlets. Working out, jogging, boxing… and yeah, I did all of that. It made me fast, lean, powerful. One night, I watched a guy at the gym hassle a woman. He followed her out to her car. Force her inside at knifepoint. Something in my brain snapped. It just fucking snapped. I followed him. He drove to a park, raped her in the backset of the car. Tossed her ass out when he was finished. Rage consumed me. The next time I saw him at the gym, I followed him home–alone this time. I hunted *him,* dragged him back to Davenport Manor, strapped him to the chair upstairs and, well," I blink away that memory,

"I took care of him. At the first drop of blood, I felt a sense of peace in my chest for the first time in years."

"You were just a little kid," she says, eyes filling with pity. "What you saw—"

"Shut up!" I release her and push her back. She slams against the wall. I rip off her blouse and pull down her skirt. Grabbing one arm and then the other, I chain her to the wall, tightening the shackles around her wrists. She stands before me, tits rising and falling with every heavy breath, her pussy barely covered by the thin strip of lace. My cock is harder than it's ever been in my goddamn life and I'd bet the last fragments of my soul that if I touch her between her legs she's sloppy wet, dying to be fucked.

"You're talking to me about misguided revenge?" I hiss. "About the psychology behind behavior? What about you, little sister? You think I don't know what this is all about? Why you let me touch you? Why you play these little games? You want to take me down for what happened all those years ago even though we both know you fucking loved every second of it."

"No!" she shouts, face turning red. "I hated it! I hated you for putting me in that position. I hated myself for fucking testing you and your goddamn rules!" Her eyes water, hot with rage and when she speaks again it's lower, quieter. "I hate the fact that ever since that night, I don't know how to be in a normal relationship, want normal things, because you're right, it changed me, what I want. What I *need*."

I close the gap between us, forcing us eye to eye. A grin spreads across my face. "Tell me what you need, Katie," I say, hand palming her tit, the hard nipple pressing into my hand. "Tell me how much you want it."

She moans, and I'm caught up in it all, caught up in the heat of it. The fear in her eyes sparks harder as they dart to something over my shoulder. But I'm trapped by her and I miss the movement that comes at the corner of my eye. When I do?

By then it's too late.

———

MY HEAD THROBS, a sharp ache spiraling from the back of my head around to my temples. I try to move but can't. Try to open my eyes but they won't. In the distance, through the groggy haze, there are voices, two, one familiar one not.

"Please don't do this."

Katie. I'd had her shackled to the wall when–I wince–trying to remember. I force my eyes open.

I see her first, still chained to the wall. A man paces in front of her. I catch a hint of his profile. It's not the guy from the bar. Not Prince Charming... Christopher Watkins.

Then who the fuck is it?

My ears ring, and I struggle to keep my eyes open. My body still won't move, but I'm aware enough to know I'm upright. Bound to something. Hands and feet. Through the fog, I'm pretty sure I hear him say, "Tell me about that night."

"What night?" she asks, her voice full of false bravado. Always the fighter. Again, I force my eyes open to get a look at her.

"The one he was talking about?" He turns toward me and I let my eyes flutter shut. "The night you've been fighting about since you were in the woods."

"I don't want to talk about that night, Ryan."

Ryan. The name rings a bell or maybe that's just the concussion. Jesus.

"I don't think you have a choice," he says. "Tell me what happened–what's the dirty little secret."

"There were rules," she says. "And I broke them."

"What kind of rules?" I hear the scratch on the cement floor. The sound of him sitting.

"I'm not–*wasn't* allowed upstairs. To the third floor where the boys' rooms were. They made it clear they were off-limits."

"But you went up there anyway?" he prompts, the knife glinting in his hand.

"Yes."

"What were they doing?

I crack my eyes open again, watching as she tells the story. Her face is pale, body trembling from having her arms extended for so long. She's cold, naked. Exposed.

"I went into Oliver's room first. He was the nicest to me, but they weren't there. I snuck through the adjoining bathroom and peeked at them. They were watching porn."

"That's all?" he asks. "There's nothing too extreme about a bunch of boys watching porn."

"It was... violent. Women being held down and being raped." She swallows. "Over and over–a gang bang."

"Ah. Well, I understand the appeal." He chuckles. "And then what?"

"They were jerking off. All of them. It was the first time I'd seen one–a penis like that, all hard and... *big*. It was shocking to see them so exposed. Red faced, stroking themselves. Even though what they were watching was terrible, seeing them like that made me feel funny. Excited."

"You got horny."

"I stayed too long wanting to see what it looked like. I knew about orgasms, how a man's body worked, but I was stupid."

"You wanted to see for yourself."

She looks away, shame written on her face.

Fuck that'd make me hard if my skull wasn't stamped with whatever he knocked me out with. Still she's a good little victim, keeping him talking like that. *Never* underestimate her.

As she speaks I remember that day–the things she's leaving out. How Davis and Paul stroked one another, exploring one another's cocks. How hard I got watching that woman on the screen get gang raped by a dozen guys. How Oliver's red cheeks were from humiliation, how he felt awkward and pressured to be there.

"I stayed too long," she repeats, her voice taking on a faraway sound. "One of them noticed me in the bathroom doorway. Davis maybe, but Jack was the one that caught me halfway down the stairs."

"What did they do?"

I can feel her fighting against me as I dragged her down the hall, her skinny body sliding across the hardwood floors. I dumped her on the floor, right in front of the TV screen where the video had been playing.

"I told you to stay out of our way. Not to come up here, you stupid bitch."

"I'm sorry."

"You're pathetic," I shout at her, knowing no one else is at home.

"Jack," Davis says, *"chill out."*

"I'm not going to chill out! She had one rule to follow, and we'd leave her alone, but she had to break it."

"Then punish her," Paul says. "We could fuck her." His cock is still in his hand. He looks at me for permission, knowing I'm the one that'll make the call. I glance at Oliver next to him and his face is pale. Worried. I realize then that Paul is right. We have to punish Katie for coming up here—but we also need to make sure that what she saw never leaves this house. It'll ruin all of us.

"We're not fucking her," I say. A flicker of relief crosses her face, but I jerk my chin at her. "Get on your knees."

"Why?" she asks, a fat tear escaping down her cheek. "I won't tell anyone what I saw. Let me go back to my room and—"

"Get on your fucking knees." I grab her by the arm and jerk her into position. I reach into my pants, pulling out my cock. It's still hard and stiff, harder than it's been in my whole life. I grip the back of her head and force her face up. "Ever tasted cum, little sister?"

Her eyes widen, horrified. "N-no."

"Well, you're about to get four flavors." I gesture for the boys to come over. "Open wide."

"Oh my god," she cries, a huge sob coming from her throat. "Please don't do this."

"Sorry, Katherine, but you were warned," Paul says, working his hand up and down his cock. "It's almost like you wanted this to happen."

Another sob shudders down her spine, but then something shifts. That fighter returns, the defiance that brought her up here in the first place. Her shoulders square and she lifts her chin.

"God you're a little fucking slut, aren't you?" Davis says, followed by a deep grunt. He's the one that brought the movie.

Evidence actually, something his father, a cop, brought home from work. Part of the thrill was knowing the video was real, that this had really happened. It made my balls ache with unquenchable hunger. Davis reaches out and rubs his thumb over her bottom lip. "Gonna fill you so much you'll choke."

Paul groans, thumb rolling over the tip of his cock. He hums and looks at Katie with half closed eyes. "You're beautiful, you know that? But you'll be prettier with my cum dripping down your lips."

The guys talk, but I keep silent, afraid of the rage building deep inside. The urge to flip her over. To bury myself inside of her—to fuck my stepsister out of my system, until she begs for mercy, is overwhelming. So much so that I don't notice Oliver hasn't joined in until Davis' palms his cock, fisting it in three hard pumps and emits a deep groan. White fluid spurts from the tip, his hand gripping her jaw, forcing her mouth open. Cum lands right onto Katie's waiting tongue.

"Swallow it," he tells her, hand wrapped around her neck. "Swallow every last goddamn drop."

She gives it a solid try. It's clear she's never had a cock near her mouth before. Maybe never even seen one. She chokes it down, only gagging once. Her eyes water, but then Paul approaches her. He fists her hair and pushes her head into his pelvis. Her eyes watch him closely but her tongue darts out and flattens as he presses the tip against the pink flesh. He groans, coming in jerky spurts, some hitting her upper lip and dripping back down.

Paul's right. She's fucking beautiful like this.

She swallows again, gags again, but takes it like a champ. I almost come just watching her force it down.

"You ready to take one more?" I ask her, lifting up her chin. I see the fear in her eyes. Not just because of what's happening, but

because it's me. I see it over the kitchen table. Passing her in the hall. When we watch TV in the den. This girl is terrified of me, and it's fucking intoxicating. "Tell me you're ready, Katie."

"Does it matter?" she says, voice hard. "You'll do it anyway."

She's right... I will. I'll do whatever I want with her, and she has no choice but to take it.

I stand over her, cock right in her face. I stroke painfully slow, letting it swell and thicken. She watches closely, like she knows not to take her eyes off it for a second. She's right. It's not just a cock. It's a weapon. One I've learned to wield by watching the monsters all around me.

She must sense that I'm close because her jaw loosens, and her mouth opens, tongue sticking out. My balls tighten and the pit in my lower belly twists like a coil. I cinch my fingers around her chin and say. "Close it." Confusion flickers through her eyes but she snaps her mouth shut. I come in an instant, hot cum spraying all over her face. Thick ropey semen marking, not just her mouth, but her whole goddamn face. It drips down her eyelashes. Arcs over the curve in her nose. Lingering in the divot of her upper lip.

Pleased, I look back at my brother, nodding at him to go next but he shakes his head and exits the room.

Shit.

I'm going to have to do damage control on that one.

We stare down at her, cum dripping from her mouth, coating her chin and sliding down her throat.

"Jesus," Davis says, zipping up his pants. "I'm starving."

"Same," Paul says. "Is there any pizza left downstairs?"

"Yeah, I think so." I tuck myself back in my sweatpants and look down at her. "Go clean yourself up." She wobbles on her knees *and I grab her arm, helping her to her feet. "Clean yourself up," I repeat. "And don't you fucking dare tell anyone what happened up here. Not one word or your punishment will be a hundred times worse. Understand?"*

"Yes," she whispers, stumbling toward the bathroom.

Katie stops, and I wait, wondering if she'll continue, tell the rest of the story, but after a beat it's clear she's not going to.

"So they performed a bukkake on you?"

"A what?"

"It comes from Japanese culture–anime really. When a group of men masturbate and come all over a woman. It's degrading and demeaning. Although," he pauses. "Some women find it very arousing."

She doesn't take the bait, but he's right. Some women do, and Katie is one of those women.

"So that man over there–your stepbrother–he's been tracking me for months, trying to catch me in the act, but you're the one that found me." I peel open my eyes and watch as he touches her cheek. Hot rage boils under my skin and when I get loose, I know I'll cut those fingers off, one by one. "Sexy and smart. I like that."

He turns and walks back to the table, picking up one instrument after the other, inspecting them closely.

"The difference between me and your brothers," he says, "is that I kill my victims and put them out of their misery. They made you live with the shame and humiliation, the dark truth. But that's okay sweetheart. I'm here now. We'll get you cleaned up, have a little fun, and best of all," he turns, eye catching mine, like he's been aware of me listening this whole time, "I'm going to make him watch."

EIGHTEEN

Kate

HERE, YOU CAN TAKE MINE. THE WORDS RING IN MY HEAD. Memories of him filter through of him standing in that bar graciously giving me his seat. My mind refuses to make the connection. This isn't the same man, not the one who acted like a gentleman, and the one who bumped into me at the diner near work. But it is him, the same kind eyes... the same careful, shy smile.

Awkward.

That's what Davis told me to look for. An awkward guy. I flick my gaze to Jack, on the floor, checking for the steady rises and fall of his chest, then I turn back to Mr. Nice Guy. Only he's not so nice, is he? Not when he has me bound and shackled. Not when he's about to do what he does to women.

My insides clench.

I need to find a way out of this. I glance at Mr. Psychotic Killer as he strides to the filthy window of the cabin and reaches out, touching a carved marking in the wood. "He was supposed to take you, you realize that?"

I jerk back to reality, trying hard to catch up to what he was saying. "He?"

Ryan turns to face me. "My brother."

Brother?

My mind races to make the connection and when it does, it's like lightning in my veins. "The photo... that's you in the picture. With Christopher."

The murderer at the window smiles. "Yes."

"He's your brother." I try to wrap my head around the information.

He nods and drags his finger across the marking etched into the wood. I see it now, see the initials. Zeros and crosses. A child's game... one you played together.

"He sent me a message that night he met you at the bar. He was so excited, '*smart and beautiful.*'"

I recoil inside, forcing the words. "I feel flattered."

The Binder, Ryan, turns to me, ignoring Jack unconscious behind him. "You should. It's not often he finds a female that makes him question whether he wants to kill her or keep her."

Keep her... the idea of that was sickening. Almost as sickening as my current situation. I force myself to not look at Jack. He's the reason I'm shackled to the wall. His stupid, petty, deranged games.

"But you disappeared, so he had to make other arrangements."

I wince and glance at the yellow shirt on the ground. Brandi. He took Brandi because I was fighting—and fucking—my stepbrother in the bathroom that night. I close my eyes. "It's all my fault."

"She knew it too," he whispers in front of me. "He told her she was his second choice, that he'd wanted you."

Something cold and sharp drags down the swell of my breast. I open my eyes and shiver, knowing that one tiny flinch and the blade would cut deep.

"You're filthy," he murmurs, eyes skimming down my body. "I don't like filthy. I like my girls clean. Sweet. A little sexy." The chain links gnash as I move on reflex, trying to escape. My pulse speeds as he glances at the shackles. "Do something stupid and I'll gut you right here, understand?"

Defiance roars in my chest and I lift my chin. His eyes narrow and the tip of the blade presses against my skin.

"Do you understand, Kate?" His voice rises, echoing off the cement floor.

"Yes. I understand."

He leans forward and then bends down, his back to Jack. I stare at my stepbrother's eyes, searching for movement. *Come on*, I urge. *Come on now!* But there is no flicker behind his lids, and no change to the steady, rhythmic rise and fall of his chest as Ryan unlocks the shackles from the wall and rises.

The metal clasps are around my wrists, the chains hanging free as he turns and motions. "Bathroom."

I glance at the doorway and the tiny room and there's something inside me that knows once I step in there, I won't come out. "We can talk about this." I start as he grabs the chain and yanks. "Talk to me... I can be a really good listener."

"Move." He growls, turning from Mr. Nice Guy to someone terrifying in an instant. My feet slide against the filthy cabin floor, desperate to drive myself away from that door. But it's no use. With a snarl he steps close, pressing the blade to my neck.

"You either get in that bathroom standing or you can go in pieces. It's up to you."

The blade presses harder against my neck, giving me no alternative. I cross the room to the bathroom. It's tiny, barely big enough for one person, let alone two.

"In," he commands. I look at the cracked filthy floor and then step inside. He reaches in around the plastic curtains and turns the tap.

The pipes howl before freezing water shoots from the jets, hitting my chest. I cry out from the shock and yank my hands high. The chain rattles as he hands me a cake of soap.

"Wash."

I stare at it, did he make Brandi wash like this before he raped and killed her?

"Do it yourself or I'll do it for you, Katie. Don't make this difficult."

I take the soap and slowly run it along my arm, shivering under the icy spray.

"Make sure you get your pussy."

I nod carefully, warmth sliding from my eyes. I hate that I cry. Hate that after everything I'm still here, under the brutal force of yet another man. I wash, slowly, methodically, bending over to scrub between my legs. He watches my every movement, but I take the opportunity to search the tiny bathroom for anything I can use as a weapon.

But there's nothing in this bare, ancient cabin that's of use and I straighten and lift my face into the icy spray. The water is freezing and I shiver uncontrollably. He looks me up and down, then turns off the water with a squeak of the faucet.

I glance at the basin and the tiny mirror above it. It's clean and I reach out, using the glass to help steady myself. In truth, I press my fingers to the mirror, hoping to leave my mark anywhere I can. Even in death, I'm determined to help catch these sick bastards.

He yanks the chain, dragging me like a dog. I'm naked, wet, freezing. I follow him back out. He points to the chair. "Sit."

Fear and the cold makes me tremble. I clench my fists, making the chains rattle. The metal set of the chair shocks my bare skin when I sit. I hear him behind me and then feel a sharp yank in my hair.

"Hold still now," he murmurs, "I don't want to snag any strands."

I want to scream when he touches me. I want to scream from all of this, but he slowly drags the bristles through my wet hair, his fingers combing through the strands. "So beautiful. I wasn't sure if you were right when we first met, but then when I saw you at the diner, I knew it was fate. Serendipity. You were chosen for me."

Shivering, I hear him move around the room again, returning with a white cotton nightie. "You're going to look so beautiful, Kate." He steps closer, holding out the fucking thing like I should feel honored. I don't understand what sick fulfillment he gets from this, but he unfolds the garment, lifting it over my head until it drops.

"Arms."

I lift one, and then the other, still shackled. He feeds the chains through the armholes like this is the most natural thing in the world. When the dress falls, covering my body he steps back admiring his handy work.

"God, you're beautiful."

He winds the chain around my wrist and yanks, pulling my arm behind me. Tears come again, only this time there's no icy water to hide their trail. A sob tears free. "Please," I whisper. "You don't have to do this."

But he doesn't answer. With a sharp jerk, he drags me back to the wall. Tendons yank taught, screaming with the pressure. I'm bound and utterly helpless.

He stands back and admires me. "Perfection."

He turns to the table of instruments; the knives and sharp tools. There's a saw and a hammer. Screwdrivers and a variety of blades. He fusses over them, trying to determine which one to use—or rather—which one to start with. He selects one and a chill runs down my spine, forcing my knees to tremble and buckle as he steps closer. I look away but his fingers graze my cheek.

"Come now. I have you all ready." The blade of the knife slides under my chin and pressed upwards, forcing my gaze to his. "You may as well look at me as I make love to you."

It's those words that stop the sob in the back of my throat. Jesus Christ, he's crazy. I hold his gaze for a second before I rear back and spit in his face. "Fuck you, Ryan. Fuck you *and* your cats."

His hand whips out, slapping me so hard my neck snaps to the side. "Don't you fucking dare slander my cats."

He moves fast, stepping close to me, something in him quickly unraveling. His hands shake as he lowers his zipper, pulling out his cock. It's small. Disfigured and something clicks in my brain.

"He'll have a scar, or some kind of deformity." Paul was right. He sure as fuck does, it's just not anywhere visible.

"Say a word about my dick and I'll cut your tongue out," he says, holding up the knife. "Say a word about how I'm not truly a man, that I do this because I can't satisfy a woman, that I'm pathetic and they will be the last words you ever speak." He lunges for the table and grabs the hammer, "I will fuck you with this and yank out your insides until they're nothing but a pile on the floor."

His rage is unparalleled, different than Jack or Davis'. It's deep-seated inferiority. There's no mission here but pain. He flips that hammer over in his hand, shoving the wooden handle between my legs. I cry out at the pressure. At the same time, I feel a pinch in my side, one that doesn't release. It's when I look down, to find him holding a knife against my side.

"It always comes to this," he says, face inches from mine, "what do I want more? To kill or fuck? The urge to both is strong, but every time killing wins."

His eyes are cold and inhuman and I realize this is it. There's no after. No getting out of this one.

"Kill me," I beg, wanting it over sooner than later. Unable to bear any more pain. "Do it."

His lip curls and his eyes widen—too wide, I realize as his neck snaps back. Pale yellow fabric wraps around his throat, twisting and cutting off his air.

A scream of rage rips through the air as Jack, alive and vengeful, chokes the life out of The Binder. "Get your fucking hands off of my sister!" he screams, slamming Ryan's body to the ground. "You fucking son-of-a-bitch! You don't get to touch her. To be near her, to defile her with your filth. She's *mine!*"

He climbs on top of him, knee in his back. He twists the shirt, *Brandi's* shirt, until Ryan's eyes bulge and his face turns blue. With one final squeeze, something snaps and his body slumps to the ground.

Jack releases him and falls back on the floor, breath coming in jagged heaves. My body shivers despite the trickle of blood dripping down my side. I want nothing more than to vanish, than to evaporate out of here. But that's impossible. I'm still chained. I'm still captive. And even though one murderer is dead, another one isn't, and now that The Binder is dead, Jackson Davenport can take his time and do whatever he wants to me.

Jack

I drag myself off the ground, stepping over The Binder's dead body. My head throbs from the concussion and my arms ache from the exertion. Strangling a man isn't easy.

I lunge toward Katie, taking in the pool of blood dripping off her ankle.

"How?" she asks, clearly in shock. "I thought you were dead."

"He had me tied to the leg of that bunk," I say, voice raw. "I was able to lift it up and get free."

It'd taken nearly all my strength, but watching him touch her, dress her...that was bad enough. But when he threatened her with that hammer and stuck the blade in her side, Jesus, I've never been so angry, so fucking *scared* for someone in my life. Well, once. That day when I hid in the secret passage off the kitchen with Oliver.

It wasn't going to happen again.

She watches me, eyes tired and wary. I deserve that. The things I was going to do to her before he knocked me unconscious. It wasn't pretty.

But now I know.

No one is taking Katie away from me.

She's *mine*.

"Jack, I know you're angry," she starts, watching as I pick the key up off the table of instruments. "But whatever you're thinking about me, The Binder is dead. I can tell the cops you caught him, how you saved me, no one needs to know what happened before he got here."

I approach her, knowing I can do whatever I want to her. I can fuck her. Make her scream. Make her beg. But the first thing I do is reach for the hem of the white dress. My fingers graze her thigh as I lift it, and I see the slick of blood running down her hip.

"How bad is it?" she asks. I press my fingers against her skin, inspecting the wound. She hisses, body jerking from the pain.

"It's not that deep." I drop the dress and start unlocking the shackles, one by one. Her arms drop, limp and useless. I grunt toward the bathroom. "Go wash it off."

She hesitates, like she's wondering if this is another game, a different trap. I thrust my hand in my hair. "Clean the wound, Katie."

Without another word, she jerkily walks to the bathroom, legs stiff from being chained to the wall. I stare at her until she shuts the door and I hear the water running. I just needed a minute without her in my face, so I can just figure out what to do. She'd betrayed me, lied to me and my brothers, snuck around and almost got herself fucking killed.

But she's also...

Goddamnit.

I step over Ryan Watkins once again and go outside, sucking in the humid night air. Rain is coming. I walk to my car and open the trunk, grabbing my black bag. When I step back into the cabin, Katie is in the bathroom doorway, shivering in that wet, bloody dress. Her eyes dart to the table of weapons and then back again.

Always a fighter.

"Come here," I tell her, nodding to the bunk. When she hesitates, I add, "I'm not going to hurt you."

The sentence feels like a goddamn lie, but it's true. Pain isn't on my mind right now. She does as she's told, sitting on the saggy mattress, and I unzip the bag, removing a First-Aid kit and a clean black sweatshirt.

"Take off your dress," I tell her, sorting through the supplies. I've got disinfectant wipes, ointment, different bandages and a stitching kit if I need it.

"You carry that around with you?" she says, hair falling to her shoulders after she pulls off the dress. She clutches the ball of cotton protectively in her chest, covering her tits. "A First-Aid kit?"

"Not every hunt goes smoothly," I tell her, opening the wipes. "Oliver almost had his finger sawed off once. Paul got stabbed. One guy had snakes and Davis got bit. Hunting rapists and killers is a dangerous job." I look over at the dead body on the floor. "As you can tell."

I clean the wound. She got enough of the blood off in the bathroom that I can get a better look. As I suspected it's not deep and didn't nick anything important. I get the rest of the blood off and unscrew the cap on the ointment.

"I shouldn't have come out here alone," she says quietly.

I dab the ointment on the cut, making her shiver. "No. You shouldn't have."

"Trying to get the jump on this. It was stupid. I spent the last week trying to get the fuck away from you all. You scare me. But I had nowhere to go and even though you think this is all about you, I grew up in that house too. Catching bad men is branded in my soul, just like yours. I just do it differently. My instincts are good, Jack, but the people I'm investigating are scary." She touches my hand, stopping my care. "The Binder was way out of my league, and when I found that clue, I should have just shown it to Davis, or to you. But most of all, I shouldn't have betrayed you."

It's a last-ditch plea. Katie knows she fucked up. Out of the frying pan into the fire. The difference is that I'm not the same man I was an hour ago.

I place a bandage over the wound and hand her the sweatshirt. She stands and tugs it over her head, giving me a full view of her body. She's skinny. Bruised. Bandaged, but she's still fucking gorgeous. Energy courses through my veins, the adrenaline from killing a man. It's savage. Feral. I feel like I'm barely holding on by a thread.

My eyes are glued to the hem of the shirt, *my shirt*, how it skims the top of her thighs, barely covering her pussy. My dick swells, pushing against the inside of my pants and all I want to do is–

"You're thinking about it, aren't you?" she asks. My eyes snap to hers. "Fucking me."

"Katie."

Now isn't the time to push me.

But she does. Always. "I know because you get a certain look in your eye. My body reacts to it. I don't want it to, I never have.

Not that night, not tonight, but I have these cravings, ones that only you and the others know how to meet."

I step forward and push my fingers between her legs. She's slippery with heat. "Jesus," I groan. "I just killed a man. I'm..." I swallow back the urge to shove my fingers in her tight little pussy. I yank my hand away. "You don't want to taunt me now. I'm not in a good place."

"You can talk to me," she says. "Use me."

I stare down at her, at those big eyes and puffy lips.

Her fingers fist in my shirt, pulling me down, mouth hot and needy against mine. "Fuck me," she whispers, looking down at the floor. At the body. Something flickers in my mind. She's got something wild running through her blood too. "Fuck me in front of him. Pour everything into me."

I hold out for one moment longer, *one*, and then grip the back of her head with my hand and crash my mouth to hers. Her lips are hot, tongue greedy. Again, I dip my fingers between her legs and feel the rush of heat, the slippery want and I groan on her tongue.

"Davis is right," I tell her, pushing up the shirt she'd just put on to get to her tits, "you *are* filthy."

But it's more than that, I know it. It's the crackle of near death between us. The bonding over shared trauma. Teetering on the fine pinpoint between life and death. I want to pound that into her, bite and bruise. I want to claim and consume.

Make her *mine*.

I release her, moving to the bunk and yanking the mattress to the floor. I unbuckle my jeans, dropping them to the ground and kicking them off. Her eyes are glued to my cock, the way it bobs against my belly, thick and long. I pull her to me, kissing her, licking her sinful mouth, and drag her down on top of me, aware of the wound in her side.

I watch as she lifts the shirt, exposing herself. I rise up, latching my mouth to her nipple, sucking and licking until she squeals. Her hips rock against me, gathering friction. It takes everything in me not to lift her up and impale myself in her, but I'm not rushing this. Not this time.

She bends, pressing those tits against my chest, capturing my ear with her teeth. She bites down, tugging at the skin. The spread of pain ripples through me. In my ear, she whispers, "How many men have you killed?"

"Ten," I reply, lifting my hips, sliding my cock between her legs. Then I glance to the side. "Well, eleven."

"And they all deserved it?" she asks.

I lick the seam between her lips. "Monsters," I say against her tongue. "Every last one of them."

She nods, still processing, still reconciling. It's more than I could ask for. She's one of us. She understands. Finally, I've had enough. I grab her by the hips and lift her over me, slotting my tip at her entrance. Her eyes hold mine and she bites her bottom lip, fingernails puncturing my bicep.

"Fuck me," she begs. "Please, Jack, don't make me ask you again."

I give her what she wants, sheathing myself with her tight, warm pussy. I slam her down as hard as I can, filling her with my cock. She cries out, still for a moment as she absorbs me, but then drops her head back and rocks her hips.

She's goddamn fucking glorious.

It takes everything in me not to flip her over and punch my way inside, but I keep her like this, sitting over me, tits bouncing with every rocking thrust. She consumes me the same way I want to consume her. Her nails leaving marks on my skin, her pussy clenching around me, holding me tight.

The animal in me roars and I grab onto her hips, fucking her like a beast. These are the hands of a killer, a monster, but this woman, she both fears and wants me. Ever since that first day. I helped mold her into the woman bouncing on my dick. I helped create the woman not afraid to take a bad man's life.

Her breath grows ragged, soft little cries tremble on her lips.

"Come for me, Katie," I say, brushing my thumb over her clit. She shudders, back arching, a long guttural moan rumbling in the back of her throat. All the fear, the anger, the terror of the night, releasing in an epic, soul-crushing orgasm.

It takes everything in me not to come when her pussy clenches around my cock. But I don't, saying, "I'm going to roll you over," and I follow through. I'm gentle on her wound, but I can't take it anymore. I need to pound into her. Stake my claim.

I push her knees back and bury myself inside. She looks up at me, eyes glaze, still riding her orgasm. I feel it in her pussy. In the way her body has loosened, the hate and anger leaving her eyes, as they flutter shut. My balls ache, seizing, and sending a jolt up my spine. My groan comes out more like a roar, the orgasm hard and fast, cum pumping into her.

"Jesus," I mutter, hips rising and falling. "Goddamn, Kate."

Her eyes flicker open and her hand reaches for my cheek. We hold one another's eyes, absorbing the aftershocks of the orgasm, the night, the dead man beside us. The *everything*.

I pull out and roll over, cradling her against my side. I've fucked women after I've hunted someone. Two or three in one night, just to get the smell of pussy on my hands instead of blood, but it's been nothing like this. Nothing so concrete and real.

Nothing that makes my racing heart slow and a sense of peace spread through my limbs.

She hits close to home and I know it. Still, I can't stop that hunger inside me. I can't stop feeling things I shouldn't...dangerous things. Dangerous for her and me.

The adrenaline fades, and the woman next to me rests her head on my shoulder. I stare at her until she falls asleep, her chest rising and falling with even breaths, realizing with startling clarity that we caught him. *Finally*. The Binder has been eliminated, and that means we can focus on our true mission, finding my mother's killer.

I JOLT AWAKE, eyes blinking into the early morning light. Sitting up, I feel the space next to me–where Katie had been all night. She isn't there.

"Hey," she says, drawing my attention across the room. She's still wearing my sweatshirt, long legs bare underneath. I woke up hard, but this is different, a tickle deep in my belly.

"Morning," I say, searching for something else to say. How do you articulate what happened last night? We killed a serial rapist and killer, then we fucked next to his corpse on the floor. I wrinkle my nose. That doesn't seem right. I glance over at the body. "We're going to have to figure that out. I'll call Davis–"

That's when I notice the phone in her hand. My phone. And I sense how quiet it is outside. Not a bird singing. My eyes narrow and I push myself off the mattress. "Katie, what's going on–"

I never get out the rest of the sentence, the door kicks open, splintering against the wall. A cloud of gas fills the room, followed by dozens of men in black uniforms, long rifles clutched in their hands. I have zero time to react, no ability to brace for the impact as I'm slammed to the floor.

I do know the last thing I see before I'm flipped over and handcuffed. Her. My stepsister, her eyes pinned to mine as she's being dragged out of the cabin door by one of the men, mouthing the word, "I'm sorry."

TWENTY

Kate

I'M WHISKED OUT OF THE FRAY, PULLED TO THE SIDE AS they haul Jack out of the cabin. The scene is chaos, men in uniform swarming the tiny building. Even though he's handcuffed, he bucks and snarls, trying to tear away from their hold.

"Get your fucking hands off of me!" he shouts, using his massive strength to break free of one of the officers. Two others jump on top of him and they scramble in the dirt. When he's finally subdued, his eyes meet mine. "Katie! I'm going to fucking kill you!"

People hover, pulling me one way, then another. I can't drag my gaze away from Jack as the lies fall from my lips. "It's him! The Binder. He's a killer."

Someone, an EMT, encourages me to sit on the ledge of the ambulance and throws a blanket over my shoulders. They inspect me next, flashing a light in my eyes, taking pictures of the sores on my ankles and wrists from the shackles. Then swipe under my nails for evidence.

"Did he assault you?" a woman asks. She's an EMT. Her eyes are kind and that's what makes me feel bad for lying. But not enough to stop.

"Yes." I know his semen is still in me. Proof. "He chained me up and stabbed me. Then he raped me."

"You'll have to go to the hospital for an exam."

I nod, wanting them to collect the sample. Wanting to prove to the world who Jack Davenport really is.

"This cut seems cleaned," she says, looking at the injury to my side.

"He let me patch it up," I tell her, scrambling for something–anything. "He said he was going to keep me for a while. To use me before he killed me. I guess he didn't want me bleeding all over."

She touches my arm and gives it a gentle squeeze. "You're very brave."

"Are you the person who made the call?" a different voice asks. I look up and see a dark blue jacket. A patch on the chest says, 'FBI.'

Across the driveway, officers drag Jack to the back of a car, again our eyes connecting. For a long beat, we stare at one another, the truth passing between us. My word against his. Neither of us look away until he's jerked by the collar.

"Yes. I called." The FBI, not the police. Davis would have intercepted that alert and things would have turned out differently. I take a deep breath, the sob I release not entirely fake. "I escaped when he fell asleep, and I was able to get to my phone. He's the one that r-raped and killed those women. The one they call The Binder."

Beyond the other vehicles, I see a Mustang pull up, tires kicking up gravel. Davis. His gaze turns savage as he looks at his best friend handcuffed.

"Can you tell us what happened?" the agent asks, jerking his chin at the EMT to give us privacy.

"He kidnapped me and my date." My pulse starts to race as I turn to the officer at my side. The lies start to gather momentum now. I don't think I could stop it, even if I wanted to. "My stepbrother... he's always been off," I whisper. "Mean and abusive, but I had no idea that he was capable of," I swallow and glance back at the cabin where investigators go in and out of the screen door, "something that terrible."

"Did something set him off?" he asks. "Has he been violent with you before?"

I bite back a laugh. "I think he just snapped. He saw me with Ryan and just... it was like a switch flipped. He strangled Ryan and told me to go run in the woods–that he wanted to hunt me." They'd find our footprints in the soft dirt, more proof. The pieces are lining up. "He chased me for what seemed like hours. I thought I had a good hiding spot but he found me and brought me back here to... you know."

He nods in understanding. "Did he say where the last victim is? Where he left her body or what he did with her?"

I shake my head, hot tears building in the corner of my eyes. "He strangled Ryan with a yellow shirt. A woman's shirt. Maybe that's a clue?"

The agent grunts and nods, writing all of this down on a little pad, before waving another officer over. They whisper to one another, but I pick up on words, 'hunt,' and 'woods' and 'yellow shirt.' I watch as the agent connects the dots, as all the pieces click into place. Jack Davenport looks every bit the killer–because that's what he is. A murdering, raping, sadistic killer.

Even if he's also something else.

The man that saved me.

I once thought I was the key and they were the locks. But maybe that's not true at all. Maybe they're just sick, deranged men who like to taunt, torture, and play with their victims. I thought I was the one who got away. I didn't, but I am the one that will stop them.

"Anyone want to explain why the FBI is here and no one called the local PD?" Davis asks, flashing his badge. "This is our jurisdiction. This is *my* case."

The agent gives him a withering look. "Not that I have to explain it to you, but the FBI got a tip about the whereabouts of a violent, deadly, killer. We followed procedure." Davis steps closer, his gaze moving from me to the agent. I can see him scrambling to find a way out of this, a way to get back in control.

"Can you at least tell me why you've arrested him?"

"They found a body inside, recently strangled. Shackles and chains on the wall. A table full of torture devices and a black bag with Davenport's belongings." The agent's eyes sweep to me. "And we have a survivor. An eyewitness that can tell us everything that happened."

I sense the moment Davis realizes the truth. Jack is going down. Not just for killing the Ryan Watkins, but for kidnapping me and a dozen other murders. There's no silencing the evidence.

There's no silencing me. For once I'm the one in control and from the hard set of his jaw and the dark flash in his eyes, I know he realizes it.

And Jesus, he's pissed.

It takes everything in me not to shout in his face, *"I'm free!"* From one of them anyway.

I pull the blanket tighter around my shoulders, using it like a shield. It's useless, and even with all the law enforcement around me, I don't feel safe. After today, I doubt I ever will. Two men tried to kill me. Two different sides of a similar coin.

The cop's walkie-talkie crackles on his hip. The agent responds, walking across the driveway, leaving me sitting on the back of the ambulance. Davis and I are alone in a sea of uniforms. It's a relief to drop the pretenses.

Can he tell that my body is still slick with Jack's cum, my nipples still tender from his mouth? Does he know what truly happened between me and his best friend? Does he care?

All I know is my soul is screaming, clawing for redemption.

"You think you're real smart going to the feds, don't you, Katie?" he hisses. "Going over my head?"

"I did what I had to do."

"Selling out your brother?" he asks. "Ruining our mission?"

"Your mission is bullshit. It's an excuse to hunt and murder," I whisper, "because you're cold-blooded killers."

"You need to watch your fucking mouth." His fingers ball into a fist. "This was the dumbest move you could ever make."

"I may not be able to take you all down," I say, lifting my chin, "at least not yet, but I'm starting with him."

"So this is revenge?" he asks, hand on his hip. I think about how rough they feel when he handles me. How he tastes in my mouth. I think about how he raped me with his gun, and they all watched. "You think you can pick us off, one by one? You think you can get the upper hand on us?"

"I think you're psychopaths. Garbage. Abusers." I stand, tossing the blanket. His eyes slide down my body–Jack's sweatshirt, my bare legs underneath. "And yeah, I plan on taking you down one by one and revealing to the world what kind of monsters you really are."

He grabs my arm, fingers digging into the soft skin. "It's going to be hard doing that if you're cut into a dozen pieces and tossed in the landfill."

I don't let him see the shiver that runs down my spine.

"Miss," the agent says, waving me over. "It's time to go."

Davis releases me, but I know his grip will add to the bruises I've acquired today. Pretending he doesn't scare the fuck out of me, I push past him and follow the agent over to his vehicle. We pass Jack as they hold him face down against the back of the car.

"You think this is it? That you're going to get rid of me, little sister?" His soft snarl carries over to me. "You forget the weight that the Davenport name carries. How much power comes with money. I'll be out before you scurry into whatever hidey-hole you think will keep you from me." He grunts as the agent roughly shoves him in the back of the car. Before the door slams shut he shouts, "You better be ready, *Katherine*, because I'm coming to get you."

My pulse races with his words, at the way he says my name.

Katie is what he calls me when he wants to torment me.

Kate is reserved for moments of sincerity. Few and far between.

But Katherine? I don't think he's ever called me that and the way he says it? It's not just a threat, it's a promise.

"Keep moving." I feel the pinch of a hand on my elbow. Davis has appeared at my side. He opens the rear door of the vehicle. His mask is firmly in place, and he's back to being the protective good guy. He jerks open the door and I get inside. Davis leans down, his gaze seething. "You may have gotten rid of one of us, but there's still three of us watching your every move."

The engine of the car in front starts before the agent assigned to me gives Davis a glare, then comes closer. "Detective. Ms. Stevenson is officially a witness in federal protective custody. If you want to speak to her, you'll need to follow procedure."

Davis' jaw tics and I think for a moment he may snap. He's not used to being told no, to having to answer to someone with more power. Quickly though, he recovers and says, "Just ensuring our witness knows that she's in good hands." He turns that glare my way, eyes narrowing. "I don't care what they tell you, we'll never be far away, Kate. Despite what happens to Jack; Paul, Oliver, and I will always be here, always watching and waiting to strike. You can rest assured of that."

Then with a hard shove, the car door slams shut. I jump at the sound. My heart punches against my chest, booming. I'm glad to be away from him, but it's not enough. I need to get far, far, away from these crazy bastards.

"You okay?" The agent glances into the rearview mirror as he slides in behind the wheel.

I nod even as I feel the warmth drain from my face. "Yes. No. God, who the fuck knows." I was hunted, tortured, almost raped, and killed, and then... well I don't know how to describe what happened between me and Jack. The way we were together–it was more than part of the game. I can admit that. The way he made me feel, the emotions that passed between us.

It doesn't matter anymore. He's going to jail and I'm...

"What happens to me next?" I ask, leaning forward. "I can't go home. His family–*my* family–is very powerful. Wealthy and connected."

"The house is off-limits. Agents are already there processing evidence." My mind races. How much evidence will point to me? Oliver? The others? "After you give your full statement and are examined, you'll be required to testify in the trial. The prosecutor will want you safe, and we'll do everything we can to protect you."

"I don't think I'll be safe in Wilmington."

He nods. "If that's true, it most likely means witness protection for at least a few months."

"So I'm not going back?"

His eyes meet mine. "No. Not until this is resolved."

I exhale, feeling the weight slowly lift off my shoulders. They can't get me. Not Davis or Paul or Oliver. Not Christopher Watkins who is out there somewhere lying in wait.

I stare out the window, watching the thick forest fades and the town of Wilmington passes by the window. I loathe this city, the hot sticky air and god, that nightmare of a house. It seems too surreal to process yet, but this is what I wanted all along—an escape. I just didn't know it'd be like this, from the backseat of a cop car.

Captured by my Stepbrothers

Foreword

Thanks for following along with the adventures of Kate, the Davenport Brothers and their psycho friends, the doctor and the detective.

This is your pre-book notice about what's coming, what to look out for and if you should turn around now.

Family Confessions is a fast-paced, book of darkness and deviancy. It was originally published on Kindle Vella as a serialized fiction.

If that's not your jam, it's okay not to read this book. These guys are terrible. Kate is in a MESS. Their relationship is capital 'C' complicated. Who wouldn't be if their brothers are serial killers and decide to use you as bait?

But, as promised, here's the notice.

T/W: dub-con, non-con, exhibitionism, overall mindfuckery, stalking, psychological exploitation, and obviously, murder.

Enjoy!

Angel & AK

ONE

Kate

____

I WAITED UNTIL HE WAS ASLEEP, HIS BREATH EVEN, FINALLY *settled from devouring one another. Because that had happened between us—a devouring—two traumatized, desperate, people—looking to satiate a hunger that could only be found in one another.*

Sex and violence was our language.

But so was betrayal.

I slid from under his arm, easing away from his body heat, hyper-aware of my surroundings. Every breath he took, the birds rousing in the forest outside the cabin, but most of all, I'm aware of the cold, dead silence of The Binder on the floor. Ryan Watkins.

I bend and search for the cellphone Jack had taken from me when we first met the night before. My hands trembled as I patted his clothes, finally finding it in his discarded pants pocket. With my heart pounding in my ears, I opened the screen door and stepped outside, pressing the number I'd programmed in the day before.

The FBI.

THAT WAS THREE MONTHS AGO—A lifetime when you're in witness protection and building a new life from scratch. The prosecutor set me up four states away in a lazy beach town called Tidewater. It's busy enough to not look out of place to have a new face in town, but small enough to know if someone suspicious starts creeping around.

They found me a job working for the local newspaper, The Tidewater Times, which is much smaller than the Gazette. I spend most of my time writing copy about the weekly farmers' market, missing pets, and parking concerns. None of this requires a lot of field work, so it's mostly just me and my laptop, drinking coffee in the tiny café.

I have no social life, but I'm also not living in a household of murderers and chasing a serial killer.

Not officially anyway.

Any prestige that would've come from taking down The Binder was lost when I went into witness protection. The less attention the better. At least until the trial.

My fingers fly over the keyboard, pulling up the latest on Jack Davenport, AKA: The Binder, a notorious rapist and serial killer. Also? My stepbrother.

A quick skim reveals that there's nothing new. His first hearing is scheduled to occur in a month. The prosecutors won't call me in to testify until the last minute. They think they're hiding me from the press and from copycats, but the truth is much closer to home. Oliver, Jack's brother and my stepbrother, along with Paul Sanders, and Davis Higgins, those are my real threats. When I betrayed Jack, I betrayed them, too. There's no doubt they're looking for me—looking for revenge.

"Can I get you a refill, Maggie?"

Still not accustomed to my new name, it takes me a few seconds before I realize 'Maggie," is me. I quickly close the tabs and smile at the cute barista I've gotten to know the past few months. "Thanks, Dave, that would be great."

He picks up my cup and nods at the laptop. "Anything exciting worth reporting?"

"Hmmm..." I tap my chin. "There is a story about a local dog taking care of a litter of abandoned kittens."

"Sounds like exhilarating front-page news."

We both laugh, and he carries my cup off, heading behind the counter. It's late morning and although summer is waning, there's still plenty of tourists that pass by the coffee shop window on their way down to the beach.

I reopen my laptop and open the encrypted file my mother and I can send messages through. The letters are monitored, checked for any information that could jeopardize the case or my location. The early ones were about how disrupted their lives had been due to Jack being arrested and how they'd been forced to return early from their trip only to find that the police had made a mess of Davenport Manor while they'd searched for evidence.

There's a new letter. I glance over my shoulder to make sure no one is watching, and only see a man across the shop in a Tidewater Beach baseball cap focused on his phone.

> Daughter,
> Hope all is well. We've had a lot of rain lately, but it's good for the garden, which I'm spending a lot of time in. The results are impressive and it's a good thing.

Going to the market is no longer fun. Too many questioning eyes and stares. Maybe I should get a few chickens and cows to round things out.

XXX is busy with work. It's that time of year when the stockholders' reports are due. XXX well, he's lost without his brother. They both maintain his innocence. Things are difficult. I know you think you did the right thing but... family should always come first. I just wish you had come to me before doing something so drastic.

Love,

Mother

The letters are all the same. Little tidbits about her life. How people judge and watch them because of *my* actions. How upset Oliver is that I had his brother arrested and how I should have given her and my stepfather an opportunity to solve this without the authorities. I don't know if she thinks Jack is guilty or not, but it's clear they don't think he's the problem, but I am.

The truth is that Jack isn't The Binder, but he is a killer—a serial killer and I'm not going to feel guilty about getting a psychopath off the streets.

"Here you go," Dave says, delivering the fresh cup of coffee.

"Thank you." I take a sip and taste an explosion of flavor. "Oh, what is that?"

"You like it?" He grins anxiously. "It's a new blend I'm trying."

"It's amazing." The sound of a chair scraping across the room draws both of our attention. Now standing, the man in the baseball cap slips a pair of dark sunglasses over his eyes. His cheekbones are sharp and his skin a warm tan. A Tidewater Beach logo is on his T-shirt.

"Have a good day," Dave calls as he opens the door. He doesn't reply. Just exits. Dave snorts. "Nice guy."

"Seems like it," I laugh. "Anyway, thank you for this. It'll make writing up the town council notes about how there are too many tourists here and how we should shut down the bridge at noon, go a lot easier." He raises an eyebrow. "I wish I was joking, but people here do not like strangers."

He gives me a slow smile and I see he has a dimple in his left cheek. "Eh, not all strangers are bad," he says. "You know what they say, 'a stranger is a friend you just haven't met.'"

I can't help but smile back at his cheesy line and there's an awkward beat between us and I wonder, not for the first time if he'll ask me out. The moment passes and he says, "Enjoy the coffee."

"I will."

He returns to the counter and my chest flutters. Was that flirting? It was right? It's been a long time since I felt something for a man other than fear. But after my stepbrothers? After being hunted? I don't know if I'll ever be able to feel anything else.

***

EVERY NIGHT after dinner I walk down to watch the sunset and then back up past the little cottages and rentals packed with tourists for the season. It's something I force myself to do. Sitting inside with the doors locked and the shades drawn would be easier, but I'm not letting my life be ruled by paranoia. I've given enough years to these psychopaths.

Not that it's that easy to shake. I'm on alert, aware of every movement, every sound. That's why I do this, take these walks down the street, hang out in the coffee shop. I'm trying to desensitize myself from the urge to flee. But every time I hear the rustle of a palm tree or spot a cat slinking under a parked car, the hair on the back of my neck stands on end, warning me to stay alert.

If anyone can find me it's them.

No, I tell myself. I'm hundreds of miles away. I'm hidden. A new name. A new life. I'm fine. Safe.

Even so, I try to be home before dark and I'm relieved when I see the house with yellow shutters and a pink door up ahead. The apartment they found for me is above the garage, tucked back in the twisted branches of weathered oak trees. I climb the steps and feel the breeze rolling in from the ocean two blocks away. It's still warm here but it's nothing like the oppressive humidity in Wilmington.

"I fixed your screen."

I yelp, the voice from below startling me. With my heart in my throat, I look over the railing and see Mr. Holbrook, the man who owns the property carrying a rake. "Sorry, I forget you're a jumpy little thing."

"It's okay," I say, trying to settle my nerves. Mr. Holbrook is an older man, in his late sixties. Harmless and a good property owner. "Did you say something about my screen?"

"On the window," he points to the window just off the porch. "It had a tear."

I look over and see the clean, non-torn, screen. I hadn't noticed it one way or the other before. Had it been there? Was it new? "I didn't realize it was torn." I force a smile. "Thank you."

"Happens sometimes, but if you're going to keep your windows open, bugs'll get in."

"Of course." That is something I know for certain. I don't leave my windows open or unlocked. Ever. "I'll make sure to keep them closed."

"Too hot for open windows anyway—not with the AC on at the same time. It'll freeze up."

I nod. Mr. Holbrook is big on not wasting the AC. There are notes by the thermostat and he's brought it up several times already. "I agree."

"Well," he says, giving me a curt nod, "good night."

"Good night."

I look over my shoulder before I open the door, watching him disappear around the corner as I step inside. I should've told him I didn't leave the window open. Or did I? I burned eggs on the stove this morning and opened it up to air out, but I know I closed it after.

Didn't I?

Locked inside the house, I check every room, every closet, even under the bed before my heart settles. Even later, when I'm under the covers and in bed, my hand keeps checking for the kitchen knife I keep under the pillow. The cool touch of the steel handle soothes my nerves and I repeat the mantra that helps me get through the night: I am strong. I am in control of my own fate. I'm a survivor.

Finally, I drift to sleep.

"COME FOR ME, KATIE."

I wake, drenched in sweat, one hand wrapped around the handle of the knife, the other tucked between my legs. My pussy throbs, caught in the dream of Jack pounding into me, drawing out the best orgasm of my life.

The dream is familiar. It's one of a few that rotate in and out of my subconscious every night. There's one where I'm sprawled on a tabletop, the guys standing over me while they eat off my body like a buffet. There's another where I'm sucking Davis off, cock buried in my throat. He comes. We both do, just as he drives his car off a cliff.

But the one with Jack rocks me the most. It's too real, and every time, I end up pushing my fingers down my panties, furiously rubbing my clit, chasing the feel of the orgasm my stepbrother gave me the night before I betrayed him.

Tonight is no different.

Except this time, I run the blade down my inner thigh, allowing the blood to drip between my legs and use the slippery fluid for lube.

When I'm done, breathless and staring at the ceiling, I know the deep, dark truth.

These men have ruined me.

SINCE THERE'S no urgency with my job at the Tidewater Times, I've created my own schedule. Get up, get dressed, take a long walk on the beach, come back and shower and eat, then head down to the coffee shop to write up my copy.

I'm searching for my hair band when I walk in the kitchen. I'd pulled it out after my walk the day before and maybe it's—

An envelope sits on the counter.

I freeze, every nerve in my body on heightened alert. From where I stand, I look at the door.

Locked.

The windows.

Locked.

For anything out of place.

Nothing.

Slowly, I reach for the envelope and see that my name is written on the front, "Katie," in block print.

Oh god, oh god, oh god…

I swallow back the fear and run my nail under the flap. Maybe it's from Mr. Holbrook. My brain screams, knowing better. Inside are three photographs.

I lay them on the table.

The first is me at the café, smiling up at Dave as he grins back.

The second is of me walking back from the beach at sunset.

The third… goosebumps rise across my flesh, and I cover my mouth with my hand, forcing back a gag. It's of me, in bed, in the dark, asleep.

I flip it over and written in the same print: *To the one that got away. I'm watching and waiting for the perfect time to strike—TB.*

Bile rolls up my throat and this time I don't fight it. I make it to the sink, vomiting down the drain. This whole time I'd been worried that the three men I betrayed in Wilmington would find me.

Apparently, I should have been worried about someone equally or far more dangerous.

TWO

Kate

I almost turn around a dozen times before I get to the boat ramp. It's far enough from Tidewater to not reveal my actual location. The narrow strip of road is mostly deserted, just a couple of fishermen down by the ramshackle old pier. A gray stray cat darts across the road and I pull the car to the side, parking it in the soft dirt.

"What am I doing..." I drop my forehead to the steering wheel and take a deep breath. "This is a terrible fucking idea."

But then again, so is being murdered.

The decision comes in a split second. I've got to get the hell out of here now, although there's no guarantee he'll help me. Not after everything I did. Running seems to be the best idea. I'll pack up and move again. Over and over. This is my life now.

I shift the car in reverse and press the gas, but just as quickly slam on the brakes, lurching the car to a stop. I'm blocked in. A large black SUV idles in the middle of the road.

A familiar man sits in the front seat. My stepbrother. Oliver Davenport.

I guess this is happening.

He makes no move to get out of his car, but he jerks his head, gesturing for me to get in the passenger side. Great. I wonder how many days it will take them to find my abandoned vehicle?

My heart is hammering as I kill the engine of my car and climb out, making my way closer, one terrifying step at a time. My fingers tremble, aching as I reach out. I clench my fist, driving feeling and blood through my body, then open the passenger's side door. The blast of AC slams into me—followed by the clean, soapy scent that lingers on Oliver wherever he goes. The smell brings back a rush of memories, mostly from that night. I can still smell his skin, warm and clean. I remember his taste. I feel the phantom pain, the humiliation, and regret.

He parks the SUV a few feet behind mine. Another stray cat darts between the palm trees. This one black and white. Oliver is dressed in a pale blue button-down shirt and khaki shorts. Sneakers on his feet. Mirrored aviators hide his eyes, but I take in the hard line of his jaw and the two-day-old growth covering his chin. He looks like a tourist.

He also looks ridiculously hot.

"Before we start," I tell him, "I left a note with someone back where I've been staying, telling them to open it if I go missing. I've included details about this meeting."

"Protecting yourself." Oliver pushes his sandy blond hair off his forehead and lifts his chin. "Guess our girl has learned a few things since you ran off."

Our girl.

"I didn't run," I tell him, although I know it's semantics. "The feds put me in protective custody."

"Yet here we are," he says, resting his elbow on the edge of the window. "Completely unprotected, which tracks. You never were one for following the rules, were you?"

It's rhetorical. I know my stepbrothers and their monstrous friends think I'm a defiant brat. Maybe they're right. I'm also a survivor, doing everything I can to live another day. This is why I'm in this car with Oliver now, despite the fact he's a serial killer in his own right.

"Here," I say, pulling out the envelope with the photos. I hand them over and he takes them out, studying each one. "That was in my apartment when I got up this morning. He was in and out like a ghost."

"These were taken while you were sleeping?" He studies the photo of me in bed. "Doors locked?"

"Yes, although it's possible they broke in and were hiding somewhere. Although I checked everything before I went to bed." I wipe my palms on my skirt. "I've been diligent."

He reads the note on the back, the threat to come for me. A rush of nausea tumbles in my belly. I rest a hand on top like I can stop it.

"You think it's him."

"Was it you?"

"No."

"Paul or Davis?"

He shakes his head. "No. We didn't even know where you were. Trust me, Davis has been looking."

My heart pounds at the confession. "Then yeah, it's him. He found me."

Christopher Watkins—The Binder—or the other half of the Binder. Turns out that Ryan Watkins had a brother, and they were both raping, murdering sons of bitches.

Oliver clenches his jaw. "I hate this mother fucker."

"That's something we can agree on."

He takes one last look at the photographs and stuffs them back in the envelope. He tucks them into his breast pocket, claiming them for his own. He shifts and removes his glasses, looking me over. "Exactly how do you want our help, Katie? Because I'm not in a particularly generous mood when it comes to you."

"I know." I take a deep breath. I knew this would be hard. Impossible. Sacrificing. "I'm asking for your protection."

His eyebrow raises and I see the small pale scar just above the right one. I remember the day he got it, coming home from football practice with a butterfly bandage affixed to his forehead. He claimed something about an illegal tackle and shot Jack a dirty look.

"You want my protection," he repeats.

"Well," I twist my hands in the fabric of the skirt, "*all* of your protection."

He's still for a moment and then his arm snaps out and slams my head into the window. His fingers cinch around my neck, tight and unrelenting. I struggle against him, clawing at him, desperate for air. He's halfway over the center console, breath hot against my cheek.

"You want us to protect *you*? The woman who sent *my* brother to jail? You lied, Katie. He fucking saved your life and you lied. Why? Because you're a deranged, petty, bitch? Or you've just been waiting all this time to get back at him—back at all of us."

He laughs, his deep voice echoing off the interior of the car. "God, you're brave. I'll give you that. And fucking insane if you think we'd ever help you."

Gurgling sounds come from my throat and I feel the life drain out of me. He stares at me then releases me with a hard thrust. I gasp for air, the sound dragging against my throat. Coughing, choking, eyes watering as I fumble for the door. The lock engages, bolting me inside.

I look over at my stepbrother and see the deep, dark, rage.

"I was scared," I tell him, voice raw and brittle. "You know that before Ryan found us, Jack followed me out to that cabin and *hunted* me through the woods. Stalked me. He didn't trust me any more than I trusted him. He chained me to the wall and was going to rape me, then kill me and dispose of me so I'd never be found again." I straighten. "So yeah, I turned him in before he could kill me himself."

I can't tell if he knew that, but I know that I've got his attention because his breathing slows, and his fingers finally unclench from the tight, fisted, balls by his side. I don't know if this is what the final moments of my life look like, or if he'll give me a running start. Finally, he speaks.

"If we choose to protect you," he says slowly, words measured, "and I mean *if,* there are no more games. No more manipulations or secrets."

I nod my head. "I can do that."

"Yeah, well I'm not done." He laughs darkly. "You'll have to recant your statement against Jack in court."

"What? I can't do that!"

"Yes, Katie, you can, and if you want our help, you will. You tell the court that you lied. That you were looking to get him back.

That you wanted to become a big name in investigative journalism. You tell them that he killed Watkins in self-defense."

"But my reputation, it'll be ruined. I'll never get a job again. All a journalist has is their word and mine will be destroyed after this."

"You're right. It will be." His tone is cold. "Everyone will know you're the lying bitch that tried to ruin her stepbrother's life. But, you'll be alive, and whoever else is on Christopher's rape and kill list will be safe."

He's right. My lie puts other women at risk. Christopher may be focused on me for now, but soon that will wane. The urge to torment and kill will grow stronger, and he'll strike again. That weighs heavy on me. Heavier than the lie... or the truth, whichever way you look at it.

"Fine," I answer slowly. "I'll do it. I'll recant my statement."

"That's not all little sister," he says. "That's the price you'll pay for us not killing you on the spot. There's another price for protection."

I swallow and meet the dark glint in his eye. "What do you want?"

"We own you, Katie. Body, mind, and soul. You belong to us, you're one of us. We drop this charade that you've ever been anything, but a Davenport—ever since that night." When he looks at me, I know he sees past the vernier. Past the college graduate, the journalist, the survivor. He sees the truth. The girl they forced to her knees and came all over. The girl Oliver...

I sniff back the tears of shame and humiliation, my world sinking into the dark, depraved hole they put me in. "Okay. Whatever you want."

"Good girl," he says, cupping my cheek with his large hand. "We protect what belongs to us. I can promise you that."

I ran out of options when I found those photographs in my rented house. Maybe long before that. Maybe I never had an option to begin with, maybe this was just fate catching up to me. "Thank you."

"Don't thank me yet," he says, dropping his hand to his buckle. "We can start now."

"What do you want?"

He looks at my mouth and then says, "We've got a long ride back. I want your mouth on my cock the whole way."

"That's hours," I say, watching him pull out his cock. It's erect. Thick. A sheen of precum oozing at the top. "You want a three-hour blow job?"

"Not exactly, sweetheart. The last few months have been stressful. I'm tense and worried about Jack. We've never been apart this long. We were forced to stop hunting because there's too much heat on the family and that... well, that took away a release. Dad... he's a mess and your mother? If she's not drunk, she's holed up in her room crying in the dark. You fucked up the family, Katie." He reaches out and cups my face, thumb grazing my bottom lip. "Feeling your mouth on me, sucking me while I drive, watch TV, pay my fucking bills... that is what you owe me, personally, for all the stress and strain."

"You want me to just like..."

"Use it like a goddamn pacifier." His other hand gently strokes his cock. "When we're together your mouth is on my cock. When I need comfort, suck it. When you're looking for something to do, come find it. When you're needy, hungry, horny... whatever it is you're feeling, you come to me."

Out of that depraved hole, I found myself some kind of sick need arises. As weird as it sounds, I kind of understand. I've been lonely. Lost. And having a little bit of family, a little comfort? I get the appeal. Is it weird? Fuck yes, but nothing about my family has been normal for a long time.

"What about my things back at the house? My car?"

"The guys will handle it. You can't go back there." He shifts, positioning himself so that his legs are slightly spread.

So now. We're starting this now. My fake life is over, and I've just agreed to let my stepbrother become a human binkie.

He pats his thigh. I pull my hair to the side and rest my head on his lap. He inserts his cock into my mouth, pushing the tip in slowly. I taste his salty pre-cum and feel him thicken. I grip the base, but his hand comes down on mine.

"Easy," he says, stroking my hair, "this isn't about me cumming. Not yet, at least."

He starts the car and I settle into the rolling motion as we ride down the road, away from Tidewater Beach. Away from isolation and back toward trouble, hopefully for the last time.

At first, I'm tense, shoulders still, awkwardly wedged between his body and the steering wheel, but the longer we go, the safer I feel. No one knows I'm in the car. Not Christopher, not the police. We drive this way for hours, the car quiet other than music on the radio and the hum of the tires eating up the road. I suck on him, nurse him, and somewhere along the way I doze off. I don't wake for hours, not until the car rolls to a stop, his cock still in my mouth. It's dark outside.

He nudges me, "Katie, we're here."

I give him one last little suck and rise, wiping a trail of saliva with the back of my hand. My mouth feels strangely empty. In the faint light of the car, Oliver looking less stressed than he did when we first met, tucks himself into his pants. He nods out the window to the imposing house that fuels my nightmares.

"We're home."

THREE

Kate

I ADJUST MY JACKET, CHECK THE BUTTONS, AND FIX MY hair. Mom reaches out, grasping my hand, pushing it down to my lap, forcing me to stop fussing. I look over at her, taking in her gaunt face and shallow cheekbones. She stinks of stale sweat and last night's alcohol, smothered with expensive perfume. I don't even know if she showered. I'm not sure she does either. But it's the glazed look in her eyes that hits me the hardest. There's just torment waiting there. Just grief. I look away, unable to face what I've done.

The truth. That's why we're here. The truth in all its sick, shameful forms. I look over my shoulder at Oliver as he sits behind me. Gone is the five o'clock shadow, and the tousled blond hair. He's clean-shaven, combed, and immaculate, wearing something expensive and tailored.

Those intense eyes find me. He doesn't have to speak, doesn't even have to nod. He makes no movement, just a stare... but that's enough.

Enough to remind me why we're here and what I'm about to do. Paul sits next to him. His expression is a mask, those aquamarine eyes giving nothing away. He's the epitome of the clinical doctor, a specialist of the mind. But I know what lingers in him, and how far he's willing to go to protect them all. They close around each other like a pack of apex predators, only now they draw me in. I'm one of them now, whether I want it or not. If *they* want it or not. This isn't out of some sick desire to murder and control.

This is the basic need to survive.

Self-preservation can make you violent and it can also make you weak. But not for me. Self-preservation is making me a whore... *their whore.* My stepbrother turns his head, meeting my gaze and I shift away, unfortunately making eye contact with Davis.

He just glares at me. Hate burns in his eyes. Betrayal. Revenge and he makes no effort to hide it from me. I swallow a shudder and turn away, catching mom stiffening at the sound of a door as it opens at the side of the courtroom and after all this time he's here.

Jack.

I take him in. The orange jumpsuit. The shackles around his wrists and ankles. The blank stare as he finds me. No. It's not that. *Looks right through me.* He does turn to his brother a ripple of kinship running through them.

"All rise!" the bailiff calls, making me jump. Mom claws my arm, her nails sharp and stinging as she jerks to her feet, forcing me to follow.

The judge strides in with a flurry, wielding his black cloak like a weapon that slices through the air before he sits. There's a hint of a scowl on his face as he glances at Jack next to his attorney. From the look of it, he's an expensive one, paid for with Davenport money.

I feel the weight of Jack's presence. I know whatever he has planned for me will be relentless and soul-destroying. The devil has nothing on my step-brother, especially when vengeance is on his mind.

"According to the paperwork, we've had a change of testimony from a Ms. Katherine Stevenson," the judge says, his dark eyes lifting as he reads my name to find me at the prosecutor's table. "In the case against Jack Davenport."

I shift my stance.

"Well," the judge sighs, glancing at the prosecutor, "let's get this over with, shall we?"

The prosecutor, Mr. Adams, stands, his chair scraping on the hard floor. Looking at me, and then back at the judge he says, "Ms. Stevenson would like to recant her statement, Your Honor."

"Are you aware of this, Mr. Harper?" he asks Jack's lawyer.

He hops to his feet. "Yes, sir. Mr. Adams informed us about Ms. Stevenson's testimony."

The judge nods for the two of them to approach the bench. They speak quietly, but not where we can't hear. "Your witness seriously plans on recanting her statement?" the judge asks.

"Against my advice," Adams says, "but she's determined."

"She's not being coerced?" the judge asks.

"No. She claims she isn't. It's her assertion that her previous testimony was a lie and that after consideration she wants to tell the truth."

"Can't put the genie back in the bottle," Harper replies with a coy smile. "It's already on the record, so if you choose to prosecute my client, I will bring this up as evidence."

The judge looks tired. The prosecutor is furious. And Harper? Gleeful.

Katherine Stevenson, the girl who fucked up the biggest case in Wilmington history.

I wait for what comes next, flinching as mom reaches out and pats my arm...

Good girl.

I hear the words in my head, and I fight the urge to pull away from her. I feel raw today and... *terrified.* I swallow the ache in my throat and for some sick reason, I miss the feel of Oliver's cock in my mouth. I need it. Want it. More than that, I hate that I think about it, especially now.

"Ms. Stevenson," the judge calls, motioning me to the witness stand.

I slowly make my way to the front of the courtroom and take a seat on the hard chair in the witness box. I automatically lift my right hand. The bailiff swears me in and I fumble through the words, "The whole truth and nothing but the truth, so help me God."

I find Jack as I utter that statement. Hate echoes back and my pulse races at the sight.

I'll take what he gives me, all the pain and the depravity... because I have no choice. Not if I want to survive.

The judge turns the questioning over to Mr. Adams. He strides toward me and begins. "It's my understanding that you're recanting your statement about Mr. Davenport's involvement in the murder of Ryan Watkins."

I run my sweaty palms down my thighs. "Yes, sir. I was telling the truth when I said Jack killed Ryan Watkins. But it wasn't because he was a murderer, it was in self-defense. I was there that day like I said, investigating for the paper. I had a hunch and it was right. Unfortunately, the Bind—*I mean*, Ryan Watkins was waiting for me. He hit Jack…" I look at him, and my voice quietens, "He hit Jack over the head."

"And do you know why Mr. Davenport was there that day?"

I nod, staring at him. "He was there because he knew I was going to go there on my own."

"Knew how?" Mr. Adams asks.

"The image." My cheeks burn red. I swallowed hard. "The one I stole from the crime scene."

I knew this was the start of the end. From this moment on, any hope of a career as a journalist would be over.

"Stole from the crime scene?" Mr. Adams repeats "Which crime scene?"

I swallow, searching the rows of spectators for the familiar, handsome, terrifying face. "I went with Detective Higgins while he was investigating the murders. There was a lead that a man named Christopher Watkins was possibly involved. Detective Higgins allowed me to go with him since I'd met him the night the last victim was kidnapped."

"This seems highly unusual," Mr. Adams says. "Taking a journalist along to a crime scene?"

"He thought I might have a fresh perspective and allowed me to go with him to Watkins' house while they were searching it."

Mr. Adams seems satisfied with that, although when he looks at me, it's with hard disappointment. "So, you stole evidence from a crime scene and then decide to track down a murderer on your own."

A soft teetering comes from the galley, laughter over my arrogance.

"Yes." I swallow hard. "Like I said, the Binder was already there. There were all these instruments on the table–tools–and the shackles on the wall..." A sob bubbles in my chest. My hands rub at the phantom sores on my wrist. "I thought he was going to rape me like the other girls. Kill me. But then Jack came out of nowhere and fought him off." I glance at Jack and then the judge. "It was a struggle. Ryan got the best of him–at first..."

There's nothing but silence now, and it's empty and hollow, waiting for me to fill it. I keep going. "Keep going," the lawyer says.

I stare at my stepbrother. "He knocked Jack out and I thought that was the end of it, but Jack woke up, they fought, and...well, he killed him."

"To protect you?"

I nod.

"Sorry, Ms. Stevenson, you'll have to speak louder for the court reporter."

"Yes," I reply. "Yes, he killed to protect me."

Mr. Adams walks over to the table and flips through a stack of papers, finally settling on one. "According to the phone records, you didn't call the police until the next day."

I shook my head. "No."

"Why?"

"I don't know." *Because that's when we really had sex, laying there with the stench of blood and death in the air.* But Christ, I can't say that. I can't tell them—that in that sickening moment, I was fucking my stepbrother. Not by force, but because I wanted it. That my entire being was desperate to have him inside me. I wanted him raw and primal, fucking me with the same hands he'd just used to murder someone.

My breaths turn shallow. I can't quite catch them. There are some things I'd never come back from, and that was one of them.

"Can you explain to the court why you lied about this?"

I shake my head, refusing to look at anyone.

Mr. Adams says, "Your honor, if I may," and hands the bailiff a piece of paper. My heart thunders. I don't know what's on it, but as the bailiff nears the judge, I can see it's some kind of report from the crime scene, and my face burns.

My mind flashes back to the police station, where they took my panties. The ones stained with my stepbrother's semen.

I can't do it. I can't say the words.

A cough draws my eyes up. Oliver stares at me. We made a deal and I have to go through with it.

The judge looks at the paperwork, then stays without looking at me. "I think it's time you told us what really happened in that cabin, Ms. Stevenson after Mr. Davenport saved you from Watkins."

I swallow hard and mumble, "Jack and I had sex."

The judge's face is hard as stone, but he says, "Sorry, you'll have to say that a little louder."

God, I wish the room would just open up and swallow me whole. I lean closer to the microphone and repeat, "Jack and I had sex."

The room stiffens. I swear I see the corner of Jack's mouth quirk into a smirk. He knows this is going to ruin me, and he's enjoying every second of it. But I don't give a shit about him. It's my mom that I look for. Mom turns her gaze away. Montie sits beside her with the same look of disapproval that never seems to fade.

"So, you had sex with your brother?" Mr. Adams asks. Do I hear disgust in his tone?

"Stepbrother," I clarify. "Jack is my stepbrother."

"Stepbrother," Adams corrects, giving a pointed look at the court reporter. "Keep going, Ms. Stevenson."

There's no warmth in the room. No soft, careful smiles from my mom. Just revulsion, from all of them, except from the four who know the truth. Oliver sits still, his gaze fixed on my mouth, and I know what he's envisioning. I doubt I'll make it home before he's sliding that big hand around the back of my head and guiding me down to his crotch.

"It wasn't the first time we've had a sexual relationship," I admit. "And the adrenaline from everything that happened with Ryan... it just sparked something." I peek at my mother. Her expression is one of shame and betrayal. "It was wrong. Disgusting. Humiliating."

Mr. Adams clears his throat. "I believe my client is possibly suffering from PTSD, your honor. Her behavior right after being attacked by a known serial rapist and killer can't be considered rational–"

"Sit down, Mr. Adams," the judge says, then faces me pursing his lips together. "You had sex with your brother and then what? You decided to call the FBI and lie instead."

"Yes. Jack fell asleep and I–I was embarrassed about what happened. I wanted to pretend it never happened, so I made it up."

"Your honor," Mr. Harper blurts, "I believe that is enough testimony to drop the charges against Jack Davenport for murder. I'd like him to be released immediately and his record cleared."

The judge takes a deep breath, but ultimately says, "I agree, Mr. Harper. Jack Davenport did a favor to our community when he rid us of one of our worst predators." His eyes swing over to Mr. Adams. "Is the prosecutor's office considering filing charges against Ms. Stevenson for lying and making false statements or for using federal funding for witness protection?"

It's a big list. A serious list and before I can even react, a wounded cry rips from my mother. Montie jerks his gaze her way. A tortured look crosses his face as he turns back. It's love that drives him to his feet. Love that makes the esteemed Montgomery Davenport clear his throat and speak out. "Please, Your Honor, if I may speak."

The judge pauses. "It's highly irregular for you to interrupt these proceedings, Mr. Davenport. Please sit."

"I know," Montie continues, "but, this whole situation is highly irregular."

The judge sighs and waves him to continue.

"My family has been through enough. I implore you and the prosecutor's office to allow us to deal with this privately." The judge fixes his gaze on Montie, and something passes between them. I don't know if it's respect or admiration, but the judge's glare softens. Montie continues, "My son did a service to the community by removing a dangerous criminal from the streets and my stepdaughter...well, has a history of this kind of vindictive behavior toward her stepbrother. We thought sending her away for college would be of benefit, that she might somehow grow out of this." A stab plunges into my chest. At this moment I see how much I hurt them—I glance at mom—*both of them.* "I'm asking the court for leniency, your Honor. Allow us to take care of this as a family."

"Your honor, I don't see how this is appropriate," Mr. Adams says to the judge. He's a prosecutor. His job is to make someone pay for the crime and that person is me. There's no way I'm going to wiggle out of this one.

There's a sound...a quiet clearing of a throat.

Out of the galley, a figure stands, and it's almost like he knew this moment was coming. He never once looks at me as he lifts his hand and speaks to the judge. "Excuse me, Your Honor, my name is Doctor Paul Sanders."

"I know who you are, Dr. Sanders," the judge replies. "And your reputation."

Paul smiles and I know it's nothing more than a physical reaction. There is no ego with him...because there's no room. The cold, calculating monster takes up all the space inside of him. "If it pleases the court, Your Honor. I'd like to offer my services to Ms. Stevenson. She's obviously experienced great trauma. A lengthy trial and jail time doesn't seem advisable."

"You're willing to take on her treatment?"

Paul nods and glances at Montie, who gives him a sad, grateful smile. "As a favor to the community and the family."

The judge considers the offer, and I'm sure he'll toss it aside. Part of me hopes he does. I deserve the punishment; in whatever form it's served.

"Ms. Stevenson," he starts, "you'll be required to attend the offices of Dr. Paul Sanders for a term of no less than a hundred hours, and I hope for your sake, that you can explore whatever darkness you have and find some clarity in how to move forward with your life."

Explore my darkness?

"Mr. Davenport," the judge calls, and Jack stands, his presence intimidating. "The case against you is dismissed, and you are to be released immediately."

He slams down the gavel, concluding court, and the galley reacts with emotion. My mother cries and reaches for Montie. Oliver and Davis hug. I start to rise, trying to gain my bearings, trying to process everything; my lies, my ruined reputation, therapy with Paul...

"Ms. Stevenson," the judge says, before I leave the stand, "I hope you realize how selfish and utterly reckless your actions have been. Not only incriminating your stepbrother in a very serious allegation, but placing your family and yourself in grave danger. You've shown little to no remorse and I hope the psychiatric counseling I've issued will assist you in realizing the effects of your actions."

"Yes, Your Honor."

"You're lucky to have such a supportive family," he adds, exiting the bench. "Be grateful for that."

"Yes, sir."

I look out at the crowd and the set of eyes that find mine belong to Paul. Only when our gaze meets, does he smile.

A coldness washes over me.

The judge doesn't know what he's done.

But I do...and I'm terrified.

FOUR

Jack

THE HOUSE IS DIFFERENT WHEN I RETURN.

Loud, bright, filled with people.

"We're so glad you're home." My stepmother's arms are tight around my neck. It's an intrusion, one I grimace and bear. "I knew we could get this straightened out. Kate just needed a little time to reconcile..." Her lips dip to a frown before rebounding, "well, everything." She squeezes my forearm. "Thank you for always being a patient, supportive big brother, even when she doesn't reciprocate."

But that's the thing. Katie does reciprocate. Her pussy clenches tight around my cock when I fuck her. Her skin burns with want.

They don't understand that part of us—the fire that flickers between us. It's not for them to know. I simply nod and slip out of her vise-like arms, futilely looking for an escape.

They threw a party, celebrating my return—my *freedom*—hosted by my father and stepmother. My brother is here. My friends. People I vaguely recognize from town. There's booze and food. I drink and eat, filling the hole of betrayal in my gut. Numbing my senses with alcohol.

I need to hunt.

That's what I've missed most while being in jail.

The hunting.

And the pussy. *Her* pussy.

She isn't down here, but I know she's in the house and I tap on the corner piece of wainscot and the secret door opens. I duck into the passage, the space tight now that I'm an adult. My shoulders barely fit, but I like it here. I like the tightness. The quiet. The invisibility. I travel through the walls. Listening. Observing.

"It's been a long road," I hear my father confide. I'm in the narrow space next to his office, the place he goes when he needs privacy. "I'm worried this one won't be so easy to wipe away. A murder accusation—which, he doesn't deny."

"Self-defense," I hear Davis say. "All charges dropped. I told you not to worry about it."

"I can't help but worry," Dad says. "I know you managed to get the upstairs cleaned up before the FBI searched his room, but it was a close call. They'll be watching him." He pauses, I assume to take a drink. "They'll be watching all of you."

"I'll keep an eye on him," Paul says. So, he's there, too. Guess they decided to have a family meeting without me. "He's resilient. You know that."

"He's been through a lot, everything with his mother, the accusations Katherine made as a teenager, and now. I thought giving her a home and education was the best thing for her, but clearly, she's troubled." His voice lowers. "And my son can't seem to keep his dick away from the family tree."

"Adjacent tree," Oliver reminds him, "but yes, he's drawn to her."

I love the way he says it like he's unaffected by Katie, too. Like he doesn't relish the torment and torture we put her through as much as I do. I saw the looks they exchanged today. Something transpired between them to make my release happen. I want to know what.

"And I understand the attraction," my father says. "She's a beautiful girl and a temptation. Jack has a penchant for going after forbidden fruit."

He's right, of course. This isn't the first predicament where my impulsiveness has gotten me into trouble. There was the preacher's daughter; I was caught fucking her in the Narthex, during service, choir robes pushed up her waist. It's not my fault she saw god when I made her come and shouted it into the vaulted ceilings. I don't forget my ninth grade English teacher, who gave me my first blow job in the science room supply closet. That lasted six glorious months until the principal caught us, and my father subsequently had the school board fire her. And then there was the time Davis and I got caught sneaking out of the Sheriff's twin daughters' bedroom, his shotgun pointed at our backs as we hauled ass down the road.

Every time my father cleaned up the mess, and I have no proof he's responsible here, but I do know he and the judge go way back and are both members of the country club.

Those girls meant nothing. Not really. Katie...she's different. She's family. She understands.

She's *mine*

"This was a close one," my father says, his voice tired. "I'm going to rely on you more than ever to make sure nothing goes awry. I know you have your mission, and I support it, one day we'll find the bastard who did this to my wife, but right now you need to focus on your brother and best friend. On your sister. And on finding the one that got away."

"Watkins," Davis says, and a few of the missing pieces slot into place. "With Katie back it shouldn't be long before he makes a move. He can't seem to control himself with her."

"No more than the rest of us," Paul adds.

I continue through the tunnels, the sounds of the party fading with every step. I turn sideways, squeezing up the hidden staircase to the second floor, and stop at the small doorway, tucked into the back of a closet. This is how I got into Katie's room all those nights.

I'm convinced all the time I spent in the narrow passageways is why jail didn't bother me so much. Tight, cramped, space doesn't bother me. It feels comforting. I don't need Dr. Sanders to explain why. It's in these same hiding spots Oliver and I hid while our mother was being beaten, raped, butchered.

We clung to one another, silent and safe, just a few feet away as she cried and begged for her life. She told him she was a mother. He slit her throat to keep her quiet. He fucked her while she was bleeding out, then carved her into pieces.

A sound on the other side of the wall draws my attention from those memories—from the darkness. I slide over the piece of paneling that allows me to look into Katie's room. She's going through the motions: locking her door, sliding the chair in front of it. Little does she know the boogie man is already in the room.

I let her get acclimated, watching her search through her bag. She pulls out tiny scraps of cotton. A tank and shorts. I watch as she reaches for the buttons on her dress, first glancing over her shoulder. Paranoid. She should be.

She checks and double-checks the lock on the door, then adjusts the curtains. It's only when she's satisfied that she's alone and unobserved that she undresses. Blood pumps to my cock at the sight of her shoulders then grows hard and thick when I see the swell of her perfect tits. The fabric slides over her hips, down to the floor. I haven't had a woman since that night with her in the cabin. I'd lay in my bunk and drown out the sounds of lock-up by thinking of how good it felt to be buried deep inside, having her clench around me, warm and tight.

From my hiding spot, I watch as she unclasps her bra. Lowers her panties. Stands right before me with all that soft, sexy skin. The urge to reveal myself is strong, it pulses in my veins, but it's too soon. Too many people in the house. Too much risk.

Quickly, she pulls on the tank and shorts. Her nipples are hard and pebbled from the cool air in the room and I wait...

For her to get into bed.

To turn off the light.

For the party to wind down.

I listen...

As people say their goodbyes.

For the sound of doors closing.

Heavy steps on the staircase.

That's when I'm ready to make my move.

But then she shifts under the covers, grabbing her phone to use as a flashlight. She rises, and tiptoes past me, unaware of the monster in the dark. Quietly she heads into the hallway, and when I hear the creak on the staircase, I know she's going upstairs.

My upstairs. My territory. My hunting grounds.

For the first time in hours, I leave my hiding spot and creep after her. Keeping my distance, wanting to know where she's going. It doesn't take long.

Her shoulders hunch as she stands outside my brother's room, tapping softly on the door. It opens and I see him in the doorway; tall, fit, hard-muscled, standing only in his pajama bottoms.

"Can I come in?"

He touches her bottom lip. "Do you need me, baby?"

I sense the hesitation in her, knowing that although she walked up here on her own, it's something darker that propelled her up the steps. I'm caught off guard when she says, "Yes."

Oliver holds the door open wider, giving her space to come in, his hand dropping to her lower back as she passes. From the dark, I watch until the door shuts behind them, closing me out.

What the hell happened between these two while I was locked up?

FIVE

Oliver

Just seeing her standing there in that little thin tank and shorts brings my cock to life, but it's the answer to my question, "Do you need me, baby?" that makes it twitch.

I told her to come to me when she needed me, but I didn't know if she'd do it. Especially not this soon, not so fast.

But it's been a few long, hard, days for all of us, and honestly? I could use a little comfort too.

"Yes."

I invite her in, well aware that the two of us are treading on uncharted territory. Well, semi-uncharted. I'd been reading in bed when she knocked. I return there now, grabbing the book spread open on the quilt, and settle back on the sheets. She follows me, eyeing the bed. We've been here before. We *started* here. But this is different.

"Tell me what you need." When she doesn't speak, I add, "Katie, use your words."

She hovers next to the bed, tears welling in her eyes. "You said I could come to you when I was feeling...I don't know...things."

"I did."

"It's just been a shitty week, you know?"

I chuckle. "Yeah, I know." I pat the spot next to me, and after a deep breath, she climbs up, the mattress shifting from her weight. "You did good on the stand. Just like we talked."

I thought I'd have to force this, grab her by the neck and pull her head down to give me the relief I crave, but she does it on her own, easing down beside me until her cheek rests on my stomach. I stroke her hair. "I looked like an idiot," she admits, her fingers curling into my cotton pants. "No one will ever believe a word I say again. And Jack. He wouldn't even look at me."

No doubt my brother is desperately trying to put together the pieces of what transpired over the past few days. I thought he'd come find me during the party, but he vanished. He probably needs space after three months in lock-up. I can give it to him.

"Shh," I tell her, rubbing little circles on her back. "Just relax."

Her face tilts up. "I don't know if I can. I just..."

"You just what?"

"Can I give you a blow job?"

I run my fingers under her chin. "You want to taste my cum, don't you?"

"I never have tasted you before," she says, licking her bottom lip. "Not that night and..."

No. I didn't give her my cum that night when the guys trapped her. She didn't deserve it then and... "Sorry, baby, I know how much you like it, but you're still being punished for running off like that and for the lies you told about Jack."

She nods, eyes welling with tears. "I know. I'm sorry."

I know what she needs, what we *both* need, after an emotionally trying day. I dip my hand under the waistband of my pants and pull out my cock. "Everything will be better tomorrow." I press the tip to her mouth, using gentle pressure to part her lips. She reacts immediately, mouth opening. Tongue darting out, tasting. "That's right, baby. That make it better?"

She nods, drawing me into her mouth. She does like I told her, nursing me instead of a full-on blow job. It's almost impossible to push past the urge to thrust, to fuck, but I've spent years honing my patience. Denying myself. And sometimes it's not about getting off. It's about feeling good. Soothing. Katie's shoulders relax, her fingers loosening, and we settle into an easy quiet.

While she sucks my head, I stroke her hair with one hand, and I hold my book with the other. Our relationship has been fraught with ups and downs, but it doesn't have to be. My balls fill with a dull, persistent ache as she nurses on me, and the sounds of her suckling fill the room.

This is new for us, but it's how I want it. I want to build something with Katie, something not wrought in violence, but formed out of a mutual need. Neither of us have a mother we can count on. Both of us have dark holes inside of us from past trauma that need to be filled. This? This is a way to relieve that as we continue on our mission, together.

NOT SURE WHEN I passed out, but it was to the soothing feel of Katie suckling my cock. It's a sensation I'd fantasied about and tried to coerce other females into trying, but nothing ever clicked. I understand why now. It's a level of intimacy only a true partner can understand. The relief I felt when I made Katie do it on the way home that day felt like a revelation. Now, after falling asleep that way, she's curled up next to me. My cock is morning hard and it'd be nice to let her work it off, but I let her sleep. She's been a good girl and deserves a little extra rest.

I stretch and adjust my pants, walking into the bathroom. I'm standing over the toilet, trying to coax my dick into functioning, when Jack walks in.

"Morning, brother," I say, stretching my arms over my head once the stream starts.

He glances down at my dick. "Thought you would've had her work off that wood."

"Not today." I finish and shake off. "Or last night, either."

"She fucking hates you, what the hell is she doing going to you in the middle of the night?"

I can feel the anger vibrating off of him. I don't blame him. He took a bullet for all of us, killing Ryan Watkins when he tried to hurt our girl, taking the blame when she lost her fucking mind and pinned him as The Binder. It was a lot for one man to carry, even Jack Davenport. "I told you I'd take care of this while you were gone. I'd get you out, fix everything. That's what I've done."

His eyes flick to my bedroom door. "Tell me everything."

I grab my toothbrush and squeeze out a glob. "Katie got sent to witness protection and none of us could find her. Not Dad, not Davis. She was locked up tight." I put the brush in my mouth and scrub. Jack leans against the counter, arms crossed over his chest. "We had no fucking clue where she was," I say through the toothpaste, then spitting, "until she contacted me."

"She contacted *you*?"

"Yep." I rinse the brush and tap it on the sink, dropping it in the cup. "Don't be so surprised, she's my sister, too." He scowls.

"Turns out that while we couldn't find her, Watkins did. And he scared the hell out of her."

"Huh." His eyebrow raises. "Scared her enough to come out of hiding. Must've been bad."

"Stalked her and broke into her house and took pictures of her while she slept. He left the photos and a note."

"I'm going to need those." He rubs his chin. "That doesn't explain how she got back to Wilmington and up on that stand."

I tell him the rest. How I went out and picked her up. How she asked for protection, and I gave her the conditions. I'm not about to tell Jack what I asked her to do, he'll mock me for being soft, so I simply add, "She and I have to spend time together, that's part of the deal."

Jack eyes me and I see the mean, belligerent glint. "So, I spend three months in jail, falsely accused by that bitch, and you get to be the hero and sleep with her at night?"

Age old irritation flickers under my skin—sibling rivalry at its finest. "I'm trying to make sure things don't go off the rails like last time. We need her. She needs us. I'm trying to build bonds, so that this time when shit hits the fan, she doesn't turn on us. Again." I meet his eye. I may be younger, and he may have twenty pounds on me, but we're the same height. I'm his little brother and I know he'll always look out for me, but sometimes, he gets so focused on his own needs he forgets the rest of us exist.

He forgets the big picture.

He sighs, not happy he isn't in charge, but that happens when you go off script. He's the one that followed her out there that night. Got involved and decided to play games.

"Look," I tell him, "I made it clear. We own her. Body, mind, and soul. Use her however you want, that's up to you, but we have to keep her whole, brother." He snorts, but I lift my chin, making sure he understands that's not negotiable. "I'm serious. Just a little bit longer until we complete our mission."

"Whatever. After what she did to me, looking at her makes me sick."

It's bullshit, but I let him have it.

"Go out and find someone else to play with for a little bit," I suggest, combing through my hair in the mirror with my fingers. "Find another pussy to tear apart, dump all that frustration into."

"Yeah," he says, rubbing the day-old scruff on his chin. "Good idea." He rests his hand on my shoulder. "Thanks for getting me out and not letting me rot in there."

"Never. I've always got your back, you know that."

We walk separate ways, him to his room, me to mine.

"Ollie."

"Yeah?"

"And once we get him, then I can have her?"

I nod, grinning at him. "After that, she's all yours."

THE BREAKFAST TABLE IS QUIET. It's just Dad, Jack, me, and Katie.

"Is my mother okay?" she asks, eyes darting to the empty chair.

"No, not really," Dad says, holding the spoonful of oatmeal midair. "She's struggling with everything that's happened."

That's an understatement. She's been barely functional since she returned home and found her daughter in witness protection and her stepson in jail, awaiting trial. "It's been very hard on her to be the subject of gossip and speculation, like this. Coming home to this kind of chaos, well, it's the kind of situation that can break a mother's heart." He gives Katie a long look, but she just stares at her plate of now cold eggs and hard toast. "She's lost friends and has been shunned by several of her women's groups." He sighs. "You know how Wilmington is—gossip spreads like wildfire. It's worse when your daughter is the one that struck the match."

Her chin jerks up, tears welling in her eyes. "I never meant—"

My father holds up his hand, silencing her. "I know you never mean to do things, Katherine, but your actions have consequences. I'm not sure you ever realize that, even after all these years." He picks up his coffee, and takes a sip. "Henry called to let me know that you shouldn't expect to return to your job. He can't afford the liability of a known perjurer on his staff."

"I understand, I'll start looking for something else right away."

"No," he shakes his head. "For now, you'll stay in the house and fulfill your mother's duties while she's under the weather. A home like Davenport requires constant management and that will be your role from now on."

"I can do that." Her voice is quiet and she looks like a small child, shoulders hunched and turned in on herself. She's lost. Under the table, I rest my hand on her thigh, palm up. To my surprise she rests her hand on top, fingers lacing into mine.

"Then, it's agreed. You'll take care of the house and obviously, attend therapy with Dr. Sanders." He looks between me and Jack. "And if your brothers need anything, I want you to be at their service. No arguments. No accusations."

"Yes, sir."

"Good. There's just one more thing." He clears his throat. "I'd like you to apologize to your brother."

Her shoulders stiffen. "I did that yesterday, in court."

"You admitted that you lied, but you did not apologize to your brother for the three months he spent in jail while you went on a government paid vacation."

"It wasn't a vaca—" she starts, then snaps her jaw shut when she sees the expression on my father's face. If anyone wants to know where my brother and I developed our hardness from there's no reason to look further than the head of the household. Katie swallows. "You're right." She turns to Jack. "I'm sorry for what I put you through. I lied to the FBI about what happened at the cabin."

"Sort of"' she wants to add. I can see it in the hard glint in her eye. So can Jack.

"I hope you can eventually forgive me."

The look he gives her is dark and terrifying. "I don't know if that's possible but," he glances at our father, "for the sake of the family, I'm willing to do my best."

"Thank you," she says, gripping my hand like a vise.

Dad smiles tenderly at Katie. "I know this has been a difficult time for you, as well, and I want you to know that we're going to get through this, as a family. We support one another through the good times and bad, don't we boys?"

"Yes, sir," I say, squeezing Katie's hand and tucking into my breakfast.

My father stares at Jack, waiting for his agreement. His eyes flick darkly over to Katie, but he finally grunts. "Yeah, just seems like we have more bad times than good, don'cha think?"

My father ignores him. They're close, but too similar. Their temperament and need to control. My father's silence is the kind of reaction that makes Jack even more annoyed and soon he leaves the table without another word to any of us.

"Katherine," Dad says, pushing his bowl forward. "Why don't you get started on the dishes?"

"Yes, sir." She pushes her chair back and grabs her uneaten meal and the other empty plates, vanishing into the kitchen.

Once she's out of earshot my father turns to me. "I don't want your sister and brother to be at odds for the rest of their lives. I need you to be their intermediary. They need you, Ollie. More than ever."

"I'll do what it takes."

"I know, son," he rests his hand on my back, squeezing my neck, "and I'm counting on you to be the one that helps keep this family together."

SIX

Kate

My life is a cycle of one deja vu after the other.
Circling in and out of Wilmington, never quite escaping.

There's one thing that's different this time. I'm never alone. To be fair, it's what I asked for; protection and my stepbrother is holding up to his word, including driving me to my first appointment with Paul.

"Do you need me to go with you?" he asks, sitting in the driver's seat. If they brought my car back, I haven't seen it. But deep down I know it's unlikely they'll give me that sort of freedom anyway.

"No." I look up at Paul's house–his office is connected to the back. I came here once before, but that was to further the investigation for the Gazette. This time I'm here by force, ordered by the court. It's a punishment. Paul Sanders isn't a good man. He's a monster with a fancy degree and too much power. He manipulates and controls, he worms his way into my head and it's impossible to get him out. I look at the clock, waiting for the second to reach its destination before climbing out of the car.

"I'll be here when you get out," Oliver says, with a smug smile. It's a warning, but he doesn't have to worry. I'm not going anywhere, not as long as Christopher Watkins is looking for me. His hand slides down and gently squeezes his cock. "Just let me know if you need a little comfort."

Bile rises in the back of my throat, and I force it back. I don't care that I'm late, but I know he will and it's not just him I have to worry about now. He'll have to send reports back to the court, to make sure I'm following the treatment plan for my " compulsive lying." Paul Sanders holds my future in his hands and there's no way out of it.

He's probably up there right now, watching the clock for his newest victim...I mean, patient.

Patient.

God the word brings heat to my cheeks just thinking about it. But that's what I am now. A patient. A liar. One who needs monitoring and treatment. To be put in my *place* after daring to cross Jack Davenport.

I climb the stairs that lead to the office, feeling a heavy weight in my chest. That's what this is about, reminding me of my place.

Clean the dishes.

Check with the landscapers.

Organize with the maid.

Suck on my brother's cock.

My legs feel like lead. Every step drags me deeper into the pit. When I finally muster the energy to approach the door, I see that it's already ajar and realize that Paul isn't sitting there anxiously watching the clock. In fact, he doesn't even lift his gaze when I enter his sterile space. Like last time, I close the door behind me and hear the lock catch.

"Sit," he instructs with a wave of his hand.

He's focused on writing something on the lined paper before him. His attention is solely fixed on the file under his hand as his fingers move with a long elegant scrawl. I didn't notice anyone leave, so is he...writing about me already? I do as instructed, sitting on the same sofa where he checked my injuries the last time I was here. The memory of that triggers a wave of anxiety.

He finally lifts his gaze and a smile brightens his face. Brightens, but doesn't warm. Underneath the tug of his lips is the cold detachment that is always there. The depth of his indifference is terrifying.

"So," he leans back in his chair and laces his fingers, "before we get started, I want to be clear that you understand why the judge issued these sessions."

"I understand."

"Explain it to me—in your own words."

My heartbeat quickens. There's a right answer, something Paul wants to hear. It's not necessarily the truth. "I uh," I pull at a thread on my skirt, "I lied about Jack and what happened in the cabin. I lie all the time." He listens, giving me no sign that I'm telling him what he wants. "I'm obsessed with hurting Jack and causing my family pain."

"That's a good start, Katherine." He clears his throat. "Although it sounds a little forced."

I stare at him blankly. What does he expect? I'm a writer, not an actress.

"I suppose, after everything you've been through, some denial is to be expected. That's why we'll spend much of our sessions exploring your need to harm the people close to you, but before we start, I'd like to get some backstory."

"What kind of backstory?" Paul knows my deepest shame and secrets. What kind of game is this?

"Tell me," he leans forward slightly, "what was it like to be on the run?"

The question takes me by surprise. "Free," I answer instantly. "And terrifying."

"Free," he repeats, rising from his chair. "That's interesting since you were forced to start a new life and hide from everyone you knew. And now?"

Now?

Now, I'm a mouse trapped in a cage with four trap doors. Each of them with their own degrading demise. "Now I'm trying to make amends."

"And stay alive," he answers with a ghost of a smile. "Can't forget that, can we?"

"No," I mumble as he rises from the seat across from me and moves to the sofa, taking the empty spot beside me. "We can't forget that."

"Because that's really the only reason you're back at all, isn't it? To save your own skin." His aquamarine eyes bore into mine. "Tell me, what's it like to be branded a liar? Not just by your family or the court, but by the very newspaper you used to work for."

I flinch both from the truth of what he says and from the way he shifts closer.

"Because you are a liar, aren't you, Katherine?" He reaches out and brushes a strand of hair from my face, fingers trailing lightly under my ear. "You are a liar and a manipulator, isn't that right?"

My heart races with his words. A liar, and a manipulator? I shake my head, my brows furrowing. "No."

"But we know what you are. You told the court, the prosecutor, and the judge." His fingers trace down my cheek and along the column of my neck. "We know exactly what you are, playing the victim when the real victim here is Jack, isn't it?"

We.

The way he says that word makes me panic.

I meet his gaze. "Jack? No. He isn't a victim."

I think about how he murdered Ryan with his bare hands. A victim? Hell no. I can't go that far.

Paul's lips pursed in disappointment. "No? Seems like he's the innocent party here to me. Spending all those days locked in a cell all because he protected you when you needed him the most."

"That's not exactly what happened."

"Then tell me what happened, Katherine. Take me back to the beginning, in your own words," he says and his voice is so soothing, lulling me, pushing me. "Describe what happened when you got to the cabin. In detail."

I shake my head. I don't want to relive any of it.

"It's why we're here, isn't it?" Paul urges, the back of his hand brushing the side of my breast. I tremble in response. "To work through your trauma. Tell me about the cabin."

"It smelled," I answer quickly.

"How?"

"Musty." I close my eyes and I'm back there. The birds chirp as I climb out of the car and the sun shines on me, warming my face. But the warmth doesn't linger when I step into that cabin. No, cold plunges into me with the pungent scent of wood and cement, and under that... under that is... "The air was stifling. Dust and...and..." Blood? That's what I smelled, blood. Copper. There were drops of it on the tarp. Places he didn't clean up. "There were shackles on the wall."

"Go on."

"There's a shirt. It's yellow. Discarded like trash." I take a deep breath. "I knew it was Brandi's. She wore it that night at the bar. The fabric was so see-through and she wasn't wearing a bra. Her tits are—were—fantastic. Jack couldn't keep his eyes off of them. *I couldn't keep my eyes off of them.*"

"You were jealous of her?"

"If I was, it didn't last long. He took her and all that was left was that shirt." I shudder, thinking about everything that happened. Jack chasing me through the woods, catching me, shacking me to the wall. Then Ryan showed up and how I thought I was finished—just another victim.

Thankfully, Paul doesn't seem interested in making me relive that. His focus is elsewhere.

"Move to the moment where Jack kills him." He circles his finger over my kneecap. "Tell me what you saw and heard..."

Get your fucking hands off my sister! Jack's roar rocks back at me. I grip the edge of the cushion under me, trying to control my body. "His neck," I whisper. "His neck snaps."

"Ryan Watkins' neck?"

I nod and open my eyes, finding Paul's. "Yes."

"He killed him to save you." His fingers rub and rub and rub, drawing that heat closer to the surface. "Wrapped his hands around Ryan's neck and strangled the life out of him."

"I don't think it was about saving me."

"Is that the action of someone who hates you, Katherine? That wants to hurt you?"

No. Yes. I know what happened that day. It was about tormenting me. Punishing me.

"Tell me about you and Jack having sex, how did that transpire, exactly?"

"I don't want to talk about it."

"Was it your idea, or Jack's?" he presses, hand moving up my leg. His movements are soothing. Soft but strong. I sink back against the leather couch.

My idea?

"No. I was still shackled to the wall when he killed Ryan. I was injured and after he released me, he cleaned my wound, and things," I swallow, "escalated between us."

"Show me."

I blink. "Show you what?"

"Where you were stabbed." I lean back and I lift my shirt, showing him the thick, puckered scar. He touches it gently, tracing over every jagged ridge. "You were very lucky this wasn't worse."

"Nothing about that day involved luck."

He shifts next to me and there's no mistaking the outline of his engorged cock beneath his gray pants, pressed against his inner thigh. "Did seeing a man being killed in front of you make you horny?"

"No," I say it forcefully, hoping it sounds true.

"Is it normal for you to fantasize about sex and death?" He trails his fingers between my legs. "There's no judgment here, Katherine."

"I don't know," I admit. "Things were confusing. *Are* confusing."

"Mmhmm," he murmurs, staring at his hand. "Everything that transpires in this office is part of your therapy, and as you know, strictly confidential."

Everything... I lower my gaze to where his fingers stroke my inner thigh, easing them apart.

"Don't you have to report to the Judge?"

"A summary," he says, nose running along the shell of my ear. "Only what I want him to know." He looks at me, eyes piercing. "Remember that, Katherine. I'm the one in control."

My pulse stutters. I nod and my clit throbs when he works his way up my skirt and under my panties.

"After he tended to your wounds, you fucked Jack, didn't you?"

"It just kind of happened. The adrenaline and..." I swallow again, trying to formulate words while his fingers push into my folds.

You're thinking about it, aren't you? Fucking me. Jack's words surface. My hand clenches around the arm of sofa. "I didn't mean to."

"Get turned on?"

I nod.

"Use your words, Katherine," Paul says and it's just like Oliver said earlier in his room.

"Yes, I wanted him to..." I lick my lips, that surge of adrenaline surges through me as I say the words. "Use me. To feel something good after so much terror."

Paul's other hand rises, working the buttons of my blouse one after another until he pushes the opening aside. "You wanted him to use your body, right in front of a dead man, and then..." He pushes the cup of my bra low, releasing my breast. His thumb grazes my nipple. "Tell me how it felt as his cock entered you?"

"Exhilarating." I moan as he rolls my nipple between his fingers. "Forbidden."

I'm caught now, trapped between the past and the present. "Is this normal for you?" He bends down and takes my nipple in his mouth, sweeping his tongue until it hardens. "Death and sex, is that what you find exhilarating?" I don't stop myself from closing my eyes and dropping my head back as his fingers find my clit. "Open your legs wider for me, Katherine."

My body responds on its own, his mouth and fingers drawing me out.

"Kill or be killed," Paul murmurs. "The desire to fuck and kill is the dark side of human nature. They're closely interlinked in the human brain, invoking the most intense arousal." He presses harder on my clit, then eases. Pulse... release... pulse... release. "It's a drug. A very addictive one."

I arch my back as he takes my nipple deeper into his mouth, latching on. I don't know if he's talking about me here, or him. Then he stops, pulls away, leaving me breathless. "Strip for me, Katherine."

"Now?" I ask.

"You showed me your scar, but let me check the rest of you, make sure you're okay."

I'm so desperate to come that I comply, rising carefully. I shrug off my shirt and unbutton my skirt, pushing it and my panties to my knees.

"That's far enough, turn around and bend over." He instructs, coldly.

I do, placing my hands on the back of the sofa, my ass and pussy on display. He runs his hands along my body; shoulders, back, over the curve of my hips and ass. He slides his finger along my crease, dipping it between my legs. I'm wet...so fucking wet, too turned on to be embarrassed. "Your cunt is dripping," he says. "Just talking about this is making you horny, isn't it?"

It's not fair, I want to tell him. The way he's touching me, talking to me. Making me remember how it felt to feel Jack buried inside of me, for the hands that just killed a man, to feel so good against my hot, hungry flesh. I close my eyes and rock against Paul, driving myself closer, seeking friction.

He pulls free, leaving me throbbing. He speaks low and directly in my ear.

"I want you to start a journal as part of your therapy. You need to explore your sexual urges and the correlation between your needs and other dark thoughts. How your stepbrothers are part of your fantasies. When that started, how it affected your other relationships, with family and friends–other men." His breath is warm and his hand lingers on the upper curve of my ass, teasing the space between my cheeks. "You need to explore how all of this makes you feel. Why you seek forbidden things–people."

I nod and say, "Okay." I have to bite down on my bottom lip not to beg him to bend me all the way over the sofa and take me.

"Bring your journal to your next session. I'd like us to explore this together."

He steps away, taking his heat, his hands. My body aches from the toying and lack of release.

"Next week, Katherine. Next time make sure you're not late."

I'm dismissed, just like that.

I straighten as he rounds his desk, and takes a handkerchief from his pocket. He wipes his fingers as I pull my panties in place and then my skirt. But he doesn't discard the fabric with disgust, instead, he looks at it, closes it in his fist, and then slides it into the top pocket of his shirt.

Keeping me and my smell close.

I tremble as he watches, adjusting my bra and rebuttoning my blouse. He sits behind his desk, picks up his pen, and starts writing once more.

It's then that I notice the framed photo on the shelf behind him. Him and another man. Paul is younger, wearing a black cap and gown, his shoulders draped with sashes and cords. Clutched in his hand is a diploma. The other man has similar features, but older. His father? My mother has spoken of him before–he's a psychiatrist as well. Paul notices my interest and clicks his tongue. "Until next time, Katherine."

Our session is over. I walk out, hating how I can feel the dampness in my panties and that throbbing, unquenched ache. He's done it again, controlled, debased. Left me horny and dissatisfied all while worming into my head and making me confused. I exit the office and start down the driveway, halfway to Oliver's car before I realize it's gone.

He's gone.

I spin, turning to head back to Paul's office–to safety–when I hear movement behind me and panic seizes me as a hand clasps over my mouth. A savage growl fills my ear. "I've been looking for you."

SEVEN

Davis

"Detective."

I look up, finding Hargreaves, my sergeant, standing over my desk...*again.* It was the fourth fucking time in as many days where he decided to ride my ass about something. He didn't meet my gaze, just scans the files under my hand, and then looks at the rap sheet on the screen in front of me.

He doesn't trust me. Not since we lost The Binder case to the FBI and it's only gotten worse since Katie's testimony to the court that I took her into that crime scene without permission and allowed her to remove evidence.

If I didn't hate that girl before, I definitely do now. She not only fucked up the case, the screwed with my best friend and now she's walked back into our lives demanding protection.

I know one thing; she was smart to call Oliver and not me because I would've dumped her body on the side of the road before making any kind of deal.

"You've screwed up filing your paperwork for the third time this week," Hargreaves says, tossing a stack of paperwork at me.

"Screwed up?" I turn my focus back to the file, not giving him a second fucking more of my time. "Can't see how. I handed it to Camilla."

"Camilla isn't your personal assistant. It's about time you stopped treating her like one."

I sigh, lean back and turn, giving him my full attention. "I haven't changed my process in four goddamn years, you gonna ride my balls now?"

There was a flinch in the corner of his eye. "Things change."

I want to dive across this desk and punch him in the mouth. But all I do is reply, "Apparently."

"People are watching us, Higgins. The state, the feds, all eyes pointed down to Wilmington." His eyes narrow. "That's because of you. You're goddamn lucky you haven't been put on suspension."

"Whatever," I mutter.

"You need to redo all the files you sent Camilla. I expect them by the end of the day tomorrow."

"There are over seventy files," I grate out. "That's impossible."

His lips twitch. "Then I expect you better get started." He turns then and strides away making sure to puff out his chest as he walks past all the others.

It takes everything in me not to run after him and stab him with the pen I've got in my grip. Right in the jugular. A nice slow, painful death.

Shaking off that fantasy, I ignore the burn in my cheeks as I turn back to the file. But I can't see the goddamn words on the page anymore. I'm angry. So fucking angry and nothing is making it go away. Not with their eyes on me, the judgment and scorn of the officers and other detectives in the building. They think I'm a fuck-up. It's in their smirks, but not their respect. One which I've deserved for all the fucking shit I'd done around this precinct.

I stand and grab my jacket.

"Davis!" Hargreaves calls from his office, but I ignore him and keep on walking.

I need to get out of here before I do something I'll regret. I stride out, leaving the precinct behind, and climb behind the wheel of my four-wheel drive. Only I don't start the engine. Not yet.

Rage boils under the surface and I tamp it down until I feel it unleashing inside of me. Like a storm, I can't hold it back any longer. *"Fucking cunt!"* I punch the wheel.

She did this.

She did this to *me*.

The instant she went behind my back, she fucked me over. She made a mockery of my badge and my authority. She fucked up our lives and then ran and hid. Not even I could find her. I tried, believe me, I fucking tried. But I was blocked at every opportunity. My name was flagged by the Bureau for Christ's sake just for inquiring about her. Now the stupid whore waltzes back into our lives and thinks she can fix everything, beg for our protection and everything will be fine.

Nothing about this situation is fine.

I suck in a hard breath and will the heat of my anger back down. It turns cold. Ice cold. An image of her face consumes me until it's all I can see. I glance at the clock on the dashboard and start the car. The automatic doors of the precinct open behind me as I pull out of the parking lot and head south.

Hargreaves waits outside, watching me. "Fucking filing," I mutter and push the SUV harder. "I'm a lead detective, not some lackey desk jockey. Kiss my goddamn ass."

Things change, Hargreaves' words haunt me. "Do they, asshole? Let's see about that."

I need to take back control. Need to go back to how it was before she betrayed me. No, betrayed us.

Betrayed us.

I'm driving aimlessly until I come to a familiar street. Oliver's car sits across from the bungalow. I pull up and roll down the passenger window. "What are you doing here?"

"Katie had her court-appointed meeting," he tells me. "Just waiting for her to finish."

I can't decide if Oliver is an idiot or a genius. He's stuck out here, driving her around like he's her guardian or something but...he also has her under his thumb.

I lift my chin. "If you want, I can take it from here."

"Yeah?"

"Sure. I need to talk to Paul anyway about a case. No need for both of us to be on babysitter duty."

"Yeah, that sounds good. I should get back and check on Jack." His mouth forms a tight line. "I don't think he's transitioning well."

"Lock-up's a bitch," I say, "but a few nights rest and some healthy meals and he'll be right as rain."

And hopefully ready to eliminate Christopher Watkins for good. Then we can get back to our real mission. Finding their mother's killer.

"Go," I say, jerking my head. "I've got this."

"Thanks, man."

"No problem."

I wait until he's out of sight before moving my car around the corner to the narrow alley behind the houses. The drive is old, unpassable in some areas, and no one but Oliver uses it. He lets his clients park out front and I park my car next to his BMW.

We've come in and out of Paul's house this way a million times, but no one else uses it. I kill the engine and go through the back gate, situating myself under the porch steps.

What these people, my colleagues, the other cops, Hargreaves, don't realize is that I'm always two steps ahead. Well, most of the time, which is why what Katie did pisses me off so much. How she got one over on me... there's only one excuse. I was thinking with my cock, not my brain, and she got one over on me. Fucking cunt.

I hear her footsteps before I see her, *smell* the cloying perfume on her skin. I react quickly, grabbing her in a tight hold. She's pissed, but that's not all she is—she's scared.

Good.

I slap my hand over her mouth. "Fight me and see what happens," I snarl, and drag her backwards.

She bucks, her heels drag on the driveway. I push her underneath the porch, against the wall, face first. The memory of the last time I had her comes rushing back. That dark alley outside the bar. I fucked her with my gun while the boys huddled around and watched. Not this time. I've got her alone and she's mine. All mine.

"Get off me!" Her words are hot against my hand. "You won't get away with this. My stepbrother is waiting for me. He'll come looking!"

"Fucking *bitch*," I snarl in her ear and push her face first against the bricks. "Oliver went home. Left you all to me."

Her body stills the instant she connects the dots. I'm not her boogie-man. I'm one of her guardians.

I shove her forward until she slams her palms against the wall.

"Davis?" Her voice is quiet.

"Finally figured it out, you stupid whore." My pulse booms with the words and I push my body against her, pressing to the moss-covered bricks.

"You *fucking bastard!* I thought you were–" Her elbow shoots out, slamming into my rib. I wince, absorbing the jab, then tighten my hold on her.

"Thought I was who?" I lift my gaze and straighten. She's too keyed up. I need to get her away from Paul's house. He may have another client coming in and the last thing I need right now is more scandal.

The knot of pain catches under my ribs, but I dismiss it, grabbing her by the upper arms and leading her back through the gate. "Thought I was *who?*"

"The goddamn Binder!"

Ah, I see it now. "You think he's scarier than I am, sweet Katie?" I grind out and spin her around, before pinning her against the hood of the SUV. "When I'm done with you, it'll make that night in the cabin seem like a sweet, soft memory."

It's a move I've done a thousand times. Every perp's face. Every dealer's mouth. Every whore's fucking screams have met the front hood of my car as dominate and control the worthless pieces of shit that mar the streets of Wilmington. *My* streets.

I wrench her wrists behind her and her back arches with pain.

"Stop! *Davis stop!* You're hurting me."

"I'm hurting you, am I?" I could hurt her a little bit more, *should,* but I release my hold just a little until I know her muscles stop howling. "You fucking cock tease." I press against her, forcing her legs wider. "Do you have any idea what you've done to me?"

"Done to you?" The glare she shoots over her shoulder is enough to get across that she's pissed. So very fucking pissed. Too bad for her she doesn't get to be angry. She made a deal, and this is part of it.

"I take it the doc's visit wasn't a success," I taunt. "Or maybe he got under your skin. Knowing him, he probably did."

The thought of that almost makes me smile. "Fuck you, Davis."

"Fuck me?" I reach around with my other hand and grasp her throat. My cock grinds harder against her ass. "How about I remind you of the arrangement you made with Oliver? That you only got to come back home in one piece because we agreed to protect you and you agreed to do every single thing we say." I push her, but I don't like the leverage here. The SUV is too high for my needs. I grab her by the hips and toss her onto the back of Paul's BMW, bending her over the trunk.

Christ, I'm hard. Having her alone with her flimsy fucking skirt. I release her hands and her palms hit the hood. "The only one getting fucked is *you.*" I reach between her legs and feel her warmth, stilling for a second. "Fuck you're wet...goddamn soaking. Don't tell me the doc left you like this? Sloppy wet? Or are you just that excited to see me?"

She shakes her head, but I'm not sure what for. Is Paul teasing her to this point? Me bending her over the trunk? I don't care. I want to hurt her. I want to make her whimper and beg. I yank her panties to the side and slide two fingers in deep. "That's right. Your cunt is fucking aching, isn't it?"

"Davis, don't." She shoves her ass to the side, trying to squirm away.

But I clamp my hand tighter around her throat and pull her back against me. "Don't?" I slide out, then yank her panties over her hips and down to her knees. I think about tearing them the fuck off and having her ride in the car with me all goddamn day. *Ride me all goddamn day.* But I don't, I slide my fingers along her slit and fuck her cunt. "That word doesn't exist where we're concerned, remember?"

Her fingers splay against the car. Her spine bowed backwards, yielding. But she can't stop her fucking need, can she? She can't stop her pussy from growing wetter as I slide out and round her clit. She's swollen, so fucking swollen, but it's not her pussy I want, not this time.

She lets out a moan and pushes backwards, but it's not to dislodge my hold. She's fucking into this. "You like this, don't you? Missed it while you were on the run. While you were *hiding.* Tell me, did you really call Oliver for protection or did you just miss this? Could you not find someone to fuck you in public like a dirty slut?"

"I was scared," she says. "He found me and I didn't have a choice."

I snort. "Oh, you had a choice. You could have called the FBI again. You could have moved. I know how the system works, Katie. I *am* the goddamn system," I hiss in her ear, thrusting my fingers in and out of her. "But you didn't want to run. You need us. You want us."

"I want your protection from Christopher Watkins."

"I can give you that," I tell her, "but I'm also going to give you something else you want." I cast my gaze toward the alley, then back toward the house. There's no one there. I slide my fingers out of her and reach for the buckle of my belt. "How long have you waited for this? Since the day you ran away?" I nudge her knees apart, unbuckling fast, then unbuttoning my pants.

With my cock out and her body pressed hard against the car, I slot myself between her legs. Her cunt is so warm as I slide against her, gliding along her pussy. "That's it, you lying whore, get me wet." But she isn't getting off so easy, not after what she did to me. *Us.*

I pull back, grip her ass, and spread her cheeks.

She bucks when she sees where I'm going, but I whisper in her ear. "You don't get to fight, you understand that? You made a deal. We protect you from your boogie-man and we get something in return. You." I let the tip of my cock swell just inside her and Jesus Christ, she's so fucking tight. She exhales when I pull out, but it's just to use her cunt again, pushing in just enough to coat the head, then I try once more. "We can do whatever we want to you, Katie, and what I want is for you to understand that I know you're a lying whore that fucked up my life when she pulled that stunt at the cabin." I lean forward, breath hot on her ear. "You fucked me, Katie, and I'm going to fuck you just as hard."

That hard ring of muscle widens just a little. Fuck she's gonna work it. I ease back out and try again, pushing slower until she moans. She leans over, pressing her face against the car while I ease back out and look down. Under the hem of her skirt, I catch a glimpse of pink. I lift the fabric, watching as she takes the head. "You're just perfect to rape, aren't you? My rape bait." I drive in deeper, forcing my way into her ass.

This time she pushes back against me, her ass widening with every slow thrust. "You're like a dog in heat, aren't you?" I groan. She is, her hands splayed and ass speared. "You're nothing, but a hole for me to fuck." I thrust harder feeling her body give. "Jesus."

That feeling is fucking adrenaline.

She gives into me.

And I take it.

"A hole for me to fuck anytime I want. I'm going to fill this hole. Going to fill all your holes, my fucking little cum slut." The words drive me harder. The need for her takes over. I know I'll remember this moment. Relive it every fucking day.

Well, until I get to her again.

She unleashes a moan and lifts one leg, her panties slide a little lower until they're tethered around her knees. It gives me the room I need, *want*, and I thrust hard, making her body buck, hard cries coming from her filthy mouth. Over and over, I pound into her until I'm hilt deep and that vein throbs, pulsing along my cock. My balls tighten and I don't want it to end, I want to be in her like this forever, hurting, feeling, cumming hard...

She moans as I unload into her, hips rocking, hands splayed out across the hood holding herself upright. One thing is obvious. She didn't get off–her needs are unmet. A need she carried from the doc's, and a need I'm not going to give her. She doesn't deserve it.

She cries out when I pull my cock from deep inside, watching as my cum drips from her red, puckered ass. I make sure I don't dirty the front of my pants. "You're gonna feel my cum in your ass, do you understand me?"

She nods like a good fuck slave.

"Don't wipe it away until you're home. You sit in it. You feel what I did to you. How I did it."

"I won't clean up," she says, turning. Her skirt slips down, covering her exposed bottom. Her eyes are ringed in red, eyelashes wet. But it's not the distress I notice. It's the soft pleading glint.

She wants praise, a "good girl" or something affirming. She's not getting that from me either.

"And don't you fucking think about touching yourself in the car. You don't have my permission to do that. If I find out that you do..." I smile at her frown. "Oh yeah, I'll find out. I'm a detective. It's my job. I have eyes everywhere." I tuck myself into my pants and rebuckle. "The next time you decide to open that whore mouth and spill your lies and deceit, just remember I can leave you out for bait anytime I want. Not just The Binder. For anyone I need to catch." I lean close, grab her jaw and force her gaze to me. "You got that? Anytime I want."

I'd like to say she's completely docile, that I extinguished the fire in her, but that's too easy. Katie is tough and beneath the need, I still see the hate in her eyes.

Fuck, she's beautiful.

I can't help myself from pressing my thumb across her lip, bruising it against her teeth forcing a wince. Just another thing to remember me by.

"Go home, Katie," I growl and step backwards, working myself back into my pants. "We're done here."

I watch her as she yanks her panties up, her mouth red, her ass shining and slippery with my seed.

I want her ass again...

And again.

And *again*.

She stumbles away, her breath ragged, the frantic sound of her accepting her harsh reality.

Only then does my mood brighten.

EIGHT

Kate

——————

THE NEXT WEEK OF MY LIFE SETTLES INTO AN UNEASY routine of managing Davenport Manor, checking in on my mother, and avoiding my stepbrothers and their friends.

All more difficult than I expected.

I never realized how much food my stepbrothers consume. I'm constantly adding to the list, ordering from the market, and cooking. This is only matched by the amount of laundry they go through. The washer is constantly running, and there's a pile of clothing that always needs folding. When I was a kid, I was clueless about everything my mom did around the house—especially after we moved in with Montie and the boys. And while I was at school, I became more independent, taking care of my own needs, but apparently, no one ever made the Davenport boys lift a finger.

Unless they're torturing someone, I guess.

But as time-consuming as that is, the most exhausting and draining part of my day is taking care of my mother. She's...well, a mess.

I had no idea how bad she'd gotten and from the line of prescription bottles on her bathroom counter, it started long before the recent incident with me and Jack. The medications range from anti-depressant to anti-anxiety, to uppers and downers and tiny green pills that knock her out for three days straight. I learned about that one the hard way after she'd already swallowed it and I'd panicked and called the pharmacy when she wouldn't wake up.

They told me to let her sleep it off.

I tossed the alcohol—bottles stashed around the room. She's thin as a rail, skin sallow and pale, and her hair is brittle, the ends breaking when I comb through it. The most disturbing part? I can see myself in her. I can see my future if I don't get away from this house and these men.

"You're awake," I call out when I enter the room carrying her dinner tray. "Hope you're hungry."

She looks up at me with those glazed-over eyes. "You shouldn't have brought that up here, Katherine. I'm not very hungry."

"It's just a little broth," I tell her, setting it on the bedside table. She no longer shares a room with Montie—his is across the hall. At some point, he moved to the guest room, next to mine. "You need something on your stomach."

I sit on the edge of the bed and lift a spoonful of broth to her mouth. She clamps her lips closed and refuses to open them. "Come on, Mom. You know you need to eat."

"I know you're the whore that ruined our family."

Her words hit me like a slap. "I—I didn't mean to hurt the family."

"Didn't you? Isn't that what you've always wanted to do? You've been mad ever since I married Montie."

"That's not true."

She holds out her hand. "Just give me my pills."

A knock on the door interrupts us.

"Come in," Mom calls.

My shoulders tense, which happens whenever I brace myself for an interaction with one of my stepbrothers, but relief washes over me when I see it's not Jack or Oliver. It's one thing when they treat me like an object when we're alone, but in front of my mom? I'm not sure I can handle that.

But it's neither of them, instead, an older man that looks vaguely familiar opens the door. He's tall with board shoulders—fit-looking under well-pressed clothes. He's handsome, very much so, with distinguished gray hair, still dark at the temples. He smiles when he sees my mother and it doesn't falter when he looks at me.

"Oh, I didn't know anyone else was up here," he says, approaching me with his hand outstretched. "I'm Derek Sanders."

His hand is warm in mine and his eyes are gentle and kind—something unexpected over the last few days. "I'm Kate. Helen's daughter." The name and face prod at my brain. "Oh, and you must be Paul's father."

"Yes, I am." He grins over at my mother. "And Helen's physician."

"Oh, well thank you for stopping by. Now that I'm assisting with her care a little more, I'd love to pick your brain."

"My brain is fully available for picking."

Okay, so this man is a charmer—way more so than his son. Sure, Paul can manipulate, but I always feel dirty afterward, like I need a shower to get the sticky residue off my skin. But his father has the opposite effect. His presence is calming. I feel better already.

He approaches my mother's bedside. "Looks like your daughter is taking good care of you."

Mom purses her lips. "I didn't ask for her help."

"She brought you some broth and tea. Both things you need to keep up your strength."

"Why do I need strength? My whole life is over." Her eyes slide past him to where I'm standing a few feet away. "She ruined it."

Dr. Sanders gives me a sympathetic look and turns back to my mother. "That situation is complicated, and you know it. Those boys... they'll try anyone that comes across them. Why do you think I've had to prescribe all this medication for you?"

I still. Is Dr. Sanders admitting that my stepbrothers aren't what they seem? Or at least in my mother's eyes...perfect?

"I need that medicine to calm my nerves."

"I know you do, but you can't just medicate." He takes her hand in his. "You need fresh air, healthy food, and some positive interactions. You're spending too much time in here."

"I can make sure she gets all of those things," I speak up. "I know my mother has had a hard time. I just want to see her get better."

Mom frowns, but Dr. Sanders pats her on the hand and stands. "I think that sounds wonderful, Katherine."

He manages to get my mother to eat, to take her medicine, and by the time he's given me a list of diet and nutritional suggestions, plus more information about her medication, she's settled down. I follow him out of the room and pause in the hallway.

"How did she get like this?" I ask once the door is shut.

"Things have been hard for a while," he says. "Montie works a lot. The boys are a handful—spoiled if you ask me." He shrugs. "I know they're good friends with my son, but after their mother died...they haven't had a lot of expectations required of them. I think your mother—and you—probably came into their lives a little too late."

I look up at this man and wonder how much he knows about his son and his friends. How they hunt bad men and have spent their life on a mission to find who killed their mother. How they're brutal and mean and terrorize the people in their lives. But he just looks back at me with a kind, supportive expression and I think that no. There's no way he knows. How could he?

"I think having another female in the house will help Helen get back on her feet." His hand rests on my elbow. "I know she's a challenge right now, but she's been through a lot lately. She just needs to know you're here for good and not leaving any time soon."

"I'm going anywhere." If I want to or not. At least not until Christopher Watkins has been found. "Thank you for coming."

"Any time." He gives my arm a squeeze. "Montie and his first wife were dear friends of mine. I'm happy to do whatever I can to help the Davenports. Please call me if you need me. Morning or night."

"Thank you," I say again, feeling warmth bloom in my chest.

It's not until he's gone that I realize how the smallest amount of kindness lifted my spirits. It's not much, but I'll take whatever I can get. Anything to survive my time in Wilmington.

ALTHOUGH I'VE BEEN TOLD a dozen times that Davenport is my home and I should treat it as such, I still knock on the hardwood door of my stepfather's office. I checked first to make sure his Mercedes is in the garage and listened for a moment so as to not interrupt something important. I've never quite understood my stepfather's business. Something with international trade. Whatever it is, he's a very wealthy, and busy, man.

"Come in," Montie calls from the other side. When I enter, he's sitting at his desk, a laptop open and a stack of papers to one side. It's kind of strange to have him back at home—coexisting with my stepbrothers and their reign of terror. I'm well aware that my stepfather either can't, or won't, make his sons behave. Like Dr. Sanders said, no one made either of them accountable for their actions and this is the result.

"Katherine." He stops what he's doing and looks up at me. "What can I do for you?"

"I hope I'm not bothering you." I take a step further into the office, tearing my gaze away from the twelve-point buck mounted behind his desk. I've heard the story of how he hunted it and took it down many times over dinner. That and the other dozen kills hanging around the room. "But I wanted to talk to you about my mom."

He leans back, the leather on his chair shifting beneath him. He gestures to the chair across from his desk. "Is something wrong?"

"No," I say, taking a seat. "Well, no more than usual. She's still refusing to eat and is very reliant on her medications. I had the chance to meet Dr. Sanders today—not Paul, but his father and he gave me a few ideas on how to assist with her care."

"What did you have in mind?"

"I was thinking something social. A dinner or maybe a small party? You know Mom loves to socialize."

"She does, but lately she's been hesitant to engage with her friends. Things were uncomfortable when Jack went to jail. There was a lot of gossip and your mother felt very ostracized." He taps his fingers on the desk. "I'm not sure this is the right solution."

His response feels like a hit in the gut, but I'm not ready to give up. "Maybe the best thing we can do is present a united front. Show the gossipy women of this town that the Davenports are not just good, but great. That we've worked through this obstacle—especially with her bringing us all back together."

It's a stretch, a long one, but it feels like the right thing to do.

"So, we pretend that your mother is the one behind all of this," he asks, eyebrow raised skeptically. "But really you're pulling the strings."

"Yes," I answer, realizing it's the truth. "We can pick a charity and use it as a fundraiser. Something fun for the fall. A barbeque?"

He rubs his chin. "Well, there is the big game in three weeks. The match-up between State and Tech, we could do something surrounding that."

Football. In the South it's all that matters and it's the one thing that brings people together.

I grin. "Yes. That's a great idea."

Montie opens his desk drawer and pulls something out. A black card. He hands it to me. "Put any expenses on here, just make sure you keep your receipts." I take the credit card, running my finger over the cool metal. "Make sure your brothers assist you. I know things are tense, but you'll need their help getting the supplies together and setting up."

"Yes, sir," I reply even though the idea makes me nauseous. I'd rather they focus on taking down Christopher Watkins than helping me order decorations. "I'll make sure everything is perfect."

He nods at me, and I stand, aware that I've been dismissed. Before I reach the door, he adds, "I like this initiative, Katherine, and the willingness to do what it takes to find your way back to the family."

"I'm doing my best." I reply, quickly exiting the room. In the hall, I press my back to the door and exhale. Another day, another charade, but in the end, I do have an obligation to my mother and this family. I made a promise and I'll do what I can to keep things running while the guys follow through with theirs.

Keeping me safe and hunting down the Binder once and for all.

I DON'T RUN into him until after until I'm almost finished cleaning up for dinner. I've just finished wrapping up the leftovers when I sense someone standing in the doorway. I look over and there he is. Huge. Imposing. Eyes dark, with purplish smudges underneath.

"Hey," I say, taking a moment to find my voice. "I just cleaned up, but if you want some dinner there's extra."

I barely see him. He leaves around the same time in the evening, going out until dawn. Then comes home, stumbles up the stairs, and closes himself in his room. Wash, rinse, repeat. Day after day, this has become his life.

He's not even hunting.

"I'm not hungry," he says, grabbing the keys off the hook by the back door. He grabs his jacket, shrugging into each sleeve while I stand there wanting to run and lock the door to my room and hide, but I don't. I can't. Montie wants us to work together.

"So, listen," I start, but he's already opening the door and stepping out on the porch. I follow him. "Your dad and I came up with an idea for a party as a way to lift mom's spirits. He'd like us to work on it togeth—"

Slam.

The door closes in my face. Hard. Final.

I hold the roll of aluminum foil in my hands and watch him out the kitchen window as he strides toward his car.

Jack Davenport has been many things to me. Cruel. Vulgar. Evil.

But never has he just ignored me. Not once—even when I would have given anything for him to do so.

Now that he has, I realize as I watch his taillights vanish into the night, I don't know exactly how to handle it.

NINE

Jack

"Hey, baby. You want to go back to my place?" A hand slides along my thigh, dragging my gaze to the brunette standing beside me.

I barely see her, not her long brown hair, tied up on one side to expose her neck, or the plunging neckline of her tight black dress that lets me know exactly what I'm getting.

I don't see her...because all I see is Katie.

Katie, as she bucked when the knife drove into her side.

Katie, as she writhed and moaned, panting as I fucked her raw in that filthy cabin alongside Ryan Watkins cold body. My stepsister is all I can see, all I can feel, everything else is gray like ash.

Fuck.

Still the brunette drags her finger along mine, the act is purposeful as she leans close, her words fighting the nightclub music in my ears. "I have a roommate who's into being number three."

Her eyes sparkle, red lips stretched wide into a smile. I want to imagine those lips wrapped around my cock, to imagine those lips wide as she screams for me, or *because* of me. I really don't care, but as hard as I try…I can't fucking see it.

"God, you're gorgeous." She breathes in my ear, the heady scent of Chanel No. 5 so strong I can almost taste the shit. "I want to watch you fuck."

Movement from a table behind us catches my eye. Three guys drinking beer under the pretense of watching the game on the big screen, but their focus isn't on the TV. It's on her. The brunette. I take her in as though I finally see her for the first time. She's stunning; full lips, nice tits, long legs, but she's not Katie.

I drain my scotch and place the glass back down before I slide from the stool. The brunette thinks we have a bargain and for a second her smile stretches and those big blue eyes twinkle with expectation.

"Sorry, babe," I tell her, squeezing her hip, "not tonight." I leave her behind, making my way past the three guys that watch with hunger. "She's all yours."

One of them gives me a nod in appreciation. The feeling of her finger along mine lingers. She was looking for an indentation, a wedding band. I may as well wear one because Katie may as well have me strapped down.

My cell vibrates in my pocket. I want to hunt…no, I *need* to hunt because this obsession with goddamn stepsister is wearing me the hell down.

I glance at the message on the screen.

Oliver: I'm out front.

I leave the nightclub behind, pushing through the glass doors and out into the night. Away from the dull throb of music. Oliver's vehicle waits against the curb, engine purring, bright white headlights shining against the cars out front. He looks my way as I slide inside.

"Have any fun?" he asks.

I don't answer, just yank the door close behind me and tug on my seatbelt.

Oliver shifts the car into gear and pulls out with tires squealing, drawing attention from people outside the club.

I say nothing, but he's acting strange. He has been ever since I came back. Is it Katie? I try not to let the idea of two of them together get under my skin. I know she visits him in his room at night. I also know she doesn't visit mine. But there's no jealousy there, if there was, this wouldn't work. Him, me, her–*us*.

She knows too much so it has to work. Either that or I kill her.

But even I know that's not what I want. Killing Katie isn't what I obsess over, I understand that now.

We drive through the city and head west to the residential neighborhood on the opposite side of town. New money houses, two-story stucco, painted white and gray, each with a manicured garden that all look the same. So very different from the creaking floorboards and hidden hallways of Davenport Manor and our dark, depraved family secrets that will never see the light of day.

We pull up outside the basic gray house that belongs to Frankie Wales. The man is a chemical engineer. A genius really, working at the nuclear facility just outside Wilmington. He's also a greedy bastard, selling bio weapons on the black market. That little piece of information was enough to leverage him into helping us get what we need, which is enough acid to burn away the bodies.

Before I went to jail, we'd been busy, but the boys had to shut down the mission while the feds were nosing around. But with Katie recanting her testimony and me being a free man... well, it's time to get back to the hunt. First off: Christopher Watkins.

I'm ready to take him on, to kill him for what his piece of shit brother put me and Katie through. But first, we need to get our operations back up and running and that means we need Frankie.

We don't go to the front door. Instead, we sink into the shadows, making our way down the side of the house, through the gate, and across the patio.

Frankie doesn't live alone, he has a family living with him, for fuck's sake. A family. I wonder if they're as fucked up as we are? The lights are on inside, although there's no movement. Despite the kind of people Frankie works with, the door is unlocked and Oliver's steps are light behind me as we move through the house. Quiet, calm, deadly.

Frankie's awful humming comes from somewhere deeper in the house. We'd been to Frankie's place twice before, each time at night. This time he was expecting us days ago, but with the attention from my hearing, we had to be careful and bailed. Tonight, we don't have an appointment, which explains why when Frankie appears in the hallway, carrying a giant bowl of popcorn between his meaty hands, he flinches. With wide eyes, he jerks his gaze from Oliver to me. "Holy shit! You scared the crap out of me."

"Your door was unlocked." I move around him and into the kitchen. "You alone?"

"Jess and the girls are upstairs asleep," he says carefully. There's a tremble in his voice, one that hasn't been there before. He's nervous.

"You worried about something, Frankie?" Oliver asks from behind me.

"No, of course not. You just surprised me."

I turn around, his eyes wide as he meets mine. Something doesn't feel right. "You messaged us, remember?"

His smile was fake and fast, tagging corners of his party mouth. "That was days ago. You never showed. I thought maybe you changed your mind."

Oliver picks up a framed family photo and studies it. "Yeah, we kind of had to deal with some family shit. You know how it is."

An awkward silence fills the space before Frankie adds, "Right." He looks me up and down. "I saw you on the news. Incredible that your sister recanted."

"Stepsister," I say. "You ready to do business or should we come back?"

"No," Frankie makes his way out of the hallway and into the living room. The TV is on, a movie paused on the screen. From the grainy film and hockey mask, it looks like Friday the 13th. "Of course not. Like I said, I just wasn't expecting you."

"Do you have our order?" I ask.

"Yep." Frankie tracks my every move. "Just like last time. Fifty percent upfront. The rest when you pick them up."

I nod. That's the same process as before. I'm about to hand him the envelope of cash in my pocket when I pause. "How about the tablets?"

Like I said, Frankie is a genius, and once he understood exactly what we needed, he created a tablet that dissolves in water and can be used to remove all traces of blood, bodily fluid, and DNA.

"Yeah, about that..." Frankie shifts his weight from one foot to the next, "...they didn't come in."

"They didn't come in..." I repeat, scanning the dining room behind me, stopping at the small black boxes stacked in the corner of the room. "You mean the ones you make in your lab?"

"Yeah, those. Things got tricky at work. My boss started asking questions about the extra materials and I wasn't able to get the formula right..."

He rambles as I take a step, moving deeper in the dining room that was set off from the living room. I pick up one of the sleek rectangle boxes and open it. Inside are packages of the tablets Frankie had shown us last time we met up. His eyes widen as he turns a shade of ashen white.

"What's going on, Frankie?" my brother asks carefully, moving his hand to his hip, revealing a gun tucked into the waistband of his jeans.

My gaze fixes on the splayed out file on the other side of the table. Black-and-white images peek out from under what looks like a police report and a photograph of Watkin's cabin draws my attention.

"Doing a little investigation of your own?" Slowly I pull my knife out, flicking the blade out with a snap. "Checking up on us? Me?"

"No." Frankie follows me into the dining room, his eyes wide and fixed on the blade in my hand.

I look down at the images, ignoring all of them, but one. Katie's in the camp cabin doorway, eyes glazed as she stares at a distant camera. She's dressed in the same clothes she wore when she turned me in.

My clothes—*my* sweatshirt. The one I gave her. I know how the bandage on her abdomen is taped, and I know what's seeping out of her perfect goddamn cunt.

My cum.

It wasn't just a wet and horny fuck. She was mine for a moment. All mine.

"It's not how it looks," Frankie tries, glasses sliding down his nose. "Just doing my due diligence. If someone is ratting you guys out, they could come for me next. I have a family. I can't just–" I don't let him finish.

I spin the knife in my palm and clench tight before I lunge, driving the fat fuck backward and burying the blade into the wall next to his head.

The room falls silent, nothing but his heavy breath filling the air.

"Jack..." Oliver warns. *Pull it back—reign it in.*

I stare into the bastard's eyes, but as always, it's not him that I see.

It's her.

She'd been wet. So fucking wet. She may have betrayed me, but I know the truth about what happened between us. She'd been turned on by what I was and what I did to save her.

God, how I wish she hadn't been.

How I wish she hadn't kissed me back. If she hadn't opened herself to me, it'd be so much easier to kill her. I could get rid of her once and for all, make it look like an accident... for her mother's sake. *Jesus.* The fact I even gave a shit about my stepmother's feelings says more than I want to admit.

"I n-needed to p-protect myself." Frankie stammers. "If you go down, then I go down. You'd do the same if you were me."

Protect himself. I glance at the file on the table. Is that all this is? Just a little self-preservation?

"You're a smart guy, Frank," I say. "I know you wouldn't do anything to jeopardize our relationship."

"No, Jack." He swallows. "Never."

"Good."

I turn and pick up the photograph of my sister. In return, I drop the envelope of cash on the table.

"Dig into our lives again and I'll come back here and get to know your family a little better. Got it?"

"Y-yes. Loud and clear."

I fold the photograph until it's small enough to go in my pocket. I can admit it now. I'm hung up on her. Hung up on the spark of desire in her eyes. I had a taste of her. A taste of how things could be, if only she allowed herself to become who she was meant to be.

Bloody.

Murderous...

A Davenport.

"Jack," Oliver murmurs beside me.

I clench my grip around the blade and yank it free from the drywall. I drop the blade to my side and unfurl my fingers from Frankie's shirt. "I'm okay," I say, mostly to myself.

Because I am. I finally know what I want.

A family. One happy, murderous family.

All I have to do now is make her want the same.

TEN

Kate

—————

"Did you hear what she said on the stand? They slept together. That's why she lied."

"I knew this was going to be a problem when I heard the girl was coming back. You can't have these blended families all living together—especially after they're all grown. It's asking for trouble."

"Or when the brothers are that handsome."

They giggle and the squeak of the shopping cart wheels lets me know they've finally moved along.

I push my own cart down the grocery store aisle, trying my best to ignore the gossiping women as they head toward the checkout. I recognized them when I walked in—they were members of my mother's book club—and unfortunately on my list of people to invite to the party.

No wonder my mother is a mess.

The ramifications of my return home follow me everywhere; in the house, with my family, during my sessions with Paul. Even here, at the grocery store where I should be able to shop in relative peace.

I'm still thinking about it after I pay and carry the groceries out to the car. Oliver waits for me in the parking lot, leaning against the car. Fair hair tousled by the wind, sunglasses covering his eyes. That woman was right. He is handsome, and right now, a relief.

"What's wrong?" he asks, as I get closer. He drives me everywhere, a constant reminder that I'm always being watched.

"Nothing." I lift the bag from the cart, but he stops me, taking over.

"You've been crying."

"No, I haven't." It's true. I want to cry. I'm on the verge of it, but I'm stronger than that and I don't appreciate Oliver noticing every goddamn thing about me. "Let's just go."

His eyes train over my shoulder. "Was it them? Did they say something?"

I look back and see the two women. They glance over at us and one gives a small, fake, smile. "Not *to* me," I admit. Oliver's jaw tics, the tight ball of muscle in the back pulsing. He drops the bags in the backseat and pushes the cart out of the way. "Wait. What are you doing?"

"I'm going to tell those women to mind their own fucking business."

I lunge for him, grabbing his arm. "You can't."

He snorts. "Yeah, Katie, I can. No one talks shit about our family." His eyes drop down to my mouth, then back up. "Including you."

"It'll make it worse—especially for Mom. I promised your dad I would try to make things better and putting those women on blast will only make things worse."

One already has her phone out, discretely held at her waist. She's most likely taking a photo of the two of us out here—proof of our family dysfunction to spread around to all their friends. I can see the caption now: *Katie and her stepbrother. Is she sleeping with this one, too?*

The muscles in Oliver's arm are tense under my hand. "It just makes me so fucking mad."

"I know. I'm sorry. It's all my fault—"

"Not all of it," he says to my surprise. "We were sloppy, even before you returned home. Bringing the men we hunted to the house. Allowing the Watkins brothers to slip through our fingers...that's on us." He gives the women one last hard look and turns back to the car, lifting the bags of groceries into the back. "If we're going to catch Christopher Watkins, we're going to have to up our game."

Catch.

He means *hunt*. For the first time the idea doesn't make my stomach turn.

Oliver shuts the trunk with a slam and turns to me, hand reaching for my chin to draw my attention away from where the two catty women have finally parted and are getting into their own cars. "We're a family, Katie. And I don't like seeing you hurt any more than I like it when it happens to anyone else in the house. You say the word and I'll make sure they pay."

His eyes are bold, bright. *Sincere.*

The thought of someone so strong and confident at my back sends a thrill down my spine, but there's something else: fear. I shake my head. "It's not worth causing any other problems."

He frowns and drops his hand. "You're probably right."

Once we're in the car and on the way back home, I exhale and say, "I don't know how we're going to get all these people to the party for Mom. I'm pretty sure the damage is worse than I feared."

His arm stretches over the center console and rests on my thigh. "I'll take care of it."

"You sure?"

He nods and squeezes his hand. "Positive."

WITH MY JOURNAL sitting on my lap, Paul and I sit across from one another.

"Have you done your homework?" he asks, nodding to the book in my lap. I bought it at the stationery store when I was buying invitations to the party for my mom. I saw it on the rack, the front and back covered in pink and orange flowers—a small strip of gold gilding the edges of the blooms. I grabbed it on a whim, wanting something pretty to contrast the dirty thoughts going inside.

Because that's what I learned about myself this week. I have dirty, depraved thoughts when it comes to sex.

"Yes. I got the survey you sent me." It came over email after our last session. A sexual inventory, which is mostly a series of extensive questions, each more intimate than the last about my sexual desires and fantasies. It started with basic things, like, "*How willing are you to explore outside your identified sexual orientation? Are certain parts of your or a partner's body off limits? What kind of sexual aftercare do you prefer? Do certain sexual acts or scenarios trigger post traumatic response? What other acts make you uncomfortable?"* And then delved into more explicit questions about bondage, blood play, and other acts I've never even considered. Until lately.

"How did you feel about exploring these sides of yourself?" I shrug hoping it's enough of an answer, but Paul's gaze is unrelenting. He adds, "Remember, I have to report back to the court that you're cooperating with therapy."

I take a deep breath and open my journal, deciding I may as well be truthful. It's not like I can hide much from Paul anyway. He always has a way of knowing my thoughts and feelings. "I discovered that I'm not really sure how I feel about sex. My experience is pretty limited and," I swallow, "as you know, my first interaction was by force."

He nods and I can tell by his expression that he's thinking back to that night in the boy's room. When I'd caught them masturbating to a gang bang video and how they'd turned their focus on me. I'd never seen anything like it, not the video, not the hard erect cocks of my brother and his friends, and definitely not the predatory gleam in their eyes when they forced me to my knees.

"I think it's fair to say that I have conflicted feelings."

"What kind of conflict?" he asks.

"Sometimes," I look down at my hands, "I confuse pain with pleasure."

He leans forward, the leather chair creaking under his weight. "Do you want to feel the pain?"

"Sometimes. I think so." Finally. "Yes."

"It says here you had sex with a man at college." He looks down at the printed survey, a peek into my intimate thoughts. "How was that?"

I think back to John and his goofy smile. He had no game. None of the extreme confidence of my brothers and their friends. "It was...satisfactory."

He frowns. "Did you orgasm?"

I shake my head. "No. Well, later, after he left. I used my vibrator."

He jots something down on his notepad and a tickle of anxiety builds in my chest. "What was missing, do you think?"

"He was sweet. Kind. He asked me what I wanted, and I didn't know how to tell him. I didn't know how to explain it." My cheeks heat. "Not without embarrassing myself."

"You find your desire for pain to be embarrassing?"

"I'm pretty sure it's supposed to be, isn't it?" I ask back, thinking of all the humiliation they've put me through. The gaslighting and demeaning. The sessions with Paul where he pushes me to my limit, or when Davis jumps me in the most unexpected places, keeping my nerves frayed and on edge. "Isn't that what you all want?"

"What I or the others want, isn't relevant." Paul leans back in his chair, legs crossed, and casual. Controlled. Always controlled. "This is about you, Katherine. Why you put yourself into situations where you feel humiliation and seek pain. If it's as simple as desire—the things that make your panties wet—then that's one thing, but if it's because you can't stay away from destructive behavior, then that's another." He rests his tablet on the table next to him. "We're here to figure out how you can control these desires. How to channel them into something that meets your needs, but keeps you out of trouble."

As always, Paul has this way of speaking that both confirms my beliefs and confuses me more. He's smart, but manipulative. I can't ever catch onto exactly what he's trying to do.

"When was the last time you orgasmed?" he asks suddenly.

"Not since I returned home." Again, my skin warms. "Before that, I masturbated—when I was in witness protection—but since I've been back, Oliver said I'm not allowed to. Not until he gives me permission." I twist my hands together. "And Davis...he also didn't let me."

"So, they're punishing you."

"Yes, for what I did to Jack and for hurting Davis' career."

He nods. "Do you think you deserve that punishment?"

There's a glint in his eye. The question is a trick—maybe a trap. I'd already admitted to liking pain. Did I enjoy this as well? All I know is my body is on a hair-trigger, my dreams filled with these men and their heavy touch.

I swallow and say, "I made a deal when I came back. You'll protect me and you can do what you want. If punishment is part of that, then I have no other choice."

"I was going to suggest that you show me your masturbation technique, but I don't want to go against the rules of your arrangement."

"Oh," I say, trying to get a handle on my emotions. I'm pent-up and horny. Dying for release. Having doctor approval would probably be the one thing Oliver would agree to. "Doesn't your position overrule the agreement?"

A small smile plays on his lips. "It does, but consequences are important, Katherine. As much as I want to see how you pleasure yourself, for therapeutic purposes, I don't feel comfortable violating the terms of your arrangement with your stepbrother."

"I understand."

"But that doesn't mean that we can't explore other avenues." He stands and walks around his desk.

My forehead wrinkles. "What do you mean?"

"I want to perform a little test." He gestures for me to stand while he rummages in the top drawer of the desk.

"What kind of test?" I ask, standing.

"To assess your pain threshold." He moves back around, stopping behind me, and rests a hand on my back, pushing me forward. "Hands flat."

I catch myself, and flatten my palms on the sleek stainless-steel surface. His fingers graze the back of my thighs before he pushes my skirt up around my waist. He yanks my panties down and leans forward, showing me a long, wooden ruler.

"This may sting a little bit, Katherine, but I think we both know you don't mind."

Smack!

I buck as the first hit takes me by surprise. Sharp and stinging.

Smack!

The second makes my flesh scream and I bite down on my bottom lip swallowing one back.

Smack!

The third compounds the second, new skin, raw and ripe. But from there each strike starts the slip into something just out of reach, something transcendent. I don't fight the cries, letting them bellow with every slap of the wood against my flesh. I'm not sure how many blows I take—how many he gives me—but by the time he stops, I'm almost flat on my belly, legs spread as he touches between my thighs. They slide in easy, gliding in the slick. The moan of want that follows comes from deep in my core.

Then he pulls away and reaches for his tablet and jots down a note, mumbling, "Subject is sexually aroused when spanked." I push up on my elbows and he glances at my chest. "Nipples erect." His eyes meet mine. "How bad do you want to be fucked right now, Katherine? Scale of one to ten?"

I don't have to think. "A ten."

My pussy throbs almost as much as the pain in my backside, but I already know he won't do anything to help relieve the aching want. He just writes down my response and directs me to get dressed.

I leave the session with my journal in my hand and a new list of questions to answer. But that's not all. Paul confirmed to me something I've been wondering about, how in line are these men with how they treat me...how they feel about me?

The answer seems universally clear.

The four of them are very much in sync.

"KATHERINE, can you hand me my hairbrush? It should be in that drawer behind you."

My mother has agreed to go outside, to take a walk around the block, for the first time in days. But first, she wants to put on a full face of make-up and fix her hair.

I open the drawer, wincing with almost every move. Paul tore up my backside when he spanked me, leaving me with purpling bruises and a few raised cuts. Every step is a reminder of what transpired in that office. It almost makes me think that was his intention.

"Here you go," I say, handing her the brush.

"You should wear lipstick," Mom says, pulling the brush through her hair. I feel her eyes assessing me in the mirror. "And maybe a little blush. Your complexion is lovely—just too pale." My mother is a pro at the backhanded compliment. She frowns when she sees a grimace when shift my weight to one side. "And why are you standing like that?"

"I slipped on the stairs," I lie. "Going down too fast."

"You've always been clumsy."

I sigh. "Finish your hair and makeup, Mom. I'll go get your shoes."

I cut back through the bedroom to the master closet on the other side of the room. Montie took a small room, intended to be a nursery, and turned it into a large dressing room and closet. Inside are rows of clothing, shoes, and handbags, all things my mother needed in her prior life as the wife of a successful businessman. She was active and involved. It's hard to imagine that now when she's so out of it most of the time.

I turn to the wall of shelves that hold her shoes, looking for the one she'll find most appropriate. Of course, the walking shoes are on the bottom row and I brace myself for the excruciating pain of having to bend.

"Son of a—"

"Katherine?"

I exhale and turn to see Dr. Sanders, Paul's dad, in the doorway, medical bag in his hand. His clothes are casual, golfing-style, like he just came from the green.

"Oh," I say, trying to keep my expression in check. "Doctor, I wasn't expecting you."

"I was in the area and thought I'd stop by and check on your mother." He smiles. "I'm happy to see she's out of bed."

"I've convinced her to go on a walk." I rest a hand on the bookshelf to help leverage myself back up. "She's in the bathroom getting ready."

"Then you've definitely made some progress since the last time I was here." He takes in my position. "Are you okay? You look like you're in pain."

I guess there's no use faking it. "I fell down the stairs. Bruised my coccyx pretty bad." With the shoes in one hand and using the shelf with the other, I manage to get back to a standing position without screaming out in pain. I give him a thumbs up. "See? I'm fine."

He watches me closely—his eyes so familiar to Paul's. "Would you like me to take a look?" he asks. "I don't mind."

"That's not necessary." He's blocking the doorway and doesn't seem to have any plans on moving. "Really, it's just a bruise that makes me walk like an eighty-year-old woman. It's more embarrassing than painful."

"Depending on how hard you landed it could be worse than that," he says. "There could be spinal injury or internal bleeding. Falls are no joke, Katherine. I'd feel better if you let me at least take a look."

His tone is authoritative—confident—and really, I am in a tremendous amount of pain. It kept me up half the night. I relent. "If you don't mind."

"Not at all."

I rest the shoes on the dressing table and turn. "It's my, um, backside, obviously."

He places his medical bag next to the shoes and touches my shoulder. "I'm just going to lower your pants, okay?"

"That's fine," I say, although my heart pounds in my chest. I'd worn leggings, something that was light and expanded around the wounds. I grip the edge of the countertop and it's not lost on me that I'd been in a similar position, *with his son*, when I received these injuries. Would he know I'm lying?

"Jesus." It's a low curse as he pulls the waist of my pants down low enough to see the first marks. "This is pretty bad, Katie."

"I think I hit every step," I say, forcing a laugh. His thumb grazes over my skin and I flinch. "It looks worse than it feels."

"Then it must feel like shit." His fingers are soft, but firm, taking care to explore each wound. Heat rises through me as he pulls my pants lower, revealing my entire backside. "I'm not seeing any permanent injury, but I have some salve that may help with the pain."

He doesn't pull up my pants, but he removes his hands, reaching for his bag. He fumbles around inside before pulling out a tube of cream. I watch over my shoulder as he squeezes a liberal amount into his hand. "This will be cold at first, but I doubt that'll be a problem." I sense his closeness when he quietly warns, "Brace yourself."

Like he said, the cream is cold, a sudden burst of iciness on my overheated skin. His touch continues to be gentle, and he rubs smooth circles into my tender wounds, spreading across my skin thoroughly. Feeling relief for the first time since leaving Paul's office, I exhale loudly and allow my eyes to flutter shut.

"Better?" he asks, fingers still massaging my backside.

"Yes, thank you." I sink into it, the soft touch, the gentle caring nature. It's only when his fingers inch closer to the divide between my cheeks, do I tense. My body freezes as he runs a finger down to the warm spot hidden by flesh. Touching the puckered ridge that Davis so angrily violated days before. *Can he feel the wounds there, too? Should he touch me like that?* But before I can overthink it, he says, "Good girl—all done," and slowly pulls my leggings back up. "I'll leave you a tube of this cream. Use it whenever you feel like the pain is starting to flare up again."

His voice is steady. Clear. Professional. I glance at him, and there's nothing amiss on his face—maybe I did imagine it. "You let me know if it gets worse, okay?"

"Yes, of course." I grab the shoes to give my hands something to do. "Thank you for taking time out of your day. You're so generous to our family."

He smiles, the crinkles near his eyes, giving him a kind glow. "I'm happy to be of service," he says, "especially for the Davenport's. I feel a special kinship to your family, and despite everything that has happened, that includes you."

ELEVEN

Jack

I SIT IN MY CAR OUTSIDE FRANKIE'S HOUSE. THE PLACE IS alight, the faint glow of the living room lights glimmer through the windows at the front of the house, even though it's almost three in the morning.

Like he expects I'll be watching and he's trying to say *'I have nothing to hide from you.'* Nothing other than the fact he went behind our backs and pulled the records of the case, spreading them all over his dining room table.

The image of Katie returns. I don't like the idea of his beady fucking eyes on her. Still, I needed him...alive preferably. Looks like he wants to stay that way. I scan the cars parked along the street in front of me taking in the license plates.

None are out of place.

I know the numbers from memory alone. The minivan is a family of six that's soon to be seven. The royal blue Mercedes belongs to the childless couple that just came back from Spain and the black Porsche is the fifty-year-old banker who runs Wilmington Municipal Bank.

I glance back to Frankie's house and start the engine before pulling away. It'd been days since our encounter, still, I can't get it out of my head. If Frankie is digging into our dirty little secrets, there has to be for a reason it.

Is this a setup?

The idea nags at me.

We take possession of the acid and the Fed's descend, taking us both out at once? It would ease his conscience. But Frankie isn't that stupid, surely. He doesn't know about Davis or Paul. We've kept pieces of information hidden. He knows who we are and the kind of reach we have.

I leave his house behind and make my way west, dividing my focus between the road in front and the few cars behind me. My phone lights up with a message. One I've been waiting for. I don't need to look. I know exactly who it is.

I head to a small warehouse on the outskirts of Wilmington and pull into the parking lot of a rundown storage facility before driving slowly around to the rear, finding Oliver's Mercedes parked outside the normally locked side gate.

He stands at the front of the car in the darkness, waiting for me.

Headlights shine over his scowl as I park and kill the engine, hitting the latch for the trunk before I climb out.

"Took your sweet time," Oliver says as I stride toward him.

I don't speak, just fish out the keys for the gate and warehouse from my pocket. "Let's do this."

My brother glances behind us then turns back as I unlock the gate and push it open. It's pitch black out here with not even a street light to guide our way. But we know this place by heart. Every sound. Every corner. We make our way between towering warehouses and turn left heading toward the warehouse at the back.

You won't find this place in any of our records. The Davenport name can't be traced back to this building or any other building we have hidden from the IRS or any other government department that wanted to poke their nose into our business. It didn't mean that I wasn't on edge.

I stop at the battered roller door at the end of the walkway. "Cameras."

My brother brings up the view of the CCTV cameras on his cell and flicks through the live views. "All clear," he says before I slide the key into the lock.

Only one other person has a key to this place, and Frankie knows he's on thin ice. We so much as get a sniff he's betrayed us, he and his family won't see the sunrise. He knows that. It's the only thing keeping him alive.

I unlock the door and lift the heavy thing. Oliver follows me inside before I yank the door down behind us and hit the light switch.

The murky amber glow barely reaches the corners but it's the two drums sitting in the middle we care about.

98% Sulphuric acid.

The shit is expensive.

But it's good.

Eating through flesh and bones in a matter of days.

We need it, especially now. With the Feds on our ass, *my ass*, we can't be too careful.

"I'll grab the trolley." Ollie heads toward the back of the warehouse.

The squeal of the wheels makes me wince. The sound carries, and I don't like it. "Don't bother," I mutter. "We can carry them ourselves."

My brother gives me a glare standing there in his Valentino shirt. "And ruin my clothes?"

"Who gives a fuck about your clothes." I head for the nearest barrel, bend and grasp the top with one hand, tilting it to grasp the bottom and heave it from the floor. "Leave it if you're so goddamn worried. You can grab the door instead."

Ollie yanks the chain, lifting the door up and I carry the damn thing out and back to Ollie's car. He follows behind me and loads the first barrel in before closing the trunk with a thud.

"You go.' I suck in a heavy breath and step away. "I'll be right behind you."

"You sure?"

I give a nod, watching him yank open the driver's door and slide behind the wheel. The engine starts and he's backing out before I head back inside. If the cops are waiting to ambush us, at least Ollie will have a head start. I go back inside the warehouse, but I don't automatically grab the second barrel of acid.

I make my way to the back of the garage and bend down, reaching to the back of the shelf hidden in the shadows. My fingers skim the soft leather. I grab the tied case and pull it free, dusting it off as I lift it to the shelf.

My fingers work the knot, unraveling the sheath to reveal the shine of steel. My fingers trace the cold metal, extracting one from the pack. I open the blade and run my thumb along the honed edge. The knife isn't new, but the grip is small, perfect really. Perfect for my murderous little sister.

I hold it in my palm and smile with the weight. It was one of the first blades I had and saved my life more times than I can remember. Now I want it to save hers. I close the others back up, tie the leather around them and stow them at the back of the shelf in the dark. The blade is clean, with no trace of DNA on any of the pieces of shit I disposed of before.

It's safe...for her.

I close the blade back up and slide it into my pocket before I stride to the last barrel. I carry it out of the warehouse and lock it in my trunk.

By the time I head out of the city, the first traces of sunlight peak on the horizon. Katie invades my thoughts as I focus on getting safely to the cabin. By the time I get there the darkened forest is a deep, sage green.

Ollie's car sits outside the barn. The door is open, waiting for me. I park next to him and climb out before making my way around the car. By the time I have the barrel of acid inside I'm sweating. Ollie waits for me. His sleeves are rolled up, and there's a smudge of dirt in the middle of his perfect white shirt. I can't help but smirk. "Seems you got dirty after all, Brother."

There's that scowl again. I missed it while I was in lock-up. I turn away, knowing before long I'd be back. This time I'll be carrying a body with me.

I let Christopher Watkins get away once, it won't happen again. I've tried to come up with a plan on just how to lure him out of hiding, but there really is no plan. It's just me and him, both hunters. Only one of us will come out of this alive and there's no way I'll allow it to be him.

Katie's face returns as I dust off my hands and chain the barn door closed. Oliver stands there waiting, that scowl now eased. I want to ask about what he does with Kate at night. What they're doing in his room, while he reads or plays video games, while they're in bed. Whatever it is, they're quiet. I've listened from behind the walls. Somehow, he's gained her trust and that seems unattainable for me.

He's getting soft with her. I can see in the way he talks about her and the way she reacts around him. She fills some kind of need for him and yet she leaves me wanting. I don't know how to deal with that, just like I don't know how to deal with them.

"Katie's been spending nights with you." The words hurt in my throat.

One brow rises as my brother takes a step closer. "Do you have a problem with that?"

"No. I just..."

"We don't fuck, if that's what you're worried about."

They don't fuck? Then what the hell do they do?

I lick my lips as the image I have of them consumes me. The fantasy I've made in my head. His hand closed around her wrists pinning them on the bed above her head. I imagine him fucking her, making her buck, and moan. Just like I made her buck and moan. My cock thickens at the idea of watching her and him. "No. That's not what I worry about."

He narrows in on me. "Then what is it?"

I want to tell him how I feel. I *should* tell him how our little sister has somehow slit my skin and crawled underneath. How she's burrowed her way deep inside my chest and at this moment is infesting my heart. Ollie above anyone else would understand. He knows me, what drives me, what consumes me. I want to tell him, but I still can't. "Nothing." I turn away.

"You're different since you've come back."

His words stop me as I walk to the car. I lower my gaze, looking down at the ground. "Something has changed and I don't know what it is. If it's Katie, then you need to get your head straight with her, Brother." He takes a step closer, crowding me. "You haven't fucked her since you got back. Don't think I haven't noticed. What are you waiting for?"

So, he's been watching me, too. "Nothing."

He shakes his head. "I know you; something is eating you, and it's pulling you away from us. Your own personal demons can make you dangerous, and force you to make rash, stupid decisions. If it's our sister's pussy you want then take it. She'll do whatever we want now. Take it any way you want to give it to her. She's almost fucking panting for it, desperate to please."

And that's just it, wasn't it?

I wanted to fuck her, I wanted to claim her. I wanted to own her in ways that shouldn't be possible and it wasn't just sex. She wasn't a Davenport. Not yet anyway and I wanted that. I lowered my hand feeling my cock harden. I wanted to keep it all in our sick, murderous family.

"You need to figure it out, Jack," Ollie urges.

I nod. "I will."

"Good."

I leave with those words ringing in my head, yank open the driver's door, and climb back inside. My headlights splash over him as I reverse and drive away. Home feels awkward to me now. I've taken to driving at night, haunting the city streets in the hopes I might somehow come across Christopher Watkins on my own.

Being so close to her and not fucking her makes me feel desperate. I reach down and touch the knife as I turn the wheel and head home.

The house is still quiet when I pull into the driveway. I automatically look at her window as I climb out and make my way inside.

I know she's no longer barricading her bedroom door. Like she's come to terms with her predicament. I make my way upstairs to her bedroom. Soft snores reach me as I slip inside, and close the door behind me.

I'm drawn to her in ways I can't fathom. I step closer, stopping beside her bed.

Her lips are parted with her heavy breaths. The sheets are kicked free, leaving her exposed. She's dressed in a dusty pink negligee; the shade reminds me of her cunt. I dig out the knife from my pocket and flick open the blade with a *snap*.

The sound is sharp and jarring. Her eyes open instantly, and those brown eyes widen as they find me. I lean down, sliding the tip of the blade under the strap of her garment, and twist, cutting it. "Have you missed me, little sister?"

Her breath catches as I slide the blade deeper, cutting through the lace until I reach the satin. It's no match for the honed edge.

"Yes," she answers.

I know it's the truth because I see it in her eyes. She licks her lips and her breath deepens. I lean down until I'm kneeling beside her. Is this where she wants me to be, on my fucking knees? The idea of that is both a punch to my gut and a surge of blood to my cock.

I kiss the top of her breast as the knife tears the material. She doesn't dare move as I lick through the torn material and take her puckered peak into my mouth. Until she does. I know the instant she needs to moan, pulling the blade away as her chest rises and the guttural sound reverberates through her flesh.

"I bought you a present." I murmur, giving the knife a jerk and cutting her negligee all the way down. "Tell me how much you missed me, little sister...tell me how sorry you are for all those fucking nights in that cell."

I lift my gaze as rage and desperation burn inside me.

I want to fuck her.

I want to hear her scream.

But more than anything, I want her to be mine, and she can't be as long as The Binder wants her, too. I bend down, watching as her breaths change, and know instantly she senses me. Her eyes snap open, and slowly she turned her head. One lick of her lips and she croaks. "Jack."

I want to do more with those lips...so much more. But I don't. Instead, I lift the knife in my hand, watching as her eyes wide. "This is for you." I start. The words are awkward and alien. I force them out because I have no fucking choice. A need drives me now and it's not the depraved bloody kind that consumed me before. This is darker, more absolute—this a need not to destroy—but to protect. I look down at the honed edge as it glints in the early morning sun. "I made my first kill with it."

She stares at the blade with fear. Her voice is husky when she lifts her gaze to mine. "Why are you giving it to me?"

I stare at the blade and scowl. "So that you're ready if I'm not there."

"Ready for what?"

I lift my gaze to hers and answer quietly. "Killing Christopher Watkins."

TWELVE

Kate

HE SHOWED UP MIDWAY THROUGH DINNER, DRESSED IN ALL black—from his fitted button-down to tight black jeans and thick-soled boots. He eases his way into a seat at the table, all charm and smiles. Before he arrived, it'd been me, Montie, and my stepbrothers, Jack and I avoiding one another's eyes as I felt the cold steel from the knife he gave me in my boot.

I'd been shaken after Jack left my room, relieved from the fact he didn't force himself on me, and also a little upset that he didn't. Who was this man? What had changed my brother? And when did he decide to give me a weapon—one that means so much to him.

And then the directive. *"So that you're ready if I'm not there—to kill Christopher Watkins."*

It's like a seed burrowed into my brain, planted and growing by the day. Is that what I'm here for? To kill the remaining Binder?

The thought lingers between us over the dinner table, as I also try to reconcile the guest who stopped by. He's nothing like the man that cornered me outside of Paul's office the week before, pushing me forward and forcing himself on me. Davis Higgins

314

knows how to work a room, especially with men like my stepfather, and before I know it, he's convinced Montie that he needs my help clearing up a few things for the Watkins' case. In a blink, he's got me tucked in the passenger seat of his car and is handing me a paper bag.

"What's this?" I ask, afraid to open it. Honestly, I regret asking him anything. Davis made it clear that he's got nothing but hatred for me. I don't get to ask questions. I don't get to say no. To speak my mind. He owns me, that's the deal I made, and I don't want him to remind me about it in his own psychotic way.

"Clothes." He starts the car. "We've got some hunting to do."

"Are we doing back to the bar?"

"Not this time." He tosses me a matchbook. There's a pinup girl stamped on the front. It's not familiar.

"What's this?"

"Our ticket inside Club Hades. Got it from one of my informants. He's a drug dealer that has a niche clientele in the scene."

I'm not sure exactly what scene he's talking about, but I open the bag and feel the pile of thin fabric down at the bottom. I remove it, holding it up to the light, and see that it's a black sheer leotard and matching mesh harem pants... "Did you buy these?"

"I got it out of evidence. We busted up a sex ring a few months ago." He gives me a smirk. "Don't worry. I had it washed."

I swallow and look out the window, noting that we've entered The Bluff's, the nicest neighborhood in Wilmington. These houses are new—not historic like Davenport Manor. Big and sprawling, the backyards overlooking the river. An uneasy feeling builds in my stomach and I glance over at the man driving the car. His jaw is set, cheekbones chiseled. His eyes take in everything, cataloging the houses, the cars, anything we pass. I finally build up the nerve and ask, "Seriously, Davis, what's going on? If you want me to be helpful, I need to know what I'm getting into."

He pulls the car into a long driveway paved in flat stones and we're waved into a parking spot by an attendant. This isn't a seedy club, it's someone's home. Someone with money and I assume power and influence. What is this about?

He takes so long to respond that I assume he's not going to, but once the car is parked, he shifts to face me. "While you were in witness protection, we discovered that the Watkins brothers were active in the kink community, mostly BDSM, but their tastes run the gamut. Club Hades is an underground, constantly changing locations, sex club. Different people host. It can be at bars, clubs, warehouses, or," his thumb jerks behind us, "million-dollar mansions by the river. You and I are going in as a couple, but anything goes." He reaches across the center console and grabs my chin. "I'm going to need you to play the part, sweetheart. No acting coy or being a bitch about it. No games. It's just sex and we both know you're a dirty slut. You should feel right at home."

I don't argue and quickly change in the dark of the car. The leotard has long sleeves and a high neck and the harem pants cinch at the ankles. It's a false sense of security since I'm bare underneath the sheer fabric and when I step outside the car, the cool fall air sends goosebumps across my flesh. I round the vehicle, Davis stares at me for a moment that stretches out so long that I'm afraid he disapproves. His tongue darts out and says, "Jesus, you're a thorn in my side, but you're perfection." He holds up his finger. "One more thing."

He opens the back door of the car and reaches inside. He hands me a wig, platinum blonde with blunt bangs.

"What's with the blonde? Watkins likes brunettes or did something change?"

"You're not the bait tonight, sweetheart. We're here to observe. See if anyone mentions him. If he shows up, I'll handle it."

He reaches into the backseat one more time and pulls out a long coat, that once the wig is secure, he drapes over my shoulders.

"Thank you," I say, surprised at his generosity.

"Let me make something clear, other men are going to want to fuck you. Probably other women too, but no one is going to touch you but me." His fingers run along my neck. "Flirt all you want, but your pussy is mine."

I clench the coat around my body and follow him to the front door. A bouncer waits, thick-necked and imposing, but he takes the matchbook without a second look and opens the door.

The foyer is huge, the massive crystal chandelier set to a low glow, and the rest of the room lit by flickering candles. Before we even leave the circular room, an attendant has taken my coat and a drink is pushed into my hand, the glass made of crystal, the liquid a golden, bitter champagne.

"How do we do this?" I ask, feeling completely out of my element. I search the room for one person, Christopher Watkins, my heart thudding every time I catch a glint of blond hair.

"It's just a normal party," Davis says, arm snaked around my waist. The feel of him so close unnerves me. He's a venomous snake, poised to strike, I can't forget that, but here he's my only protection. "But, according to my contact, sex isn't a maybe, it's a definite." His hand runs along my back and my nipples tighten. "Straighten up. Look confident."

I have to give it to Davis, my outfit fits in perfectly with the other women in the room, and I get more than a few appraising looks. I feel like I'm naked, and basically, I am. Every inch of my skin is visible under the thin shadow of fabric.

"You go left. I'll take the right," he says, hand on my ass. The bruising finally feels better—the cuts healed. The ointment Dr. Sanders gave me helped tremendously. But there's just enough sensitivity that when Davis gives me a firm squeeze before walking off, that I feel dull pain. It travels along my nerves, right to my core, confirming Paul's suspicions. Pain and pleasure go hand in hand.

We part, and I work my way around the massive living room, taking in the opulence as much as the guests. Honestly, it's like three rooms combined into one, with various sitting areas, a bar, and a double-sided staircase on one side that leads to the second floor where people lean over a balcony railing. I snag another drink from a passing waiter, keeping my eyes peeled for Christopher's handsome face. "Prince Charming" is what I'd called him before I knew he was really a villain. Shiny blond hair, bright blue eyes, and an aristocratic face that belongs in a live-action Disney movie.

It's not easy to snoop in a crowd like this, the lights are dim, and men and women huddle close together, exchanging flirty touches and smiles. There's an energy in the room—a vibration —like Davis said, people seem focused on connecting, and as the minutes pass, I notice couples and threesomes, sometimes larger groups head up the staircase and vanish to the second floor.

I spot Davis across the room holding a drink in his hand and talking to a woman dressed in a latex body suit. His hand is on her waist, and she smiles at whatever he says. I wonder what it would be like to be on the receiving end of that charm for once and not the venom. It's a foreign thought, something I can't quite imagine.

"Going upstairs?"

I turn and see a man—handsome with a smooth, dark complexion. He's dressed less risqué than some—more like Davis in all blacks and dark gray. The style is sexy on him though, his hard muscles straining at the cotton on his shirts. "I'm thinking about it. What's up there?"

"Ah. First time?" Although I feel naïve, I nod, and he grins back. "We've all been there." He offers me his hand. "I'm Marcus. Would you like me to show you around?"

"I'm uh, Ashley, and um," I glance across the room and see Davis still involved with the woman in latex, "sure. I'd love a guide."

He offers me the crook of his arm and together we climb the staircase to the second floor. "Depending on the space, Club Hades is always a little different, but there are always a few consistent features. There's always the main lounge and bar area, and then smaller, more intimate theme rooms." We pass by a small sitting area at the mouth of a hallway where a trio, two women and one man take turns kissing one another. I draw my eyes away.

"It's okay to watch," Marcus says. "If they didn't want an audience, they would've found a more private space. Voyeurism is a big turn-on."

I look back over my shoulder and see the woman pull the man's cock out of his pants and lick the tip. Warm heat spreads across my flesh and when I turn away, Marcus has stopped and opened a door.

"Oh wow," I say quietly, taking in the room. It's set up like a library, complete with an old-fashioned librarian desk. A female librarian sits behind it with a tight bun and glasses perched on her nose. A man stands before her, handing over a stack of books. Everything about the scene appears normal, other than the fact the woman is in a bustier and fishnets and the man has on black leather shorts and is slowly stroking his cock.

Marcus raises an eyebrow and grins, stepping back into the hallway and closes the door behind him. He leads me down the hall, into one room after the other, each room an elaborate setup. There's one with a massive bed, the comforter pristine while with big fluffy pillows. Two men hold down one man, while a fourth uses a long white feather to tease his skin.

"Tickle fetish?" I ask, watching as the man being teased squirms with pleasure.

"Yep."

The following room is for people with a foot fetish, then another where everyone is dressed and acting like cats, down to cleaning and eating and drinking from little bowls. No one seems bothered by us observing, a few even noticing Marcus and giving him a small nod of greeting.

I'm fascinated by every room—by each fetish, some more appealing than others. Like the cat one, not sure I can get into that, but then Marcus opens a door and I see oversized baby furniture and a man wearing a diaper sitting on the lap of a woman rocking in a chair. His mouth is latched to her breast, suckling. There's part of me that wants to judge, but then I feel the familiar heat rolling up my spine and I think about the way Oliver has me nurse on his cock, using it as a method of comfort.

I step back abruptly, aware of the desire stirring in my lower belly, and Marcus touches my arm. "Everything okay?"

"Yeah," I say, hoping he can't see how red my cheeks are in the dim light, or how erect my nipples are under the thin mesh. "It's all just so...raw."

"Seeing people's true inner desires is definitely something to get used to." He leans against the wall, a huge painting of landscape next to him. "Out in the real world, people keep these inclinations to themselves, afraid of judgment, but at Club Hades anything goes."

"You know a lot about it. Do you come often?"

He smiles and his eyebrow quirks. "Since we're being honest, I run Club Hades."

"Oh, gosh, I had no idea." Now I'm *sure* he can see my blush. "You shouldn't have wasted your time showing me around. I'm sure you have plenty to do."

His eyes twinkle. "I have a very capable staff. There's nothing I love more about my job than showing off my hard work." He nods to the room we just left. "The rooms rotate, and I try to keep them fresh from scenes in real life or that I've seen on the news or on TV. The feline room is from this amazing little cat café that I visited while on vacation. The baby room from my sister's house. The library...well, we've all spent time in a library. That was just my favorite—"

"Downtown Wilmington," I blurt.

He grins. "Yes, exactly."

"I recognized the setup." The tension that I carried in my shoulders eases. "Well, it's amazing. I genuinely had no idea what to expect when I got here, but definitely not this much thought and creativity."

"What did bring you to Club Hades, Ashley?"

I feel bad lying to him, so I take the easy way out. "A friend suggested we come. He thought it would be something that interests me."

"Have you been exploring your desires?" His eyes dart down to my chest and then back to my face. "Looking into your fantasies?"

I think back to the time I've been back with my stepbrothers—the things they put me through, and the things I crave. "I've been testing myself." I look down the hall at the doors we've passed. "I'm not quite sure what I like. Not yet."

"There's no rush," he says. "It can take time to really understand who we are sexually, emotionally. We spend so much time repressing our true desires that it can take a while to peel off the layers to discover what truly, uniquely, turns us on."

"Thank you," I say. "For all of this. The tour and your insights."

"Please, I get to spend my evening with a beautiful woman. It's not a hardship."

His compliment makes me feel both good and nervous. I glance over my shoulder making sure Davis is nowhere around. Would he misinterpret Marcus' attention for something else? Would he lash out and punish me?

"Are you ready for the final two rooms?" He points and I see that there are two doors remaining. One on each side of the hall. I choose the room on the right and he opens the door.

I realize it's a mistake the instant I step in the room. A thick, choking lump lodges in the back of my throat—the only thing that contains my scream. The walls are made of planks of wood, bunk beds in the corner. A table sits in the middle of the room, the top covered with shiny instruments—tools. On the wall are shackles—wrist and feet, a blue tarp on the floor.

"What is this?" I manage to whisper.

"You've heard about The Binder? How they caught him at Clearwater Creek? I had the idea to do a true crime room. I managed to get my hands on some police photos and replicated it." He glances at me, his smile fading. "Ashley?"

"Oh, God." I take a step back, falling over my feet and running to the closest door. I fumble with the knob, but get it open and enter a quiet room filled with hundreds of candles and a wide, soft chaise.

Marcus follows me in. "Ashley, are you okay?" A tremor runs through my body. "What happened? What's wrong?"

He sits next to me, his hand resting on my upper thigh. The room is quiet, soft music playing from an unseen speaker. Next to the chaise is a small table, filled with candles, some lit, some waiting. Before I can react, the door flies open, slamming into the wall. Davis stands over us, expression grim and focused on the place Marcus touches me. "Hands off."

"Look man, I was just comforting her." Marcus lifts his hands up. "She got upset."

"She's mine to take care of," Davis barks. "Go. Leave us alone."

"Ashley? Do you want me to go?"

Do I want to be left alone with Davis Higgins? No. Never. But I don't get that choice. Not after making the deal with Oliver. "It's fine. We're...family friends."

Marcus stands, giving Davis a narrow eye, before turning back to me. "You need anything, tonight, tomorrow, any other day, you come find me. Okay, Ashley?"

"Yes, thank you so much. I'm sorry I panicked, that room it just—"

He cuts me off. "Everyone has triggers. I apologize for setting yours off."

Marcus gives Davis a curt nod and exits the room. Once he's gone Davis looms in front of the chaise.

"I'm sorry," I apologize. "Marcus was giving me a tour and then he showed me that last room and it—"

"I know." He runs his hands through his hair. "I saw it."

A sob runs through me. "It just took me by surprise, and I freaked out." I take a deep breath. "I'm sorry if I fucked up the investigation."

"You didn't." He sits at the foot of the chaise, his features even more prominent in the flickering candlelight. "I lost you downstairs and came to find you. I saw you run in here." He swallows. "With *him*."

There's a tone. A hint of anger and something else. I look up at him, trying to figure out how to respond. "He's the owner of the club. Maybe a good contact."

"He was touching you."

"Because I was upset." I sit up. "Nothing happened. We'd only been in here for a minute."

Davis reaches for one of the candles on the table next to mine. He holds it in his fist and then turns it, allowing the wax to drip on the back of his hand. I watch in horror, waiting for a reaction, a flinch or even the tic of his jaw, just exhales and continues to press his thumb into the soft wax dripping down the candle.

"Doesn't that hurt?" I ask.

"No." I watch as the wax cools and he peels it away. There's a faint red blister underneath. Leaning over I press a fingertip to the warm skin and he says, "This is a room for wax play."

"Wax play," I repeat. I'd been in such a rush to get away from the true-crime scene that I didn't even notice. I just thought all the candles were soothing, but of course, like everything else, it's a kink. "You like that?"

He shrugs. "I like a little pain." His eyebrows raise. "Just like you do."

I've never sought pain, I've just taken what's been given to me by men like Davis, Paul, and my stepbrothers. But there's a flicker of curiosity in my belly, the same heat that ran through me as Marcus showed me all of the rooms.

"You like the idea, don't you, little slut," he says, grabbing me and pulling me against his side. In my ear he whispers, "You want to feel the burn?"

"I don't know," I admit truthfully. There's no use lying to him. "What if it hurts?"

His fingers pull at the zipper holding my leotard up and pushes it off my shoulders. The flicker of candlelight is the only thing that clues me onto his movements, and I lurch forward when I feel the first drop hit my shoulder, followed by a steady, hot, rain. "Oh," I cry at the burn. The warmth seeps into my skin, peaking my nipples and settling at my core. "Do it again."

"Ask nicely." He nips at my ear, the sharp sting of the bite adding to the mix.

"*Please*, Davis, do it again."

This time I feel the hot droplets down my back, followed by a soft touch. A kiss? Is he kissing me? Whatever it is, it feels good, and I don't fight when he pushes me on my back and pulls down the leotard, exposing my breasts. I watch as he reaches for a new candle, lighting it off one of the others, the wick sizzling as it flares to life. This time he starts on my chest, splashing droplets of wax over the swells of my tits, each one providing a shock of pain before they slide down my cleavage.

Davis hand pushes between my thighs, feeling the heat through the sheer pants. "Always so fucking wet."

My hips rock upward, seeking something—some kind of relief after days of withholding.

"You're so horny you'd probably let me fuck you with one of these candles, wouldn't you?" Davis asks, leaning forward and dragging his tongue over my nipple. "Oliver still withholding from you?"

"He thinks I don't deserve any pleasure after what I did to Jack."

"And what you did to *me*," he reminds me, mouth moving to my other breast. His teeth clamp down on the nipple and I cry out in pain. "You deserve nothing but torment, little slut." He lifts the lid off of a circular container sitting next to the candles. He pulls out a piece of ice and pops it in his mouth. He takes a fresh candle and holds it over my tits. "This one may sting a little," he says, before slowly dripping wax just over my areolas.

My fingers grip into the fabric of the chaise, bracing myself for the sting of pain. It comes, fresh and raw, blinding over the sensitive skin. "Too much," I cry, chest heaving.

Davis bends, freezing cold mouth latching on with sweet, perverse, relief.

"Jesus, Katie. Never in my wildest dreams would I foresee you becoming this."

"Become what?" I ask, watching him as he flicks the cooled ice off my nipple.

"My darkest fantasy."

My eyes widen at the confession, but he continues to drip hot wax down my belly, watching it dribble and cool over my skin.

"Do you know how much I want to fuck you now? Ignore Oliver's punishment and just fuck you until your pussy clenches around me, milking my cum." He lowers my mesh pants, pulling them over my hips and I think, finally, *finally* someone will take this ache away. "I want you bouncing on my cock, those magnificent tits in my face, calling out my name so that every bastard in this house of depravity hears you."

He pushes my thighs wide, and I'm not embarrassed at how wet I am. I want to get fucked. I want to feel everything he just described. I need his cock inside of me.

"Is that what you want, little slut?"

I nod.

"Oliver will understand, won't he?"

"Y—yes," I stutter, unable to speak in full sentences, but when he moves it's not for his buckle. He goes for a candle and in my lust-fueled haze, I react too slow, screaming when I feel the hot drizzle of wax over the lips of my pussy.

"*No!*" I cry out, the scalding heat blistering the sensitive skin. He bends, blowing air on the cooling wax, and I grab his arm and bite down into the soft flesh of his forearm. He laughs, loving every minute of my pain and long after the wax has cooled, I feel the pulse of the burn between my legs.

"Oh, little slut, when are you going learn that I'm bonded with my brothers. We'll never betray one another. If this pussy is off-limits to one of us, it's off-limits to *all* of us. This," he runs his fingers down the sealed shut slit, "is just a little reminder that your cunt is closed to business." The heat fades quickly, but the burn continues. "Although," he stands, hand on his belt, thumb pushing at the buckle, "No one ever said you can't pleasure me." He drops his pants and his cock bobs heavily. He grabs me by the neck, pulling me forward until his dick slaps me in the face.

"Open wide, Katie, we're not finished until you swallow every last drop."

I take him by the base, guiding his thick cock into my mouth, tasting him on my tongue. I realize this is my life now, my penance, pain, and suffering—servicing.

Davis groans, rocking back on his heels before thrusting to the back of my throat, I don't fight it—not just because I'd agreed to it—but because I want it. I want his cock, I want the pain, I want to feel him explode in my mouth and then consume him.

I want what they want, and Jack confirmed that to me when he gave me the knife.

I'm not just their little sister anymore, I'm one of them, and I'll take everything they give me, including death.

THIRTEEN

Jack

I'VE ADDED PINING NEEDY STALKER TO MY REPERTOIRE.

I'm not proud of it, but as the saying goes, it is what it is.

I park my car across from the grocery store, watching Kate climb out of hers and go inside. My knuckles turn white gripped around the steering wheel as I remind myself for the millionth fucking time why it's bad form to follow her inside.

I'm not this man; one who obsesses over a woman...even if it is my stepsister.

I lift my gaze to the front of the grocery store, watching the automatic doors close behind her and unleash a low, sickening sound before I yank the door handle and step out of the car.

Goddamnit.

The door closes with a thud and I cross the street and cut across the parking lot. There are other cars parked alongside hers. I search for them as I pass. We don't know what kind of car Watkins drives now. It's all for show anyway. Deep down I know it. It isn't the idea of him coming after her that pushes me to watch her.

I just want to.

Shoving my hand in my pocket, I lower my gaze to the ground, tormented by my own fucking realization as I step through the automatic doors and head for the nearest aisle.

The knife I gave her isn't enough. I thought it would be. But what is a knife against someone like Watkins?

Nothing...that's what. If he decides today is the day for retribution, then a slice of steel won't save her, but I will.

I keep to the outside of the store, haunting fruit and vegetables and make my way toward the refrigerators at the rear of the building. Flesh and blood wait, drawing my gaze before I look away.

I walk slowly, glancing down the aisles as I flank the outside of her. I'm a predator in my own right, stalking my prey. Only this one I don't want to hurt or terrorize. No, this one I want to protect with every ounce of my being and the idea of that sends chills down my spine.

I am not the same man I was before. Some would say that prison changed me, but I know different. It's her. It's always been her. My Katie...

I clench my fist in my pockets and grind my jaw as I catch the word, "Slut."

The word is so jarring at first, that I think I misheard. When another comes, I narrow in on the sound.

"Brother fucker."

Sonovabitch.

It's a man's voice. Faintly familiar. I search my mind for a face to match the sound and narrow in. A twitch spasms in the corner of my eye. I know that voice... I hate that voice.

I move a little faster, rounding the end of the aisle of detergent, and looking to the right. Raymond Pressler has my sister pushed up against the corn chips, one hand blocking her escape against the shelving as he crowds her. She has a basket between them, using it as a barrier, but he pushes against it, driving it into her side. "I gotta say, sweetheart, if you're fucking Jack, you must like it rough, too."

The fucker brushes a strand of hair from her face and the sight of that unleashes something savage inside me. No one touches her like that...no one who isn't family.

"Get away from me, you pig." She shoves the basket at him and pushes him away, making her escape toward the front of the aisle and disappears. The dumb-fuck bastard follows her, crowding her steps.

It's a wonder he's alone and not with his asshole buddies Dale Crawford and Sebastian Brooks. I wonder what his prissy little housewife thought of her husband chasing after women in the damn grocery store? I doubt Sophie Pressler cares. The last time I saw her, she was flirting with Oliver in the bar the day after our little sister came home. Now her fucking husband is cornering Kate against the goddamn corn chips.

"Come on, Kate." His voice carries. "Where the fuck are you going?"

I move faster, striding out, my mood darkening as I step around the front of the aisle, but stop short as a cart cuts me off. Anger flares. I jerk my gaze to the person responsible for the intrusion and still. "Mrs Bilford?"

"Is that you, Montgomery?" She squints, peering at me.

I straightened. "No, it's me Jack."

"Jack?"

I look over my shoulder, trying to track the sound of their footsteps as I force the words through clenched teeth. "Yes, Jack Davenport. Now, if you'll excuse me." I step around her, hearing their footsteps fade.

I move fast, hunting. But she's not amongst the freshly baked baguettes and glazed croissants, and neither is he. I glance at the rear of the store and the hallway that leads to the warehouse as Ray disappears.

He's following her.

The bastard is actually fucking following her.

"Why are you running, sweet thing? It's not like you're particular. I have a question, though." His voice carries and the squeal of a door hinge follows. "Did you just sleep with Jack or was Oliver there, too? Is that why they don't date the women in Wilmington? Too busy creeping in their little sister's room at night?"

After the trial, the whole world heard what happened between me and Katie in that cabin. The truth is out there and we can't go back. But that's between me and Katie, not some asshole like Ray. And if he thinks he can use it against her...well, I'll stab the fucker in the face for that alone.

I catch sight of him as he rounds a pallet of fresh produce sitting there ready to be unloaded.

"You're putting out for him. How about a little for me?"

Mother. Fucker.

I see him lunge around a forklift sitting in the middle of the warehouse. He shoves her against a stack of toilet paper. Packages fall to the ground, but he doesn't even notice.

*Hurt him...*the snarling command rises. *Stab the knife I gave you between his goddamn ribs. Show him who you are, Kate.*

But she doesn't do any of those things. Instead, she unleashes a cry as he grabs her arm and slams his body against hers. "You fuck your brothers, so why not me?"

Ray is so focused on my sister that doesn't see me coming. I grab the bastard around the neck and yank him backwards.

"You want to know why?" I snarl. "Because unlike you, I know how to fuck a woman right."

I shove him away. The bastard stumbles backwards. His wide eyes fixed on me. He tries to straighten, to gain his composure to what? To pretend this is all just a mistake?

"Jack. Hey man..."

I don't answer him, just look at her. Her chest expands with a heavy breath...but it's the wide, terrified look in her eyes I settle on. The kind of fear I've seen before in that filthy cabin. Does she think I'm going to murder this asshole?

I want to.

Christ, I want to.

I know just how her terror tastes, too. Salty on goose-bumped skin, heady and slick as she comes hard. Fear turns my little sister on, but I don't want that. I want the rage to unleash her darkness. I wanted savagery to make her fuck and I want to be the one ready for when that moment happens... and it *will* happen.

Just not today.

"Are you okay?" I ask her.

She nods. "Yeah."

"Pressler?" The low growl comes behind me.

I don't need to turn around to know who it is. It seems like the piece of shit bought his pathetic possie, after all. I cut a glare over my shoulder at Sebastian Brooks as he glances from me to Ray. "What's going on here?"

"Yeah, Ray, what the hell is going on here?" I ask, giving him the opportunity to hang himself.

He turns to his friend. "Ray?"

The bastard just brushes the wrinkle from his shirt, looking all pissed now he's cornered. "It's nothing."

I'll take a step forward. "No, it's not nothing. Do you always corner women in public places? Or do you just like to stalk them through grocery stores and call them filthy names?"

"Only the ones who deserve it," he snorts.

And there it is, that jealous, rejected bite in his tone as he looks at my sister. So, he has a thing for Kate? The idea of that would make me smirk if I wasn't slammed with the image of him...all over her.

I slide my hand into my pocket and wrap my hand around the grip of the flick knife as Brooks comes closer. "I'm sure it's just a misunderstanding."

"No." I answer coldly, staring at Pressler. "No misunderstanding."

"Seeing as though you're here," Pressler grins. "How about telling us the truth? How does your sister fuck?"

I slide my hand out and lunge. I press the blade against the side of his neck in a heartbeat. "How about I tell you something different? How about I tell you how it sounds when a man whimpers like a pathic child as he bleeds out? How about I tell you about the last whisper you'll have will be for a mother who can no longer save you?"

He pales...and his knees shake.

I don't look at Kate, but I'm aware of her every movement. She doesn't flinch, doesn't even look at the asshole I have pressed against the stack of paper napkins. She is fixed on me.

"I can definitely tell you how fast it takes for a man to die from a stab wound? All it needs..." I press the edge harder until blood beads and races down the blade. "Is a little pressure."

Pressler isn't game to move or whisper.

His buddy does it for him. "He didn't mean it."

"Stay out of it, Sebastian" I murmur, my focus on Pressler, "or you can be the on the other side of this blade."

He knows now. Sees it in my eyes and it's mirrored back in all its terrifying beauty. He knows how far I'll go to protect her. How a word, or a fucking look her way, will end up with him in a body bag.

"You going to chase her again?" I ask. "Follow her around and harass her?"

"No." The word is a whisper.

"Get the fuck out of here." I ease the blade away. "And if you want to keep tabs on a woman, tell your slutty wife to stop hitting on my brother."

I take a step backwards, but the bastard doesn't move until I lunge and bury the blade into the napkins next to his head. He cries out and his knees buckle, leaving him to hit the concrete floor.

Cold, cutting rage moves through me as Pressler scurries away and pushes to his feet. I stare at the blade burrowed between some ugly floral design as those two fuckers scurry away.

The squeal of the door hinges cuts through as I fight the need to hunt those fuckers down. "The knife." I force the words through gritted teeth. "Next time, use the goddamn knife, Kate."

I yank the blade free, slicing through the napkins as I turn.

"Jack," she calls. "Wait."

Silence is heavy between us. She doesn't like this awkwardness, not when she expects violence. She's prepared for me to fuck her, take her hard, but this... she doesn't understand.

Neither do I.

"No one speaks to you like that." The words feel alien as I speak them. "Not while I'm around." I swallow and meet her eye. "And I'm always around. Remember that."

Then I leave, battling the twitch in the corner of my eye as I make my way out of the warehouse and into the store. Pressler and his asshole buddies are nowhere to be seen. I cut across the parking lot and climb back into my car.

And I wait.

Watching her.

Waiting for her.

Obsessing over her...

FOURTEEN

Kate

____

"Hey," I say, walking into the den. Oliver's playing a video game, eyes focus on the big screen hanging on the wall. The flatscreen is the only thing that's changed since I lived here before—a time capsule of comfortable couches for the boys to hang out.

His eyes dart away from the screen to meet mine. "Hey."

"There's a piece of key lime pie left." I hold up the plate. I've been practicing different desserts for the party coming up. I know Oliver loves key lime pie and saved him an extra piece.

"Seriously?" His eyebrows shoot up his forehead. "God yes, I've been thinking about it since dinner." He pats the couch next to him and I sit.

"Where do you want it?" I ask, then add, "The plate."

His hands are full, fingers moving quickly across the controller. His lip quirks. "You can feed it to me."

It's not a suggestion, it's a command. I see it in the dark glint in his eye. I cut off a piece and hold it to his mouth. He hums and

337

chews slowly. "So good. Tart, but also sweet." He smiles over at me. "It's perfect."

"Thank you," I say, cutting off another small piece. "I'm thinking of making these little shooters for the party with graham cracker at the bottom then pie filling and homemade whipped cream."

"As long as you save me a dozen of them," he says, opening his mouth. I pop in another piece, and he slowly sucks the pie off the fork. My insides warm at his teasing—at his *compliments*. "Jesus, you're a good cook, Katie."

"Well," I say, making sure I get some of the whipped cream with the next piece, "Mom and I were alone before she met Montie. She had to work a lot and I had to learn to cook. Not just for myself, but for her, too, since she was tired when she got home."

He takes the next bite and chews it slowly, savoring it. His eyes are on the game, the light flickering with the changing scenes. I'm surprised when he says, "I miss my mom's cooking."

"You do?" I ask. It's barely a whisper. The boys never talk about their mom—unless it's about revenge. "You remember it?"

"I remember she made an amazing chocolate cake and spaghetti and the best hot dogs around."

I bend and tuck my legs underneath me and rest a hand on his thigh. "I bet she loved cooking for you."

"She took care of us," he says, "I know that. Tucked us in at night, read us books...always made sure I had my blanket."

I've seen pictures of Oliver as a child: white-blond hair, big blue eyes, a ragged blanket always in his hand. "I'm sorry about what happened to her—and you."

His expression tenses. "She's why we do what we do."

I pick up the last piece of pie—mostly crust—and hold it up to him. He looks down and takes a bite, licking my fingertips in the process. He eats until he's finished, until my fingers are licked lean. His tongue is warm, and I ache—not just because I'm horny after so many days of teasing and taunting. I ache for the little boy that lost his mother—who saw her butchered while his brother hid him from danger.

I set the plate to the side and run my hand from his thigh to his, his crotch, rubbing it gently, but I know what he wants—and I think I understand it a little better. Somewhere inside, Oliver is still a little boy who needs soothing, needs someone to take care of him. His breath hitches as I unzip him and pull him out. He never once takes his eyes off the game, or skips a beat on the controller, just lifts his hips so I can reach him better.

"You want me to suck you?" I ask, rolling my finger across the sticky tip.

"Yeah, I do."

He's always sweet about it. He doesn't force me—or maybe it's just that I don't make him. I like the way he feels in my mouth. Maybe, like Oliver, I just need a little soothing of my own. I curl on my side laying my head in his lap, pulling his cock to my lips. He's always erect when we start and gets harder and harder. I know he's denying himself—the same way he's denying me.

I know what he's punishing me for, but what did he do? Why does he think he deserves this pain?

I suck him gently, the way he likes, tugging at the tip, using him like a soothing ring. My body lights on fire, every nerve set on edge, my nipples hard, my pussy wet, but I know better than to try to relieve the desire. What if he takes this away, too?

As if he can hear my thoughts, he drops a hand into my hair and smooths it away from my face. "You're such a good girl," he says, smiling down at me, before going back to his game.

His words of praise do something to me, and I remove him from my mouth, kissing the tip gently. Tilting my head to face him, I ask, "Oliver?"

"Hmmm?" His nose wrinkles at something happening in the game.

"I understand why you're punishing me." I swallow, tasting the salty precum on my tongue. "But can you tell me how long it's going to last?"

He looks down at me, then back at the game, then finally presses the button that pauses the action on the screen. He focuses his attention on me, his hand sliding down my head to settle on my neck. His thumb strokes the hollow of my throat.

"I know you're trying," he says. "You've been attending therapy with Paul, going undercover with Davis, and keeping things civil with Jack. You're very attentive to my needs." He licks his bottom lip. "I've noticed how much you've taken on in the house, but you haven't earned the right of pleasure, Katie. Not yet." His thumb applies the slightest bit of pressure. "You caused a lot of pain when you turned in Jack and as much as I wish that I could, I can't guide you down the path of absolution for your sins. You've got to figure that out on your own."

His eyebrows raise, wanting me to tell him that I understand, but every frayed nerve in my body wants me to hop on his dick and ride him until I soothe the aching desire that has overtaken my body. In the end, though, the words that come out of my mouth are, "I understand."

"I don't think it'll be much longer, Katie. I think you're going to do the right thing."

"What if I can't figure out what the right thing is?"

"I believe in you, because deep down you're a Davenport and this family... we're strong and resilient. We take care of one another."

He runs his thumb over my bottom lip and parts my mouth, lifting his cock to press inside. Once I've got him between my lips, he twitches eagerly but just exhales deeply before going back to his game. As much as I hate myself for it, hot tears burn at the corner of my eyes. It's more frustration than anything else and I pull him closer, needing the feel of him in my mouth.

Oliver has faith in me, which means I can figure this out.

Maybe I can make my stepbrothers forgive me.

THE IDEA COMES to me in the shower, mid-shampoo. I barely get the soap out before I climb out of the tub, wrap a towel around my body and run up the stairs. I'm out of breath when I fling open Oliver's door.

"What the hell, Katie?" he asks, eyes roaming down my body. Water pools at my feet and I pretend not to notice that he's cleaning a very sharp knife.

"Get dressed," I tell him. "And meet me downstairs in ten minutes." I take in his T-shirt and shorts. "Wear something sexy."

I leave before he can ask more, rushing back to my room to change.

I dress quickly, changing into one of the black dresses the guys gave me and a pair of thigh-high boots. When I get to the foyer Oliver is in a black button-down and dark jeans. He's also not alone. Jack stands next to him in a tight dark gray sweater, his hair damp and combed.

"What—" I start, but Oliver cuts me off.

"Wherever we're going, Jack's going with us."

"What's this about?" Jack shrugs on his leather jacket.

"Combining what we do best—hunting and investigating."

Oliver's eyebrow raises. "You have a lead?"

"Where?" Jack asks, his tone hard and suspicious.

My heart thuds in my chest. I know that once I lead us down this road, it's truly going to happen. I'll become one of them and there will be no turning back. As I open the door and lead them into the night, the truth burns in my chest; I won't become one of them. I *already* am one of them.

JACK MAKES a call to Davis and soon we're downtown, looking for the right building.

"This is it," Oliver says, peering out the window to get a good look at the building. He glances over at his brother. "Remember the last time we were here?"

"Yeah." His jaw clenches. "It's where we found that fucker that'd been killing hookers."

Oliver eyes flick to the rearview mirror, meeting mine. "You think we can get some information here."

"Yeah, I do."

It's an old hotel—a landmark. The Wilmington Inn. A half-century ago it was where wealthy people stayed when they came to town. Then it became a flop house for prostitution and one-night stays. Now, according to Davis, it's under renovation to become a permanent location for Club Hades.

It's where I hope to find Marcus.

They probably wouldn't have believed me on my own, but since Davis agreed it was a solid lead, they've been cooperative. "I met this guy the other night at one of his locations. He was really chatty and took me on a tour." I tell them about the different rooms, including the cabin. Jack doesn't react at all when I reveal that detail—doesn't move an inch—but my heart pounds so loud I wonder if they can hear it. "He didn't know who I was—I had on a wig and gave him a fake name, but I got the feeling he knew a lot about what happened at the cabin, which makes me think he may know more about the Watkins brothers than he let on."

Oliver and Jack share a look and Oliver says, "It's better than anything else we have."

"Okay." Jack turns to face me, his leather jacket creaking as he moves. "But you stay close. No games. No manipulations."

"I'm here for the same thing you are, big brother, don't worry about that."

It just slipped out—supposed to be sarcastic—but his eyes darken at the words, 'big brother' and my heart lunges into my throat. I do the only thing I can, I exit the car and pretend it never happened.

Oliver and Jack follow and at the entrance, Oliver steps ahead of me to open the door. It leads to a lobby, renovated to fit the time period of the building, 1920s art deco. Everything, from the light fixtures to the carpets and furnishings fit the vibe. There's a front desk, and a woman positioned behind it.

"May I help you?" she asks, eyes skipping over me to my brothers.

"We're looking for Marcus. Is he here?"

Her gaze slides back over, smile firmly in place. "And you are?"

I start to say my name but then remember he doesn't know it. I swallow it back and say, "Ashley. Tell him it's Ashley. From the other night."

"Just a moment."

She picks up an old-fashioned phone handle off the desk and slowly dials.

A hand settles on my lower back. Oliver leans in and asks, "Ashley?"

"We were undercover."

"Excuse me, but there's a woman here to see you. Her name is Ashley. She says—" her eyes meet mine. "Yes. Of course. I'll send them right up." She hangs up. "He'll meet you on the mezzanine."

She points in the direction of a wide staircase, to a level with an open balcony. The boys let me take the lead, which is a weird feeling, but it's also nice to know for once they're at my back. I have no idea what I'm walking into. Marcus has proven he's into some dark things—how far does it go?

I see him the instant I reach the top of the steps. He's as handsome as I remember, maybe even more so in this softer light. His forehead creases when he sees me, confused at first. I remember I look different—no wig. More clothes. That doesn't keep him from raking his gaze down my body, taking me in, inch by inch.

"Ashley?"

"Yes," I say, but then add, "and no. I'm the person you know as Ashley, but my name is Kate. Kate Stevenson." I glance at Oliver and Jack. "These are my stepbrother's the—"

"Davenport's." Marcus steps forward with an outstretched hand. "I know who you are." He shakes Oliver's hand first and then turns to Jack. "I followed your case." He looks between me and Jack, recognition clicking into place. "Then that means you're the sister that—"

"Recanted my testimony. Yes."

"—fucked your brother next to a dead body."

Jack stiffens next to me, and Oliver takes a step closer. Marcus holds up his hands and grins. "There's no judgment here. Not in Hades. Not from me. Everyone has that dirty little forbidden fantasy. You two actually claimed yours."

My skin heats, but this isn't why we're here. I clear my throat and say, "We're not here about our...relationship. We're here looking for some information about The Binder."

"The Binder? He's dead." He looks at Jack. "You killed him."

"I killed Ryan Watkins," Jack says, "who was a raping, murdering son of a bitch, but he's not the only one."

"We're looking for his brother, Christopher," Oliver says. "We heard a rumor he frequents your club."

"Do you know him?" I ask.

"I do know Christopher," he says. "And you're right. He is a regular. Although, I haven't seen him recently."

"Tell us everything you know about him," Jack demands. "Everything."

Marcus looks at my stepbrother and smiles. "It's possible that I have some information that may be of interest to you."

Relief washes over me. "Thank you, I can't tell you how much it means—"

He interrupts. "For the right price."

"How much?" Jack reaches into his pocket and pulls out a fat clip of cash.

"You misunderstand," Marcus says. "I don't want your money. I want you."

"Us," Oliver says.

"Your unique and eclectic relationship to one another. It's a perfect representation of Hades." He starts walking, gesturing for us to follow. Both Oliver and Jack look hesitant, but I know we have no choice. We've reached a dead end on Christopher and I'm tired of being the bait. When I look back again, they've started following us. Marcus speaks as we walk. "I have a group of potential capitalists coming tonight that want to see what they're investing in. I'd planned on just taking them on a tour, but you may be able to provide me with something more valuable."

"What is that?" Jack asks, now walking next to me.

"A show." He stops outside a pair of ornate doors.

"I don't understand," I say. "What kind of show?"

"My job—my *passion*—is fulfilling fantasies. The three of you...you have something burning inside of you. I smelled the embers on you the minute you cleared those stairs. I'll give you the opportunity to fulfill that need, give my investors what they want, and in the end, I'll send you away with the information you need."

"How do we trust that you have the information we need?" Oliver asks.

"I know everything about everyone that enters my club." Marcus looks at me. "Why do you think I showed you around? You gave me everything I needed to get to know you better. What interests you—what doesn't. What turns you on." He smirks. "You think it was an accident you and your friend ended up in that wax room together?"

Heat burns my cheeks and I ignore the way my stepbrothers assess me. I never told them what happened. I guess Davis didn't either.

"You like pain, Kate," Marcus says.

"W-why do you say that?"

"You wouldn't have come back to Wilmington, to your stepbrothers, if you didn't."

The statement hits hard, and I have no idea how to respond. He's right. I do like pain, there's no denying that anymore, but whatever he wants us to do, I know it won't happen. My brothers won't allow it.

Except...

"What exactly do you want us to do?" Oliver asks.

Marcus grins, showing bright white teeth. He opens the double doors and reveals a theater. Rows of seats on a slight incline, ending with a stage at the bottom of the slope. "This room has had many uses. During prohibition, illegal drinks were sold behind the bar. After that a gentleman's club, with a burlesque show. Then during the shitty days, a strip club. I'm bringing it back as a way to showcase what Hades does best, fetishes."

"So what?" Jack asks, nodding at the stage. "You want us to fuck up there?"

"You know," Marcus says, tilting his head as he assesses the three of us. "I'm going to leave that up to you. Whatever feels authentic between the three of you. I'm not about force." He chuckles. "Well, not if that's not your thing. I'd rather be surprised anyway."

"Um," I say, needing a minute, "can we talk about it first?"

"Of course. I have a few calls to make." He pulls at the door handle and steps back into the mezzanine.

Once we're alone I face Oliver and Jack. Neither look happy and if they're going to take their irritation out on anyone, it'll be me.

"I'm sorry," I say. "I had no idea it would go this way. We should get out of here."

"He's a smart guy," Oliver says. Jack grunts in agreement. "He's got leverage."

"I'm surprised Dad isn't one of his investors. It's a good business plan."

I blink, trying to process what is happening.

"Are you serious?" This is where my brothers confuse me. I thought they'd be pissed but... they're impressed? "You want to do this?"

"We want the information, Katie. Isn't that why we're here?" Jack asks.

"Yes, but—" Oh god. They want to do it. They want to get on a stage and let them do whatever they want to me. *Fuck.*

"Nothing comes free, little sister," Jack says, "you know that."

"What about the fact that I'm being punished?" I blurt. "You've been denying me pleasure for weeks. You're just going to give that up?"

Oliver steps closer, closing the distance until we're only a few inches apart. His hand cups the side of my cheek. "Remember how I told you that you'd figure out a way?"

I swallow and nod. "Yes."

"It's a tradeoff, one we're willing to make. You give Marcus what he wants, and he gives us what *we* want, then maybe...we can finally give you what you *need*."

Heat rushes through me, landing hot and wet between my legs. If I wasn't so desperate, I'd run. But I am. I'm desperate for the information. I'm desperate to get back in my brother's good graces, but most of all, I'm desperate for release.

And I guess now I'll see if they'll finally let me have it.

FIFTEEN

Oliver

Marcus led us backstage and left us in a changing
room with makeup mirrors and a closet full of costumes. Jack
picks through the clothes, passing by the leather and heels, away
from the dresses and corsets. He pulls out four pieces. A white
lace bra and panty set, a white button-down, and a plaid
schoolgirl skirt that has barely enough fabric to cover her ass. He
drops a pair of sheer thigh-high stockings on top and grunts at
her to get dressed.

"You sure you're okay with this?" I ask, putting on a dress shirt
and tie. Yeah, we're dressing up, too. It's fetish-play, Marcus
explained. We're either all in or the deal is off.

"It's fine." He strips off his shirt and pulls a football jersey over
his broad chest. I get a flashback to high school when Jack was a
first-stringer. There were scouts around but he wasn't
interested. The mission always came first. And I know, even
though my balls ache when I look over at Katie and see her
adjusting that tiny skirt, that this is what tonight is about, too:
the mission.

It's just that exhibitionism is my thing. Although with the way my brother creeps around the secret passages in the house, I think he's got more of a voyeuristic kick than he'd like to admit.

"How far do we want to take this?" I ask.

"I don't know, Ollie. You ready to fuck her or are you still playing petty games?"

My punishment of Katie isn't a game, but my brother rules more with brawn than his mind. I want her compliant. Hungry. So strung out she'll do whatever we want. I need her to know her weakness—and that there's no one out there that can fulfill her needs like we can. There's a method to my madness, but tonight is different. Anything goes.

Jack's hand comes down on my shoulder. "You got me out. You got her to cooperate. This is on you. Whatever you want, baby brother. I'll follow your lead."

Across the room Katie bends over, flashing those white panties and slides on a pair of saddle oxfords. My dick gets painfully hard and Jack's body tenses.

That's the little sister we remember. The one prancing around the house taunting us in her school uniform. The one unaware of how much she was driving us crazy with her flowery scent and soft skin. The one barging upstairs, catching us, forcing us to enact vengeance.

Jack mutters, "Fuck," and turns to me. "I just want to be inside her when I come. I don't care what hole."

I nod and we bump fists, deal in motion. He walks into the bathroom and shuts the door.

Fully dressed, Katie walks over, twisting her hair into braids. "How dumb does this look?" she asks. "I feel like an idiot."

"You don't look like an idiot," I say, eyes glued to the low cut of her shirt. The white bra lifts her tits into the most fuckable cleavage. Jesus. "You look hot. Sexy."

She looks up at me, eyes big. "You think?"

"Every teenage boy's fantasy."

She gives me a long look and then walks over to the dressing table, sitting down to finish her hair and makeup. I watch her, unable to stop thinking about that night and what happened between us all those years ago. The night everything went to hell.

I watched as my brother, Paul, and Davis jerked off and dumped their cum on Katie, filling her mouth, coating her face. When it was my turn, I froze, cock hard in my hand, but unable to go through with it. It was fucking stupid. I wanted it—God how much I wanted *her*—but that was the thing. I wasn't content jerking off and walking away. I wanted her to be *mine*. I was in love with my stepsister.

As I watch her apply eye makeup, the night comes rushing back to me...

After I left Jack's room, I heard the guys go downstairs, leaving Katie to clean herself up. She entered my bathroom and I stood on the other side of the door, listening as she cried with deep heaving sobs.

Her cries tugged at me, pulled at the threads of my heart, and even though I knew Jack would be pissed I opened the door. She was sitting on the floor, still sticky with cum. A mess, physically and emotionally. I grabbed a clean washcloth and ran it under the faucet.

"I'm sorry," she said when I couched down, curling toward the wall. "I shouldn't have come up here—in here. J-Jack told me to clean up and..."

"I'm not mad," I told her. I hold out the cloth and wipe the sticky residue off her cheek. It took a few minutes, some dried quickly, but got her clean and helped her to her feet. In the vanity drawer, I found a new toothbrush and handed it to her. "Brush," I said, and left the room. I returned a moment later with a T-shirt. One of mine. Across the front, it said, Wilmington Soccer, with a ball flying across the chest. My heart pounded as she pulled it over her head, standing in front of me looking small and lost.

"You need to go back to your room and keep your mouth shut. This never happened." I was sure my brother already warned her, but I needed her to understand. She could never tell anyone what happened. The consequences would be devastating; for both of us.

She hesitated and whispered, "What if they find me again?" Another wave of tears built in her eyes. "What if I see Mom or Montie, and they ask what I'm doing?"

I frowned—neither of those would end well. "Fine. You can stay up here."

She looked across the room, past the messy video games and school work, and soccer equipment. "In your bed?"

I almost said that I'd sleep somewhere else, but that flicker of heat still burned deep in my balls. I wanted Katie in my bed. I wanted her to choose me. Maybe this was how I made that happen.

"It'll be okay," I promised. "I can protect you if they come back."

My cock thickened as I watched her climb in my bed, white panties peeking out from under my shirt. I got in next to her, pulled up the cover, and turned off the light. In the dark I heard her soft cries, sniffing back the tears.

"Hey," I said, caught in a war of emotions. "Come here." I pulled her to my chest, and I wrapped my arms around her. "It's going to be okay."

She shook her head, but didn't speak, just pressed her tight body into mine. I ran my fingers down her hair, smoothing it off her neck. The skin was warm, smooth and I pressed my lips softly against the flesh. "I won't let them hurt you, again."

I waited for a response, for her to run or to turn and slap me. She did neither, just gripped my arm closer and pushed her ass into my throbbing crotch. I kissed her again, this time on the jaw, another on the cheek. I rose until I was over her, kissing the soft swell of her lips. Her mouth parted and she opened for me, and my heart pounded against my chest so hard I thought it may break free.

Katie wanted me, too.

It should have stopped there, but then I saw the panel that led to the secret passageway in the wall open, the one my brother used to spy on everyone in the house. The one we hid in the day my mother was killed. In the dark of the room, our eyes met. His shone with pride. With expectation. Even though I was scared out of my mind, I knew what I had to do.

I ran my hand down her side, grazing her breast, and pushed up her shirt. "Can I?" I asked, looking down at her tits.

They were soft and full and in the dark, I heard, "Okay."

I almost came in my pants when I touched them for the first time, my balls about to explode. I conjured up the porn we'd been watching, all the stories Jack and Davis told about girls they fucked and I dropped my mouth to her nipple and sucked. Underneath me, Katie moaned.

Jesus Christ.

I took it further, sliding my hand down her flat belly, pushing my fingers under the cotton of her panties. I felt the damp heat between her legs—she's wet—my brother would have called it. Soaked. It meant she wanted me. In her ear, I whispered, "Can I put it in you?"

She stiffened, thighs clamping around my hand. "I don't know."

If I'd been alone in that room, I would have stopped, been happy with what she'd given me, but my brother was watching. He'd never let me live it down. "We don't have to," I said, "but you know they're not going to stop until one of us does it. Jack won't let it go. Neither will Davis. You let me...then I can tell them to leave you alone."

She turned to face me, eyes shining in the pale light. "You'll make them leave me alone?"

"I promise."

I'd wanted to take my time, but the instant she gave me the go-ahead, I yanked down her panties and slotted myself against her pussy. It was clumsy and fast but, Jesus, it felt so goddamn good when I pushed inside of her. When she cried out in pain, I covered her mouth with my hand, telling her, "Shhh, quiet. If they hear you, they'll come in." I thrust in, pushing past that tight, almost impenetrable barrier. "It won't take long. Just," thrust, "let," thrust, "me," thrust, "in..."

I came quick, fast, too early, but finally. I wasn't a virgin anymore, and I'd proved myself to my brother and...well, I was with the girl that I loved and now...now she'd be mine.

Except, she started crying again, and this time when she got out of the bed, leaving a stain of blood on the sheets. She ran out the door, not caring who saw her or who knew. Two days later, shit hit the fan and she was gone.

Until she came back.

"They're ready." A hand lands on my shoulder. "Are you?"

I turn to face my brother, who is undoubtedly remembering that first time too, when I ran. There's no running tonight. Not for poor Katie. I'm no longer that scared little kid. I'm a man who has spent the last few weeks denying himself the pleasure of release. This may not be the way I thought I'd break her punishment but when she looks at the two of us from across the room, her eyes wide with worry, I know it's right—for all of us.

THE SET-UP FEELS STRANGELY intimate with a large bed in the middle of the stage and dozens of candles surrounding the area, giving it a warm, sexy glow. Katie waits for us, lying on her stomach, flipping through a magazine, playing the innocent teenager. The only thing amiss is the swell of her ass and those godforsaken white panties, peeking out from underneath.

If there's really a crowd out there it's hard to know. Bright lights shine down from the ceiling, making it impossible to see past the glare, and music plays from hidden speakers, blocking out any noise. The truth is that I'm only focused on the girl in front of me, proving to her and every perverted asshole in the room who she belongs to: The Davenports.

Jack and I circle the bed, but I approach her first. "Hey, little sister."

"Hey," she looks up at the two of us and I notice the shiny red sucker in her mouth. Fuck, every inch of this is a cliché, and every part of my dick just got bigger. "What do you want?"

"Just wanted to see how you're doing." I sit on the edge of the bed and reach out, tugging at the hem of her skirt. It barely moves. There isn't a centimeter of extra fabric, but it's just an excuse to touch her. "How was school today?"

She sits up, flashing her ass and pussy when she does it. "It was okay."

Jack towers over the bed. "Did something happen?"

She shrugs. "Some kids were making fun of me."

"For what?" I ask, falling into the role play a little bit more.

"Being a virgin."

Over her head, my eyes meet Jack's. Jesus. It's like she plucked it straight out of our fantasies.

"It's not like I want to be," she continues, toying with a button on that low-cut shirt. "It's just...who wants to have sex with me? I don't even have a boyfriend."

"Little sister," Jack says, lifting her chin with her fingers. "Do you know how many times I've jerked off thinking about you? This week alone? How many times have I thought about coming into your room at night and pulling those white panties off of you and claiming you?" She swallows and shakes her head. His fingers drop, running along her throat, down her chest, and between the V in her shirt to her cleavage. "Dozens of times. Sometimes twice a day."

"You do?" Her voice is innocent, but Jack and I both know he's not exaggerating. I've noticed the extra showers. The amount of time he spends in his room. The hours he goes missing in the walls, creeping around, watching her while she sleeps.

"I can assure you the other guys at school are, too."

Her eyes widen. "I don't know. No one seems interested."

I laugh. "They're interested they just—"

"Ollie," Jack warns. He knows where this is going, but there's no reason not to tell her the truth.

"None of the guys seem interested in you because we've told them not to date you."

"What?" She rises to her knees. "Why would you do that?"

I grab her hand. "Because you're ours, Sis. And if we can't have you, no one else can either."

"Y-you..." she stammers, but there's a dose of reality here. A truth that can't come out unless we're playing a game, and Katie knows it. "You don't mean that."

"We do," Jack says, grabbing her by the shoulders. He's still standing and even though she's on the bed, on her knees, he towers over her. "You belong to us, Katie." His hand runs down her back to squeeze her ass. "Body, mind, and soul."

"I didn't know. I thought you hated me," she admits.

"We hate the fact we can't have you," I say, knowing Jack never would confess. Katie bites down on her bottom lip, worrying the pink, plump flesh. Her fingers lift to her blouse, toying with that button again. "But what if you could?"

"Is that what you want?" Jack asks, taking her hand and pressing it against the front of his pants. "Is this what you want?"

She nods, coy and sweet, but with enough conviction that a switch flips between us, the three of us all in sync. Jack and I descend on her, kissing her mouth and her neck. Katie moans from our attention, goosebumps rising on her flesh. Jack pulls at her shirt, the buttons straining and then popping off, scattering across the bed, then removes his own. Her hands land on his chest, running down his hard muscles and I push my fingers under her panties, yanking them down to her knees. While my brother massages her tits, I get the panties off and push my fingers between her legs.

Always wet.

"What are you going to do?" she asks, voice a quiet whisper.

"I'm going to fuck you so hard you see stars," Jack says, spinning her around. He pushes her forward, and she lands against my chest, her face inches from my own. "And you're going to suck Ollie off until you choke on his cum."

She looks down at me, at the hard bulge in my pants that strains to be freed. "We're doing this then. In front of all these people?"

"What people?" I ask, kissing her mouth. "It's just you, me, and Jack."

She nods. Over her shoulder, Jack lowers his jeans, his belt buckle clinking as it hits the floor. I push down my pants, my cock bobbing with relief as it lets loose. Katie reaches for me, but hisses, signaling the moment my brother has pushed his cock between her legs. I look down and see the tip, gliding in the slick heat of her pussy, getting wet.

She and I reposition, me on my knees, her on all fours. This way, he can reach her, and she can reach me. My spine seizes the moment her tongue touches the head, the instant her mouth takes me in, I know this is different for us. It's not about soothing, or nursing. It's not about taking care of one another. This is about our primal instinct—the need to get off and fuck. To *claim*.

And that's what I do. I grab her by the back of the head and fuck her face. I know the moment Jack slams into her. She gasps, breath hot around my cock. She's stunned by the force of him, and it allows me to go in deeper, pushing to the hilt.

This is what I always wanted. What we always wanted. The two of us filling her at once. Pumping her full of cock and cum. Owning Katie, the two of us, balls deep.

The world falls away as we succumb to one another. Jack hovering over us, one hand on her hip, the other around her throat. I reach down and grab her tit, taking the nipple between my fingers and twisting hard. She cries out, jaw slack, and I go in deeper. Katie's eyes water at the intrusion, but she doesn't resist. She's been wanting my cock like this ever since I picked her up on that side road, begging me to save her.

I allow Jack to set the pace and he hammers into her until his spine goes rigid. "Hold on, baby," he says, tightening his hold on her hips. She looks up at me, mouth full as he groans, spilling into her. "Jesus Christ, she's tight."

"You feel him in you?" I ask, pulling out just enough for her to answer. "You feel that cum you've been begging for, little sis?"

"Yes." Her gaze holds mine. "I want to taste you, Ollie."

I run the tip over her swollen lips, then push it back in. "Don't you fucking dare waste one drop, understand me?"

She nods and it only takes a few more thrusts before I groan, hot jerky spurts of cum filling her cheeks. She sucks me off, taking every last drop, her neck muscles rippling as she swallows.

Jack pulls out, his body slick with sweat. When I'm spent, I do the same, removing my dick from her mouth. She doesn't move, just stays on all fours panting to catch her breath. I see a thick drop of white fluid drip down her leg. Jack and I share a look, it's time to give our sister what she's been begging for.

"Come on," Jack says, pulling her against him.

"What are you doing?" she asks, as he cradles her against his chest. I center myself between her legs and spread her thighs with my hands. Jack's fingers run down her sides and rest above her knees, holding her wide. Her pussy is wet, red, and swollen, sticky with my brother's cum. I rub my fingers along the dripping fluid, scooping it back up.

"Not one drop," I remind her, bending and kissing her inflamed pussy, pushing the cum back in her cunt with my tongue. Jack's semen is salty, thick, and tangy against the taste of her pussy. She moans, fingers thrust in my hair, hips rising to meet my mouth. She fucks against me, desperate, body quivering with want. Jack's hands reach for her folds, and he holds her open for me and I lick and suck until she's crying, "Stop, god, please stop, I can't—oh god, I can't—oh god..." while never letting go of my head. The groan that follows reverberates in my chest, deep and feral. Against my tongue, I feel the result of a woman teased and taunted—*denied*—to a place of no return.

I don't move away until she's finished riding it out, her thighs going slack and her breath turning steady. The three of us lie on the bed, trying to regain function. My jaw hurts from eating her out and I'm sure she can say the same. I look up at her wanting to say something—do something—but then the music shifts and the curtain falls, and I remember where we are and what we're doing.

Jack rises first, lifting Katie off his chest. "I'll go find Marcus. For that, he owes us every goddamn piece of information he has."

He bends, grabbing his jeans off the floor and walks toward the back of the stage.

My eyes meet Katie's for a quick moment before looking away. Information, that's what this was about.

The mission.

It's always about the mission.

SIXTEEN

Jack

______

THE INFORMATION MARCUS HAS BETTER BE FUCKING
worth it.

Not that fucking Katie was a hardship. God, I'd been dreaming
about it for weeks, feeling her warm pussy again, watching her
as she trembled with ecstasy. But this wasn't how I wanted to do
it, not with the three of us being put on display like that. It's
evidence of how desperate we've become to find any scrap of
information about Watkins that I'm willing to allow the three of
us to be put in a position like that.

Tossing the football jersey into the corner of the room, I grab my
clothes and yank on my trousers and shirt. "I'll deal with
Marcus," I say, as the two change back into their clothes. My
eyes skim Katie's naked body, cock twitching at the sight. She
makes no effort to hide. After what just happened between us,
all pretenses of modesty are gone. "Get your stuff and meet me
at the car."

I leave before they can argue, but I don't need to be around
either of them right now. My body pulses, ticking like a bomb
from being balls deep inside Katie. It was the first time I'd had

sex since being in prison, still, it barely scratched the itch where she's concerned. And watching her get her pussy devoured by Oliver?

Jesus.

I had no fucking clue how hot that would be.

Running my hand over my face, I try to get my shit together before I approach Marcus to finish our business. Voices drift down the hall and I catch a feminine tone as I round the corner. "Is he for sale?"

"Jenna," Marcus' voice carries. "*Everyone* is for sale; it just depends on the price."

I grind my jaw and stride toward him, both of their heads turning my way. The woman is the first to smile and coy interest flares in her eyes. Her tits push at the neckline of her blue dress, their exceptional buoyancy giving away the fact she bought them for a pretty penny.

"You're just delicious, aren't you?" she purrs.

Delicious?

"Jackson," Marcus says, voice oozing with charm, "That was an outstanding performance this evening. Very...enthusiastic. I'd like you to meet Jenna Kilpatrick. One of our potential investors."

"Name your price," she whispers, dragging her gaze down to stop at my cock. "Whatever it is, it'll be worth it."

Any other time I might be smug from the attention. But not tonight, especially with my sister's cum still cooling around my cock. "I don't think so."

She smiles, teeth white against her red lipstick. "That was an impressive show," she says, running a sharp, manicured nail down my forearm. "Your body is exquisite. So powerful. I could feel the tension all the way in my seat."

I don't give a shit how this woman feels about my 'performance.' All I want is what we came for, but as the saying goes, you get more flies with honey than vinegar, so I give her a smile and say, "Thank you, ma'am, but unfortunately, my services aren't for sale."

"Oh," she pouts. "That's too bad. I was going to pay double your regular fee since you're a celebrity."

Celebrity?

Then I realize it: the murder trial.

"I don't have a fee, but if I did, I don't think you'd want to pay it."

The rock on her wedding finger tells me that whomever she's married to is rich as fuck. She's probably used to buying and selling whatever and whomever she wants. My threat doesn't deter her, and she leans forward, now gripping my arm. "I'm happy to pay for your brother as well, even if he isn't like you."

"Like me?" I ask.

"A natural-born killer."

I snort. If she only knew, but it clicks. She's attracted to the killer in me. The hunter. This woman is a goddamn fool.

"Sorry, Jenna," I reply, gently removing her hand. "Tonight was a one-time thing."

"Don't be too quick to turn her down," Marcus says, eyes greedy like he's planning to get a cut. "You *were* a natural out there. All three of you."

Because it had been a genuine moment. I'd been dying to get my hands, and cock, back in Katie again. No one makes me feel like she does and tonight proved it. Her pussy is divine and now that I've had it again, I just want it more.

"As flattering as that is. It's time to settle our business." I give Marcus a hard look. "*Now*."

He gives a small laugh and shrugs. "If you'll excuse me, Jenna."

"Oh?" She takes the rejection well, her smile widening. "Pity. Well, Marcus knows how to get in touch with me if you ever change your mind. And I *do* hope you will change your mind, Jack."

I turn to Marcus with a clenched jaw. He gives a nervous smile in return, finally realizing my patience is waning. "Yes, well. If you'll please excuse us."

Marcus leads me to a shell of an office where there's a desk in the middle of a room and two cheap chairs on the other side.

"Sorry about the furniture." He gives a wave of his hand. "We're still decorating."

Now that we're alone, my patience has reached the limit for pleasantries. I'm silent, trying my best not to stab the fucker in the side of his neck and watch him bleed out on this bare concrete floor. "The information about Christopher Watkins," I say, forcing the name through clenched teeth. "And I'm telling you now, this better be fucking good. Or you can expect another performance from me, one more suited to my particular skill set."

His breath catches and he gives a slow nod of his head. I know he's smart. He's a successful businessman. Hades is a brilliant idea. The last thing he needs is a setback while all those investors are still in the building. He licks his lips and pushes past me, heading to a file cabinet in the corner of the room.

Metal grinds as he yanks open a drawer and extracts a thick file before placing it on the desk. I grow cold, staring at it as he flips open the cover and pushes the contents aside. He wasn't lying about having information. "We keep dossiers on our guests, both current and previous. Club Hades prides itself on crafting a distinctive, personalized experience. The only way to do that is by knowing everything about the people who require our services."

"Sounds like you're justifying invading your customers' privacy."

"Not at all. We do thorough background checks on our members who have more... exotic desires. For safety and liability reasons. We need everyone to feel secure when they walk through the door of our establishment. Christopher's check revealed several holdings—properties—some of which I'm sure you're aware of, but my associates don't stop on the surface. I specifically remember that he owned a parcel of land..." he pulls out another file, "it's owned by a trust."

The hair on the back of my neck rises. "Where?"

"A warehouse in the Grange Point District. I didn't realize the importance at the time." He grabs a small piece of paper. "Ah. Here it is."

He hands it over, but right before I take it, he snatches it back. His eyes are wild and cunning.

The bastard is a snake. I knew that. I didn't know how much until now. His eyes glint, his cheeks are flushed underneath a pale pallor. He's nervous and excited.

"Give me the address," I tell him, hand reaching for the gun at the small of my back. Marcus stumbles back when he sees the weapon. "I'm not in the mood for games."

"Wait!" Marcus' hands fly in the air, palms forward. "I just want to make an offer," he says with a rush. "The house from last night hasn't been cleaned out. I can take you there if you like. I'm sure you'd love the room I showed your sister. Maybe the two of you can relive your fantasies?" His head tilts. "On camera this time?"

The room designed like the cabin—the one that sent Katie into a panic. I jerk my gaze to his. Hunger and violence ignite inside me like a Molotov cocktail. I lunge at him, driving him back against the desk. "You want to torture my sister? Make her go through the pain and terror again."

"Isn't that her kink? Pain? Because I know that she and her friend had fun in the wax room right after."

Heat wells in my chest. Katie does get off on pain. Paul's been testing her for weeks. It makes her hot and horny, but that side of her belongs to us. It's never going to be used for someone else's pleasure. "You'd like that, wouldn't you?"

"Yes," he answers, breathlessly. "Desperately."

I clench my fist, forcing myself not to pull out my gun. Marcus is a sick son of a bitch, but as much as I want to hurt the bastard, I know he can be useful. He has dirt on everyone—a treasure trove of information. I press forward, making his spine bow backward until he's almost laying on his desk. I lash out, and snatch the address from his hand.

"Let me explain something to you," I say, so close I can smell his expensive aftershave, bought from exploiting the perversion of others. "The Davenports are not the family to fuck with. Not me, not my brother, and definitely not my sister. Not if you want this hotel of depravity to stay open. I'm happy to come through here and pick off one deviant at a time, exposing them the way you exposed me." He trembles under me. It would be so, so, easy to get rid of him right here. Right now. To watch the blood drain from his face. But that's not what I'm here for. It's not the mission.

He doesn't check the boxes.

Instead, I grind out, "Do you understand?"

He nods. "Yes."

"Good."

I stuff the paper in my pocket and head outside, finding Ollie and Katie waiting for me. I want to say I've calmed down by the time I'm outside but the way my brother eyes me, I know he can tell. "Everything okay? You got it?"

I glance at Katie with her red lips and her flushed face. Kate, who I can still feel clamping around my cock as my brother filled that beautiful mouth full of come. Christ, I'm getting hard again already. I lift the piece of paper in my hand. "I've got an address."

"*His* address?" Katie asked, avoiding his name.

I give a slow nod. "*An* address, yeah. Some additional property. He could be hiding out there."

"I'll call Davis." Ollie takes the paper out of my hand and pulls out his cell as he turns away to make the call.

Katie comes closer, her expression wary. "You look...something." She tilts her head. "Worried?" She glances back at Hades and says carefully. "Should we be worried?"

I know what she's asking even as her focus moves to my hands. She's searching for a sign that I had resorted to violence, concerned that I killed Marcus and left him bleeding out in his office. Our little sister knows me too well. "No," I answer. "You shouldn't."

"Davis is going to do some research and a little recon," Ollie says after he hangs up. "We'll go tomorrow night."

As much as I want to go now and end this once and for all, I know it's foolish. We're strung out from what Marcus put us through, emotionally and physically. Watkins is savvy. He's eluded us this far and I'm not walking in there without a plan. I get in the driver's seat and Oliver sits next to me, but my eyes are trained on Katie as she gets in the back. *Should we be worried?* Yes, they should be. I'd murdered to keep her safe before.

But this...

This what feel is far beyond anything I'd ever experienced before. It's dangerous. Dark, even for me. It's consuming my soul. I don't start the car. I sit there, staring at the wheel until Ollie asks carefully, "Jack? You okay?"

I look his way, then to the rearview mirror where I catch her eye. "I'm fine. I'm just ready for this to be over."

She doesn't speak, but knowledge passes between us.

She's ready for this to be over, too.

SEVENTEEN

Kate

"I'LL BE IN THE CAR."

It's the only thing Jack has said to me since we got home from Hades. To be fair, what do you say to your sister after you had a threesome with his brother in front of a crowd of people at a sex club?

That stays with me as I gather my things and head to the driveway. If Jack and Oliver had their way, I'd never leave Davenport Manor. They'd lock me up safe until they found Watkins. But the court has ordered me to attend therapy and I have no choice.

I'm definitely not going anywhere unchaperoned.

We don't speak on the way over. After what happened at the hotel, what I did with both Oliver and Jack...what is there to say? I'm as filthy and disgusting as everyone thinks. I let Jack fuck me. I sucked Oliver's cock and let him eat me out. I can pretend it was for a higher cause—to stop a serial rapist and killer, but deep down I know it was for my own dark desires. My pussy throbs just thinking about it and if Jack forced himself on me right now, I don't think I'd fight back.

370

What started out as pretend, a show for Marcus' investors, for a way to get information, quickly turned into something very, very real.

God, I think, looking out the window at Paul's house. I really do need therapy.

Too bad my psychiatrist is a monster, too.

"Thanks for the ride," I say, instantly feeling ridiculous. Our boundaries are getting twisted and turned. I wait outside of the car and take a deep breath to clear my mind. I need to have my thoughts about me when I enter Paul's office. Because it's a battleground...just like everything else.

But we're not fighting each other anymore. We've got a common foe. And it's not just my life that's on the line now, is it?

Jack's haunting eyes come back to me. I'm slipping and I know it. I came here to use them for protection, now I'm caught in their web, only now I don't know if I'm the fly...*or the spider*.

I make my way along the sidewalk to the entrance, but the moment I step inside, something feels off. The door to Paul's office is open, but everything is too quiet. I slowly make my way forward. But he isn't there.

He isn't anywhere.

"Paul?" I call out tentatively.

When there's no reply, I turn around, scanning the waiting room. It and the office are the only areas I've ever been to in Paul's house. Everything else has been off-limits, until now.

I stop. What if it's The Binder? I spin around, glancing over my shoulder at the open office door. What if he's been here? I snatch a decorative vase off a side table and clutch it in my hands. I can use the knife I have tucked in my boot, but what if I'm over reacting and stumble into Paul carrying a cup of coffee?

"Paul?" I call out again and head along the hallway to the door that connects to his house. I test the knob and to my surprise it turns. Behind it, I find the kitchen and it's also quiet. It's dark other than a light over the stove, the coffee maker switched off as though no one has been there all day. I glance across the room, toward his living area.

Fuck. I should just turn around and leave, go wait in his office. Go get Jack. But I don't—*can't*. I stare at the threshold between rooms and a voice inside my head whispers, *you're bound by the court to stay here. One report from him and you'll find your ass thrown in jail, who will protect you there?*

I hate that voice. It's one of truth and lies all muddled together.

Only I don't know which is which. But I can't stand here forever. I take a step forward, crossing the precipice of violating his privacy and calling out once more. "Paul?"

Silence answers.

I move, knowing once I do, I can't ever go back. This is too personal. Too vulnerable. Too *altering*. Again, I tell myself that I should go back outside. Go to the car. Find Jack. I should, but don't, swallowing hard, grit my teeth and step forward into his domain.

Moody amber and smoky black decor fill the space. Like his office, it's immaculate, but I knew it would be. Everything about Paul Sanders is cold and calculating, even when he's being gentle and patient. I bet there isn't a speck of dust in this place. Not one thing out of place, or a long, perfect hair left by one of his women...I mean, *victims* left behind.

Because without a doubt they'd be victims where Paul is concerned. Even if they don't know it.

"Paul?" I make my way further through his house, passing what looks like an expansive guest room to the bedrooms further back in the house. "It's Kate. We had an appointment. Are you here?"

One door is open, and a shadowy, barely it room waits for me.

My heart is in the back of my throat as I near the doorway. It's in the murky gloom that I find him. Paul is a dark silhouette as he sits on a chair in the middle of the bedroom, his legs crossed, his gaze fixed on me. "Jesus Christ," I mutter, lowering the vase. I set it on a table by the door. "You scared the shit out of me."

"Katherine, I thought I heard you stomping around out there." His eyebrow raises. "But you found me. Tracked me like a good little huntress."

"I was worried and thought maybe—"

"No excuses, Katie. I just gave you a compliment. Don't ruin it."

"What are you doing back here? Don't we have an appointment?"

His tone chills. "I thought this room may be better suited for today's session."

I glance at the bed knowing exactly what kind of session he has in mind. I don't take another step. "I can't imagine what kind of session would occur in your bedroom, Paul."

His chuckle is deep and devoid of emotion. Aquamarine eyes pin me to the floor.

He says nothing, just watches me, picking apart every tick my body makes and cataloging it in his mind. Safekeeping for later. I take a step forward drawn by my own sick desire to be both used by him and by them all. I don't understand the ropes I'm bound by but I feel the choke.

"I heard you had quite a night at Club Hades."

I frown. It's not a surprise that my brothers told him, but he can't know everything. "It was..." How do I describe it? Wrong. Disturbing. Transcendent? There's no reason to lie to Paul. He'll know. "It was confusing."

"I know you'd been desperate for release. How did it feel to get fucked by both of your brothers? To have them come inside of you, to feel Oliver's tongue on your pussy?"

Okay, so he does know everything.

"Overwhelming," I admit. "But it felt good to finally have an orgasm."

"Even if it was at the stake of your dignity."

I rankle at that comment. "It was at the stake of us finding out what we need to stop Watkins," I say. "A sacrifice for the greater good."

His lips quirk at the corners. "A sacrifice. Is that how you see it?"

I exhale. "I don't know. I don't know what you want me to say. I'm just trying my best to get through the day knowing that a terrible, horrible person is out there, and to stop him, I have to do whatever it takes."

"How does that make you feel that he has so much control?"

He? Watkins? Jack? Oliver? Davis? *Him?* The list of people controlling me is endless and under the numb sensation I've been existing in for weeks—*months*—I feel something else.

"Pretty fucking pissed off," I admit. "I'm tired of living like this, feeling like a trapped, scared, little rabbit." The truth of my words hammers home. "I'm ready for this to be over."

"How will it be over?" He leans forward. "What's the next step?"

"Killing him." His eyebrow shoots up and in the shadowy room it makes his face handsome and chiseled. I clarify, "Killing Watkins is the only way for this to be over."

"Could you do it, if you had to?"

Without hesitation I respond, "Yes."

"Interesting." He shifts in his chair. "What kind of weapon would you use?"

"A knife." I say, bending to reach into my boot and pulling out the blade Jack gave me. A glint of light runs down the steel. I love the weight of it in my hand, the power it gives me. "I'm prepared to do whatever it takes to stop him."

"Yet you carried a vase for protection through my house, not the knife."

"I—" Shit. He's right. The knife, although it feels good in my hand, I'm not sure I could use it if I had to.

"I see." He reads my thoughts. "Show me how you'd use it."

"What?"

"Show me," he says, standing, *towering* over me. "How would you kill him?" He makes a stabbing move. "The gut?" Then a slash across the throat. "The jugular?"

I stare at him, trying to figure out the game.

"I'd do whatever I had to," I say. "Do whatever it takes to get away."

He steps toward me, my hand grips the blade, but he doesn't attempt to take it away. "So, what you're saying is that you're ready to take control of your life."

"I am." My heart pounds as he gets closer, his scent washing over me. This game feels more familiar. Paul wants to fuck with my mind as much as he wants to fuck with my body. He's testing me. How much can I take? How much pain can I handle? How much do I want it?

"My goal this whole time wasn't to 'fix' you, Katherine," he says, grazing his finger along my cheek. "Or help you toward rehabilitation. It's been to break you down, push you past your boundaries, help you see who you really are." His hand drops to where I'm holding the knife. He lifts it between us, pressing the steel against his chest, unafraid. "Can you see it?"

I nod slowly. "I think so."

"Tell me who you really are, Katherine."

He'd said the word when I entered, but I was too busy trying to calm my nerves to hear it. But I do now and it rings clear in my ears.

"I'm a hunter. A *huntress.*" Even with that admission, Paul isn't afraid I'll stab him. He shouldn't be because Paul isn't my prey. I have one person in my sights now. Kill him before he kills me. "Just like my brothers."

His eyes light up. "Ah, there she is. The real Katherine Stevenson."

"No," I say, swallowing thickly, "the real Kate Davenport."

He looks impressed. Surprised. My heart thrums. "So, you feel it? The connection to your brothers? To their mission?"

"I feel everything," I tell him. "Anger, fear, hate, rage."

"Would you like me to help with that?" His fingers trail down my arm. "At least temporarily?"

There's the kindness he likes to show, the caretaker, the good guy, the doctor. It fucks with my mind and body and it's why I can't help myself. I answer, "Yes."

"Remove your clothes."

Instinctively, I look over my shoulder.

"No one will interrupt us. You should know that by now."

It's part threat and part assurance. As usual, I'm helpless to resist and lift my fingers to the buttons of my blouse.

"Every piece," he says, nodding at my shirt. "But leave on your lingerie. I want to see it."

He watches without lifting a finger as I peel the cream-colored satin from my body and let it fall. It hits the floor behind me softly, leaving me to reach for the zipper at my hip. I slide it down, pushing the black skirt until it too crumples at my feet.

And as he steps away, he motions deeper into the bedroom. I follow, feeling the coldness of his gaze taking in every inch of my body from the black lace bustier on the French lace black panties that hug the cheeks of my ass.

"You dressed for me," he says quietly.

Maybe I did. Maybe I knew it would come to this. The way his eyes drink me in, tells me that he's realizing that, too.

"Tell me, Katherine, where does it hurt? Where can I soothe your distress? Make you feel better?"

"Make it hurt," I beg. "God, just make it hurt."

The man gives no emotion at my request, not even a hint of the hunger underneath the mask. But I know there is a hunger, because why else would I be here?

"Hands on the bed."

I do as I'm told, placing my hands on the end of the bed and bend over slightly. I wait for a strike—a punishment, but when he moves close, his fingers gently touch the skin on my ass where he brutalized me the week before. I'm healing, but there are still lingering marks. They may always be there—a reminder of how far he can bend me. How much I can take. I feel him trace along the edge of my panties, fingering the lace.

"You have Jack twisted into knots, do you know that?"

His question catches my breath. But I don't dare move. I keep my gaze fixed on the soft gray mink blanket underneath my hands as he continues. "I know he wants me."

"It's not just want. It's so much more."

"I know. He hates me and wants to kill me, but he can't. Not yet, not with so many people watching us." My pulse races. Heat follows moving through me at Paul's touch.

"You know that saying, don't you?"

"What saying?"

"There's a thin line between love and hate."

My heart kicks in my chest at the thought. But he's wrong. Jack doesn't *love* anyone. Because my vicious stepbrothers don't care about anyone but each other. I know that for a fact.

Still, Paul's words worm their way into my head. Jack's stare haunts me as Paul slides his finger along the crease of my panties and pushes deep against my opening. "Your pussy," he says, bending down and inhaling, "is fucking delicious."

He dives his fingers under the elastic of my panties and plunges in. I close my eyes and clamp around the invasion. "Were you wet like this for Jack? For Oliver?"

If *I* was the therapist here, I'd say Paul is deflecting—focusing on my brothers and not his own desires.

"I'm wet all the time," I say over my shoulder. "Horny. Needy. Please, Doctor, make it better."

I brace myself for the desire that will rage unquenched by the time he's done. For him to tell me he can't satisfy me, but it never comes. I just hear the clink of metal that makes me shiver and the slow slide of his zipper that drives me back against his fingers as they thrust. I moan, but the sound barely escapes before he pushes my face into the mattress.

Paul is on top of me in an instant, a different man than the one I've come to know. This one is more like when we were kids. He grasps my wrists, pinning them above my head with one hand as he reaches between us with the other. Behind me, he savagely tears the lace of my panties, ripping them to the side. "I could hurt you," he says, yanking me to my knees and lining his cock up against my pussy, "but pain is pointless. You inflict that better than anyone else. You're the dangerous one here, with your soft, mouth, perfect tits, and tight cunt." He laughs. "Your body is a weapon. Your appeal...a nuclear bomb. No wonder Watkins is obsessed with you. We all are."

The truth is we are dangerous to each other and even more dangerous *all* together.

None more so than now. I wait for his cock to enter me, I open my legs wider, welcoming the brutality. It's familiar. Warm. Easier than the confusing rage I've been carrying. I allow him to become a cage around me. Shackles of flesh and bone and malevolence under an icy exterior. I welcome it all, letting the rush of hunger sweep me away. I have just enough time to catch my breath and melt into this before it changes.

He pulls away, stumbling backwards. I suck in hard breaths, stunned for a second before I realize he's gone and glance over my shoulder.

What I see unnerves me. Paul is gasping for breath. His cock is erect, bobbing heavy between his legs, slick with precum. His eyes are wide, staring at me as though I'm the monster. I see it so clearly now. He's tortured. Consumed. He doesn't want to want me—but he does. I'm the one in control.

Like he said, this was never about fixing me. It was about breaking me down. Turning me into something else.

Mission accomplished.

I push upwards and turn, sliding my fingers under the ruined elastic of my panties and push the remnant down. "You want this," I whisper. "I know you want this." I lean against the bed and slide backwards, lifting my feet until my heels dig into his expensive as fuck rug. I'm going to ruin this rug...*I'm going to utterly destroy it.* "You want *me.*"

His focus shifts to my thighs as I show him more.

Who's in whose head now, Doctor?

He unleashes a snarl like a man possessed and closes the distance between us in a heartbeat, crawling along the bed to grab my calves in his cruel grip and yank me back under him.

I raise my hands over my head as he finally, *finally*, takes me. After all these years, all the teasing and taunting and torture, Paul Sanders impales me on his cock, driving it in with a deep, feral groan. I cry out, scratching my nails along his back, holding on tight. He makes the wait worth it, taking me hard, and I welcome the feel of his cock inside, stretching and filling me. Becoming part of me. This is what we are now, rutting, beasts. Hunter and huntress. Mindfuckers.

Killers.

The mattress bounces with every thrust. I bite down, swallowing every whimper, and stare into his eyes. That aquamarine blue is no longer arctic. It's...melting *for me.* Against the force of my teeth, my lips curl at the edges. I smile as he slams into me. We are joined. Him. Me. *Them.*

Another link, another piece.

"Katherine." My name is a growl as his big, thick cock drives in deeper. "You've crawled under my skin." *Thrust.* "Climbed into my head." *Thrust.* I close my eyes pushing back against every impact. "You can't escape us," he growls, "no more, it seems, than we can escape you."

My pussy clenches greedily and I bite back a savage, animalistic sound.

He drops his head, unable to meet my gaze a second longer, and gives one hard thrust before he moans, coming inside me. Punctured breaths consume the space. But I remember everything, how my stomach coils, how stars burst behind my eyes, how I clench around him as I come with him inside of me. Two bodies, consumed with one another.

It's in every glint of hunger. Every twitch his body makes because he can no longer lie to me. Now I see the truth. Slowly, he releases my hands and pulls out. At this moment Paul is no longer the therapist, nor is he the hunter. He's just a man who's fucked. Welcome to the party.

He looks down at me, his gaze lingering between my slick thighs to the cum that leaves my body with him and he swallows hard. I think the sight of that excites him more than he realizes.

He likes it in my mouth, in my pussy, anywhere where he can get it in.

"The bathroom's through there if you wish to clean up," he says carefully.

"No." My chest rises hard and falls. I'm still breathless when I command, "Clean me up."

Our eyes hold for a beat, and I think he's going to snap, thrust a hand out to my neck, and strangle me on the bed. How fucking dare I tell him what to do? But then, to my surprise, he turns and walks into the bathroom. I can hear the water running, and he returns, holding a wet cloth. I spread my legs and he wipes me clean, removing every visible trace of him. But he and I both know that he's marked all over my insides; my pussy, my flesh, my mind.

He takes the cloth back to the bathroom and returns.

I ask, "Is today's session over?"

"Yes."

I rise from the bed and walk over to where my clothes are in a heap on the floor. I don't waste a second, sliding my skirt on, zipping it, and pulling my blouse back on.

"You're ready," he says before I step into the hallway. I glance at him. "To kill Watkins."

I swallow and leave, my fingers working the buttons as I walk from his residence and back into his office once more.

Even though he cleaned me up, I can still feel him between my thighs. I make my way through the connecting door and into the reception, then freeze. His father, Derek, is sitting in the waiting room, legs crossed, hands clasped in his lap waiting patiently.

"Kate." His tone implies that he's aware of everything that just happened.

Did he see us? Hear us? The idea makes me panic. "Dr. Sanders." I answer, trying to quell the thunder in my chest. "How are you today?"

"I'm fine, thank you." My skin burns as he lowers his gaze to the crumpled fabric of my blouse and my skewed skirt. "I hope the ointment helped your bruises."

"Yes, it was a relief." I can't manage more than a nod of goodbye, and rush to the door, making my escape outside. There, I lean against the side of the house, catching my breath.

What the fuck just happened?

What the *actual* fuck just happened?

EIGHTEEN

Davis

Grange Point District isn't just low-income housing. It's gangs and violence. A perfect place to hide out, especially if he paid the locals to keep him safe.

I follow Jack's sleek, expensive Audi through the streets. It stands out like a goddamn sore thumb. Locals lean against darkened buildings, eye-balling us as we drive past, more curious than threatening. Leaving the housing area behind, Jack pulls up against a row of empty warehouses. I double-check the address that Marcus gave Jack and spot the rusted numbers hanging on the chain link fence. Marcus was right, the police hadn't uncovered this property—or the trust.

I hop out of the Explorer, waiting for them to get out of the car. Jack and Oliver get out of the front. To my shock, Jack opens the back door for Kate. Her shoulders are rigid—stiff—clearly not used to Jack being nice, but there's something different about her. An eerie calmness behind that sexy exterior.

Things are changing between them. It doesn't take a detective to sniff it out. There's less animosity. More...connection. I heard all about what happened at Hades the other night. I don't like it. I don't trust it.

I don't trust *her*.

Unlike the Davenport brothers, I don't let my cock rule my emotions.

I haven't seen her since the wax room when I sealed up her pussy. The memory sends a shiver up my spine, the urge to inflict pain and hurt the little betrayer. Her eyes cut in my direction, a haughty dismissal, but I know she remembers how it felt to have me inside of her. How she fucking begged.

No. I'm not letting my guard down around her. Not a chance.

The gates are all locked. The yards are empty, metal signs hang from the fence warning: Private Property Keep Out.

"Looks like this is it," Ollie says. "If his intention was to hide, then this would do it."

"We'll need the cutters," Jack says.

Oliver moves to the back of the car, opens the trunk, and rummages inside. The Davenports don't go anywhere without their bag of tricks.

Oliver makes short work of the steel links, snapping tight and leaving the chains to fall. In the distance, cars race up and down the street, the rumble of their engines bouncing off the asphalt. Tires squeal and they vanish, headed out to terrorize some other part of the city.

I pull out my Glock, knowing we could very well be walking into a trap. Marcus could have sold us out or Watkins may be that paranoid. He's been quiet for weeks, but like a festering boil, he'll come to the surface at some point. I just hope we get to him first.

Ollie shoves the gate open and steps inside.

Jack gestures with his gun for me to go next, while holding the fencing back. "Go on, Katie," he urges, indicating he'll come in last.

She hesitates and I realize that it's not nerves and fear holding her back. One lick of her lips and I can tell it's excitement. She's wrestling a monster. A monster we've created by forcing her, one step outside her comfort zone, at a time.

"Do you have the knife I gave you?" Jack asks.

"Yes," she answers without hesitation.

She looks around nervously, then bends and pulls out the knife from inside her boot. It takes all my will not to smile. Jack isn't successful, a proud smirk teasing his lips.

"Good girl," I hear him murmur. "Keep it ready."

The two of us watch her back as we step around the corner of the warehouse and step into the gloom. The knife in her hand glints and it sets my pulse racing.

"You really trust her with that?" I ask, keeping my eyes on both the knife and the sway of her ass in the tight black jeans she's wearing.

"Yes." His answer is definitive, but I'm not buying it.

"And you think she'll use it if she needs to–on Watkins–and not to slit your throat."

"Paul thinks so."

I can only imagine the battery of tests that Paul put her through to come to that conclusion.

"I don't know," I say, keeping my voice low. "She's screwed us before."

He grunts and then adds, "She doesn't know it yet, but she's on her very first hunt."

A chill runs down my spine, and I look at her in a new light. The lift of her chin. Her squared shoulders. She's not shaking or wary or worried. She's strong. Capable. A flicker of desire bubbles in the pit of my stomach as I view her in a different light. I still don't trust her but, I can't deny that it's fucking intoxicating.

It's dangerous to be high on a mission like this. It'll get us all fucked.

Up ahead, she and Oliver scan the buildings, stopping at the corner, glancing around before surging ahead. When we catch up, I hear the snap of a lock before the rumble of a warehouse door. Jack keeps his eyes peeled behind us, making sure we aren't followed. By the time I get there, Ollie is walking out, shaking his head. "It's empty."

Something about a small building to our left draws my attention. It's not a warehouse—but a side building. A garage maybe. I leave the others, and make my way across the crumbling asphalt, the cracks weedy with overgrowth. It's then that I smell it. Something dank fills the air, and I inhale, catching the pungent scent of rotting trash. God, I hope it's trash. I continue until it's so bad that I cover my nose with the collar of my shirt, only dropping it to holler, "Over here."

Davis strides forward, but it's Katie who stands at my side as Ollie snaps the lock and they yank the door upwards.

"Christ, that's rank." Jack's face twists in repulsion, and turns away, wincing at the putrid smell.

It's the stench that alerts me to the fact that we're on the right path. The door is padlocked, but Oliver quickly steps forward, snapping the metal in two. With the nose of my gun, I push the door open, the rusted hinges screaming. I step inside, taking in the overflowing trash piled at the front of the garage. Unlike the others, this one isn't empty, nor is it for storage. I hear Oliver behind me, and Katie follows. Jack lingers at the door, making sure we're still alone. Light flickers at the far end of the room, an old fluorescent, sputtering in and out of life. There's a room. A small office.

Someone has been staying here.

A cot is shoved against the wall on one side and a makeshift sink along the far wall. There's a row of knives, weapons, hunting gear, and a heap of other gear that I don't care about. My stomach drops. Fuck, the weapons are the least of our problems.

I turn to tell them not to come in, but Katie is already behind me, gravitating toward the far wall at the end of the room. I shoot Oliver a look, but it's too late. They all see it. Even Jack has come into the room, gun lowered, jaw tensing in disbelief.

"I checked the trash. There's a body in there. Older male. Maybe a vagrant? Or someone found him back here?"

His words barely filter through. Watkins has his own murder board—but this one isn't filled with just his victims—although they're on there. Photos of women, naked and chained to the wall of the cabin. Others dirty, pleading on their knees. One is in a cage, a collar around her neck like a dog. More show images of the aftermath, bruised bodies. Sores and lesions from the chains. Hollow, empty eyes. Pinned around the photos are various trinkets: jewelry, torn panties, a license, or scraps of paper.

I expect all of this, the trophies. We'd been looking for it, ripping up floorboards in Ryan's house, searching for evidence. He laid it all out for us, but that's not what forces me to swear.

"Motherfucker," I snarl, staring at the surveillance images. There's one of me, from two days ago, outside the police department. There are two of Jack at the supermarket, his face angry and tense. Another of Oliver at the post office. There are none of Paul, but he's done his best to lie low, keeping his professional distance so the court doesn't come sniffing around.

It doesn't matter, because there are plenty of the rest of us. All invasive. All close proximity. Taken as we go about our daily business. But none of them are as fucking terrifying as the blown-up image in the middle. It's an image of Katie, a closeup, with her face hacked and sliced into shreds. Mangled. Words scrawled in red around it: *DIE BITCH!*

"Fuck you."

My head snaps and I look toward the voice. It's low. Whispered. Female.

"Fuck. *You*," she says again, this time a little louder. Her hand grips the handle of the knife, and she stares at the wall. "Fuck you, you goddamn monster. You son of a fucking bitch!" She spins, eyes wild, looking around the room. "Can you hear me, you fucking coward? Are you watching? All these fucking pictures? These trophies? You don't get to keep them. Not anymore!" Her arms fly wildly, the knife slashing through the air, she cuts down the image of her face, creating a jagged tear.

"That's evidence!" I shout, jumping between her and the wall. The blade slices through the air, cutting the leather of my jacket. "Jesus Christ! Stop her!"

Jack jumps after her, circling her with his arms, but she fights against him, screaming, "We don't belong to you. You don't own us. I'm going to kill you!" The words a strangled cry. "I'm going to fucking make you beg for your life and then I'm going to slaughter you like the dirty, filthy, pig we know you really are."

"Katie, stop!" Oliver shouts, managing to grab her wrist, forcing the knife from her grasp. "Fuck," he says, realizing she nicked him. He tosses the knife on the desk and wraps the hem of his shirt around his bleeding wrist. "Shit."

The blood is the only thing that gets her to stop fighting against Jack. She stills, but only long enough to let out a blood-curdling scream. The sound of her voice—her rage—echoes off the metal building, vibrating back into our souls.

She heaves in his arms, chest rising and falling, her hair wild. Over her head, Jack and I share a look.

Paul was right.

She's ready.

NINETEEN

Kate

The images on the wall of the garage stay with me all that day and the next. I try my best not to think about it as I move around in a dream-like state, preparing for the party. The big game is this coming weekend and I've been pleasantly surprised at the number of guests that have RSVP'd. I don't know if they're attending out of true friendship for my mother or to witness the spectacle of the Davenport family.

Probably a little of both.

While the party, and all the finer details, loom over me, I'm trapped in my own private hell, one where Christopher Watkins carries out his threat.

DIE BITCH!

My pulse skips and my hands shake. The glass in my hand falls and shatters against the floor. "Shit."

I crouch, gathering the shards, slicing my finger. Blood blooms and runs in a bead down my thumb. Black polished boots move into my view and I slowly lift my gaze past pressed black trousers and the black cashmere sweater to the bottomless, steely eyes of my stepbrother.

Jack looks at my hand and then slowly reaches down. But it's not for the slivers of glass in my hand. His thumb glides along the edge of my jaw and catches my chin tilting my head even higher.

It seems so poignant.

He captures me even without violence.

Still, it's never without a little pain though, is it?

He grazes his thumb over my mouth, bruising my lips against my teeth. I don't wince, not anymore, not from his brutal ways. My heart pounds instead. Only this time it's for an entirely different reason. Pain. Pleasure. I am caught in this trap.

"You need to be careful."

Those words hold even more meaning than any threat he's ever given me.

I need to be careful.

And not just because of The Binder.

Every boundary established between us, natural or self-made, has unraveled. There are no more pretenses. I like the way fucking Jack feels. I like the pain inflicted by his friends. I go soothe myself on Oliver's cock, allowing the feel of him in my mouth to ease me to sleep.

I close my eyes and hang my head. I can feel Christopher closing in, gathering momentum like an on-coming storm, and this time I don't think even my stepbrothers can help me. He was so close—following me and the guys around town—always just a few feet away. We were clueless, feeling safe in our bubble. I should know better. If a Watkins' wants something—someone—they'll do whatever it takes to get her.

The clock has been ticking since I left witness protection. Probably before.

Jack notices, dropping his hand from my cheek to check my wound. The sting is cutting. Something ignites inside his eyes, and it burns with passion as he meets my gaze once more. He catches a droplet of blood with his fingertip.

"You go take care of this," he says, jerking his head toward the bathroom. "I'll clean up the glass."

Jack has never offered to help me with anything. *Ever.*

But his tone isn't pleasant. It was an order and I follow it. It takes me a minute to clean the cut before securing it with a bandage. When I come back, Jack is gone. The floor is spotless.

A strange feeling blooms in my chest, one I've never associated with Jack, or anyone else in this house.

Gratitude.

***

THE AFTERNOON IS SPENT SETTING up the yard, hauling out tables and chairs in the warm fall air. The weather forecast is perfect for the party, and I go all out, arranging a viewing area for an outdoor screening of the game, along with long tables for a buffet of barbeque and a bar for drinks. The rivalry between the two schools is epic, and it's not uncommon to have mixed allegiances in each family. I decorate with bold colors, celebrating both.

"Why didn't you go to college?" I ask Jack as he helps set up the speakers. Oliver ran into town to get a few last-minute supplies. I had planned on going, but they both agreed that with Watkins lurking around, it would be safer for me to stay home. "I know your grades were good enough."

Squatting behind the electrical unit, he connects a black wire to a red one and shrugs. "College was never my goal. We had a mission."

"The mission to find your mother's killer."

He grunts in response, then points to a small box. "Hand me that, will you?"

"Sure." I hand it over and our fingers touch, setting off a spark that travels up my arm. If he feels it too, he doesn't reveal it. "Can I ask you something?"

"Didn't you *just* ask me a question?"

"Yeah but...I don't want you to get mad."

His eyes flick up, and I expect them to be dark and angry. Instead, they're amused. "I'll do my best."

"Don't you find the way you treat me a little..." I choose my word carefully and settle on, "...ironic, since your whole mission in life is to stop the person that raped and killed your mother?"

To my surprise, he stands and runs a hand through his dark hair. His eyes remain cast on the ground. "The rage...it's not something I can turn on and off. It bleeds from one situation to the next. A violation is a violation—and that night you broke the rule by coming up to my room. In my mind, there was no other option than punishment—swift and severe." He swallows, his Adam's apple bobbing. "It's a place I've had to go in order to complete my mission—to find the son of a bitch that did that to her." His eyes raise and meet mine. "My hands are bloody, Katie. I'll never deny that. And sometimes emotions get confusing. *Urges* get confusing." He lifts his hand and cups my cheek. "You trigger something in me, little sister. Something both dark and feral. I tried, but you didn't heed my warnings."

I'm not sure if it's a confession or a justification. Mostly, it's the rambling admissions from a tortured man, who has sacrificed his soul for vengeance. I can understand that. I can feel it bubbling under my own skin—the need to rid the world of The Binder—despite what it may do to me.

"There's so much evil out there," he continues, thumb stroking my cheek, "it spreads like an infection. I thought I was hunting one man, but it turns out there are so many more. And the thought of one of them taking you from us..." A shiver runs down his spine. "I can't allow it. I won't."

"Do you hate me?"

"God, no." The wind blows, ruffling his hair. "I never did. Not really. I hated what I couldn't fucking have. I hated that you weren't damaged like me and Oliver were, that you were innocent and pure. I hated that you could see right through me, that you were brave and didn't give a fuck about my rules and commands." He presses his forehead to mine. "I hated the fact you made me hard every time I saw you; that all I wanted was to defile and damage you—*ruin* you the way we'd been ruined."

My breath catches, his confession is raw and real. Jack is a terrible man. An evil man, but that flicker of desire burns ever present in the pit of my belly. I'm drawn to the badness in him, in this brother and friends. I'm drawn to their mission—to the hunt to rid the world of dangerous men.

I rest my hand on his chest. "You didn't ruin me," I tell him, understanding it a little better, "you transformed me, taught me who I really am."

His lip quirks. "Who is that?"

I push up on my toes and kiss the point of his chin. "I'm no longer your prey." I kiss the side of his jaw. "I'm your sister." I brush against the soft spread of his lips. "Your lover." I smile up at him. "I'm a Davenport."

His movement is quick, hands circling around my wrists, tight like a vise. I love his strength, his size, the feel of his cock against my belly. "I can't relax until I catch them."

"Them?" I ask.

"Watkins," he says, face tensing, "and my mother's killer. I won't stop until they're dead and in the ground."

"I don't want you to," I tell him, wrapping my arms around his waist. "And I don't want you to think you're alone. After seeing that wall with all our photos, I realize this is about so much more than me. It's about all of us, and I'm not willing to lose you either. Any of you."

He kisses me, hard and undeterred, everything about our relationship having shifted. I was right, I'm no longer his prey. But I want to be something else. I lick his lips before pulling away.

"Teach me," I say. "Tell me everything I need to know to bring this asshole down."

AFTER COOKING DINNER, cleaning up, and helping my mother, I head to my room. The party is set for tomorrow afternoon, and a good night's sleep is what I need to pull it off. It's not just me being judged here, it's the whole family and I don't want to let them down.

I open my closet door and as my eyes adjust to the dark, the shape of a body forms, hand reaching out to grab my arm. The scream, the ability to move, all of it shuts down as I realize I'm not alone. That he's here.

The Binder.

I'm envisioning my death, being chained to the cabin wall, feeling his bindings around my wrists as he violates me, when the grip loosens and I hear, "Hey, it's me."

It's me.

Through the fear, the voice clicks, and I blink, trying to acclimate to the shadows.

"Jesus," I choke out. "You scared the shit out of me."

Jack doesn't apologize, just pulls me deeper into the closet. It's when we go further than the back wall that I realize we're behind the wall. He tugs me out of the way and slides a door shut. Suddenly all the late-night intrusions in my room, even with a locked door, makes sense. He had a way in and out the whole time.

"What are you doing?" I ask, my heart still thudding in my chest.

"You wanted to learn about how to stop Watkins. I'm going to show you."

"By creeping through the walls?"

"By opening your mind to the options all around you." He turns on his phone flashlight, illuminating the space. It's cramped and has a thick musty scent. "I was there the whole time. Watching you. You never noticed."

But... "Sometimes I sensed it."

"You did," he agrees. "But not enough to figure out what was bothering you." He holds up a finger. "The first rule of hunting? Be aware of your surroundings. The second, trust your instincts." He shines the light back and forth. The passageway goes in both directions. He jerks his chin one way. "Follow me."

We go down, not up, which is the way I'd assume we'd go if we were headed to his room. His fingers link with mine and he guides us, turning sideways occasionally to get his broad shoulders through the narrow passage. Along the way, he points out different hidden entrances: Montie's room. Mom's bedroom. The living room and kitchen.

"Has this always been here?" I ask.

"Original to the house. My great-great-grandfather incorporated them, as a way to spy on servants to make sure they weren't stealing from him." I'm about to suggest that it can't be all, not with access points in the bedrooms, and he adds, "Among other things. From everything I've heard, the old guy was a pervert."

The final staircase is steep, and Jack is forced to let go of my hand. I grip the walls as I take each step, hoping not to brush against a spider's nest—or worse.

When we get to a landing, no wider than three feet wide, he stops and says, "The third rule is don't forget your resources."

He taps softly on the wall and a small piece comes loose. Jack wedges his fingernail underneath and slides it back, revealing a room in the basement, I know about, but haven't ventured into. The guy's workout room.

But it's more than that.

It's a full gym, with weights and cardio machines lining the walls. A wall of weapons hangs in a case by the door. Across from it is the murder board that used to be in Jack's room upstairs. In the middle of the floor, is a sparring mat, and the three guys are standing on the smooth, flat surface. Oliver's T-shirt is soaked through with sweat and Davis and Paul are shirtless, both only wearing workout shorts.

Holy shit.

Both men are incredibly fit with rippled muscles running up their abdomens like carved marble. Davis' chest hair is dark and thick, his shoulders broad and powerful. I've felt that power as he used it against me, but to see it exposed... I realize how easily he could force me to his will if he wanted.

But it's Paul that surprises me the most, his shirtless body shockingly sleek and hard. My eyes skim over the sinewy muscles in his arms, lean and cut, down to the hard planes of his chest. I swallow at the deep set 'V' tapering below his waist, revealing a masculinity I didn't know he possessed.

Jesus Christ.

All three guys look over as we step through the wall, none surprised to see me.

"You moved everything down here?" I ask, dragging my eyes away from them, and looking at everything that used to be upstairs.

"We managed to salvage most of it before the FBI got here," Oliver says. "The gym has always had a secure, secret entrance, but we only come in and out of here now through the passageway."

"Wow. Okay." I'm still trying to process it when Jack walks across the room and grabs a life-sized dummy out of the corner. Straining, he wraps his arms around it and lifts the form, carrying it to the middle of the room. Once there, the other guys help him hang it from a hook in the ceiling.

"What's that for?" I ask.

"You asked me to tell you everything about how to catch the Binder, but that requires four steps."

"How to hunt," Davis, a small grin on his mouth.

"How to kill," Jack adds, revealing his knife and stabbing it into the heart of the dummy.

"How to dispose of the body," Oliver says, wiping the sweat off his brow with the hem of his shirt.

"And how to mentally prepare yourself to do it," Paul adds, crossing those magnificent arms over his chest.

"That's too much to learn."

"Sweetheart," Oliver says, walking over to me. "We've been teaching you all along."

"The bars and Club Hades. Pretending to be bait and allowing you to go on investigations with me," Davis says, his eyebrow raised. "All of that was teaching you how to hunt."

Oliver looks at me, lifting his chin. "Those nights up in my room, quiet and careful, patient and diligent. Denying your own urges. Those are the skills it takes to go through with this."

A strange feeling creeps down my spine. The awareness that all of this has been orchestrated, that they've been grooming me for this moment.

"You're strong," Paul says. "Unbelievably strong. Mind maybe more than body. We've tested you. I've tested you, because that's what Christopher will do to you if he catches you. He'll fuck with your head and your body—pushing you past all of your limits." His eyes are soft when he looks at me. "You passed every test I gave you, Katherine. You're ready."

Hearing that makes my chest swell with something akin to pride. God, they're fucked up and twisted, but I see it. I see how they've been preparing me for a moment I wasn't fully aware was coming.

Jack approaches me, holding out the knife. I recognize it—it's the one he gave me—the one from his first kill. He must have stolen it from my room.

He flips it, grasping the blade and offering me the handle. I take it from him, and I see it now for what it is, a test.

"What do you want me to do?"

"First, understand that we're here to protect you. If everything goes to plan, we'll get to him before he ever gets anywhere near you."

Anywhere near me?

That doesn't sound good at all.

Davis grunts, a flash of irritation on his face. "But so far nothing has gone according to plan."

"He's right," Oliver says. "We have to be prepared for anything —an unexpected attack."

"He's watching all the time."

A shiver washes over me, but I realize that here we're safe. Tucked in this secret room, all together.

"The hardest part of this is the first shot. Killing a man isn't easy —physically or mentally. Especially your first." Jack presses his hand to my lower back and guides me to the dummy. "Watkins is only going to give you one chance, Katie. You can't blow it."

The dummy is made from a mold, life-sized—I suspect exactly Christopher Watkin's weight and dimensions. His face is non-descript, but I don't need to imagine what my stalker looks like. I see him all the time, like a ghost over my shoulder.

Jack moves behind me, wrapping his arms around my body and closing his hand over mine. He guides me, showing me over and over. "Stab and lift," he says. "Don't yank it out—jerk it up. Do as much damage as you can. Unless you hit the heart," he flips my hand, shifting the blade down. "Then drag it, slicing him up as much as possible." He pushes my hair off my neck, and I feel the heat of his breath. "You ready to give it a shot?"

He steps back and I'm alone on the mat. I raise the blade, trying to push aside the feel of their eyes watching me. I rush toward the dummy, stabbing the blade in the modified flesh.

It barely sinks in.

"Shit," I say, blinking at the tiny cut. I lash out again, stabbing closer to the heart. The blade slices over the skin, a flesh wound. "Oh my god."

I'm not ready. There's no way I'm ready.

"Do it again," Jack commands, his voice tight.

"Ahhhh!" I scream, putting some punch behind it, but again the blade barely nicks the skin.

"This is stupid," I say, letting the knife fall to my side.

To the side, I hear a scoff. Davis. "I should've known she'd be too weak to pull it off."

It's not a surprise he's being cruel. When isn't he? But I am shocked to hear Oliver add, "She can't help the fact her hands are better for jerking off a cock than killing a man." My eyes dart up to his and he looks back defiantly and shrugs. "Prove me wrong."

"Shut up," I say, overwhelmed and exhausted. "I didn't ask for this."

"Guys," Paul says in that even, soothing tone, "give her a break. This is a lot of pressure. Killing someone is hard, and Katherine's used to receiving the pain, not inflicting it." His conniving blue eyes meet mine. "It's what she craves. She'll probably fuck the whole thing up just so she can feel Watkin's wrath."

I narrow my eyes at him. "That's not what I want."

"No?" The way Davis says it is a challenge. "Honestly, we should just get this over with now. Fuck her ourselves and kill her. Fill every fucking hole in her body with our cum and drown her." His voice turns impossibly crueler. "Teaching a whore to be a hunter and killer is futile. She wants to live like this. It's why she came back. It's why she called Oliver. Katie is nothing, but a whore who wants to be fucked and tossed aside. I vote we do it before he does."

The room spins around me. All that stuff they said before, about preparing me, about how strong I am, was nothing, but manipulative lies. It's the same bullshit they've fed me my whole life; that I'm worthless and useless, here for one thing only: to fill their needs.

I hate them. God, I fucking hate them. I hate their faces and their bodies and their stupid vengeful cocks. I hate the way they make me feel and the desperation they've created, the addiction. The reliance. The room fades out of view, overwhelmed by white-hot-rage. My hand tightens around the knife and I charge forward, screaming as I slash the blade at the nearest person. The tip lands, sinking in, all around me voices shout and yell, but I don't give a fuck. I want to hurt. I want to destroy.

I want to kill.

I want to rid myself of this pain: the abuse and humiliation. The taste of their sticky, salty cum on my tongue. I hate how I want it. I hate how I need it, and all of that bitter rage unleashes. There's no measure of time to my assault, I strike, swing, jab, jerk, attack, attack, attack...until my arms feel like anchors, dragging me underneath. I fall to the ground, breathless, sweating. The knife dropping with a hard clatter.

I blink past the tears, hot and burning, and see four faces, staring back at me, eyes wide. Blood drips from a cut on Paul's chest. More from Davis' forearm. Oliver watches me, with his arms crossed over his chest, his lip swelling with a growing bruise. When I finally get the courage to look at Jack, I don't see any injury—just that cold, dangerous expression.

I didn't hurt them. Of course not.

"I'm sorry," I whisper, knowing their vengeance is coming. "I'm..." What I am is too tired to go on. "Just do it. Get rid of me. Fuck me, drown me, toss me aside. I'm no good to you."

Jack walks over, his scuffed boots in contrast to the clean mat. He stands over me and I brace myself, waiting for his wrath. I shiver, both out of exhaustion and fear, as he kneels next to me. His warm, calloused fingers touch my chin and he turns my head.

Just past him is the dummy, shredded into pieces, huge chunks of the polymer on the floor.

"You did it," he says, quietly. "You dug deep down and found that place—the one we all have to reach for when we kill a man."

"I did it?" I ask, trying to process the demolished dummy. *I did that.*

"You did it," he repeats. Fingers fanning to cradle my face. He pulls me to him, breath mingling with mine. "And it was the sexiest fucking thing I've ever seen."

His kiss is hard, bruising, but it feels so good against all the other emotions. Jack's hands lower as he kisses down my throat to my chest, but I feel another set settle on my shoulders, easing me back into a hard chest. I look up and see Oliver's handsome face, including his swollen lip. I reach for it and he winces when I touch the tender flesh. "I'm sorry."

"Don't be," he says. "You were on fire."

His hands snake under my arms and he grabs the hem of my shirt, dragging it roughly up and over my tits, as Jack continues to kiss his way down.

"What is this?" I ask. My stomach quivers when Jack's tongue dips into my belly button.

"After a performance like that," Oliver says, thumbs circling my nipples. Davis and Paul come to my sides bending to their knees. "You deserve a reward."

Before either man touches my skin, a shuddering exhale rushes through me. Davis bends, licking and suckling my nipple. Paul's hand reaches between my legs, spreading the warm, liquid heat with his fingers.

Jack looks up my body, a wolfish grin on his mouth. "Spread for me, baby." I let my legs fall, but it's not wide enough for him and he gestures for Davis and Paul to grab my upper thighs, holding me far enough that I feel the stretch. My pussy is exposed, the cool air of the room mingling with the heat from Jack's breath. His tongue licks a hot path against my seam, and he chuckles. "God, you taste fucking amazing."

"He's been jealous since I fucked you with my tongue at Hades," Oliver says, dipping down and kissing my mouth. His fingers tug and pluck at one of my nipples while Davis lathes the other with his tongue. I wrap my hand around his forearm, holding on as Jack, sucks on my clit. My body tenses with all the attention, the feeling of their hands on me all at once, almost too much to bear.

Paul shifts and moves down near my waist, fingers inching along. I squirm, ticklish near my hip, but they've got such a tight hold on me that I don't have much leeway. Paul holds my gaze as he drags my thigh into his lap, and he lowers his hand under

Jack's body, seeking my entrance. He toys with my pussy before he pushes his fingers inside, two, then three.

"Oh god," I moan, as I stretch to fit him. "God, don't stop."

There's been so much denial, so much pain, that if they hold out on me now, I think I may die, *actually die*, from deprivation.

"No one's stopping until you come," Oliver tells me, kissing me again. His mouth moves with mine, giving me breath when I can't find my own. Teasing the same way he teases my nipple. Sparks flicker with every touch, every stroke, each kiss. "Make her come, big brother," he tells Jack. "Let our girl go."

Somehow, they all fall into rhythm—the four of them. Kissing, sucking, licking, fucking. My body quivers, caught up in the sheer torture of it all. They know me. They know what I want, just like I've learned to know what they want.

We're the same.

We're hunters.

Lovers.

Deviants and freaks.

Davis' teeth clamp down on my nipple and I cry out, but the scream is coaxed away by Oliver's tongue. Paul fucks his fingers into me at the same pace Jack flicks my clit. My belly winds, coiling tighter and tighter until there's nothing left to give. I buck against their touch, and cling to them as the orgasm releases, spreading out across my nerves, shooting stars behind my eyes.

It's the second time that night, that I've blacked out, my senses overwhelming me. This time though, it wasn't born in hate, but in passion.

I float down, every inch of my body used and abused, humming with delight.

Because that's how I like it. Pain mixed with pleasure, and I know now that these men, my brothers, my tormentors have trained me right.

I'm ready for whatever comes my way.

TWENTY

Oliver

The party is loud, bright, the opposing team colors collide in a way that makes it feel cohesive–decades old rivalries that bring friends and family together in the perfect sort of dis-harmony. Sure, people drink too much, make stupid bets, and get pissed at the refs, but that's the glory of college football.

It's the one thing southerners can agree on, young and old, rich or poor. It's a unifier and after the stress of the past few months, I can see why my stepsister decided to use this event as a way to mend fences. It's hard to say mad when you're drunk, full on good food, and cheering on your favorite team.

I don't care about any of it, my eyes focused solely on the dark-haired woman flitting around the yard. Katie's in blue dress, neutral colors for the event. As the hostess, she doesn't want to pick a side. I like it though, blue looks good on her, bringing out the flecks in her eyes. It's tight enough to show her curves, but not too revealing, which she's aware will send her brothers and their friends into protection mode.

Not that we're not. She's got three sets of eyes on her. Me, Jack, and Paul. There's not an angle of this event that we don't have covered.

My favorite part of the outfit though are the cowboy boots. Sexy. Fun. Good for kicking ass. Fuck, what I'd give to throw her down on one of these tables, pull them off right now, one after the other, and bury my cock into her.

Katie has done a good job, organizing the party down to the tiniest detail. Colorful tablecloths—divided out by team color. Bright party cups, filled with alcohol-laced punch. There's a keg by the deck, Jack's been manning it for the last hour, handing out beer after beer. His attitude is better than it's been in months. Even though we haven't caught Watkins yet, things feel settled. Easier. For once we're not fighting with Katie, but working *with* her, and it feels good.

The game is playing full blast. Montie unleashes a roar, jumping up from his seat. "Are you kidding me, ref?! That was out of bounds!"

"Are you blind?" Paul's father, Derek, shouts. "His foot was firmly planted inside the lines."

"I know you're a doctor," Montie says, "but you really should get your eyes checked by a professional." They bicker, good-natured. It's been this way for years. After mom was murdered, weekends watching football with the Sanders became the norm. Montie went to State, while Derek got his undergrad from the University. Sinking into the game was a way to forget the bad stuff, the loss, even if it was just for a few hours.

"Let me refresh your drinks." I hear Katie offer over the argument. She's speaking to two women from Helen's book club. Although the party is a success, she's still on edge. Her laughter is just a little too sharp—too shrill. Her movements too quick. My sister's learned a lot since she returned, but all of that is falling apart under the scrutiny of her mother's socialite friends. We learned a long time ago not to care about what the people in town thought about the Davenports and our friends. She's had a lot less practice.

I watch from the back steps, taking in the party, my family, but most of all my stepsister. This is my preferred spot—observer. Voyeur.

Katie goes to the table and fills three cups with the sickly-sweet punch, squeezing the plastic in a tight triangle to keep from dropping them. Her nervousness shows as she keeps glancing at her mother, overcompensating for *everything*. The cups slosh in her hands, punch threatening to spill with every step, as if she takes a breath the whole party will fall apart.

She's nervous, scared, and that high energy draws Jack's attention. His stony eyes say nothing. But I know him, better than he knows himself. There's a twitch at the corner of his mouth. Displeasure. But it's not Kate that's pissing him off.

"For Christ's sake!" Montie shouts when the instant replay confirms that the player was, in fact, *in* bounds. "This whole game is rigged!" He turns, his face ruddy from the alcohol. "Katherine," he grabs her on the way back from the book club women, "get me another."

He pushes the empty cup in her hand and by the deck Jack's eyes narrow. As much at the demand as the way our father sways on his feet.

"Jesus," Davis says, dropping to the step next to me. "How many drinks has dear old Dad had tonight?"

"Enough that if he doesn't cool it, he'll be too shitfaced to finish the game," I reply. I look over at him. He's not dressed for the game—but in work clothes. "You just get here?"

"Yeah." His lips form a hard line. "There was a fire down at Grange Point last night."

"The warehouse district?" It's not my real question, but I can't ask it here. Can't say it in front of these people.

"The very one we went to. The whole place went up like it'd been doused in lighter fluid."

"Fuck."

We'd sat on the warehouse discovery for a few days–not reporting it to Davis' superiors. He'd been monitoring it, hoping maybe Watkins would reappear, give himself away, but he hadn't. The plan had been for CSI to go in tomorrow morning and process the evidence at the crime lab.

"Yeah. It's like that bastard knew we were closing in." He shifts. "If the eyewitness report is correct, that fire started while your brother had his tongue an inch deep in your sister's pussy last night."

"You mean, while we were all busy."

He nods.

I scan the area behind the yard, back at the tree line. I keep finding myself doing it–looking for him. I know he's watching us, but how? When?

"Looks like Katie pulled off the party," he says, drawing my attention away from the yard. "Her mom like it?"

"Hell if I know."

While our father has turned into a lush, unable to hold his damn alcohol, Helen has continued her descent with pain killers and Valium. The two of them are quite the pair, and as Katie walks over to Jack for a refill, our father bends and kisses his wife on the cheek.

Helen smiles up at him weekly. But that faded glint in her eyes tells me that she is too far removed to enjoy the party her daughter worked hard to put on for her. Pills. Booze. She's more detached than a damn corpse.

God, we've always had that tragic family thing going on; murdered mother, the troubled sons, a tormented stepmother, and the forsaken stepsister. Gothic tales have nothing on us.

Jack hands Katie fresh drinks, their eyes meeting over the keg. He's on edge as much as she is, and if something doesn't give, one of the two will surely lose it before the game is over.

"She seems stressed," Davis says. "Edgy."

"It's all these fucking nosy housewives. They make my skin crawl."

Davis claps me on the shoulder before walking over to Jack for a drink, passing Katie on the way. The two make eye contact, but there's no warmth. Davis has been hard on her—as hard as the rest of us, if not worse. He doesn't trust her—anyone really. And even though he knows he needs her to find Watkins, I don't think he likes it.

My eyes skip from him back to Katie, watching as she hands a cup to my Dad, who gives her a sloppy pat on the back, before moving to her mother. She holds out the red cup, but Helen doesn't take it. I doubt she barely knows it exists until Kate pushes it into her hand. "Mom, are you okay?"

"I'll take it," Derek says, hovering just a little too close. He waves my sister off. "You've done a wonderful job with all of this. Go. Enjoy the game. I'll see to your mother."

He leans close whispering something in Helen's ear. Whatever he says seems to do the trick. Katie's mom lifts her head, smiles at her daughter, and nods. Her pale lips move, murmuring something under the deafening roar of the TV.

Across the yard, Paul is tight-lipped as he watches his father. Montie on the other hand doesn't seem to mind as he leans forwards and claps Derek on the back. I turn back to the game and take a swallow of beer. My father's shouts and roars seem to mingle into one another, even Davis joins in barking his displeasure at a referee's call and downs his beer. I don't participate in the excitement. Instead, I occupy myself watching our sister, remembering how she kicked and clawed, stabbing that mannequin in the gym last night.

She's a little hellcat. One bent on utter destruction. My cock pulses, balls tighten, making me shift uncomfortably. I want more than I've allowed her to take. I want more than to soothe her. I watch her like a hunter, like she's my prey, trying to anticipate her next move. Her weakness.

Derek says something to her and something shimmers in her eyes when she looks at him, before she looks away, her cheeks reddening with embarrassment. What is that about? I search for the meaning, but the deafening roar of the game booms from the stereo and Katie heads back into the house as if nothing happened. I follow her in.

I step through the doorway, following the sound of her steps to the kitchen, and stop in the doorway. She's frantic, rushing from one bench to the other, placing tiny quiches on one tray before scrambling for some kind of spinach rolls with the other.

"Katie," I call her name. But she doesn't stop, just flutters around frantically. *"Katie."* This time a little louder.

She flicks a gaze my way. "Have you seen the extra container of sauce? I know I bought it."

I close the distance grabbing her hand as she rummages through the cabinet. She's a damn bundle of nerves when I pull her against me. "There's plenty of food out there. Everything is fine." I soothe her by stroking her hair. "The party is great and your mum is enjoying herself."

She shakes her head against me.

"Look at me," I demand, pulling away a little. "Hey, look at me." When she does it's with nervous tension. "The party is great," I say again, hoping she hears me this time. "Your mom is having a really good time. Dr. Sanders makes her feel comfortable. I mean, Dad's fucking drunk off his ass, but at least she's out there."

Pretending. We're all just pretending to be one, big, happy, functional family, complete with a medical doctor and a psychiatrist, and cop hovering around to keep us together.

I don't say that though. I don't think she can handle it.

She sighs. "I'm glad she's having a fun time, but..."

"But what?"

"Rivalries and football and all of this seem a little insignificant when I know he's out there...waiting for one of us to give him the opportunity."

"That's what's bothering you?" Fucking Watkins. "Sorry, sweetheart, but he doesn't get to ruin everything." A cheer rises from the yard–a sure sign that State just scored a touchdown. "Especially football." I smile, trying to coax one from her in return. "No one is bigger than football, you know that, not in Wilmington."

"Tell that to the women he's killed," she says. "I've spent the past few days wanting to pour bleach into my eyes to get the images of what Christopher Watkins did to those women out of my brain."

She pulls away and I let her, watching as she reaches for a bottle of pomegranate juice on the counter. Only the lid is off. The blood-red liquid sloshes when she shakes, spilling over my shirt.

Her eyes widen. "Shit," she whispers, staring at the stain. "God, Oliver…"

"It's fine." I reach for the buttons. "Don't worry about it." But her eyes glaze and her bottom lip trembles. "It's fine, Katie."

I peel off the shirt and make my way to the laundry room off the kitchen, tossing it in the basket.

"Let me do that," she says, following me in. "It needs stain remover and should soak for a while and–"

I spin and grab her by the elbows. "I don't care about the fucking shirt. I'll buy another one." Cupping her cheek, I add, "If you want to make it through two more quarters, you've got to chill out."

"I know. It's all just hitting me. The party, those pictures," she glances over her shoulder. "The way he's been watching us."

"You're safe. We're all here. Today is about you and your mom. Showing the community we can get out shit together and behave like normal people."

I laugh, because God, I'm pretty sure that ship has sailed. I tilt her face up and search for a smile, but her eyes are worried. Stressed.

"Ollie." The hitch in her breath surprises me. She's so wound tight, almost ready to snap.

"Yeah?" I answer.

She looks down at my crotch. "I need…"

She doesn't finish the sentence before my balls tighten and there's that coiling in my belly. She wants me to soothe her. I've trained her to want this—to *need* this. And Jesus, she's asking for it. Meek and trembling.

I've never been so hard in my fucking life.

One nod is all she needs. She crosses the laundry room, closes the door, and returns, sinking to her knees.

I look down at her brown hair all swept up in a messy bun on the top of her head. She works the clasp of my belt, then unbuttons my trousers, dragging the zipper down. I reach for her soft strands, sinking my fingers in deep as she pulls down my boxers and draws out my cock.

This time it's different, there's more than being her walking pacifier. Now when she brings her mouth closer it takes everything in me not to fuck that pretty mouth. But she doesn't take my cock inside. Instead, she dips her head down, gently placing each of my balls into her warmth before sucking. I lurch forward, steadying myself on the washer when she grips the base of my cock.

Her eyes dart up to mine and she exhales a, "Thank you," before bending and licking her tongue along the underside of my shaft, following the vein in complete and utter gratitude. "You don't know how much I needed this."

My stomach tightens and my fingers curl, gripping the back of her head a little harder.

"Fuck, Katie." I moan as she traces that thick vein with the tip of her tongue and takes me into her mouth. "This isn't what we agreed on." She's supposed to suck. To nurse, but my little sister is on her knees taking me in whole. I growl, coming apart under her hunger.

Shit, this isn't what we agreed to *at all*.

She takes me deeper, driving her clenched fist along slick skin to the base. That desire turns from giving her comfort to filling her mouth with cum. Movement catches my gaze through the glass panel on the laundry door. I still.

She pulls back, and I look down, eyes wide. "What?"

My gaze darts back to the window but whatever, or whomever I thought was there is gone. I stroke her chin, coaxing it back open. "Nothing. Open up."

Her jaw drops and she takes me back in and I'm lost in the warmth of her mouth.

I clench my hold tighter, thrusting into her mouth. Little sister picks up her pace, working me harder.

"Don't gag." I force the words through clenched teeth, driving her head down. "Don't—" I grunt. *"Fuck."*

She doesn't, gag. Hell no. She's a queen when she's on her knees. All these weeks of practice–of deprivation, the two of us teetering on the edge. I realize that she was playing me as much as I was playing her. How fucking much I needed this–her–to feel her mouth around me.

Her nostrils flare as she sucks in hard breaths and I come... *hard,* spilling deep in her throat. I watch as she swallows. Once. Twice. My breaths are heavy when I focus on her throat. "That's it, little sister. Swallow it down."

The words haunt me, echoing from that night in Jack's room so long ago. They're the same words I use now releasing my hold. I expect her to jerk backward, but she doesn't. She stays there as my cock softens in her mouth. Her tongue tickles the shaft as she licks the softening length before she kisses the tip, taking the last traces of me, and finally pulls away.

"Better?" My voice is husky.

She slowly rises, smoothing down her dress as she straightens. "Yes, thank you."

Thank you...

My thumb caresses her cheek. "Such good manners," I murmur. If we had time, I'd bend her over the washer and work out any remaining tension, but the party is her priority, not fucking her brother in the laundry room.

"Clean up. I'll cover for you if anyone asks." I yank my pants to my hips. "But hurry. Jack is probably already freaking out we've been gone this long."

That gets a laugh. "He probably is."

I catch her by the shoulder. "I hope that helped."

"It did. So much."

I press a kiss on her forehead. "Good. Try to relax and enjoy yourself."

She nods, giving me a hint of a smile. This time it's real, not forced like it was before.

I reach down, tuck myself back into my pants, and zip my trousers before working the clasp of my belt. "I'll see you outside, okay?"

"Okay." She licks the corners of her mouth, still shiny from sucking my cock.

I grab a clean shirt hanging on a rack in the corner of the laundry before slipping it on and walking out. My half-filled cup waits on the countertop. I down the contents and made my way to the bar outside catching Jack's eye as he searches the party.

I walk over and thrust out my cup.

"She's fine," I tell him, letting him refill my beer. "She'll be out soon."

"Good," he says, pushing the cup back. "I don't like it when one of us doesn't have eyes on her."

"She just needed a minute to chill out."

"I assume that has something to do with the smug grin on your face."

I laugh. "I can't help it if sucking my cock makes her relax."

"You literally trained her to do that."

I shrug, not giving a shit. He's right. I worked hard to get Katie in this position. As hard as he worked to get her to use that knife. We've molded her into the perfect girl–the perfect Davenport.

Across the yard, Montie lets out a cheer, punching his fist in the air in hollers, *"Touchdown!"*

I raise my drink and shout with him. Tonight, we're all winners.

TWENTY-ONE

Kate

I watch Oliver's broad shoulders as he shuts the door behind him and heads back to the yard. I exhale, needing a minute to compose myself, and lean against the kitchen counter.

I can still taste him in my mouth.

God, I'd been craving his dick for days. The taste of his cum. The feel of him thickening, swelling against my tongue. He finally gave it to me—for once without a fight. No begging, just him. Me and his delicious cock.

It's wrong—in so many ways—but I feel better. More steady. Calmer. All those weeks of sucking on him, using him to soothe my anxiety. It helped more than any therapy session with Paul. Although—as I've learned, that's not what those sessions were about anyway. They were to test me—push me. See how much I could take.

A lot, I realize. So much more than I thought possible.

I reach for the plate I'd been arranging before we went into the laundry room, and it hits me. The extra sauce is in the extra refrigerator in the garage. I rest the platter back on the counter and pass the laundry room, taking the back door into the garage. The sauce is right where I left it. I grab it and an extra bag of ice from the freezer, then reenter the house. As I pass the laundry room again, I see a figure inside.

I slow when I see the white shirt, butterflies whirling in my belly, and ask, "Come back for more already?"

"I mean if you're offering blow jobs, I'll take two."

The voice sends a tremor of terror up my spine. It's not Oliver waiting for me. It's another blond—although his golden hair and tanned skin are less shiny now. Christopher Watkins is in my laundry room. He's here, with dark smudges shadowing the skin under his eyes and his smile a little off kilter, less charming than it had been the night I met him at the bar. The night he kidnapped Brandi. The night he was supposed to kidnap *me*.

My breath catches in my throat, heart pounding. I drop the bag of ice, and blindly throw the container of sauce at him. He easily bats it away.

"Hello, Kate." His eyes rake down my body. "Is that how you greet an old friend?"

I will my body to react—to run—and although it takes everything in me to make it happen, I do it. I run, pushing past the fear throbbing in my chest. I race to the kitchen, grabbing a knife off the counter.

He rounds the corner and I lunge, using the method my brothers taught me. Stab, lift. But the tip of the blade catches on the fabric of his shirt, snagging the cotton. Christopher's hand clamps around my wrist and easily, too easily, he overpowers me. I drop the knife, letting it fall to the ground and kick it with the toe of my boot. If I can't have it, neither can he.

"Should we do it here?" he asks, looking past me at the kitchen table. He still has a tight grip on my wrist, bending it so that one sharp twist would snap it in half. "Splay you out like their mother? Recreating the scene. I've seen pictures. Marcus showed me. He has a whole mock-up, ready to design for Club Hades." His eyes light up. "It would be absolutely poetic."

I glance behind me at the table, recalling the stories about how she'd been killed right here. The boys...they'd hidden in the passageway. My eyes dart to the wall, to the area where Jack showed me the panels opens.

"You're more original than that," I say, trying to keep my voice steady. "You're the Binder—well one of them. Copying another killer's methods seems...derivative and uninspired."

Watkins' eyes narrow, I'd called him out and I've hit a nerve.

"I mean, you and your brother already have the exact same style. He's the one that will go down as the original, right? Copying another famous Wilmington killer seems weak."

He twists my arm and I cry out, but at the same time he throws me off, like he can't stand to touch me. "I'm the master behind the Binder. I created his methods, the way we stalked, bound, raped, and killed. That was all me. I'm the one that taught Ryan everything—at least until he fucked up and got himself killed." My eyes dart to the back door. Music and cheers carry from the party. At any minute someone could walk in. They could, but they're not. He shifts around, blocking the exit. "Don't you dare try to minimize my glory."

A loud cheer erupts outside—a touchdown—I assume or some kind of tackle. It's loud enough to distract him. I bolt down the hall, by passing the passageway in the kitchen. But there are more—Jack showed them to me. If only I can get to one, I can buy some time. Then maybe one of them will come looking for me.

I stop at the living room, searching the wainscotting for the panel. Is it to the left or right of the television? Shit. Think Katie. *Think.*

Watkins' heavy footsteps echo off the hardwoods. He enters as I'm running my fingers over the molding. I spin and say, "I told my brother I'd be right out. He'll come looking for me."

"Will he?" he asks, shutting the door behind him. "I watched you. Getting on your knees and giving him what he wanted. You may have been the one to ask for it, but trust me, sugar, he wanted it."

"Shut up," I say, repulsed that he watched.

"Why would he come back?" he continues. "He's out there with the rest of the good 'ole boys, watching the game, getting drunk. There may be a whole party going on out there, but no one is coming for you. Not until they want something from you, a hole to dump their cum in, will they come looking." He grins. "By then it'll be too late."

"Why?" I ask. "Why are you doing this? Why me?"

"Why? You have to ask?"

"Is this about Ryan? He gave us no choice. Jack killed him before he killed the two of us."

"I have no doubt about that. Your brother is a worthy opponent." He takes a step closer. "Ryan died because he got sloppy. He was too obsessed with you. You were all he could think about." He tilts his head. "Personally, I don't get it. A little too skinny for me. You know how I like my girls. Brandi was perfection."

He'd kidnapped Brandi while I was letting my stepbrother violate me in the bathroom of the bar. Her death is on my hands, like so many other things that have happened.

"Then why not leave me alone? I never told the police about you. I kept it quiet. You're the one that followed me to Tidewater—that stalked me and left me photos. You're the one that drove me back here—back to my brothers."

"I don't know, Kate. Maybe I just like to finish the job, tie up all the loose ends. Or maybe I know that the best way of getting back at Jack Davenport is by hurting the woman he loves."

The declaration stuns me. "Jack doesn't love me."

But it's twice now that someone has said it. First Paul, now Watkins. Can they see something I can't? Do I not understand what love looks like? Feels like?

I stare at the man, closing in on me, his hands balled tight at his sides—I can't imagine this man understands what love looks like either.

"At the very least," he says, rounding the couch, "I can honor him by finishing the job."

I reach for a vase on the table and grab it, tossing it at his head. I don't stay to see if it hits, but I hear it smash, clattering to the ground, I run to the foyer.

It's in that moment I make a decision. I can run, getting out of the house going for help. I'd expose the whole party to danger, or worse, prove me once again a liar and fool, when Watkins vanishes as easily as he came. No. This ends tonight. This ends and I'll be the one that finishes it.

I spin. *Where are you? Where are you?* I ask myself, searching for a way out. What's the point of these fucking secret doors if no one can find them? Bright light casts the afternoon sun through the front door, spreading it across the wall like a rainbow. The contrast highlights a darkened smudge on the corner of the wainscotting. I dive for it, wedging my nail underneath and it gives. I duck inside just as heavy footsteps come into the room.

I hold my breath, not daring move—terrified I'll reveal myself. On the other side of the wall, I hear Watkins searching. Circling the table in the foyer. He talks the entire time.

"Was this what it was like with my brother? When he hunted you through the woods? Is this what it felt like? Did your heart pound with excitement? Did your pussy get soaked thinking about what would happen when he finally caught you?"

I hear him walk around the room, getting closer. Even though there's a wall of plaster and lathe between us, I stand completely still.

"I did some research on Davenport Manor. Did you know that this used to be a cotton farm? There were hundreds of acres sold off years ago. The hot, humid climate is perfect for the crop. Elijah Davenport, that's the man that built this house, built the farm." I hear the sound of his hands on the wall. "He owned slaves. Dozens of them. He built this Manor on the backs of those men and women, with their blood, sweat and tears." A loud bang reverberates, knocking plaster dust to the floor. "I learned that he had them add secret passageways all through the house. You see, like the rest of the men in this family, he had an obsession with the women in the house and wanted access to them. Day. Night. Whenever the urge called. Those women made the perfect mistresses, unable to say a word." The sound of picking carries through the wall as he tests the corners of the wainscotting. "His wife was clueless, or at least she pretended to be." His voice lifts. "Is that what your mother does? Pretends her stepsons aren't creeping through the walls, defiling her daughter at their whim?"

I don't know what makes me run, the story he spins, the accusation, or the fear of him discovering me. I squeeze through the dark passageway, inhaling dust and spiderwebs, slamming into the beams that hold up the walls. I trip, my cowboy boot banging into a step. Swallowing back a cry, I know there's no direction to go but up, so I climb, hoping he hasn't breached the walls and is following me.

I'd known the Manor was a house of horrors, but the story Watkins told chills me to the bone. Murders. Rapes. Enslavement. The evil has worked its way into the walls, the floors and foundation. It's wormed into the boys, their friends, and as my heart hammers in my chest, I know it has infected its way into me, because all I want is to get my hands on him. To drive my knife into his chest and watch him bleed out on the floor.

When I reach the top floor, I stop.

I stop because there's nowhere else to run. I stop because I'm tired and out of breath.

I stop because no one is coming to save me.

But most of all, I stop because I realize I can't kill him if I'm hiding.

I turn and take a deep breath, reaching for the latch in the wall. I push through the panel and step into the one place I'm not allowed in—*ever*.

Jack's room.

Over in the corner, his bed is neat. All of the items that were there before are gone—the murder board and weapons are now downstairs, tucked away where the police and any other nosy visitors will find them.

I hear his footsteps on the staircase and as much as every nerve in my body screams for me to run, I stay bolted in place.

I'm tired of running.

He can come to me.

TWENTY-TWO

Jack

It's been ten minutes. State has scored twice more. My dad has consumed two more drinks and Helen fell into a blissed-out haze right after halftime.

"It's been ten minutes," I say to Paul while keeping my eyes on the door.

"Do you think there's something going on with my father and your stepmother?" he asks, taking a calm sip of his drink. Sip is being liberal. He's been nursing that cup since he got here, focused on his father's every move.

"I don't give a shit about your father and Helen," I say, shooting him a glare. "Oliver came out here ten minutes ago. He said Katie would be out here in a few minutes." I rub my sweaty hands on my jeans. "She's not here."

"He's been her doctor for years, and obviously our families are close, but his attention seems excessive. Have you noticed anything unusual?"

I glance over as he speaks, noticing nothing unusual. Sure, Derek has been around a lot, but that's not usual. He's not just our family doctor. He's a family friend. And yes, he's the one prescribing all the pills, but Helen has been a basket case since my arrest. Either he medicates her, or she does it on her own. I'm not sure which is better, nor do I really care.

"What I noticed is that Katie hasn't come outside yet." I step away from the keg. I'd only offered to take the job of pouring beer because she asked me to. It doesn't hurt that from this spot on the deck I can see everything—and everyone at the party. I grit my teeth. "Yeah, your dad is around a lot—handing out pills like a goddamn candy man. But Helen? She's a fucking disaster. Dad has no idea what to do with her and she's become a lot of work for Katie. I think, under the circumstances, your dad may be a guardian angel to both of them."

Paul's eyes narrow and he hums, like he's mulling it over. I don't have time for his analytical shit. Not today.

"Take over for me," I tell him. "I'll be back."

Before I get to the door, Davis walks up. "Jesus, you look like your team is losing." He nods at the big screen. "Spoiler—they're up by thirteen. What's going on?"

He's right. It's been a good day. The party went over well. The neighborhood harpies have kept the gossip in check, acting on their best behavior. "Just checking on Katie. She's been in here for a long time."

I step into the house, going straight to the kitchen. It's empty. A platter of food sits on the counter. "Katie?"

Davis circles around me and walks into the small hallway off the kitchen. A second later he calls, "Jack—in here."

In the middle of the floor is a bag of ice. It's still frozen, mostly, but there's a growing puddle of water underneath. I turn and look back into the kitchen where a glint of silver on the floor catches my eye. "Look," I say, pretending my heart hasn't kicked into gear. "What's that?"

Davis gets to it first, and my heart plummets when I see it in his hand: a knife.

Shit. Shit. Shit!

"Maybe she just dropped it," Davis says, but his eyes are darting around—going into detective mode—cataloging the room.

"Or maybe she didn't," I say, exiting the room. I walk past the laundry room, ducking my head in. A dirty wet shirt is in the sink. Oliver's. So that's why he changed.

Davis splits off to the garage, I take Dad's office and the small bathroom off the hall, before darting upstairs to check her bedroom.

It's empty.

Everything is empty.

It's all empty.

I run back downstairs, into the foyer, just as Paul and Oliver come in.

"What's going—" Oliver starts.

"She's gone," I say, pacing the small space while Davis fills them in. Thank God his brain is working because mine has stopped. Feral instinct races through me.

"It's him," I say. "He got to her. Right under our fucking noses." Hot boiling rage surges under my skin. "In our house. Our goddamn house."

"I was just with her," Oliver says. "We were together. She was anxious, but we worked that out in the laundry room—"

He stops.

"What?" Paul asks.

"I thought I saw someone pass by the door while we were together. I figured it was someone at the party." Even though we had signs up asking guests to use the carriage house facilities and not to enter the manor. Oliver pales. "She was sucking my—"

I charge over, grabbing my brother by the collar of his clean shirt. "You let your fucking dick get in the way of keeping her safe!"

"You're talking to me about keeping her safe! That's fucking rich!"

His fist swings out, but a hand shoots out and blocks it. Paul wrestles him back while Davis and pulls us apart.

"Stop!" Paul shouts. "Jesus. This is not helping find her."

I'm breathing heavy, amped up, and eyeing my brother. I know it's not his fault. It's mine—I got distracted months ago by Katie and let Watkins grab Brandi right out from under me. I should have looked for him harder these past few weeks. I should've—

"Paul," Davis says, taking over, "stay outside and make sure no one gets in or out. Don't let anyone in the house, and keep your eyes peeled for someone trying to get out. No matter what, make sure Montie and Helen do not come inside."

"Got it," he says, striding out the foyer, just happy to have something to do.

"Oliver, you stay down here, keep an eye on the main floor and all the exits, check any little hidey-hole you can think of. This place is filled with them.

Hidey-hole.

"Jack—"

I've already pushed open the panel in the kitchen, ducking into the walls, ignoring Davis. I showed her these passageways. Taught her how to move around the house on her own. If she could remember how to get to them... maybe she got away.

The dust isn't unsettled, making me think she didn't come in here. Fuck. Where is she?

I squeeze through the narrow passageway, not needing my flashlight to take the familiar route. I can't move too fast, my shoulders are too broad, but I know these hallways like the back of my hand. I see the smallest sliver of light in one of the doorways where someone didn't close it all the way. Carefully, I push it open and look into the living room. It's empty but I see the pieces of a broken vase scattered across the floor.

A sharp twisted rage fills my chest.

I pull out my phone and shine the light on the floor, revealing the disturbed dust. The mess leads to the staircase going up. I climb, stopping along the way to check different rooms. There's no sign of her—or Watkins anywhere, not until I get to the third floor—to the secret entrance to my bedroom.

Carefully I wedge my finger into the corner. The doorway slides, pocketing itself into the wall. As I ease it away, over the pounding of rushing blood to my ears, I hear her voice.

"I'm not afraid of you," she says.

"You should be," Watkins says. Just hearing his smug voice makes me want to smash through the wall, but I'm a hunter. I'm patient. Bursting out of here will endanger us both. Endanger *her.*

I nudge the door open a fraction wider, enough that I can see the two of them. They're standing in the middle of the room. Katie in that blue dress and cowboy boots. Her shoulders are back, chin up. It's an offensive posture, but she looks tiny compared to the blond man across from her. He's at least six feet and it's obvious, despite the wild exhaustion on his face, that he's fit. Those days of following us constantly and living in the warehouse have caught up to him, but not enough to make him less of a threat.

"Well, I'm not," she replies. "You know why?"

Watkins crosses his arms over his chest, his expression amused. "Please tell me. I'm dying to know."

She ignores the sarcasm and continues. "Because I live with two psychopaths—four if you count their friends. Every hour, every minute of the day, is me waiting for them to pounce. To use me as bait. To teach me a lesson. To push me past my boundaries. But mostly they just want to make more like them. They'll use me to catch you and then toss me away like garbage." She snorts. "Compared to them, you're a walk in the park."

Listening to her say these words brings out mixed emotions. A psychopath? That hurts a little. Everything else? Well, little sister isn't completely wrong.

"Every day in this house is pure hell," she continues. "*Torture.* My mother has slowly gone insane. My stepfather is rich and entitled. Manipulative—but lost. I *hate* living here. I feel my soul-sucking away with every passing minute." She looks around, spreading her arms at my room. "Just being up here? In Jack's room...God," she laughs nervously, "do you know what he'll do to me when he finds out?"

"What?" he leans forward, eating up her words.

"If I'm lucky he'll just rape me. If I'm not, I'll pay in blood."

"That's a very compelling story." He steps toward her. Confident, like a cat stalking a mouse. "But, I think you underestimate your brothers, Katherine."

"That's the very last thing I'd do." She bends, scratching at the back of her knee. "I learned a long time ago what they are capable of, Christopher, and I promise you, I'm more afraid of them than you."

"Then I'll make this quick." He lunges for her, but she's ready for it, dropping to her knees, just out of his reach. She slides her hand into her boot, lifting the handle of the knife I gave her.

Kill him. Kill him, Kate. Claim him as your first trophy.

I exit the hidden passageway, prepared if she fails. Watkins will not get away this time. One of us will kill him, but in my heart, I want it to be her. I want her to know what it feels like—to have that power—that control.

Like she said, I want her to be one of us.

Neither of them notices me as I enter the room—too caught up in their fight. Her movements are quick and sure. Zero hesitation.

"I hope you rot in hell," she screams, stabbing at him. I watch as the sharp steel lands, and she doesn't stop. She's not afraid. Katie shoves the blade into his abdomen, then, like I taught her, jerks it upward, slicing deep.

"You fucking bitch," he says, clutching his stomach as blood spills between his fingers. "You cunt."

He falls to his knees looking down at the blood in shock. Katie stumbles backwards, jaw dropped in shock over what she's just done. I step through the panel, just as Davis barges through the bedroom door, his chest heaving from running up the stairs. Our eyes meet, and Katie looks between the two of us, horror etched so deeply on her face it may never go away.

"I did it," she whispers.

"Hey, bitch," Watkins says, drawing all of our eyes to where he kneels on the floor. He has one hand on the wood, holding him up. The other behind his back. "This is for my brother."

"No!" Davis yells, but not fast enough. Not faster than Watkins pulls the gun from the waistband of his pants. Not faster than he levels it and pulls the trigger. There's no bang. No loud shot. A silencer covers the nozzle, just the soft "thwick" of the bullet exiting the gun and Katie's gasp as it tears through her flesh.

Davis dives for him, while I lunge for my stepsister, catching her before she falls to the ground. I hold her in my arms, pressing my palm against the bloody wound. It rushes out too fast—too slippery. I can't make it stop. Footsteps pound in the hallway and Oliver appears, wild-eyed and panicked. He looks at the carnage.

"Call for help! We need an ambulance!"

He fumbles for his phone, fingers stabbing at the screen.

"Jack?"

I turn back to my girl, her shirt soaked in red. "Yeah?"

"Did I stop him?"

I look over at Watkins. He's flat on the ground, Davis' boot on his chest, lying in a pool of his own blood.

"Yep." I brush the hair off her forehead, smearing blood across her fair skin. "You got him."

"Good." She smiles weakly. "He can't hurt anyone else."

There's the difference between us. We claim we're in it for the community, to stop the bastards before they tear apart families and lives, but at some point, that shifted and it's as much about the blood lust as anything else.

That difference is why we need her. A beacon to bring us back home—back away from the edge of darkness—and back to our true Mission.

To find our mother's killer. This time with our sister by our side.

Saved by my Stepbrothers

Foreword

Readers!

Thanks for following along with the adventures of Kate, the Davenport Brothers and their psycho friends, the doctor and the detective.

This is your pre-book notice about what's coming, what to look out for and if you should turn around now.

Family Confessions is a fast-paced, book of darkness and deviancy. It was originally published on Kindle Vella as a serialized fiction.

This is the final book in the series and things don't let up, so if you're hesitant check out this list:

T/W: dub-con, non-con, exhibitionism, overall mindfuckery, stalking, psychological exploitation, and obviously, murder.

Enjoy!

Angel & AK

ONE

Paul

____

"What's taking him so long?" Jack paces the hallway like a cat in a cage, moving from end to end, eyes dark and furious. "It's just a shoulder wound!"

"Maybe you should go help Davis and Oliver," I say as gently as possible. I understand Jack's impatience. It's killing me not to be inside the room with Katherine right now. She's hurt, traumatized, and alone...with my father.

"They can clean up just fine on their own."

If everything is going according to plans, Christopher Watkins' body is halfway to the Davenport house basement, courtesy of the secret passageway that runs from the top to the bottom floor. That passageway has a lot of uses, but one of the best is that it's an amazingly easy way to get rid of bodies. It's how we've used Jack's room over the years to interrogate suspects as well as remove them after.

"Yes, they are perfectly capable." I eye my lifelong friend. "I just think you'd feel better if you were doing something other than waiting."

He stops abruptly. "You're right. I would." He lunges to the bedroom door. "I'm going in."

I block him, not foolish enough to know he wouldn't try. Everything about Jack is predictable, from the consuming anger he has due to his childhood trauma, to his violent manifestation of that pain, to his current obsession with his stepsister. Everything lines up neatly. I see it, we *all* see it, everyone but him.

And maybe Katherine.

I press a hand against his chest. I'm no slouch, I'm just as fit and in shape as he is, but we both know he could pick me up and toss me down the hall if he wanted. A dark rage consumes him and it fuels him. I make eye contact and carefully say, "My father is doing us a favor by checking on her here and not sending her to the hospital where there would be a million questions and the police would automatically be involved."

The only reason the police haven't been called is because Davis *is* the police.

I'd heard the gunshot from outside, faint and obscured by the sounds of the football game playing on the big screen. Everyone else was oblivious, including Montie and Helen. I ran inside to find Oliver also racing up the stairs. When we got to the top floor, Davis was standing over Watkins' dead body and Jack held onto a bleeding Katherine.

My heart plummeted—the events of the last few months flashing before my eyes. We'd trained her, harassed her, hardened her up. We set this day into motion and now that it finally transpired... I didn't expect to see her covered in blood, hurt, and possibly dying on the floor.

I wasn't prepared for the sight of it, or the emotions it brought to the surface. Memories of how I was with her the last time surfaced. I wrestle with that beast, knowing that somehow Jack's stepsister has somehow chipped away at the icy exterior I'd honed all these years. She shattered me and crawled under my skin. I don't know how to deal with that myself.

The last time we were alone I'd completely lost control, succumbing to the desire to possess her and in turn allow her to possess me. She knew in that moment she had the upper hand. And seeing her like this, injured because of what we'd led her into...it gave me as much of a thrill as it did terror.

A plan was created quickly—that's not a surprise—Watkins isn't our first dead body, but Katherine... I realized the answer was down in the yard, buzzed on alcohol. My dad. The physician.

He'd come quickly when I told him it was Katherine that had been hurt. He liked her. Liked her mother, Helen, to a point that I'd become suspicious. What was going on between him and Katherine's mother? He doted on her. Plied her with drugs. Oversaw her treatment single-handedly, even though it's more than obvious the woman needs psychiatric help.

My father had been horrified when he walked into Jack's bedroom, stricken at the blood and violence. I wish I could say we hadn't had to go to him before, but there had been other injuries over the years. Davis took a hit with a knife two years ago when he cornered the drug dealer handing out Rohypnol-laced Fentanyl to high school girls. And there was the time Jack got shot in the leg by an asshole child molester trying to fight back. Dad had helped us out then, just like he did now, with few words and a steady hand, sewing stitches and prescribing antibiotics. He also didn't ask questions.

Ever.

Jack exhales and relaxes. "Will you at least go in and check on her?" he asks.

"Absolutely." I grip his shoulder. "She's going to be fine." His jaw sets and he nods, but I can tell he won't believe it until he sees her himself. "Seriously, go check on the guys. There are still fifty people in the yard and a body in the walls that will start to stink if you don't come up with a bigger plan. I'm sure they could use your help."

"Fine," he relents. "But if there's anything—"

"I'll let you know." I rest a hand over my heart. "I promise."

He steps back, and I wait until he's walked down the hall and turned the corner to the staircase. Only then, do I open the bedroom door. The sharp scent of antiseptic fills the air, bloody rags tossed on Jack's bedside table. While my father ran upstairs, I went to get his bag from the car. Oliver also handed over a first aid kit before he vanished to finish cleaning up.

Dad glances up, barely acknowledging me before refocusing on Katherine.

"How is she?" I ask, pushing my hands into my pockets.

"Lucky," he says. "Two inches down and it would've been her heart." Anguish pools in my stomach, dark and acrid. "I gave her some meds to knock her out while I examined her, but it was through and through." He nods to the wall. The bullet hole is small and dark, barely noticeable. "Davis will want to collect that for his report."

I take a step forward. Katherine is resting in the bed, her skin paler than usual, her eyes closed. My eyes travel to the bandage covering her shoulder. Her shirt was torn off and tossed in the trash. I see the rise and fall of her chest, confirmation she's still alive. "Listen," I say, moving next to him, "about the report. We aren't going to make one."

His eyes jerk up, not faltering this time. "What are you talking about? A man was killed here. A serial killer if you've been honest with me." The *if* is accentuated. "The police should know."

"No one is aware Christopher Watkins exists. Davis never told the police. They were so focused on his brother, Ryan, being The Binder, that they never considered another option. Davis was going to have his team go in and process the warehouse he'd been hiding out in when it went up in flames. There's no trail here." I look down at Katherine. "Just her word against a dead man. A known liar." I pick up her hand, pressing my fingers against her wrist. I need to feel her pulse. "There's no way they'll believe her."

My father wipes off the instrument he's holding. "This is very risky, son."

"I know you've been working closely with her mother—do you really think Helen can survive any more scrutiny? Can Montie? Their lives have been turned upside down since the trial."

He sighs. "Fair point. Any more and Helen would probably lose her mind completely. She's already touch-and-go as it is."

He should know. He is the one, after all, plying her with pills just to get through the day.

"I appreciate you coming up here and helping Katherine, but I need you to trust us on this. It's for the best," I brush her hair off her forehead, "for her and for the family."

He drops the last of his supplies back in the bag and faces me. We've never been exceptionally close, but we've always been similar. We both rule with logic and take our vows to our patients seriously. The rules surrounding our professions. Those have always been a little easier to manipulate. I can only hope he's willing to bend them now.

"I'll keep my mouth shut," he says, "on one condition."

"Of course."

"You keep me apprised of her health and let me follow up with her regularly."

"Sure, although I don't know if that's necessary—"

"I'm aware of the little games you've been playing with her, son. I saw the bruises on her backside—the ones she claimed were from a fall. Those were strikes." I swallow, feeling the heat of his gaze. "And yes, I heard the two of you during your 'appointment.' She's as vulnerable as her mother, Paul. The female mind can only handle so much trauma—so much abuse. They're fragile beings and if you push her to close to the edge, she may never come back."

I can't tell if it's a warning or a prediction, or how he presumes to know the mind of women. I clear my throat. "I hear you, *Dr. Sanders*, but your job is to heal her body. Mine is to nurture her mind." My shoulders push back, and face to face he's not so intimidating. "I'll make the decision on what is considered too far for my patient."

"So smug," he replies with a dark chuckle.

I grin. "Wonder who made me that way?"

He shakes his head. "She needs rest. *Complete* rest. That injury is going to be sore." He hands me a bottle of medication. "This is for the pain."

I take it and slip it into my pocket. "Thank you."

He grunts and exits the room, leaving me alone with Katherine. I stand over her, stroking her cheek with the back of my fingers. My father is wrong about her—she's not fragile. She's strong and her trauma only makes her stronger. We made her that way, built this girl from a slip of nerves and insecurity to a hard-ass killer.

I've never loved a woman more.

TWO

Kate

There's movement in the room. I'm aware of it, even before I crack open my eyes. It's a *shift—a settling*. Like a ghost of this old house that has come to life. But this is no ghost. The energy is subtle and dangerous, like a viper ready to strike. Cold settles in my lungs with a heavy breath. There's no scrape of shoes, no rush of an exhale. Just a presence. I slowly open my eyes and my focus moves to the end of the bed, where Jack is watching me.

The drugs Derek gave me have worn off enough that I'm awake, but not so much that I can feel the pain in my shoulder. It feels numb. That's not the only thing. The upset I should feel about killing a man isn't there.

Is that the drugs or the satisfaction?

Maybe both.

"How long have I been out?" I ask, feeling the dry ache in the back of my throat.

"Since last night. Thirsty?" he asks walking around the bed and picking up a glass from the dresser. He doesn't wait for my response. Instead, he slides his hand under my shoulder, gently lifting it with one hand while he aims a straw at my mouth with the other. I take a sip, the cool water a relief.

I look around his room. Jack's room. The place I'm not allowed to go into. The place that has seen so much pain and anger and death. I look down at my hands, expecting to see blood. They're clean.

I push up again, this time feeling the burn in my shoulder, but don't let it stop me.

"What the fuck are you doing?" he asks, watching me struggle.

"I shouldn't be in here," I say, gritting my teeth. "I know you don't like people—*me*—in your room."

"Jesus Christ, Katie. You think I don't want you here?"

I blink. I don't know what he wants. Everything is blurry. Everything hurts.

When I don't answer he grunts, "You're staying in my bed until you heal."

I'm not used to this side of him. This *caring* is almost too cruel after everything we've been through. Is it a trick? A trap. I fall back, the pain too much, but he catches me, eases me back down to the pillow, and moves closer.

His fingers graze my chin. "Too much?"

Too much...

Not too much water, but too much pain. That's what he's asking.

Is this another test? Seeing how much I can handle? How much until I break? I slowly shake my head. "No. Derek–Dr. Sanders–he gave me the good stuff."

He places the glass back beside the bed and I'm drawn by the movement until a glint steals my focus. It's a knife. Not just any knife...*the* knife. In a blinding second, it all comes back to me.

You fucking bitch! Christopher's screams invade. *You... cunt.* The sound of his body being ripped in two. The sound of him dying.

"He left the painkillers if you need more."

"No."

"No?"

"I don't want them." I shift my focus to him and lick my lips. "I want to be in control."

He sits on the end of the bed, and the mattress dips. "Go on."

"Tonight," I glance over to the spot on the floor where Christopher died, "something changed."

"You killed a man."

"I did, and–"

He interrupts, his forehead creased. "You're upset. It's understandable. My first time... I still wake up to the feel of his blood on my hands."

"I'm not upset." I grab his hand. Two clean hands gripping one another. "It was exhilarating."

His eyebrow raises. He's not in a position to judge, we both know that, but I can tell from the way the crease in his forehead deepens, he didn't expect that to be my reaction.

"Holding the knife, the way you showed me–the way you all prepared me–for once in my life I wasn't just afraid. I was powerful."

"I saw you," he admits, and it surprises me. I didn't know he was there. "I was tracking you—through the passageway. I saw you cut him open. It was breathtaking." He cups the back of my neck, rubbing his thumb down the column of my neck. "I've never seen you look more beautiful."

He shifts and I glance down, seeing the hard bulge in his pants. Only Jack Davenport, my psycho stepbrother, would get hard describing a murder.

And only I would feel the twist of want deep in my belly. The hot heat of forbidden desire.

God, we're a nightmare.

"I don't want more drugs," I repeat. "I want to plan."

"Plan." The way he repeats me is careful like he's the one holding his emotions in check.

My heart races, like a shotgun blast in my ears. I don't know how he'll react. But all of this meant something, right? The hunting. The killing. The training. It had a purpose, and it isn't about Christopher Watkins or The Binder. It's about the *ultimate murderer*. The man they've been searching for.

"What are you planning, sweet, little Katie?"

The way he says my name is different. There's a softness to it now, a warmth that hadn't been there before. He's pushing me, forcing me to say the words and as much as it terrifies me, it also excites me.

"The man who killed your mother is still out there." I slowly sit upright, ignoring the gnawing throb in my shoulder. His hand clamps around my waist and steadies me. "He's still out there, hunting, watching, hurting other people, other mothers. I know you've all been searching for him, but you've been distracted. Focused on the Binder. But he's gone now, and I want to help."

He tilts his head, those brilliant eyes piercing my bravado. "You've killed one man, and that was more dangerous than any of us wanted it to be. How do you plan on taking down the man that has eluded us for almost two decades?"

"You can use me–like you did with the Watkins brothers. I can investigate. Use my resources to dig up what I can."

"You think Davis hasn't already done that? We have files of information. We've followed every lead." He sounds dejected. I get it. He's searching for his white whale. He's tired.

He holds my neck with those strong fingers, stroking my throat. It's a bold statement and I wonder if I said the wrong thing. "Let me help you," I say again, swallowing the heartbeat lodges in my throat, "if you think that's a good idea."

"What I think, Katie, is that you proved yourself tonight." Jack drags the edge of the comforter down, revealing a faded black T-shirt that clearly came from his closet. My dress from the party is long gone–disposed of along with all the other evidence of the murder. I tremble as the warmth of his hand hits my thigh. "If you want to help us track my mother's killer, you can. But if you want to be used...well, I don't like the idea of other men using you. That's something between the two of us."

A shiver runs up my spine and I wait for him to act on this heat building between us, but he pulls the blanket back over my legs, smoothing it out and tucking me in.

"You need to rest," he says, standing.

My pulse throbs. "You're leaving?

"No." He sets the knife back on the table. "I'll be close. If you need anything, call me."

"But—"

"There will be plenty of time for planning, little sister." He bends and presses his lips against my forehead. "But not until you heal."

He walks away, but even after he leaves the room, I still feel the lingering heat on my forehead, burning from the kiss. It was more than affection. I understand that.

It was a promise.

"YOU NEED TO TAKE IT SLOWER."

I grind my jaw and jerk a savage glare at Oliver. "You *need* to get out of my way."

"Kate." He clucks his tongue. "You were shot, it's not a criticism."

"*Katie,*" Jack says a little more carefully, "he's right."

Because he knows. It's been three days. Three days of sleeping in Jack's bed. Three days of recovery, weaning off the painkillers, of hiding my injuries from my family.

Three days of pushing *his* boundaries for once. The Jack that has taken residence by my sick bed, is a different sort of man. He's still angry. Volatile. I mean, he did throw a prescription bottle across the room when he couldn't get it open.

Now, he and Oliver are both here, insistent on "helping" me.

I grip the edge of the bed and inch lower. Letting my shoulder take a little more strain. It hurts like a bitch, but I'm not letting go. Not yet.

My arms tremble.

My belly is rock hard.

I start to see white sparks behind my eyes as sweat runs down my brow and I collapse back against the mattress.

"Jesus. Help me get her back in the bed," Jack snarls at his brother and strides toward me. "I told you, babe, you're not fucking ready." He slides his hands beneath mine and lifts, plopping me back against the mattress.

"You'll tear something." Oliver reprimands as Jack moves out of the way. "None of us want your recovery to last longer than it needs to."

"And you sure as hell can't get an infection. It's way too late to go to the emergency room," Davis chimes in. "So far it seems like we're in the clear, but a gunshot wound? That would bring up a lot of questions."

"They're right," Paul chimes in, "there's no need to rush it. Recovery takes time."

The last three days have been surreal. Jack and Oliver hovered nearby. Davis popping in, making sure we all have our stories straight about what happened up here and that no one saw them dispose of the body. Paul drifts in and out, fussing over my wound and mental state.

I suck in hard breaths, ignoring the way they hover around me. "It's been three days, and if you're not going to let me out of the bed, can we at least talk?" I glance at Paul, hoping he'll back me up. Talking is his thing. "I'm tired of sitting here."

"What do you want to talk about?" Paul asks. He sits on one of the chairs brought up from downstairs. I'm not exactly sure what story my brothers concocted to explain my absence, but they've made it clear everything is handled. Even the laundry and cooking. *"We took care of ourselves before you came home, Katie. We can do it while you heal,"* Oliver told me.

"I want to know more about our next target."

The four of them still. Jack turns, facing the desk between the windows, busying himself with something. Oliver focuses on the package of bandages in the medical kit. Davis glares, jaw tight with his arms crossed over his chest.

Finally, Paul speaks. "It may be too soon for that."

"It's not too soon. I told Jack I want to help find the man that killed his mother." I glance at Oliver. "Your mother." I swallow. "With the Binder gone, we can focus on him."

"Katherine," Paul says, leaning forward and taking my hand. "This man...he's a phantom. We've used every resource at our disposal."

"We don't even know if he's still in Wilmington," Oliver adds. ""He could be dead."

"He's still here," Jack says, not facing us. "I can feel it."

Davis exhales. "Feeling or not, we've got nothing."

"Then let me look over the case. Give me everything you've got." I look at each of them, boring a hole in the back of Jack's head. "If you're going to force me to stay in this bed, you have to give me something to do."

Jack's shoulders tense, like a cord coiling between the two blades. He's pissed. He doesn't like me meddling in his business. He never has. My heart pounds at his reaction. I keep waiting for the day he'll toss me out of here—that everything will go back to "normal." Back to when he ignored and tormented me.

But he doesn't kick me out, he just turns and walks out of the room, slamming the door behind him.

"I'm sorry," I say to the others. "I didn't mean to upset him. We talked about it the other day and he seemed okay with the idea."

Oliver gives me a small, tight, smile. "He's not used to someone pushing him so hard."

"You're persistent," Paul says. "That's his thing."

Guess that's another thing we have in common.

"Shit." Davis looks at his watch. "I've got to get back to the station for a meeting in thirty minutes." His eyes dart to mine. "Whatever you need, Katie, I'll get it to you. I've spent my whole damn career looking for this bastard. Maybe a fresh set of eyes will help."

I stare, shocked at the offer. Davis has been...*nicer*, I guess, the last few days, but our relationship has never been anything but malice and hate. I force out, "Thank you," and watch him leave.

"I should go, too. I have appointments all afternoon," Paul says, squeezing my hand. "I talked to the court and told them about your health. They've agreed to put your therapy on hold until you get better."

"I appreciate that."

He picks up the bottle of painkillers his father left me. "You want me to refill this?"

"It's fine. I already told Jack I want to be clear-headed."

"At least take the supplement he left. It's good for inflammation." He reaches for the bottle of green capsules. He hands me a pill and I take it, swallowing it back with the water on the bedside table.

"Good girl," he says, igniting a spark in my chest. He lifts my hand and kisses the back. "I'll be back tomorrow. Call if you need anything."

"I will."

Once he's gone it's just me and Oliver. "This is weird," I confess.

"What's weird?"

"All of you, being nice to me."

He doesn't deny it. "You proved yourself to us, Kate. You took a fucking bullet for the mission." He stands over me, hand stroking my hair. "We've always known you were one of us, but you didn't. You fought it. Fought us."

But now I don't.

"I want to do this," I tell him. "I want to help you, for real. And not just investigating. Hunting."

"It'll happen when you're healed." He lifts my chin. "But I promise you, we won't go after him without you, okay?"

"Okay."

"You look beat. We'll try again tomorrow, okay?"

I draw in a breath, ignoring the sledgehammer in my shoulder, and nod. I will try again. I'll brace my hands against the mattress and dip until my body shakes. I'll push against my limits. *Then, I'll smash all the way through.*

I'M NOT sure what time it is when I wake up, but the room is dark other than the warm yellow light coming from a small lamp on Jack's desk. I blink, acclimating my eyes to the room, searching every corner as I lie completely still, the sound of my heart beating in my ears. The paranoia of being watched never goes away. PTDS is what Paul would call it.

When nothing emerges from the shadows, I exhale, releasing all the tension. I roll to my side, looking for the clock. The dark shadow next to me takes shape.

"Shit!" I shout, jerking upright despite the searing pain in my shoulder. My hand flails, searching for the knife on the table.

"Babe," a voice says, along with strong fingers clamping around my wrist. "It's me."

I barely hear him over the terror in my ears. *Me.*

I blink again, allowing the figure to come into focus. Jack.

"You son of a bitch!" I shout, beating his chest with my fist. My shoulder seizes and I cry out, flinching in pain. "You scared the crap out of me."

He sits on the edge of the bed, arms encircling me. "I'm sorry. You were out and I didn't want to wake you."

He's warm and solid. Safe.

Safe?

Jesus.

Over his shoulder, I see something on the chair. "What's that?"

His muscles tense and he pulls away. I lean back on the pillow, rubbing my shoulder. He picks up the packet on the chair. "It's my personal file on my mother's murder."

I take the packet from him, marveling at the weight. The investigator in me flickers to life. This is what I do. Who I am. I hunt people, just in my own way.

"Thank you for giving this to me." I hold it to my chest. "I know that isn't easy for you."

He runs his hand through his dark hair, bicep tensing with the move. He's a beast, muscle and brawn, rage and darkness, but I see something else in the man sitting on the edge of the bed.

A little boy that lost his mother.

"She hated this house," he says suddenly. "My mother. Loathed it."

My eyebrows raise. "She did?"

"She thought it was dark and gloomy. The dark woodworking and the big trees outside. She said she couldn't get enough light, no matter what she tried. She added lamps everywhere, opened windows, even had a few trees cut." He spins the silver ring on his finger, the raised edges of the 'D' shining in the lamplight. "Nothing worked. It was the design of the house, the architectural elements she couldn't change." He swallows, his Adam's apple bobbing. "She tried to get my father to sell it before she had Oliver."

I laugh. "God, I bet that didn't go over well."

"No." His lips tug upward, but it's not a real smile. "I remember them fighting. Their voices echoed all the way up the staircase." He glances up at me. "She joked that the house was sucking the life out of her. But in the end, she was right. Living here killed her."

I rest a hand on his forearm. "The house didn't kill your mother, Jack."

"The house didn't, but if we'd moved, she wouldn't have been here that day." His voice is hard—tight—like it could shatter. "We would have been somewhere else, living a brighter happier life." He turns to face me. "We wouldn't still be in the darkness, living and breathing in the same house where she was slaughtered."

I know Jack and Oliver were home, hiding in the secret passageway when their mother was attacked in the kitchen. She was raped, butchered, and left for him to find. He was just a little boy, but he lost his innocence that day. He protected his little brother. He ran to get help.

"The darkness of this place seeps into you, little sister. You were doomed the minute you walked into this house. You can become a killer or be killed. I had no choice but to test you, see which way you would bend." His hand pushes under the blankets, resting on my thigh. "The house either consumes or evolves. You've evolved."

I'm not sure how to respond, but the weight of his hand on my thigh sends heat through me. His confession, the revelation. I feel closer to him than ever. Jack Davenport is a complicated man.

"You said you wanted to be used," he says, pushing the hem of the shirt up my thigh. "How would you like me to use you, little sister?"

There's a dangerous edge to his tone. A shiver rattles the agony in my shoulder, shaking it alive. I wince and bite down on a groan, forcing my attention to his hand. This is the darkness he's talking about. How living here changes you. *Evolves.*

"I'm not going to hurt you," he says. "Not unless you want it."

Not unless I want it?

To get off. Is Jack asking if I want to feel pain? Is he giving me an option? He glances toward the knife I'd just been searching for, and I know what he's thinking.

"Yes." The word leaves my lips without a thought. I quickly add, "Just a little."

"Just a little." He drags the knife along the tabletop and the sound sends a shiver along my spine.

I close my eyes, my senses consumed by the sound...until there's silence. Seconds hang suspended. I wait for the touch of cold steel and flinch when the blade presses against the inside of my thigh. He glides it higher. "Do you know how incredible you looked when you killed Watkins? Like a goddamn queen." He leans in pressing his lips to my throat, sucking the skin. "I'm proud of you."

Elation surges inside me. I open my eyes, finding him.

"So fucking proud of you, *my Katie.*" He slides the blade higher until the spine is against my entrance. "Does it make you wet thinking about how you took a man's life? That you secured his final heartbeats? Stole his last breath?"

"It makes me glad," I tell him, knowing he's aware of the pooling heat spotting the crotch of my panties. "He was a monster."

He reaches with his other hand and tugs the elastic of my panties outward. One slice of the blade and they spring back, ruined. *Oh God.* Fuck yeah. I'm wet when he sinks his finger into me. Wet when he spreads my pussy and rests the cold steel against my warmth. He's so careful...so very careful when he drags it higher. There's a tiny sting. A *bite* of steel before it's gone. Then it's just him. He slides his finger knuckle deep, then looks down.

"Oh," he says quietly. "Looks like I nicked you." He presses the knife into the mattress on the outside of my thigh, bracing as he dips lower. "I'll kiss it better."

If this is what darkness feels like, I embrace it like a hug.

I almost come when he licks me, the tip of his tongue dancing across my labia. My hips rise, meeting his mouth, and I slide my fingers through his hair. He pulls back, teasing.

"Jack," I say, tone full of warning, "I want to feel your mouth on me."

"Fuck, I love it when you beg," he murmurs, moving just a little to lick my entrance. His tongue darts into my pussy, pushing between the folds, I squirm against him, dropping my head backward and tightening my grip on his hair. I don't want to beg anymore.

And I don't want to plead.

I want to fuck.

And be fucked.

I open my eyes and look down. "Eat me."

He flicks that dangerous stare to mine, a slow smirk tugging at his slick lips. "Whatever you want, little sister."

Our gaze collides as he dips once more, driving his tongue inside.

"Oh, fuck." My hips jerk off the bed. I open my legs wider, letting my panties roll around my waist. I don't care about anything other than my stepbrother's mouth on my cunt. I need him, the warmth, the suction...the *swallow.*

He grips my thigh, widening the gap between my legs, the knife pressing against the inside flesh drawing me back to the danger and to him. I grind his mouth against me, lifting one leg higher, to ride that delicious tongue. I'm so close. So fucking close.

The pain.

The pleasure.

The climax.

He snarls and the sound vibrates, sending me to the crest. His hot breath and the slick heat, tip me over, crashing to the edge.

One final buck and I come. "Oh fuck...*oh fuck.*" My thighs clamp around his ears, warm and burning, his fingers dig into my backside as I ride his face until the pleasure turns to numbness, to blissful oblivion.

I fall back down, my body limp and throbbing. Jack rises from between my thighs and licks his lips.

"Jesus, girl." His dark eyes meet mine. "Promise when your shoulder is better, you'll ride my cock with as much enthusiasm." His mouth is shining, salty, and sweet as he leans down and kisses me.

It's more startling than feeling his tongue on my clit. He never kisses me, not like this. Not like a lover should. He lifts the steel blade from my flesh, and places it back against the dresser as rolls to the side, falling to the bed. We're silent. Spent and awkward. Waiting for the other person to say something.

"Jack—"

"I love you," he says, cutting me off.

It takes me a second. A long second, before I turn my head. But he doesn't meet my stare. He can't. Instead, he whispers the truth to the ceiling, and I can only lay here and wait.

"I think deep down I've always loved you, just now, it's..."

"Exposed," I whisper because I feel it, too. This deep longing, this need for connection with this man I've known for so long. The tendrils of darkness tying us together.

He nods and closes his eyes.

It's exposed between us, cracked open, pulsing like a nerve. Jack loves me. *Jack loves...me.* He shifts his arm until it's pressed against mine and I can't do anything but close my eyes and relish the connection. This isn't how I thought love would feel. This is a savage love. A dangerous love. *And I want it.*

THREE

Davis

"WE'VE BEEN WATCHING YOU."

The statement makes my hackles rise—every self-protective nerve rising to the surface. I don't show it. I can't.

I take a sip of the shitty police station coffee sitting in front of me and ask, "And why's that?"

"After the Ryan Watkins situation, the Feds decided to take a deeper look into the other missing men in Wilmington." The guy across from me, Special Agent Jacob Holt, methodically lays missing person reports, investigation files, and several front pages of the Gazette on the table. "There's something bigger going on here and we think you know more than you've been saying."

I pick up the paper, noting it's about Michael Holland, the last man killed in Jack's bedroom before Christopher Watkins. The day Katie came back into our lives. I take my time, pretending to read, my mind running a million steps ahead. *What do they know? Did they find something? Why am I here?*

"I took the report," I finally say, "and followed up with the family. There were no red flags."

He slides another file toward me. This one is for Bruno Kingsfield. We caught him drunk in his double-wide, stacks of child pornography hidden under his filthy couch. "From all accounts, he was a drunk. Probably fell off the bridge walking home from the bar."

Holt nods, his chair creaking as he leans back. "So, you have no leads."

"Nothing credible," I admit. Nothing that hasn't been tossed in the swamp or liquified by chemicals out at the farm. "Why?"

"It seems like the families aren't happy with the police response."

I match my stance to his, making sure not to cross my arms over my chest. I keep my position wide—open. It's a body language tactic Paul taught me. Crossed arms imply a closed, defensive mindset. "They're not wrong," I admit. "Understaffed, underpaid, low morale, high crime. You know how it is."

"I do." He organizes the edges of the papers, lining them up in a row. It's a tell. He's anxious. Compulsive. "After the publicity of the Watkins case and the botched trial with Jack Davenport, your Chief feels like your precinct needs a win." He touches Holland's photo. "And we feel like the families need some answers."

"So, you're taking it over?" I ask, trying not to let the territorial flare consume me.

"We're offering you help." Holt lifts his chin. "And we'd like you to take the lead."

"With the Feds?" I blurt. Fuck. It's not a reprimand. It's an opportunity.

"Yep. You have good instincts," he says. "You're easy going and the community likes you. People have nothing but good things to say about Davis Higgins. That's the kind of police-community relations we're always looking for." He grins. "That's also the kind of attitude that gets people to talk."

I gesture to the information. "And you think we need to get more people to talk."

"The answers to where these men are is close by. I have no doubt about that." He scratches his jaw. "You're right about there being no leads, but that, in itself, is an issue. Men don't simply vanish. Not this many."

"Sounds good. I'm happy to help." *Continue to cover our tracks.*

He stacks up the papers into a neat pile, slides them into a file folder, and hands it over. "One thing," he says. "No one can know we're working together. If the locals or press find out the Feds are sniffing around, whoever is behind these disappearances may get spooked."

"Sure. No problem."

He gives me a hard look. "I'm serious, Higgins. Not a word can get out. Not to your mother. Your girlfriend or the pussy you're fucking on the side."

I smile. "No worries. I don't have any of those."

What I have with Katie is undefinable.

"Good." He thrusts out his hand for me to shake. "And another thing..."

I raise an eyebrow. "What's that?"

"You solve this case, there's a position waiting for you in Quantico, I guarantee it."

A position in DC. With the Feds.

A surge of power runs through me—pride—but even I know it's too soon to make plans.

I shake Holt's hand, my grip tighter than steel. "Let's catch this bastard."

I'M NOT surprised to find Katie still in bed—her brothers have shifted into overprotective mode. But when I walk in I'm impressed to see that she's sitting up, legs crossed, with a stack of papers spread across the blanket.

"Hey," she says, looking up. Her hair is twisted up in a messy bun. Her tank is thin, comfortable, tight enough that I can make out her nipples through the cotton. My eyes dart down to the bandage on her shoulder and push aside thoughts about how it could have been two inches lower. What would've happened then?

Some of the uneasiness between us has begun to fade. We had each other's back that night at Hades and I can't deny that every time we have sex, or something close to it, the world tilts on its axis. What started out as a game, a way to fuck around with Jack and Oliver's stepsister, has turned into something else.

What, I haven't quite figured out.

"I brought you something," I say, lifting the strap of my satchel over my head. "Everything I have on the Davenport murder."

"Oh!" Her eyes light up like I've just brought her a gift. "Hand it over."

It's a thick file. Three really, but it's smaller than I'd like it. "The case is cold. No, not cold, frozen, like a witch's tit." She snatches it from me the second I get it within reach. I nod at the papers on the bed. "Some of that may be duplicates with what Jack already gave you."

"That's fine. I'll make sure I keep them separate." She starts making organized piles. "Since you're here, can I ask you some questions?"

"Sure," I reply, sitting in the chair next to the bed.

"The other day, you called him a ghost. But really, who do you think did it? Where do you think they are now?"

"I have no fucking clue where they are now. If I did, we would have caught him." I sigh and rub my forehead. "As for theories... Jack and Oliver don't like to hear them."

"I'm not Jack or Oliver. It's not so personal to me. Tell me what you think."

Fair point. "I think it was most likely committed by someone she knew."

"You think she knew the person that killed her?" She leans forward, dragging that shirt a little tighter, making her nipples a little more visible. I guess a bra is out of the question with her shoulder. As usual, Katie is fucking clueless about how hot she is and continues with her questions. "Why do you say that?

I pick up the file and open it to the photos of the crime scene. They're gruesome. A complete bloodbath. I point to the kitchen countertop. "See that? Two glasses."

She peers at the image. "Could have been for one of the children?"

"No, those are nice tumblers. Filled with iced tea. I came to this house as a kid. We drank out of plastic cups and were strictly fruit juice. No tea." I make a face. I still hate the taste of iced tea.

"So, she wasn't alone. Montie?"

"He was at work—two towns over. Alibi checks out."

She wraps a strand of hair around her finger. "A friend?"

I shake my head. "Not that ever came forward."

"I see your point, but there could still be a simple explanation." She drops her finger, hair springing in a coil. "Is there anything else that makes you think she knew her killer?"

I pull out a photo of the body. A lump rises in my throat knowing it's my best friend's mother, but I swallow it back and push myself to the zone where I'm numb to scenes like this. "The act was excessively violent. He butchered her. He mutilated her genitals. It takes a lot of rage to do something like this. Everything in my gut tells me it was personal."

"Your gut? Gut checks don't hold up in court."

I look at her. At her wide eyes and not-so-innocent expression. She's changed in the last few months. Hell, *days*. She killed a man. She took a bullet. She's sleeping in Jack's bed. He's *letting* her sleep in his bed. Things I never would've seen coming.

"My gut is all I have, Katie. It's what helps me track killers and take down the bad guys." I rise, moving next to the bed. I take her hand and press it against my stomach. It's rock hard, toned from hours in the gym downstairs. "It's what tells me what moves to make and when to make them." With my other hand, I brush my thumb over her cheek. "It's what keeps me and the people I care about alive."

Her fingers curl against my shirt and she looks up at me, tongue licking her bottom lip. "What move is it telling you to make now?"

"God." I chuckle. "Even now, wounded and surrounded by photos of a butchered, mutilated woman, and your pussy still can't get enough."

Her legs slide together like she's easing the pain between them. "Are you saying you don't want me?"

"I'm saying now probably isn't the time." I glance at the door, knowing one of her protective big brothers is likely going to come through the door and they'll be pissed that I'm not treating her like a porcelain doll. But I'm a dumb ass, who rules with one thing other than my gut.

My fucking cock.

I take her hand, the one pressed against my chest, and drag it down, lowering it over my cock. I'm hard as lead, straining against the seam. She spreads her fingers across the space and grips me. *Fuck.*

"Let me taste you," she says, thumbing at the button. "Oliver, he hasn't been letting me..."

"Suck on him?" I ask, well aware of their kinky habit.

"He worries it's too strenuous."

I cup her chin. "No, baby, he's worried he'll lose control and fuck your mouth so hard you'll reinjure yourself."

A glimmer of want heats her eyes. "I can take it."

Hell yes she can.

I nod, giving her permission to lower my zipper. A gust of air escapes my lungs when she takes me out, heavy and thick in her small hand. I massage open her jaw with my thumbs and she looks from my cock up to my eyes. "You're not worried about me getting hurt?"

"Nope." I smirk. "My gut tells me you know how to handle my cock."

Her lips part and her hand slides down my shaft to cup my balls. I grunt, aiming my cock for the back of her throat. The rush of warmth from the inside of her mouth, sends a thrill up my spine and my balls clench as I struggle not to buck into her— out right fucking her face. Oliver's right, she is still healing, but Katie's proven repeatedly that she's tougher than she looks.

"God, your mouth is perfection," I tell her, sliding my hand around to the back of her neck. "It was made to take cock, you know that?" She nods, eyes watering from the invasion. "You're such a dirty, sexy, slutty, girl."

One hand grips the base of my shaft, and the other reaches for my hip, nails pressing into my skin. Her nipples are hard, tight pebbles peaking against her shirt. She whimpers, and I think it may be the pain in her shoulder, but I catch the shimmer in her eye. The want.

"You horny?" She nods again, never losing rhythm. "Of course you are. I bet your pussy is aching. It's been days since you got fucked, right?" I think back. "Down in the gym?"

A wet, "Yes," comes from around my dick.

"Show me how wet you are."

She dips her hand between her legs, pushing her fingers beneath her panties. She pulls them back out, sticky and slick. I squeeze her neck, indicating I want her to open up. Her jaw drops and I pull out. "Rub that on my cock."

She dips her fingers in again and they come back out shiny. She coats my shaft, adding it to her spit. "That's a very good girl," I tell her, tugging at her jaw. "Now, suck it off."

She takes me—and her taste—back into her mouth, moaning as I push inside. All of this is just teasing and taunting, but the base of my spine feels like it's on fire, my balls ready to explode. It only increases as I watch her, fingers plunging into her pussy, little cries of pleasure warming my cock as I bury it down her throat.

"I'm gonna cum," I grind out, threading my fingers into her hair, "and you're gonna take it. Every last drop."

She nods, eager for my seed. Her fingers pump faster as she builds to her own orgasm. I slow to her rhythm, wanting to barrel toward this together. Wanting the feel of her all around me, her pleasure mingled with my own. Her breath comes short, quick, just like the motion of her mouth, her fingers, our bodies writhing as one. Her eyes flutter shut, and a long, deep moan rises from her chest, and I know she's there, and I follow her, cum pulsing down the back of her throat.

She shudders, the orgasm rippling through her, and her jaw slackens, going limp like the rest of her body. I take her fingers, the ones that had just been inside her, and suck them clean. "You taste good," I tell her, licking between the crease. "So fucking good."

"You do, too," she tells me, lips blistering red. I bend down and kiss them, tasting myself. Tasting her. She groans. "I can't get enough."

I pull away, running my hand through my hair, looking down at this girl who went from fighting me over everything, to giving me all she's got. I don't hate it. No, hate isn't the feeling building in my gut, not anymore. Not when it comes to her.

She leans back, wincing at a sharp stab of pain in her shoulder. I grab the bottle of pills. There are two left. I hold one out.

"I'm not taking those," she says. "They make my mind fuzzy."

I thumb her lips apart and push it inside. "Trust me, babe, after that, you're going to need something to take away the pain."

I hand her the glass of water and reluctantly, she swallows it down. I give her the supplement and make sure that goes down too. The motion of her throat makes me think of how my cum fills her belly.

"Don't tell Jack and Oliver we did that," I say, running my hand down her hair. "They'll get pissed."

"I won't," she says. I believe her. She doesn't want them mad at her, but she really doesn't want me mad. This place, this uneasy truce where we fuck and solve crimes together, commit a little payback?

That's my happy place.

Shit, my dick twitches, ready for her again, but I've got work to do. Important work, things that can take me to bigger and better places than Wilmington—things that will make me choose between my brothers and my job.

Things that'll make me go against my gut.

FOUR

Oliver

"ARE YOU SURE YOU'RE READY FOR THIS?"

She looks up at me, those wide brown eyes sparkling. "More than ready."

The excitement in her voice is addictive. I crave more, but there's a flicker of uncertainty inside me, one I can't help but act on. "Maybe we should wait for Jack?"

Only it's too late, she's out of bed, her steps stronger, her knees no longer weak as she paces the room and works her shoulder. "You make me stay one more day in that damn bed and I swear to God, I'll burn this entire house to the ground."

She says the words with a smile, but there's an edge to the threat. She means it and I realize we've pushed our little Kate as far as she can take it. "Then if you're sure," I start carefully. "I have a surprise for you."

Kate spins, excitement sparkling in her eyes. "Oh, I love surprises."

I cross the room and caress my thumb along her jaw. "I know you do."

I also know surprises aren't the only thing our little sister likes. She likes licking and sucking. She likes swallowing and doing all the sick, little things we have between us. But this isn't about that. I step backward and motion to the pile of clothes I placed on the end of the bed. This is a reward and our sister deserves it. "Then let's get you dressed and we'll get out of here."

"We're finally leaving the house?"

She says the words as though she's been a prisoner. Maybe at first, now she's freer than she realizes. "Yes, Katie. We're finally leaving."

It's just for the day, but it's more than she's had in the last week. I glanced at the thick stack of folders of our mother's case file on the bedside table. With all that horror and death, she must be going stir-crazy.

I help her out of the flimsy pajamas. The sleeves of her shirts are a little tricky, but we manage. By the time she is dressed, and her boots are laced, she's a little wobbly on her feet, but she tries to hide it from me. Her gaze is steely when it connects with mine.

"Ready." She gives me a weak smile.

I shake my head, staring at the woman who was once a liability and now someone I didn't want to be without. "You're incredible, I don't think I've ever mentioned that."

"No, but feel free to remind me as much as you want."

I give her a chuckle, then take her hand. "I'll keep that in mind."

I lead her out of the bedroom, then out of the house to my car parked in the drive. She winces as she slides into the passenger's seat. I hate that flicker of pain and lean down, tugging the seatbelt across her and snapping it into place.

That tight feeling stays with me as I climb in behind the wheel and head out of the city. The drive is quiet and she's unsure, scanning the houses and then the trees as we slowly make our way toward the farmhouse. When I take the dirt road, she's surprised, cutting a careful glance my way.

She knew we had a place somewhere. Although, she's never been out here. I guess we're moving into a deeper level of trust.

"This is yours?" she asks when I pull into the driveway and head along the worn track to the barn.

"Yep. It's been in the family for generations–although not under the Davenport name. It belonged to my mother's family."

"Hmm." She seems to sense the importance. "And this is where you..."

I kill the engine and turn to her. "Yes. This is where we complete the missions."

Her eyes widen and she manages a soft, "Oh."

I help her out of the car and take her hand as we make our way to the farmhouse. She takes her time, taking in the barn and the surrounding forest, peeling back the layers of our world as I open the locks and step inside.

The place is clean and neat, and undisturbed. I drag in the musty scent of the place and it hits me how long it's actually been since we've had to use this place. It's been months since we hunted anyone other than The Binder. I glance toward her...well, and Katie.

I feel that familiar ache rise inside me. The one that always emerges when we come out here. That sense of purpose. The drive. "I figure being out here may help with your training. You know, getting a better understanding of where we work, how we operate."

Her gaze instantly drops to my cock. As much as I'd love my sister to sink to her knees in our house of bloodlust, I have other reasons for being here in mind. Instead of opening my fly and letting her ease that tension inside me, I cross the living room to the locked cabinet fixed on the wall and I punch in the date of my mother's death to release the lock.

Inside are the weapons we keep out here and I wrap my hands around the cold steel and drag the Sig out. There's a catch of her breath behind me. I grab three loaded magazines and turn around.

Her eyes are wide, fixed on the gun in my hand. "You're going to teach me how to shoot?"

"Yes," I close the cabinet and head toward her. There's a flicker of fear in her eyes, one she smothers by straightening her spine. The act is damn cute. "Don't tell me knives turn you on, but a gun fills you with fear?"

"I'm just nervous," she whispers, then chews her lip, "that's all."

I tuck the magazines in the waistband of my trousers and take her hand in mine. "That's why we practice, sweet Katie."

I lead her away from the farmhouse and deeper into the forest, where we bury the bodies. Somehow, she knows. Does she sense it? The dead trapped out here? She rubs her arms even though I don't feel the chill. "How many are buried out here?"

I guess that's a yes. I glance her way, watching her reaction. "A lot."

"A lot," she repeats, still there isn't fear in her tone. More like an understanding.

I slow down when we near the large rotting tree trunk that had fallen long ago. There are already tin cans with bullet holes laying in a heap on the ground from the last time we were here. I hand her the Sig, watching her stare at the weapon like it's about to bite her. I turn and walk away.

It's more than a measure of trust. It's a test. My senses are heightened as I stride to the tree and slowly pick each can up, sitting them on top. But there's no internal screaming, no chills racing down my spine. There's nothing out of place as I turn around and see her watching me with the gun pointed at the ground. I gave her the best opportunity to end this, to end me...to finally run, but I know her heart by now. I know she won't betray me.

Because she's one of us.

I move behind her to lift the gun, helping her wrap her fingers around the grip, and then her own hand with her other. "It's all about the tension, you see. Tension in your shoulders." She flinches when she pulls back. I know her shoulder must be in pain, although it's not with her dominant arm. "Tension in your breath."

I suck in my own breath, let it sit heavy in my belly then slowly exhale. "Push with one hand and pull with the other."

I guide her finger around the trigger, taking aim. "Then it's just...squeeze."

Crack.

The gun kicks in her hand. The shot misses, going completely wide. But that doesn't matter, I would be more surprised if she managed to hit it. I lower the gun and turn to her. "How was that?"

She's slow to respond at first. I worry until with a rush she whispers. *"Oh my God."* Pride blooms inside me as she meets my gaze. "That was *incredible.*"

I smile, maybe knives aren't her only kink. "Again?"

"Yes."

I move back to the same hold, creating tension in her shoulders and in her grip. This time she's the one who slips her finger around the trigger. "About this time, we aim for the can?"

She just gives a nod, and I can feel the sense of concentration inside her as she takes aim.

Crack.

She misses again, bits of bark fly out next to the can instead. I'm impressed. "Almost," I murmur against her ear.

I don't need to ask her if she wants to go again because she's already adjusting, easing her hold against the trigger, and this time when she fires it's all her.

Crack.

The can flies backward and I stare dumbfounded. My sister is a natural. "Well done, Kate."

She beams as I motion to the rest of the cans already lined up. "Go your hardest."

She gives the nod and sets back to the task.

Crack.

Crack.

Crack.

The shots ring out. She misses it first and then adjusts and she doesn't miss again, puncturing the metal with nice neat holes. I stride forward, gather the cans and line them up again and when I come back, she's already focused.

But this time when she fires, she misses. "Shit." She snaps and tries again. Misses again, and then again and growls in frustration. I can see the tremble in her hand and know her shoulder must be screaming, pushed to its limit.

"Maybe that's enough for today?"

She shakes her head. "No."

I step closer and place my hand on her arm. "Katie, we have plenty of time. The cans aren't going anywhere."

"I know that"" She doesn't look at me, frustration seethes in her voice as she stares at the fallen log.

There is something she's not saying. Something that's lingered the entire trip here. "Do you want to talk about it?"

"Things are changing with us and I'm just trying to adjust. Trying to find a *balance*."

Get shot in the shoulder and become the center of attention of four dangerous men. I see how she would be stumbling.

"What kind of balance?" I ask, needing to hear her say it. This isn't the time to be coy. She's right, things are changing and that includes how we communicate.

"The balance between us. The mission." Her eyes dart down to my crotch and back up. Her nipples tighten, pressing at the cotton of her shirt. She hasn't worn a bra since the shooting and the injury makes everything more sensitive. "How we respond to one another."

"Like, adjusting to our physical needs?"

I can't believe we're talking about this. This is something she'd normally explore with Paul, but here she was, confiding in me.

"It's more emotional than that," she says quietly. "Not just physical but...how I feel about you."

I stiffen, my senses narrowing in on the glassy sheen of her eye. I've seen it when she's suckling on my cock, gazing up at my face. I've noticed it when she looks at Jack, embracing his gruff, dangerous exterior. It flickers when Paul takes care of her, and

Davis brings her information to investigate. So far, I've attributed it to Stockholm syndrome.

But there's something now that gives me pause. Is our little sister falling in love?

Fear punches through me, the question gnawing at my soul. Which one of us has she fallen for?

But the question is stupid because I already know the answer: Jack.

"If it's any consolation, he feels the same way," I admit, knowing my brother is probably too much of a pussy to admit it himself.

She turns toward me, her eyebrow lifted in a perfect arch. "You do?"

You do...

The words slam into me and my heart pounds in response. I assumed she was talking about Jack, my mouth suddenly dry, my cock hard as steel. I fight to find the words. "Yes," I answer, "I do. Always have."

A smile tugs the corner of her mouth and her fingers thread through mine. "Good."

I pull her hard against my thrumming chest. I can't believe I finally admitted the truth, because fuck, I'm a pussy too. I'm in love with her. It's not just her body, her mouth, the way her skin turns pink when she's excited. It's the fire burning inside, the dedication and intensity. The loyalty.

She looks up at me, her long hair hanging down her back. My cock presses into her belly, stiff and eager. She rubs against me in encouragement, and she drags her hands up my chest slowly. She pushes up on her toes, kissing me. Her tongue is warm, and it should be a gentle moment, but I'm hungry for her and deepen the kiss into something rough and violent. God, she tastes so fucking good.

"I've missed you in my bed," I tell her, licking a hot path down her neck. "I know Jack gave you his bed to recover in, but I think about you every night."

"I think about you, too," she says, pressing her tits against my chest. "I miss having you there to comfort me."

I push her hair back, fisting it in my hands, and laugh. "It can't be too much. You've been passed out every time I come up."

"God, I know. I stopped the painkillers, but I've just been so tired." She tilts her head. "I've been reading a lot."

The case files. "I've noticed."

My chest constricts every time I see her pouring over it. I know she wants to help—Jack gave her his reluctant blessing—but it still makes me uncomfortable. I don't want Katie tainted by the darkness of my mother's death. I like her as she is, shiny and new. Different.

Ours.

But I guess that was lost when she killed Watkins and I know there's no going back. Would I even want to? No. This girl. This is the one I love.

"What do you think?" I ask, curious to hear her opinion.

"I think I'm going to help you find your mother's killer," she says, with complete confidence. "And we're going to track the bastard down, hunt him, torture him, and make the bastard pay."

My dick twitches. No one has ever said something that sexy to me. Not in my entire fucking life. I spin her around, pressing her against the blind, hands pushing at the waistband of her leggings. "I love you," I say to her, not ashamed or embarrassed to admit it. "I fucking love you, do you understand?"

"I love you, too," she says, fighting with my belt. "I need you in me, Oliver. Fuck me."

I push down my pants and yank her panties down, then lift her in my arms. Guiding my cock to her entrance, I groan when I feel how wet she is for me. "Jesus," I mutter, capturing her lips with mine. "Get on my dick, baby."

She lowers herself down at the same time I rise up, our bodies colliding in the middle. "Goddamn," I say, feeling her stretch around me. "You good?"

"So good," she replies. Her cheeks are red, her pussy is hot, and her legs wrap around me, drawing me as close as I can get. "Fuck me like you love me, Oliver."

I grin, aware we're out here among the dead—the piles of victims underfoot, decaying, and rotting, their souls burning in the depths of hell. Each one a symbol of a successful hunt and kill.

This, I think, thrusting into her tight pussy, *isn't hell.*

If it's anything, it's heaven, and I'm going to let my girl ride me all the way there.

FIVE

Kate

WHAT THE BOYS DON'T UNDERSTAND IS THAT I TAKE MY JOB seriously.

I understand their mission better now. I get the compelling urge to hunt, but even the taste of blood doesn't dampen my true passion: crime investigation. I realize now that this curiosity—this need for the truth—must have been ingrained in me from the moment I moved into Davenport house and learned what happened to Jack and Oliver's mother.

Yesterday, out at the farm, learning more about the boys' mission and learning to shoot had been magical. But even more so? Hearing Oliver tell—no *show*—me exactly how much he loves me.

God. I'm the luckiest girl.

Today, the house is quiet. Jack and Oliver left in the SUV early this morning. Paul and Davis are at work. Mom's health improved after the party and with Derek's encouragement, Montie took the opportunity for them to go on a short trip to their house on the ocean. Really, it's an opportunity for my stepfather to play golf, but mom likes the ocean, and the fresh air can't hurt. I keep thinking about what Jack said about his mother—how the house was filled with darkness. Is that what has consumed Mom? Her problems started long before the trial. Maybe it's the house. The darkness. I feel it in my chest every morning when I wake. There's a difference, though. I like the way it feels, pushing and tugging at my skin.

I spread the files out on my bedroom floor, arranging them in the way that makes the most sense to me. Jack likes his murder board, but I like to spread it out and stand over it like I'm looking down at the pieces of a puzzle.

For so long no one spoke of Olivia Davenport in this house. She was just another mystery—a ghost—one that haunted every soul that lived here. Particularly her sons.

According to the notes, she was thirty-five when she was killed. Mother of two, Jack and Oliver. Wife of Montgomery Davenport. She came into the house with her boys when the killer ambushed her. The boys managed to hide, Jack dragging his younger brother into the dark passageway. They heard everything. The way she and the intruder fought, the violent way he raped her in the kitchen, the hacking sounds as he unleashed his rage on her body, leaving her on the butcher block to be found by her sons.

Davis and Paul both witnessed the removal of the body—their fathers, Davis' a cop, and Paul's the family doctor—had both been called to the scene.

I search for the smallest clue, the tiniest scrap of evidence—anything to give us a new lead. I pick up the photograph Davis showed me in Jack's room. Was there something to the theory about the second glass? Was Olivia killed by a friend? An acquaintance?

Whoever it was took their time. According to the coroner and crime scene scientists, it took at least an hour for her to die. That's an hour of torture and pain. An hour of the boys listening.

Jesus. I toss the photo on the pile and rub my neck. I've been sleeping weirdly—good. Super deep, but with intense dreams. I wake up twisted in the sheets, my neck at a weird angle. I stretch and spot a form I haven't read yet: interviews with witnesses and friends.

It's the usual. Neighbors, the postman, and anyone Olivia had contact with in the days before her death. The grocery clerk. The teller at the bank. The dry cleaners. None say much. Olivia came in and out, doing her business as usual. The boys were with her. *Did anything seem unusual? No. Did it appear like she was being followed? Not that they could tell.*

Everyone says the same thing: Olivia Davenport was a nice woman. Pretty. A good mom.

I pick through the sheets until a name catches my eye. Holly Goodwin. Next to her name it says, deceased best friend.

From the report, it seems like Holly was too hysterical to give much information. I look to see if there was a follow-up.

There wasn't.

"Kate."

Startled, I shoot up, heart in my throat. "God, people have to stop doing that to me," I say, hand over my chest. It's Dr. Sanders.

"I'm sorry," he says, giving me an apologetic grin. "I knocked, but no one answered. I was concerned that maybe you couldn't get to the door and I let myself in."

I take a deep breath, exhaling out the nerves. "It's fine. I was just engrossed with my work."

He looks down at the paperwork, expression never faltering. "You're working on Olivia's case? For the Gazette?"

"Well, no. I was fired from the Gazette," I admit. The perjury charge and subsequent probation from Jack's dismissed case made that an impossibility. "I thought maybe I could sell it independently, or make a podcast or something. True crime is pretty big right now."

None of that is true, not really, but I can tell Derek buys it.

"I came by hoping to check out your wound—see how it's healing. Although I admit you look like you're feeling much better."

The other times he came to see me I was upstairs, still in bed. "I feel much better."

"Good." His eyes flick to my shoulder. "Still, I'd feel better getting a look at it."

"Of course," I reply, sitting on the chair that he gestures to. "The muscles are still tight, and I don't have a huge range of motion yet." It hurts worse after shooting guns with Oliver. The kickback was more powerful than I expected. "But I've been doing the exercises you suggested, and it seems to help."

"You're an excellent patient," he says, looking down at me. "Can you unbutton your shirt a little, and give me a better view?"

"Sure." I fumble with the buttons. I'm not wearing a bra, the straps are too restrictive on my shoulder, making it ache. I loosen the buttons enough that I'm able to drop the collar over my sleeve. Derek's touch is gentle. His hands are always warm and soft—reassuring.

He examines my shoulder, carefully removing the bandage, and inspects the wound. I glance away from the injury. The gnarled flesh makes my stomach turn. My eyes land on the paperwork spread across the floor and back up at him. "You were there that day, right? When Olivia was murdered?"

"After," he says, gently assessing my arm. "I got a call that Olivia was hurt, and I rushed over. It was obviously too late by the time I got here." He swallows thickly. "It was the most disturbing thing I've seen as a doctor, before or after. The way she was cut up."

He pales, but he has the information I need, so I change tactics but press on. "There are a lot of speculations about what happened—*who* killed her. Was it someone she knew? A friend? An acquaintance? Or maybe it was completely random. Do you have any theories?"

His expression sours, lips curving downward. "Olivia was a devoted wife and mother. I can't imagine anyone that knew her wanting to hurt her. It's unimaginable." He pauses. "I need to test your range of motion." He lifts my arm, drawing it out of my sleeve. I clasp a hand over my breasts, trying not to feel modest. Although he's a family friend, he's also a doctor. He lifts my arm, seeing how far I can raise it over my head. "Good, good." He presses his fingers into the side of my breast. "Any tenderness here?"

I stiffen at the intrusion, despite the gentleness of his touch. "No. It's fine."

He drags his fingers away, moving toward my back. I exhale and ask again, "Do you? Have any theories, that is?"

He stills, releasing my arm and stepping away. "Some questions will never be answered, Katherine. And maybe others should never have to be asked in the first place. It conjures up too much pain."

I frown. "Are you saying that you think I shouldn't look into this?"

"I think old wounds, like new ones," he looks at my shoulder, "need to heal. This case has been opened time and time again. Nothing ever changes, other than the anger and resentment it causes. That just seems to grow."

There's something pointed in his statement. I stand and slip my arm back into my shirt and ask, "You mean the boys."

He holds my eye. "They aren't well. I suspect you know that."

"They..." I search for the right words. "They were traumatized that day."

He watches as I rebutton my shirt, eyes glued to my fingers. I shift away, and when I glance back, I can't help but notice him adjusting himself. A chill runs down my spine, but before I can react to it, he clears his throat. "This is awkward but..."

Oh god, I think. Fuck. What is happening?

"...as a doctor, I feel mandated to ask, are your stepbrothers holding you against your will?"

The question stuns me. I blink, trying to process it.

"What?" I finally blurt. "No. Of course not." I hope he doesn't notice the red in my cheeks. "Would they leave me here alone if I was being held captive?"

Our eyes meet, and I don't look away. "They're complicated young men," he says, nodding to my shoulder. "With a lot of secrets."

I tug at my collar. "They're protecting me. We're family and they're protecting me. Paul and Davis, too."

The tension leaves his face—well some of it. "Good. I apologize for asking—and yes, I'm aware my son is involved. I just... I just want you to be safe. First Olivia, and now your mother with her fragile health." He reaches into his bag. "This house isn't kind to women."

"Everything is fine. I promise."

A smile tugs at his mouth. "Good. Now, I know you're resistant to the painkillers and if you think you don't need them, that's fine." He holds out a bottle. "But please keep taking the supplements. Inflammation is real and can cause a lot of other problems."

I take the bottle, his fingers grazing mine. That same chill from earlier settles in the base of my spine and it doesn't leave until I've watched him get in his car and drive away.

HOLLY GOODWIN'S house is located on a treelined street tucked inside a gated community. I called ahead, asking Olivia's best friend if we could meet. She was pleasant enough, but I heard the hesitation in her voice. "The family knows I'm doing this," I told her, hoping that helped. "They just want answers."

Jack parks the car in the circular drive and I collect my bag from the floor. Reaching for the handle, I notice he's not moving.

"Hey, you don't have to go in there if you don't want to."

He'd offered to drive me—said he wanted to come. I know he's antsy to make some progress and find a new lead. Talking to Holly is a long shot, but it doesn't look like the cops did a thorough job.

His jaw is tight, eyes facing forward. "It's not that I don't want to," he says, "it's just always weird talking to people that knew her."

I nod, resting my hand on his forearm. "I'm sure it's surreal, but if it helps, I think she felt more comfortable talking to me knowing I had the family's support. You being here may get her to open up."

The muscle ticks at the base of his jaw. Jack is rash, impulsive and I can see this whole thing blowing up, but he just lifts my hand and kisses the back. "Let's do this."

The heat of his kiss travels up my arm, spreading across my body like wildfire. He hops out of the car and circles the front, opening my door before I get there.

"Thank you," I say, letting him help me out.

"I just hope this isn't a waste of our fucking time." His arm slinks around my waist and he keeps me close as we walk to the massive front door, even after he presses the bell, I tuck against his side, inhaling his warm, amazing scent. This closeness, it's something I didn't know how much I craved. His hand rests on my hip and it doesn't move when the door is opened by a pretty woman with ash blonde hair.

"Kate?" she asks, giving me a wide grin. "Nice to meet you, I'm Ho—" Her eyes shift to Jack, and she reaches for the door jamb, smile faltering. "God, sorry, you look just like her."

Jack stiffens next to me and his fingers curl into my waist. He's not the one holding me up this time—I'm supporting him. I take his hand and thread our fingers together.

"It's the eyes, right?" I say, trying to ease the tension. "I've noticed it, too."

Holly nods, slowly regaining her composure. "It's uncanny," she says, taking a step back, to allow us to come in. "You look so similar yet it's like I can still see that little boy in there."

Somehow Jack regains his composure and says, "Well, this little boy could use a drink, got anything?"

She blinks, then laughs. "I'll have Margo bring something out to the patio—sangria?"

"Whiskey. Straight."

She winks. "Gotcha."

We follow her through the well-appointed house—decorated in warm beiges and blues. The windows are massive and large mirrors hang from the walls. It's the opposite of the gloom at Davenport House, and that is only accentuated when we step through the backdoor to the patio that overlooks a garden blooming with flowers.

"This is lovely," I say, clutching my bag to my side. "So pretty."

"I'm enjoying it as long as possible." She gestures to a love seat. "Winter is coming and I'm dreading the cold weather."

We sit, Jack and I next to one another, his hand clamping down over my knee. We make small talk until the housekeeper emerges a few minutes later with a tray filled with crystal glasses and a pitcher of lemonade. There's also a bottle of whiskey. Jack grabs the bottle and pours it himself, taking a long swallow to settle his nerves. If Holly is offended, she doesn't show it. She exudes the sort of easy grace that my mother has always wished she could muster.

I wonder if Jack's mother was more like Holly or more like my mother?

"Again," I say, eager to get started, "I appreciate you talking to us."

"I'm not sure I have much to offer." She tucks her hair behind her ear, revealing pearl earrings. "It's been so long, and I spoke to the police at the time."

"Actually," I say, unzipping my bag. I pull out a file of papers I gathered just for this meeting. "According to the police reports, you were very upset at the time, and they decided to come back later when you were less emotional." I make a show of flipping through the papers. "It seems though, that they never came back. Do you know why?"

"Other than shock, I didn't know much." She reaches for her glass of lemonade. "Olivia was an amazing person. We met at the women's society she first moved to town. We were both newlyweds, didn't know anyone, and needed a friend. She was free-spirited and strong, but not used to being a wife to a prominent man." Her eyes flick to Jack. "Don't get me wrong. She loved being a wife and mother. She and your father were a perfect couple."

Jack swallows the remainder of his drink and sets it on the table. Abruptly he says, "No."

Holly and I exchange a confused look. "Excuse me?" she asks.

"They weren't perfect." He grows still, every muscle in his body tense. "They fought. A lot. I could hear them up in my room." His fingers tighten on my leg. "About the house and how she wanted to move. She hated Davenport Manor." His eyes glaze over, deep in thought—or maybe a memory. "She threatened to leave. To take us with her and he...well," he swallows, "he didn't like it."

I rest my hand over his. "Do you think your father was angry enough to hurt her?"

He shakes his head. "I don't know. He has an alibi, right?"

I nod. "He was at a meeting in another town, with a dozen witnesses."

Holly clears her throat. "There may be something I haven't mentioned."

"What?" I ask.

"She never told me anything specific but... I think she was hiding something—maybe someone? She asked me to watch you and Oliver once or twice...for appointments, but it seemed weird at the time. She was dressed up and never gave me much information. I don't know."

"You think she was having an affair?" I ask.

"I have no proof but..."

"But what?" Jack growls.

His menacing tone startles her, and her hand flutters to her neck, toying with her necklace. "One night she called and asked me to come to get her. It was late, and completely out of character, but I did it. When I got there, she was upset but refused to talk about it. I drove her home, she thanked me, and we never discussed it again."

"Where did you pick her up?" I ask. My pulse quickens—a sign that we're onto something. A clue. An unexplored avenue.

Holly abruptly stands, and walks into the house and over to a large desk. We can see her through the window as she pulls out a drawer and fishes something out. She walks back out holding it in her palm. "She left this in my car that night."

She reveals an old matchbook. Jack reaches for it, flipping it over.

The Wilmington Inn.

"This is where you picked her up?" I ask. The Wilmington Inn is the former name of Club Hades. I flash back to the night I went there with Oliver and Jack—the night we fucked on stage for strangers to get information from Marcus.

"Yeah, it was this super shitty old hotel." She grabs Jack's glass and fills it with whiskey. She tips it back, wincing as she swallows it in one gulp. "I have no fucking clue what she was doing there, but it couldn't have been good. That is not a part of town someone of her stature should have been in."

"Did you ever tell anyone about this?" I ask.

"No. no one. I probably should have, but I knew Olivia would have been humiliated, and Montie... I don't know. It felt wrong to smear her publicly after everything that happened."

I look at Jack, unable to read his expression, he just flips the matchbook over in his fingertips. I sense the tension boiling under the surface. I know him well enough to recognize the signals that he's on the edge.

"Thank you for speaking to us," I say, standing. I tug Jack's hand and he follows. "I know it's hard bringing up all these memories."

She wraps her arms around her thin frame. "Hopefully it helps."

Neither of us speak until we get to the car. That's when Jack turns and a chill runs up my spine. Is he angry? Will he take it out on me?

The thought both terrifies and excites me.

Instead, he pulls me tight against his body, wrapping his arms around me.

"Thank you," he says, kissing my throat.

Startled, I ask, "For what?"

"Never giving up, even when it's obvious you should."

I laugh. "You know I'm at my best when I'm breaking the rules."

His mouth meets mine, and I know what he wants—needs—comfort, stability, assurance. What Holly told us inside is a revelation. One that may not lead us where he expected. Jack spent all those years trying to squash my independence, my rule-breaking, but every time I did it led me back to him.

I can't help but wonder if Olivia had the same streak and if it led her to her death.

SIX

Jack

Kate mumbles in her sleep. I stare at her, watching her twist and turn, fighting demons I can't quite reach. That aching thud slams into my chest like fists against my ribs. Against the moonlight that streams in through my bedroom window, sweat glistens along her brow, a bead runs down her temple, then her cheek like a tear.

She twists, restless, and wound up ever since the meeting with my mother's friend Holly. That makes two of us. I'd always known my mother hated living here, but to find out she was involved in something—maybe someone—at the Wilmington Inn.

I haven't slept at all.

"Katie." I reach up and brush the hair from her face. "Babe, you need to wake up. You're having a bad dream."

But she doesn't wake when I brush her face. Or when I move closer and wrap my arms around her, pulling her tight against me. She's been sleeping hard since the injury. It makes sense.

She needs to heal, but I don't like the dreams. They're fucking with her.

Us.

"Maybe the house..." she whimpers.

"I know." My voice is a murmur. "It's fucking the house."

I look up at the high ceilings, the thick crown molding, and arched doors. This place has always provided me comfort with its many rooms and secret passageways. There are times when I think I can still see her here, feel her presence—it's held me together like glue, committed me to my mission. But the more I draw on the memories of that day, watching Katie pour over the files, pictures spread across the floor, looking at it from her fresh point of view, the more this idea tumbles in my brain like a clattering bell.

Maybe it's the house.

I give my girl what little comfort I can, but it's never enough, not when she fights the demons lurking in her dreams. I've got her right where I want her, following me down the rabbit hole of my life's mission, into the depths of violence and vengeance, but I don't like that it causes her so much grief. I lift my gaze to the stack of files sitting beside her on the dresser. I should never have given it to her. I should never have let her in. Not because I'm afraid she's too close to me. There's no fighting that, not anymore. But I'm afraid the evil of my past will tear us apart.

There's a balance to being a hunter. I've got to teach her how to manage it.

I watch her while the moonlight slowly brightens until the yellow glow of sunlight fills the room, and the perspiration dries on her brow. I hold her as her breaths become faster, shallower, and she finally surfaces. Then with a tiny flutter, she opens her eyes. There's a second of surprise and fear as she registers who I am, and then that ebbs away as she realizes what I am.

I'm her protector.

I'm her lover.

I'm her stepbrother.

"Morning." She tries to give me a smile, but it comes off as a wince.

"Morning." My voice is husky.

"How'd you sleep?" she asks, her body trembling as she stretches like a cat, her tits pushing at her shirt.

I don't answer because I don't want her to worry. "You were dreaming last night."

Surprise widens her eyes. "Was I? Did I keep you up?"

"Nah." It's not a complete lie. My own dark thoughts made sleep elusive. "You were talking about the house."

Her eyebrows furrow. "Really? I don't remember."

"Yeah." I run my hand down her arm. "It's stressing you out, isn't it? Investigating Mom's murder?"

"It's just..." she searches for the right words. Her eyes meet mine. "It's just so important."

I brush a strand of stray hair from her face. "You're more important."

"Sometimes I get a little too deep in the material, I guess."

I'm glad the thoughts don't haunt her sleep during the day the way they do at night, but it's strange. They seem so vivid, her eyes moving beneath her lids, her body tense with stress. I haven't slept with Katie enough to know if she's like this when she works on every case. Maybe she just gets so into it, that she can't get back out.

But she's here now, and although I don't think Jack Davenport can be the light, I can give her what she needs—help her ease that tension by shifting the sheets aside and climbing on top of her glorious body.

Her hand reaches out for me, my cock has been hard for hours now, lying so close to her, smelling her, feeling her heat. I reach down and cup her pussy. She doesn't wear panties to bed, just for me. Because she knows how I need her, how I want her. She's learned to be ready.

"I know how to make you clear your mind." I slide my fingers inside, feeling the tight warmth surrounding them.

Stars sparkle in her eyes, and she arches her back. "God, yes."

I thrust my fingers, watching that reality give way to pleasure and I circle her clit. My balls tighten. My cock gets even harder. I'm turned on by just the thought of her, by the stroke of her. By the scent of her.

"Fuck you feel good. You look even better," I murmur. "Just like this, just woken up, all for me." I crush her mouth with mine, moving between her thighs until I buck my hips and thrust upwards. I drive into her, slamming home. Because she is home. I know that now.

Fuck this house. Fuck the darkness and the wrath it takes out on women. I'll be her home, her base, her foundation. Slow, hard thrusts draw me closer to that hunger. But she's not moving, she's not writhing. Instead, she's laying here, soundless, eyes narrow with worry.

I try to hold off, my damn fingers fumbling as I stroke her clit and thrust deep into her with my cock. Still, it doesn't draw her out of her head.

I pull out and slide down between her legs.

"Jack." She reaches for me. "It's okay, I'm just in a weird place. You're probably right—it's the investigation. It'll get better when we catch him."

"Well, I'm not okay with it," I growl through gritted teeth and move lower in the bed. I don't like her like this, lost in her fears.

With a push of my hand, I open her thighs and slide her top higher. I spread her slit, staring at the tiny hood, then lower my head and lick her slow and gentle. Her body tenses and her hands fist the sheets as I drag her clit into my mouth.

"Oh, God," she whimpers.

I'm definitely not okay with her not coming. It matters a whole fucking lot. I want to feel her fall apart on my cock, her breath heavy and lost. I want her consumed—with me—not some fucking case. I slide my fingers inside her as I suck, waiting for her hips to rise from the bed. I know her now. Her body. Her mind. I know her better than she knows herself.

She jerks and shudders. "That's it, little sister, come for me."

Her hand slides around the back of my head, pulling my face against her pussy. I open my mouth, sucking, drawing her into me. The saltiness. Her sweetness. Her cum. And with a low, guttural moan, she releases, her thighs squeezing my ears, her body pulsing against my mouth.

I swallow, again and again, closing my eyes and relishing the taste of her. Her hold against the back of my head eases, she strokes me, gliding her fingers through my hair, praising me almost. Good job. Good boy. Good brother.

I open my eyes and lift my head, finding her smile. She reaches for me, pulling me upwards. "Come inside me."

My arms are a cage around her as I rise and use my knees to push her thighs further apart.

I'm merciless, barely in control as I stare into her eyes and push back in. I don't take it easy on her—I never have—and fuck her hard. I feel the stretch of her pussy as I pound into her, the way she opens and envelops around me. I'm caught in her, my tongue in her mouth, when my balls tighten and I groan, emptying inside.

"Jesus," I mutter, rolling over. I look down at the glistening trail of cum slipping out of her pussy along with my cock. I'm captured by the sight. I want her more now than ever before and I don't care how. I slide my fingers to the slick, pushing my come back inside. I want it there; I want it so far in there it stains her scent.

She shifts, hips moving as I stroke, wanting me inside of her as much as I do.

"If this is what waking up with you is like, I'm not going to make it through the day without crashing."

I lift my gaze to her. "Same, baby."

She gives me a slow, sexy smile. "Maybe we can have a midafternoon nap?"

We both know nap is just another word for fucking.

I raise an eyebrow. "I thought you were busy today?"

"Damn, you're right, I am. Maybe a rain check?" She pushes up and slides her legs around me before climbing from the bed.

"Sure." I answer.

A raincheck.

I listen to her bare feet as they thud against the floorboards as she makes her way into the bathroom. The hiss of a shower comes soon after and I lay there in the bed, imagining my life without her.

It's too hard.

It's too heavy.

I clench my fist, capturing the crumpled sheets she left behind.

Maybe it's the house...

That haunting feeling propels me out of bed and into the shower with her. I'm still under the spray when she kisses me and walks out, towel wrapped around her sexy body. When I come out, she's already gone and so are the files next to the bed.

I may be clean, but I feel the dusty, musty air. I need to get out. I need to save this woman before it takes her like everything else.

"I THOUGHT I may find you here."

I don't need to turn my head to know who it is. His steps are soundless on the lush grass. But Paul's deep, somber voice carries on the wind. He stops next to me, not saying a word.

I like the silence and the peace out here. I like the birds chirping in the trees and the hills in the distance. I've always liked this place although it's been a long time since I've been here. I can't remember how long this time, two months, three...*is it longer?*

The flowers are dead in front of me. Brown and crumpled at the bottom of her stone. The sight of that pisses me off. Where are the groundkeepers? The fucking men we pay to take care of her? I clench my jaw that ache flaring. It's too familiar now, too painful.

"You know this is nothing like her, don't you?"

I nerve ticks in the corner of my eye. I jerk my gaze to his. "What did you say?"

Paul nods to my mother's gravestone. "She is nothing like Katherine."

Maybe it's the house...

"Isn't she?"

The question intrigues Paul. Does it rub against his own fear? "Do you think she is?"

"I don't know, you're the fucking shrink. You tell me."

"With the Binder really gone, Katherine healing and working on the case, and all of this new information coming to light, it's going to bring feelings of loss and loneliness back to the surface." He places a hand on my shoulder. "But you're not alone here, brother. You get that right?"

I know I'm not alone. I have my brother. My dad. I have my friends, and now I have Katie. Despite that, I've always felt alone, deep down, I've always been...flawed.

I thought that flaw would keep us protected.

I thought that flaw could right the wrongs of my past.

I thought that flaw could become me.

Until Kate came into our lives.

Then I realized I was wrong.

"Even if she survives this, she's going to leave me. I just know she is."

"Why do you say that?"

I can barely look at him. Instead, I fix my focus on the dead flowers at the feet of my mother's gravestone. "She's independent. She has a career. Dreams and ambition." She's not going to want to live at Davenport House forever, chasing ghosts. "She's better than us."

"Yet she sleeps in your bed every night, doesn't she?"

It's not enough. He knows this. "Physically, yes. But she's not there, she's not with me. She's caught in this case—asleep and awake."

"You feel like you're losing control?"

I don't have to answer, because he already knows.

"Davis isn't around much anymore," I answer. "Oliver is sniffing around behind her, helping her with whatever she needs." My fingers curl. I need to punch something. Hurt someone. But who? There's only one person left on the list and he's a fucking ghost.

"You're afraid that once we find your mother's killer and we no longer have our mission, you'll lose everyone." I don't respond, but I see him staring at the grave. "I suppose there's no irony that we're standing at the foot of your mother's grave trying to come to terms with loss and abandonment."

Fucking Paul.

Why the hell is he so good at his goddamn job?

"It's like I'm on edge," I confess. "Unraveling. Every time I talk to her, fuck her, taste her pussy on my mouth, I feel like I'm losing a little bit more."

Paul leans against the iron gate surrounding the family plot, his arms crossed, looking at me. "Could it be that you're not losing anything, but opening yourself up? Allowing someone else inside that cage you've built around your heart and that scares the fuck out of you?"

The blood in my veins rushes, pounding in my ears like a hammer on a nail. I clench my hands against my sides. "My mother had secrets," I tell him. "She was probably fucking someone else. It may have been what got her killed."

His back straightens. "She was cheating on your dad?"

"She was doing something down at the Wilmington Inn." Fucking and fighting were about the only things happening in that hovel at the time. He and I both know it.

"The Wilmington Inn?" he asks, eyebrows furrowing. "The same place that Club Hades is running out of."

"Yep." I know I'm changing the subject, but at the same time, I'm not. Women have secrets. They have lives and desires and dreams outside of one man, one house, one family. My insecurities run deep; I don't need Paul's psychoanalyzing to tell me that. I like control. For things to be the way they've always been, but he's right. Opening my heart to Katie is the most terrifying thing I've ever done.

And it may be easier to push her away before she does it first.

SEVEN

Kate

It's strange to think how uncomfortable Paul's office used to make me. How these court-appointed meetings rattled me to the point of panic attacks and nausea. How his probing questions and ability to see deep into my psyche shook me to the core.

Now, I sit across from him a changed woman. We have to keep up the appointments—the court has no idea Christopher Watkins is now dead or that our elaborate plot to draw him out is complete.

That doesn't stop Paul from taking the appointment seriously, or me from fucking with him. His eyes keep dragging down to my short skirt, picked out, especially for him. I'm not wearing panties—teasing him occasionally with the idea of my bare pussy as he asks me about how I feel in the aftermath of killing a man.

"I've never felt more powerful," I tell him, toying with a button on my blouse. It's loose, hanging by a thread, abused by Oliver this morning while I was getting dressed. I can still feel the sticky residue of his cum in my pussy, kept warm by the heat of my core. I may be playing games in an attempt to push the good doctor over the edge, but I'm not here to lie. "Everyone is worried about me, but it's unnecessary. I was tired of feeling scared."

I shift, slowly crossing one leg over the other. His pen pauses on the notepad, eyes zeroed in on my crotch. He's hard. I can see his erection tenting his expensive tweed pants.

"And you're no longer scared?"

"No," I reply. "Why would I be? My stalker is dead."

"There are other scary things out there, Katherine. You should know that by now. Watkins wasn't the only monster out there. The world is full of them." His eyebrows raise. "Two may live in your house."

"And one may be sitting across from me." I laugh. "Monsters stopped being scary, Paul, when I became one of them."

"So, you're saying nothing scares you?"

His head tilts, signaling the importance of the question. He's probing. Trying to dig into my psyche. Peel back that layer, and an uneasy feeling blooms in my chest. I refuse to give in to it.

"What should I be afraid of?"

"You did get injured. If Davis and Jack hadn't been there, it's possible things could have been worse. You could be dead right now."

"But they were there." And I have no doubt they always will be, they proved that. I uncross my legs and keep them that way, with a slight gap between my thighs. "Can I ask you a question?"

He draws his eyes away from my breasts. I didn't wear a bra either and the satin of my shirt rubs against my nipples, drawing them into hard points. "Sure."

I can't help the smile toying on my lips. "What are *you* afraid of?"

I assume he'll tell me it's not the point of the meeting. This session is about me, not him, but he sets his notepad on the table next to him and leans back. "In the past, I didn't have many fears. Things were very much under control." He looks up at me. "But lately..."

"Lately what?"

"Did Jack tell you I'm the one that suggested he start hunting as a way to deal with his emotions?"

"He did."

"For the longest time, we had a system that helped Jack settle his rage. Davis and I drew suspects from our respective positions. Oliver and Jack having the freedom and accessibility to pull off the plan. We worked cohesively, cloaked by our standing in Wilmington, no one the slightest bit wise to the fact we were ridding the streets of dangerous men." His arms rest on the side of the chair, giving a glimpse of the muscular, broad shoulders hidden under his button-down. "Murdering those men gave Jack and Oliver a sense of control in their lives that they hadn't felt since the day their mother was taken from them. But now things have changed."

"How?" I ask.

"Everything changed when you showed up, Katherine. It caused an unbalance. All the energy and focus we had for the mission, all of Jack's rage was pointed in one direction— completing his mission by finding his mother's killer."

"You think that's changed?" I ask, trying to follow him. "Because we're working on it. I've been investigating—"

He laughs and asks, "You don't see it do you?"

"See what?" I'm not fully following him, and that familiar anxiety creeps up my spine. "What am I missing?"

"You make us vulnerable."

It's my turn to laugh. "That's ridiculous."

"Is it? Since you returned, things have become very public. The cabin with Ryan. The court case. The publicity. The break-in, *during a party*, by Christopher. Before you came home, we were untouchable, but now things are different. Jack, a man who needs to kill to stay sane, hasn't had blood on his hands in months. Oliver, who spent all his time and energy helping his brother, is now completely focused on making you part of the family. Davis is under immense pressure at work to solve the missing men cases—men he was intimately involved with murdering."

"What about you?"

"Every interaction I have with you is one step closer to me losing my license."

I stare at Paul for a moment, trying to assess where he's going with this. Everything this man does is a test. Something to push my boundaries. What he says rings true, that Jack needs to kill. Oliver does spend as much time as possible with me—and I've noticed a shift in their relationship. The Gazette had a front-page article on Davis being tasked with solving the missing men murders, and Paul...he's right. Every exchange we have violates the oath he took as a therapist.

Under all the accusations, I hear the truth in his words and it propels me to my feet. I close the distance between us and he watches me, eyes wide as I sling one leg on each side of his, straddling his lap. His hands shift to the back of my thighs and push the skirt over my backside.

Paul swallows. "See? This is what I mean."

"How so?" I sit, rubbing my core over the hard bulge in his pants. I move to unbutton his shirt, pushing the fabric aside to feel the hard muscle of his chest. "Is this kind of thing frowned upon?"

"This kind of behavior would have my license revoked." He licks his lips and reaches for my blouse. The loose button breaks free, clattering to the floor, and his hand slips under the silk, cupping my breast. "You're a dangerous woman, Katherine Stevenson."

"What you're really saying is that I have control." I kiss him, and he tweaks my nipple forcing my back into an arch. Heat surges between my legs. "And it makes you nervous."

"All I am," he replies, voice husky, "is ready for you to get on my dick."

That makes two of us, and I rise up, giving him room to free his cock from the confines of his pants. He slips his fingers between my legs, checking to see if I'm ready but Jesus, I'm soaked. I've been that way since I walked in here. "Hurry," I tell him, impatient and demanding. "I want to feel you inside."

There's no hesitation as he lines the tip to my entrance and then holds onto my hips, pulling me down. My pussy becomes a sheath, enveloping him as deep as he'll go. I let him stretch me before rocking my hips. His mouth clamps down on my breast, suckling, and tugging at the nipple. God, he feels so good.

I ride him hard, spurred on by his fingers clawing at my ass and the way he drives into me like he's trying to drill all the way through. His teeth are on my neck, nipping at the lobe of my ear, tugging at my nipple. Each bite, every nibble, sends a shockwave down my spine. He's so handsome like this, jaw tight, eyes dark with want. His lips are red, his tongue hot. My orgasm creeps closer, and I close my eyes, letting my head fall back in anticipation.

Then he stops, easing me off his cock.

"What?" I ask, eyes popping open. "What are you doing?"

"Showing you who's really in charge," he says, moving with quick reflexes. A heartbeat later, I'm spun on all fours, and he moves behind me, spreading my ass cheeks apart. His cock is slick from my pussy, but that doesn't stop the gasp when he invades me with a sharp, invading, punch.

He falls straight into a rhythm, taking me with a commanding forcefulness that knocks the breath out of me. His fingers search for my clit, finding the hot bundle of nerves wet with desire. He stimulates me, claims me, and asserts dominance in a way that I feel all the way to my bones. I want to fight back, and rebel, but it's impossible. Paul bucks into me and the orgasm that rushes across my body is powerful and strong. That intensity breaks over me, shattering like glass, I cry out, chasing it as long as it'll let me until he unleashes, three final thrusts, each one harder than the other, resulting in a loud, guttural groan as he spills his seed inside.

We pant, stuck together like mating dogs, his cock swollen and full and now so is my ass. Slick, dribbling.

"Jesus Christ," he says, finally pulling out. He crashes to the ground, curled on his side, his body shiny with sweat. "You keep this up, you're going to destroy us, Katherine."

Because he can't resist me. Not even for his job, for his friendship, and probably his family. I understand it, it's why I'm still on my knees, the desire to keep his cum in me as long as possible. To maintain that fullness, the feeling of being claimed with brutal ownership.

"Mutually assured destruction, I feel like that's a better term for the five of us."

He laughs, rising up to kiss me. His mouth is soft, his tongue gentle. The complete opposite from a moment ago. I ease into him, falling into his lap. His fingers stroke my hair, ghost over my breasts. This is the Paul I know, the one that soothes and dotes. That hurts and then heals.

Jekyll and Hyde.

Our kissing slows and I rest my head on his broad chest, feeling his heart pound under his hot skin. Under the coffee table, I see the shiny pearl button that fell off my shirt. My eyes shift upward to another glint. Something silver, the size of the button but stuck to the underneath. Leaning forward, I press my finger against it.

"What's that?" Paul asks, hand sliding down my backside.

"I don't know." I pluck it off, feeling the hard pebble between my fingertips. "Shit."

"What?" he asks, sitting upright.

"It's a camera," I say. "Did you put that there? Are you recording us?"

It wouldn't be a surprise. Paul would want to study our sessions, and use the information to dig into my brain over and over again, but the expression on his face is one of shock. His forehead is furrowed and a deep frown sets on his handsome face.

"No, I didn't bug my office." His eyes flick to mine. "I promise. What happens in here is between us and us alone." He flattens his palm and I set the camera in the middle.

The same question ripples between us.

If Paul isn't filming his sessions, then who is?

EIGHT

Davis

______

Jack:

> Meeting. Gym. Now.

I stare at the message on my cell and try to interpret the message. Does he know? I don't know how, but I can feel it. That icy, crawling sensation that inches up my spine. Intuition. It's what's kept us alive and free all those years, and now it's telling me that Jack has figured out that I'm working with the FBI and this message? The summons?

He's calling me on it.

I want to ignore the message, giving him a *fuck you, Jack.* But that's just the guilt speaking. We've never kept secrets from one another and this one...it's big.

"Christ." I push away from my desk and reach behind me to grab my jacket. I'm being paranoid. How could he know?

Which means, I'm going to have to tell them. Sooner than later. They're going to feel betrayed. There's no two ways about it, but it's time to deal with it.

"Going somewhere, Davis?" I close my eyes for a heartbeat, then open them and push my chair in. Hargreaves peers out at me from his office. "I need the report on the Johnson break-in."

"Bite me," I mutter, snatching my keys. Then louder, "It's on your desk."

Ever since the FBI came to town, Hargreaves has been forced to take a step back where I'm concerned...and he doesn't like it one little bit. Sure, he still tries to control me with his petty little demands, probably pissed they skipped him and asked me instead. The Feds wanted me for a reason. I'm good at my job.

At least I hope that's the reason because otherwise we're fucked.

I pull out of the parking lot and head toward Davenport Manor. What I'm going to have to explain to them is that a better opportunity for me is also a better opportunity for them, even if they can't see it at first.

I know all they'll see is betrayal. We've always worked together as a team, but if I take this job, I'll won't be around to protect them. Won't be around to clean up their goddamn messes, or to feed them information. But the FBI database...fuck, it's glorious. I've been given access to help with the local cases and the amount of intel they have is a goldmine.

All those sadistic assholes out there, just waiting for someone like us—and now we have the inside information to make hunting easier. That's how I have to sell this. It's not a betrayal. It's an opportunity.

I clench my grip around the wheel and turn the corner, pulling into the familiar street. My gaze lifts to Ollie's car parked behind Jack's, then Paul's black Range Rover parked behind them. It looks like everyone is here. Fuck. Maybe this is an ambush after all.

I park the four-wheel drive and climb out. One hard exhale and I climb the stairs, then make my way inside the house. It's quiet, other than the *whoop whoop whoop* of an oversized ceiling fan doing its best to cool the sticky, humid air. I don't enter the kitchen like I normally would to rifle through their refrigerator, picking at their leftovers like a damn vulture. Jesus, Katie is a good cook. Today, my stomach is hard like a fist as I make my way to the secret paneling and into the musty, dank space.

Memories invade. The dark. The dank. The sounds of Kate as she screamed with violent fury. It's no surprise Katie's been having nightmares living in this old house with its damn ghosts. Ghosts that seem to multiply.

Muffled voices stop the moment I push open the paneling that leads to the basement gym. Jack's dark eyes jerk toward me, I catch the unhinged gleam as I let the paneling fall back into place. My heart kicks in my chest. I can handle Jack on a good day, fuck, I might even be able to handle him on a bad day. But handle all of them? Especially when the air is charged like it was right now.

No, I don't like that idea at all.

The conversation dies instantly the moment I step into the room. Jack turns on me, anger seethes in his stare as he lifts a device in his hand. "Do you know anything about this?"

I bite my tongue with the accusation and stare at the thing...it's a bug. Expensive by the looks of it. I step closer, taking it from him, finding the serial number engraved on the back.

I roll it over my fingers. "Where the fuck did you get this?"

"Answer the question," Paul says. "Do you know anything about it?"

I blink, trying to assess the tone, and the mood. "No."

"It's not one of yours? The police?" Oliver's voice takes an edge. He's worried.

"How about you guys tell me what's actually going on and then maybe I can answer your questions?"

Katie clears her throat. "It was in Paul's office. I noticed it during our appointment."

"Your office was bugged?" I ask, still looking at the device. It's not Wilmington Police, but it could be the FBI. Maybe. "Fuck."

"I have no idea how long it's been there," Paul says. His complexion is pale, sallow. He's panicking—and he should be. "It could've been weeks—or longer."

My mind spins. The shit that goes on in Paul's? It's not exactly legit. I know he fucks Katie in that room and that alone is a violation of his license and oath. But he also "treated" most of our missing men. It's how we got in their heads, how we knew exactly the best way to hunt them.

"It's not one of ours," I tell them. "We don't have the budget for this kind of equipment."

"What about the Feds?" Jack asks. "They're the ones that put Katie in witness protection. Maybe they were following up on her appointments, seeing if she was revealing anything else?"

The Feds. Shit. Shit. *Shit.* Is that all this is? Are they playing me? Is this job offer just a scam? That sense of paranoia rolls over me again and I try to squelch it. I close the device in my palm, placing it in my pocket. "I'll find out."

"How?" Oliver asks. "Why would they tell you?"

I could tell them now. Reveal everything, but what if I am being played for a fool? I can't admit that. Not yet. Not to them.

"I have contacts," I say, looking at Paul. "Go over your office and house, make sure nothing else is there." My eyes flick to Katie. "No more fuck sessions at his place. Keep the meetings, but make them legit. Benign. Boring as hell."

"God this never ends," Katie says, wrapping her arms around her upper body. Oliver steps close to her and pulls her against his side. "This is about me, isn't it? They know I killed Watkins."

"No," Jack says. "This is about the missing men. You said they're reexamining the files—that they put you back on them." I'd shared that much—I'd had to in order to explain my absence. "They know Paul is one of the connections."

"That makes sense," Oliver says, running a hand through his hair. "It's like everything is catching up to us."

He's right, and we all know why. Things got too public with The Binder. With the court case and Katie's involvement. It exposed us to the public, to scrutiny. But we can control this. I know we can. I know *I* can.

"That's enough," I say. "We're not going to panic. I'm going to figure out who planted this then I'm going to put a stop to it."

"What about us?" Katie asks. "What do we do?"

"You keep investigating Olivia's murder. It's important and it's the mission. You hunt. I keep the trouble at bay. That's how we operate, right?"

Katie nods, and the others do, too. Even Jack grunts his agreement, but I hold his eye and gesture for him to follow me into the passageway.

"I know this is hard for you to sit back and let me do this," I tell him. "But I will figure out who's behind this and we'll handle it."

"I know you will," he says, jaw locked tight. "Because even though I said otherwise in there, this is about Katie. I can feel it in my gut."

"You think?"

"She didn't need to hear it. She's barely sleeping and stressed out."

I'd noticed she looked tired, but I was too busy juggling my job —and all the *lies*—to really let it connect. "But understand, I'll let you do your thing, but if *anyone* touches a goddamn strand of hair on our girl's head, I will murder every single person that is involved."

I swallow and nod, hiding my unease under the dark gloom of the passageway.

Jack just made it clear. If the FBI planted that bug, and Jack finds out?

My best friend is going to kill me.

NINE

Kate

You didn't have to come," I say, as we walk into the records room at the courthouse. It's quiet in the room, but there's the soft shuffle of footsteps a few rows over and the occasional roll and snap of a file cabinet opening.

"It's no problem," Oliver says. "Unless you don't want me here."

He's been aloof all morning. Distant.

I frown. "Of course I do. I love having your company." I look down the rows and rows of cabinets. "It's just pretty tedious work. I'm sure there's something better you can do with your time."

He shrugs. "I thought I could be helpful, but if you don't want it—"

"Hey," I say, turning to face him. I search his face, trying to glean something from his expression, but his eyes are shuttered. "What's going on with you?"

"Nothing," he says. "Tired maybe."

I want to say that if he was tired, he should have stayed home. Now that both Binders are gone, the guys have eased up a little on letting me drive around alone, but when I grabbed my keys to head downtown, Oliver insisted on coming.

"Well," I say, pushing up on my toes to brush my lips across his, "this is a low-energy activity." I nod over at the chair in the corner. "You're welcome to take a nap."

He accepts my kiss, but it's lacking enthusiasm. I shake it off, thinking maybe this is because I've started sleeping in Jack's room more. Maybe he's feeling neglected after all those weeks of having me alone in his bed for comfort.

"Come on," I say, tugging him into the room. "Let's see what we can find and get out of here. Go home and get naked."

His eyebrow rises at that, and he nods, following me down the aisles. We pass a woman flipping through a stack of newspapers and turn the corner, toward the W's.

"So, what are we looking for exactly?"

"Information on the history of the Wilmington Inn. Deeds, land titles, police reports, photographs." I approach the file cabinet the clerk suggested the paperwork would be in and pull the handle. "It's a needle in a haystack, but at this point, any new lead would be helpful."

I flip through the files and find several thick ones that look promising. Oliver reaches over me and grabs them, tucking them under his arm. "Where do you want these?"

"We can spread them out over here," I say, pointing to a worktable at the end of the row.

"Do you think my mom was cheating on my dad?" he asks after he's left them on the table.

"Oh, um, I don't know. Holly seemed to think something was going on." And Davis is convinced there was an invited guest at the house when she was murdered. "It's important to explore every lead."

He grunts and grabs a file, flipping the cover.

"Hey," I grab his forearm, "is that what's bothering you? The idea that your mom cheated?"

"I don't know, Katie, would it bother you to learn that your mother is a whore?" he snaps. "Or maybe it wouldn't because it means you can be one, too."

"Whoa!" I cry, but then lower my voice since we're not alone. "What are you talking about?"

"Davis says it all the time. That you're a dirty slut. Maybe he knows something the rest of us don't."

His accusation stings. Oliver is the kindest of the men in my life, but something is wrong. "Davis is...well Davis. You know that. He likes belittling people. He gets off on it."

"And you don't like it when he talks to you like that? I've seen how wet you get for him."

I face him, his chest heaves, and his cheeks are red. That blank expression from before is gone and he looks wild and angry. *Paranoid.*

"Ollie—" I start. "I don't know what this is about..."

"I know what you're doing," he blurts.

"Doing?" I repeat. "I'm going to need more than that."

"You want to solve this case because then you can leave." He swallows. "Like her."

Her. Olivia—his mom.

"She didn't leave, Ollie, she was *murdered.*"

"But she was going to, right? She hated the house. She was cheating on Dad. She was miserable and if she wasn't killed, she would have run, probably off to some other man who didn't strap her with two kids." He blinks, eyes wet. "You've already run before—twice. Just like you're going to do once this is solved."

Footsteps echo on the concrete floors. A man appears at the end of our aisle and we're both silent until he passes, moving to the next row. The sound of a file cabinet opening echoes across the cavernous room.

"Big brother," I say quietly, placing a hand on his chest. "Where would I go? Like you said, I left twice before, and what happened?"

He looks up at the ceiling. "You came back," he admits, "but only because you were desperate and scared."

"That's not the only reason," I say. "Who takes care of me? Who taught me to hunt and kill? How to protect myself?" I drop my hand to his crotch, cupping the hard length of his cock. "Who taught me how to ease my worries? Showed me how good it feels to give in to desires?"

He swallows, Adam's apple bobbing in his throat. His cock thickens in my hand and I stroke the length.

"Who, baby? Who taught me those things?"

"We did."

I smile. "You did. You boys unleashed something in me, something raw and intense. I *never* want that to go away."

He searches my eyes like he's trying to discern if I'm telling the truth. I give his cock another stroke and he crumbles, hands cupping my face. His mouth crashes to mine, hard and desperate.

I suck his tongue, loving the way he feels against me—how hard he is—how much he wants me. His hands drop to my hips, and he spins me around, bending me over the table. His fingers push between my legs, and he shoves my panties aside.

"See?" he says, feeling the warm heat. "You like being called a whore. It makes you wet."

I shudder at the feel of his fingers rubbing my clit. There's nothing but the sound of our breath and the clink of his belt as he releases himself. His cock slides between my legs.

"Oliver," I hiss, glancing over my shoulder. "We're not alone."

"Don't fucking care, baby. They can watch or leave, but I'm not stopping." His teeth bare down on my shoulder, sharp and painful. It sends a shock of want between my legs. I press my ass against him, needing him as much as he needs me. "I want to feel your pussy clench around me."

My hands splay on the table, the files pushed aside. He enters me without hesitation—the urge to claim me greater than anything else. I gasp when he enters, full and stretched. "Tell me," he says, mouth close to my ear, "tell me you'll never leave again."

"I-I won't leave," I promise, my hips slamming into the edge of the table. He pushes me farther, flatter on the surface until my cheek is pressed against the wooden surface. "I'll never leave you, Oliver."

"Call me 'big brother,'" he commands, looking down on me like a god.

"I'll never leave you, big brother," I repeat. His hips hammer against my backside and just when I get used to him, he pulls out and does it again, each time burying deeper inside. "I'll never leave," I promise again. "Never."

Not as long as he's fucking me like this.

The rhythm builds, the unmistakable sound of his body pounding into mine. I bite down on my bottom lip, holding back the cry of pleasure as my orgasm rushes through me. It starts at the base of my spine, spreading toward my pussy, leaving me a shuddering mess.

"That's it, little sister," he groans, thrusting one last time. "Fuck, that's it."

I feel him empty inside of me, pulsing and hot, and my pussy holds onto him, because I mean it. I'll never leave this man. He needs to understand how much I want, no, *need* him.

He pulls out, leaving a trail of hot cum oozing down my inner thigh. I don't move, still splayed over the table, my bones molten.

Not until I hear a footstep, and jerk upright. The man from earlier rounds the corner just as I lower my skirt. He eyes the two of us, very aware of what we were just doing, but Oliver just grins. He loves getting off in public. He feeds on it.

"Need something?" Oliver asks.

The man blanches, and scurries off.

I look up at my stepbrother. "Feeling better?"

"Yeah." He runs his hand through his hair. "Guess I was feeling insecure."

"Don't," I tell him. "I love you. I love how you make me feel. I love how you take care of me." I glance down to where I can see the outline of his cock again. The guy catching us made him hard again. "I love your cock, so fucking much."

"I love you, too." He kisses me, gentler this time, but no less claiming. When he pulls away, I add, "We're going to find the person that killed your mother and after that, I'll still be here. Promise."

TEN

Kate

______

Wilmington Inn is a minefield of information, handed from one seedy owner to the next, but it's one I'm determined to navigate. Over the years it went from an upscale hotel to hourly stays. Prostitutes and drug dealers spent their time meeting customers and selling their bodies and drugs while the burlesque show ran in the club.

Olivia would have been there during its less impressive days and it makes me wonder who she was meeting. Was she the client or was she selling something?

I flip to the front of the file again, ready to dive back in for the hundredth time since Oliver dropped me off, but the creak of footboards upstairs sends my heart lunging to my throat.

I'm not alone.

Quietly, I walk across the kitchen, the sound of my heart throbbing in my ears. I grab a knife from the butcher block and I'm pulled toward the stairs.

"Hello?" I call out.

No one responds, so I continue one step at a time, taking care to avoid the stairsteps that creak. Darkness shifts in the gloom on the landing of my stepbrother's floor. I grip the banister and take the final step up, stopping as that darkness moves closer.

For a second, memories of Christopher Watkins invade, making my pulse stutter. But then it's washed away as Jack exits his room, leaving me to shudder in relief and lower the blade.

"Katie?" Jack steps closer. "What's wrong?"

I shake my head, giving him a smile as I exhale. "Nothing. I just—"

My stepbrother's eyes flick to the knife. "Planning something?" he asks, a small smirk on his lips.

"I thought I was home alone," I explain. "Then I heard a noise and..." I glance down at the weapon.

"You were prepared."

I nod. "Always."

I won't get caught off guard again. The dreams make it worse. The fuzzy shades of paranoia lurking in my sleep. The mysteries of the house. The death seeped into the very essence of the structure.

A shadow shifts behind him and I realize he's not alone. Paul stands a few feet away, watching me carefully in that intense and analytical way that makes me feel naked even if I'm fully clothed.

"Everything okay?" he asks, eyes dropping to the knife.

"Katie was just making sure we were all safe," Jack says, taking the knife from me. He pulls me to his side and kisses me on the forehead. "She's a natural."

I notice the small black wrapped bundle in Paul's hand. "What's that??"

"We're heading to my office to double-check for any other planted devices."

"Oh?" I glance from Jack to Paul as he steps beside my brother. "Can I come?"

Jack shakes his head, giving my cheek a brush as he passes. "No need. We've got it"

"But I want to," I say. Wanting to go with them. *Be* with them. "Remember, I'm the one that found the bug in the first place."

Jack nods. "If that's what you want."

I think about Oliver's concerns, that I'll leave him once this case is solved. I want to be there for them, whenever they need me. I'll be so damn present in their lives that they'll realize I'm not going anywhere. I stop for my bag downstairs, stashing the paperwork inside. I'm not sure when mom or Montie are coming back, it could be another week, but I sure as hell don't want them stumbling on my investigation.

Paul lets me sit in the front, while Jack drives. I tell them about what Oliver and I found at the courthouse.

"So, nothing concrete," Jack says, glancing away from the road.

"No. Just a lot of deeds and title exchanges. A few permit approvals. I'll have Davis do a record check on arrests and police activity," I say, assuming that with the history of the place that'll be a slog to get through. I rest my hand on Jack's. "We'll find something. I can feel it."

We arrive at Paul's house and Jack parks in the back alley. Once we're inside the office, Jack murmurs, "Stay close to me."

I don't need convincing, not after what I found crawling around on the floor the last time I was here.

"Absolutely," I answer.

"Ready?" Paul asks, punching in the code.

"As I'll ever be," Jack mutters, glancing back at me as he follows him inside.

But Paul doesn't go straight to his office. He makes his way through the front of the building checking the break room before making his way to his office at the end of the hall. I hang back, leaving them to check the rooms before Jack calls out. "It's okay."

Only then do I step into the office, my gaze moving to the corner of the sofa where I'd been crawling around, searching for the button on my blouse. Jack unwraps the black wrapping, pulling out some kind of monitor that he switches on.

"What's that?" I ask.

Jack lifts his finger to his lips as the thing switches on in silence. Green lights flash, bouncing to yellow as he moves around the room. Paul and I watch him as he moves around the room, holding the device against the walls and anywhere else a bug might be planted. It takes him a good thirty minutes to search the room completely from top to bottom and when he's done, he switches off the sensor. "It's clear."

"So, there was just one bug?" Paul asks, shaking his head. "Doesn't make sense."

"No," Jack answers. "It doesn't."

A flicker of anger passes over Paul's handsome face. "I can't trust that there aren't more in the house."

I understand his anger. His private rooms could also be bugged. My cheeks burn remembering what we did in his room. How he bent me over the bed and fucked me. Then later, how he gently cleaned me up.

Paul glances my way. He's thinking the same thing too.

"What do you want to do?" Jack asks.

"The only thing I can, clear out. Go to a hotel or something, I guess."

"I can just see you asking your very private clients to go traipsing through a hotel foyer on their way to their appointments."

"Shit, you're right." Paul rubs the back of his neck. He seems rattled, something I've never witnessed before.

Jack glances at me. "You could come to Davenport. We've got the room."

"Thanks, but, as you said, my patients expect some privacy and after all the drama with your trial, I'm not sure they'd feel safe." He thinks for a moment longer. "There's always my father's place. He has an office out front. It's better than nothing."

Jack places the sensor back onto the sleeve, wrapping it up. "The way I see it, you're out of options. Guess you're headed back to daddy's."

"Dude, you never moved out of your father's house. Are you seriously mocking me?"

Jack grins. "A little."

"Asshole," Paul mutters. "Will you at least wait until I get my things?"

"Sure. Katie and I aren't in a hurry." Jack looks my way with a wolfish smirk. "Are we, babe?"

"Take your time," I say and Paul leaves the room, headed back to his residence.

It's the first interaction I've really seen with them that doesn't involve twisting my brain or body in a thousand knots. Usually, Paul is so aloof and confident. He's quiet and assessing. And Jack? Well, Jack is coiled tight like a viper ready to strike. But now that someone has violated Paul's privacy–*my privacy*–I see the concern Jack has for his friend. He'll do anything for him. Protect him, just like he would Oliver.

Jack wraps up the sensor, then grabs me by the waist, dragging me close. He kisses my neck and whispers in my ear. "How many times did you and the good doctor fuck during your sessions?"

I tilt my head up to get a good look at his face. "Do you really want to know?"

"Nah," he laughs. "But I don't like the fact someone we don't know was watching you." His hands drag down my ass, squeezing. "The thought of someone seeing you like that makes me so angry."

"Hey," I say, touching his chin. "We'll find him."

"Hell yeah we will, and when I do, I'm going to enjoy making the pervert pay."

Jack's tongue is hot and, in my mouth, and his erection is pressing against my thigh when Paul returns a few minutes later, with his laptop under one arm and an overnight bag in the other. "That's all I need for tonight. I'll figure out something else tomorrow."

"Until we find this fucker," Jack reminds him. "Then you're good to come home."

The drive to Derek Sanders' house is quick and I'm surprised at how close Paul's father's house is as we pull up outside a stately, slate stone large home. It's old, almost as old as Davenport Manor. The grounds are immaculate, reeking of old money.

I follow the men to the arched entry, falling in behind Paul as he opens the door calling, "Dad?"

There's no answer. The place has a coldness about it. An elite emptiness I feel as soon as the door shuts behind us. There's no soul in this house. And I return back to the words the doctor said to me, *"Maybe it's the house."* Those words haunt me. If the Davenport house isn't kind, then this place is damn near hostile.

I shiver, wrapping my arms around my body.

"He must be out," Paul says. "The guest wing is this way."

I've never asked about Paul's family life, nor Davis'. I've only known Derek Sanders as a family doctor and not much else. A kind man who helped my mother. Who helped *me* in a time of trauma and need, but as I follow him past a spotless, stark kitchen I realize that his childhood must've been incredibly lonely. There are no pictures of Paul as a child or of his wife. There are antiques and paintings, vases, and cut glass, but as I pass the hallway, I see one image hanging on the wall. It's framed, a photograph of Dr. Sanders and a young Paul in the background standing next to Jack. Montie and Olivia Davenport are front and center with Derek.

Jack doesn't pause at the picture like he's seen it a thousand times. But I haven't. I stare at the casual family portrait. Jack's mom laughs standing between Montie and Paul's dad. It was taken at a beach, her wind-blown hair cast across her face while the kids stood ramrod straight and awkward. "God, you were so young. All of you."

Footsteps stop. Both Paul and Jack turn at the same time, finding me.

I motion to the image.

"Your mother, Olivia, she was so beautiful."

They look at it, saying nothing. Just turn away. Happier times are painful times.

I follow them into Paul's bedroom. I expect a desk and a bed and stark walls. But the room is surprisingly warm. Old baseball posters are still stuck on the wall. A worn sofa on one side and a queen-sized bed on the other. It's the only thing in the room that looks like it's been updated in the last ten years.

I grin.

"What?" Paul asks, dropping his bag on the end of the bed. "What's that grin for?"

"You," I say, taking in the room. The trophies on the shelf. The award for perfect attendance. It's a peek inside Paul's psyche, something he constantly does to me. I nod to a plaque. "Valedictorian?"

He shrugs, sliding his laptop into the middle of an undersized desk. "Not all of us could be football stars," he says, a clear jab at Jack. "Someone had to level up the test scores."

"He's just pissed because I was more popular than him. Chicks don't give a shit about grades." Jack touches a photograph stuck to the mirror. From my position in the room, I see it's of the four boys, younger and more carefree. They look like I remember, back before they cornered me in that bedroom. Before they became hunters.

"Right," Paul says. "I guess this is home for a day or two. At least until Davis can track down who planted the bug."

"At least you can see your clients in the office," Jack says. "Do your mindfuckery so they spill all their dirty thoughts."

"All those dark, forbidden, secrets will be safe once more," I add.

Both of them turn to me. Dark twinkling in their eyes.

"Speaking of dark forbidden secrets," Jack says. "My cock has been hard since we left the other house."

I know that look in his eyes, know that desperation, and it echoes in Paul who watches us carefully.

"Here?" I glance at Jack.

"Always wanted to fuck someone in this room," Paul says, coming closer. "So much goddamn porn. Fuck if I ever thought I'd have Katherine Stevenson in here. I probably would've injured myself."

"Fuck her," My stepbrother says. "You're okay with that, Katie?"

"Only if I can have you both."

The therapist and the serial-killer stepbrother? My breath hitches as heat moves through me. Yes, please.

Although I'd just had Ollie at the courthouse, my body warms with the thought of the two of them.

"I've always wondered how your sessions go," Jack murmurs, pushing my hair off my shoulder. "I guess now I'm about to find out."

Paul steps behind me, the two of them caging me in. I feel his hands on my hips, his lips on my neck. His voice is gravelly when he asks, "How about it, Katherine? Do you feel like baring your soul to us here in my bedroom?"

A shiver passes through me. "Depends on how deep you want to go."

"Oh sweetheart," Paul says, "don't tempt me."

Jack moves quickly, hands sliding under my shirt to pull it over my head. Paul's fingers slide under the lace straps of my bra, slipping them over my shoulders. I'm consumed by the heat of the men surrounding me. Jack reaches for his cock, stroking the length under his jeans. I spot the bulge and my mouth waters.

"Fuck, little sister."

Paul's nimble fingers unhook my bra, dropping it to the floor. My skirt goes next and Jack hooks his fingers in the sides of my panties, impatiently yanking them down. "I fucked Ollie earlier," I tell him as he fists the panties. "I'm sure his cum is still working its way out of my pussy."

"You fucked him?" Paul asks. "Where?"

"In the records room," I tease, remembering how he took me hard and fast against the table, witnesses a few rows over, listening as he claimed me.

Paul's fingers trail down my backside. "Do you like it like that? Out in public? Where you can be seen?"

"It's exciting," I breathe, watching Jack shuck off his pants, cock springing between his legs. He's so thick. So hard. "Thrilling."

"How did my baby brother do it?" Jack asks, fisting the base of his cock. Pre-cum glistens at the tip and I lick my lips, dying to taste it. *Him.*

"Hard, from behind."

Paul's fingers linger at my waist. "He bruised you." A sharp pain surges through me at the spot where Oliver held me down. "But I know you love a little pain with your pleasure."

"More than a little," I admit, knowing that if I tell them how I like it, they won't hold back. Neither of these men will withhold from me. They can't help it. They want me too much.

The corner of Jack's eye twitches. "Get on the bed, Katie."

He lets out a snarl when I don't move fast enough, taking a step forward and forcing me backward. My knees hit the mattress and I fall back, legs spreading wide for the men in the room.

"Jesus, you're soaked," Paul says, eyes on my pussy. I start to close my legs, but he lunges forward, dropping to his knees to hold them apart. "Slick and wet." His eyebrow raises. "Is that Oliver's cum?"

"Maybe," I say. I didn't clean up, liking the way his seed felt between my legs. "You can taste me and see."

From the corner of my eye, Jack breathes hard. He's triggered by the sight of me like this; naked and exposed. Wet and ready. I drop my fingers to my pussy getting them wet, then I hold them up to Paul's mouth. His lips part, tongue darting out for a taste. He groans and grabs my wrist, pushing my fingers deep in his mouth, sucking them off.

I glance over at my stepbrother and see him watching, cock still in his hand. He's jealous of his friend. Of his brother. I grab Paul by the neck and pull his face between my legs. "Eat me."

My hips rise, meeting Paul's tongue, but while the good therapist ravishes me, I keep my eyes on Jack. This is all for him. The primal fight. The battle of wills.

How long before he loses control, claiming me like I know he wants?

I fall back, letting Paul pleasure me with this tongue, bucking hard against his face. His fingers are bruising, digging into my thighs, keeping me spread wide. His tongue pushes into my pussy, making me close my eyes and moan. His grip is unforgiving but his mouth...*oh Christ his mouth*. Fingers join his tongue, sliding along my crease. "I can still taste him," Paul growls. "His cum still inside you." He slides his fingers along me, finding my clit. "Good, sweet girl."

I arch my back, then open my eyes sensing movement. Jack moves, stepping around the bed, watching me. I lift my gaze to him as Paul presses his face against me once more, face pressed harder, tongue fucking me. I widen my knees. *That's the way, get all the way in there.*

"So fucking good," I say, tugging at Paul's hair. "The goddamn best."

I feel the build-up, the orgasm flirting around the edges. Just when I think it's going to take me, I'm lifted from the bed and flipped over. My head snaps back at the force and I cry out at the loss of release.

"Not yet, little sister," Jack says, grabbing my hips off the bed. "You'll come when I say so."

Paul stands on the opposite side of the bed, his hands fumbling with his buckle. I watch as he drops his pants, revealing his magnificent cock. I rise up, grasp the back of his neck, and pull him down to me. "Kiss me."

He does, lips crushing, teeth gnashing, the taste of my pussy on his tongue. I break free and gaze hungrily at his cock. "Feed me."

As I take him in my mouth, my tongue running along the ridge under his head, Jack's hands clench around my hips and I feel his hard length slide between my legs. I push back, loving the feel of him against my folds, the way the tip of his cock nudges at my clit. He pulls back, but then suddenly drives into me, entering me with a hard thrust. His cock is thick, stretching me wide, the force punches me forward, forcing Paul's cock deep down my throat.

The invasion steals my breath. Jack's hand smooths my hair, running his hand down my back.

On all fours, I take them both. Paul fucking my mouth. Jack deep in my pussy, my body driving back with every brutal thrust. They need this. They need me. Paul's hand smooths my hair, cups me under my chin, and forces my eyes upward.

"Look at me while you suck my cock, Katherine."

Tongue flattened, the blunt smooth head pushing all the way to the back. I breathe through my nose as Jack grips me from behind, his pace hard and rhythmic.

My body is so needy, desperate, and aching. Paul slides his fingers through my hair cupping the back of my head, thrusting down my throat. I'm overcome with the sensation. My body tenses. I try to hold on as both Paul and Jack pick up the pace.

I whimper, barely able to breathe around Paul's cock.

"You're ready, aren't you? Ready to be filled with our cum," he growls, driving himself into me, over and over. He grips my hair. "Beg for it."

Paul pulls out, just for a moment, his chest heaving, his cock red and blistering. "I want it," I say, not by force, but by sheer desire. "I want you, all of it. I always have. Ever since that night." The flash of the three of them, pumping their cocks, cumming all over my face, forcing me to taste it. Swallow it. That night changed me. Tonight, will change me.

These men have ruined me, and I want nothing more than to wallow in it.

Paul's thumb runs beneath my chin, pulling my mouth back open. He slots his cock back on my lips and thrusts in.

There's nothing but deep breaths and the sound of flesh as the three of us fall into the heat of the moment.

"Hold on, sweetheart," Paul says, his groan guttural as he spills into me, filling my mouth with hot streams of semen.

Salty.

Tang.

It fills my nose as I breathe.

I swallow...

And swallow.

Trying not to choke on the force of it, but keep it down as he falls back, chest heaving, watching as Jack continues to pump into me.

"Such a good little sister," Jack murmurs in my ear. I feel his hard muscle on my back, the power in his long limbs. "Letting my best friend come down your throat."

Saying the words spark something in him, and he comes hard, thrusting so forcefully I fall forward on the mattress, pussy clenching around his cock.

I cry out, hands fisting the comforter as my pussy throbs. Jack senses this, sliding his fingers in as he pulls out. I moan, my body twitching as my orgasm races through me.

Finally, Jack pulls away, leaving me to gasp and suck in the air.

"How was that, Katie?" My stepbrother groans. "For the first session with the doctor and me?"

"Jesus." I moan, my legs falling to the side. "I'm just glad no one recorded that or Paul would lose his license for sure."

They both laugh, Jack pulling me hard against his chest while Paul climbs into the bed, throwing his leg over mine. We're sticky and satiated, but I've never felt safer.

ELEVEN

Kate

I fell asleep with the heat of Paul and Jack's bodies pressed against me. Now, with the early morning light peeking in the bedroom window, I realize I'm alone.

And I smell bacon.

My clothes from the night before are in a wrinkled, wadded-up ball on the floor, so I open the top drawer of Paul's dresser. Inside, I find a soft, worn, T-shirt with the faded words *Wilmington High* across the chest, a baseball logo nestled underneath. It's big and hangs to mid-thigh, which is good because, after a thorough search, I can't find my panties.

"Okay," I say, turning the corner to the massive kitchen and spotting Paul's broad shoulders bent over the stove, "what the hell did you do with my panties?" He turns and— "Oh fuck. Oh my God."

Blue eyes look back at me, similar to, but not Paul's. Derek appears frozen as he takes in my appearance. The threadbare shirt, my bare legs, the admission I'm naked underneath.

"Good morning, Katherine," he says, easily regaining his composure. "Paul is in a meeting with a patient and Jack left a few hours ago. They both said to let you sleep."

"Oh." My cheeks burn from complete humiliation, but Derek continues on with his task as if nothing absolutely horrifying hasn't just happened.

Which is further compounded as he holds up the frying pan and asks, "I was just making breakfast, would you like some?"

"Sure, um," I tug at the hem of the shirt, "maybe I should..."

Go change? Drown myself? Sneak out the window?

"Sit," he says, voice firm. "I'm sure you're hungry."

For some reason, I follow his command, taking a seat at the long wooden plank table, and pressing my inner thighs together. He fills the plate with strips of still-sizzling bacon and a pile of eggs.

"Toast or biscuit?" he asks, opening the oven door and revealing a tray. The biscuits are a warm brown on the top and my mouth waters.

"Are those homemade?"

"From scratch," he says with a smile. "My mother's recipe."

He drops two on the plate and brings it over, sliding it in front of me. The smell is amazing. *Comforting.* It's been a long time since someone fixed me breakfast.

He's not done, bringing me a steaming cup of coffee and a small pitcher of cream along with butter and jam. He fills his own plate and sits on the opposite end of the long table, and I busy myself with my meal. Behind the table is a wide window that overlooks the grounds.

"Your property is beautiful," I tell him, trying not to scald my tongue on the coffee.

"It's a bit large, especially now that Paul has his own home, but I can't bear to part with it." He butters his biscuit. "It was nice to see his car in the driveway last night—to hear your voices in the house."

He takes a bite of his breakfast and I do the same, letting the butter coat my tongue. Derek rests his forearms on the table and asks, "How is the search for Olivia's killer going?"

"Slow moving," I admit. "Although, I did learn something interesting."

"What's that?"

"She had a friend pick her up once at the Wilmington Inn."

There's no need to extrapolate. The Inn's reputation is well known. A woman like Olivia Davenport should've had no business there.

"Interesting," he says, stabbing a forkful of eggs. "Any idea what she was doing there?"

I shake my head. "Not a clue. Instead of narrowing down possibilities, it seems to only expand them."

He's quiet for a moment, eyes focused on his food, although his fork is still.

"Derek?" I ask, wondering if I've somehow upset him.

"I feel like I'm in a bit of a hard place."

I frown. "What kind of hard place?"

"As you know, I was her doctor," he says. "I knew things about her. Private, personal things that I'm sworn to keep confidential."

I nod, but the investigator in me can't help but ask, "Was she having an affair?"

"Not that I know of."

My mind churns. "Then why else would she go to the Inn?" I ask, more to myself than him. An idea flickers. "Drugs. Was she using?"

He takes a deep breath as if he's struggling with something internally. Finally, he admits, "She came to me a few months before her murder, complaining of depression and dark thoughts. I thought it was probably hormonal. Oliver was still young—postpartum depression wasn't out of the question. She asked for a prescription, and I gave her one—30 days of a lose-dose anti-depressant. Another for Valium—just to take the edge off."

"None of that seems out of the question," I reply, picking up a piece of bacon.

"It wasn't until she finished her prescription early and wanted more. I was concerned about her reliance on the medication and recommended she find a therapist."

"Did she?"

He chuckles darkly. "God no. She became enraged at the idea. Terrified, I think, of someone finding out she needed help."

I think, considering all the options. "Do you think she found access to drugs elsewhere? Maybe from a dealer at the inn?"

"It's possible." He folds his napkin and sets it next to his plate. "I never thought about it."

"Thought about what?"

His expression crumbles. "That I could be the one that sent her down this path. That by not prescribing her the medication she wanted, she made desperate decisions that led to dire consequences."

A drug dealer? Could that be who killed Olivia? Why not? It's as logical as anything else. But Derek's fault? No.

I stand, the chair scraping the hardwoods, and approach him. I ignore the way his gaze focuses on my legs, on the hem of my short shirt, and the bareness underneath. "You can't blame yourself for this. You were trying to do the right thing. Olivia, if she pursued drugs illegally, well that was her choice."

His eyes are rimmed with red, and he sniffs, but nods. "You're right. I know better, but the weight of this job can be a lot to carry sometimes."

I touch his forearm and squeeze. "You're a doctor. Not a god."

His eyes meet mine, and a familiar flicker runs through them— one I've seen when I'm with Paul when he's analyzing me, looking deep into my psyche. "You're right," he says. "Of course. I'm a mere mortal."

The smile that follows doesn't reach his eyes.

"Oh, speaking of prescriptions," he says, standing. His body brushes against mine, dragging the hem of my shirt up. Quickly I cover myself, watching as he opens the cabinet next to the sink. He extracts a bottle and opens the cap. "Don't forget your supplement. I suspect you didn't remember to bring any with you when you decided to stay over."

"You think I still need them?" I ask. I don't confess that I've been a little slack lately.

"Inflammation on a wound like yours can take months to go down. Better safe than sorry." He holds out the pills and I take them, swallowing them down with a glass of water he presses in my hands.

"Thank you."

"You're welcome, Katherine." His hand darts out and he pushes a strand of my hair behind my ear. "You may not be a Davenport by blood, but you're still part of the family." Paul's voice echoes down the hall as he says goodbye to his client. His father's gaze darts toward it, then back at me. "Maybe both our families, if I'm reading things right."

My cheeks heat. Not out of shame, but because Derek's father was so aware of my relationship with these men. Maybe it's that awareness that surprises me. The Davenports live with secrets and exist in denial. But the Sanders? Paul and Derek?

They reside in a place of healing and care. Mental and physical. It's a comfort, one I desire.

"Ah, well, I have a full day of patients to see." He looks at the mess on the stove. "I should clean up."

"I'll do it," I say. "You go."

"That is much appreciated." He smiles. "A hug before I go?"

He spreads his arms, gesturing for a hug. I feel uneasy with it, but he did make me breakfast and gave me a solid lead. I step into his embrace, feeling the warmth of his breath on my neck. His hands are low on my back—almost too low. Before I can react, he pulls away.

"Have a good day, Katherine."

"You, too." As I watch him leave the kitchen, my brain is already sorting the small pieces of the puzzle that make up Olivia's murder, the tiny clues that make the picture clearer. A direction to go in, and I know exactly who can help me find it.

I HAVEN'T BEEN in the Wilmington police station since the night Jack killed Ryan Wilcox. Back then I was seen as a victim, now, after everything that's happened, officers and staff give me a wary look as I approach the front desk.

"I'm here to see Davis Higgins." I peer around her to where the desks are situated in an open concept. Davis' desk is near the back wall. His chair is empty.

"He's in a meeting right now," the woman says peering down at me through the half-moon of her glasses. "Would you like to leave him a message?"

I pause. I would like to leave him a message about the information I need to look up, but not to this woman. "Can I leave him a note on his desk, maybe?"

She frowns. "You can leave it here. Visitors aren't allowed to—"

"Davis!" I shout, spotting him walking out of an office. His eyes dart up to mine and a flicker of emotion crosses his expression. First, it's the heat I've come to expect from him—the hunger—of where our interactions tend to go when we're together. Dark and dirty. It sends a flicker of desire to my core, but just as quickly, that want vanishes, eyes shuttering.

He looks over his shoulder, saying something to the person in the room. I ignore the clerk's command that I wait and stride across the room. To be an investigative journalist, you need a sense of ambition and relentlessness.

"Hey," I say, pretending like every cop in the room isn't watching me. They all still think I'm a liar. A liar so in love with her stepbrother, so humiliated by the truth of our relationship, that I'd do anything to keep it a secret. "I need to talk to you—run something by you."

"You shouldn't come here like this," he says, voice low, "not while I'm working."

"It'll only take a minute. I just need to see some arrest records from—"

His hand clamps around my bicep, fingers digging into the flesh. It stings because it's the arm that was injured by Christopher Watkins. I suck in the pain and let him drag me out of sight, to a narrow alcove of the bullpen. "I'm not your fucking lackey, Katie. I'm not sure why you think you can come into my station and boss me the fuck around."

I'm used to Davis being an ass. To him calling me names and treating me like shit, but this feels different.

"I have a possible lead on Olivia's case. Well, an idea more than a lead. I was talking to Paul's dad and—"

"And I don't have time for this now. This is my job. I have more cases on my desk than a twenty-year-old cold case." He glances around the corner, back to the office he came out of. I catch the profile of the man inside and a twinge of familiarity nudges my brain. "Important cases."

"You can't be serious." This case is part of The Mission. The case that brought them together. That colored every moment of their lives. "I wouldn't let Jack and Oliver hear you say that."

Zero guilt reflects on his face as he says, "Olivia Davenport has been dead for a long time, Katie. One more day isn't going to be the end of the world."

"Wow," I say, completely stunned. Not because he's being a dick. He's *always* a dick. But because his priorities are not aligned with the rest of us.

"For god's sake." He runs his hand through his hair. "Don't give me that look."

"Sorry, Detective Higgins. I thought we were in this together. I thought you were a hunter. I guess you're just another lazy cop who doesn't give a shit about the victims."

His eyes narrow, giving me a flash of the dangerous man I've come to know. When he speaks his voice is gravelly. Dangerous. Familiar. "You think that because we're in public—in a police station—I won't put you in your place. But you're wrong, little slut. I will ruin you in front of every person in this building."

"Is that a threat or a promise?" I ask, licking my bottom lip.

"Katie," he says in warning.

I glance around the corner, back to where he keeps looking, to the man I recognized immediately. "Is that who you're worried about seeing me? The FBI agent?" He stiffens and I laugh. "Yeah, I recognize him from the night Ryan Watkins was killed. He was on the scene."

"If anything, he's probably wondering why I'm talking to a known liar," he snaps. "You need to leave before you tarnish my reputation the way you've done to your family."

Something in my head clicks. His absences. The extra time he's spent at work lately. His attitude right now. "You're working with him, aren't you?" I ask, curious now. "Why? The Binder case is closed."

His jaw sets like he doesn't want to answer but ultimately says, "They asked for help on some other open cases."

"What cases?"

"Missing persons." He rubs the back of his neck. Sweat beads on his forehead. He and I both know the missing person cases in Wilmington all lead back to one place: Davenport Manor and the four hunters that use it as their home base.

"What have you gotten into?" I ask quietly. "What have you told them?"

"Nothing!" he hisses. "But you coming here, it's not helping anything!"

"Higgins," the agent calls from the bullpen. "We're ready to get back to it."

"Be right there," Davis shouts back, before turning to me. "Tell me what you need, and I'll make sure Alyssa, at the desk, gets it for you." He swallows. "But Katie, you show up here again, unannounced, and you and I will have to handle this at home."

A shiver runs up my spine and there's no doubt that is a promise. A promise I'm not so sure I don't want him to keep, but I nod and say, "Thank you."

He walks off, shoulders tense with his jaw locked hard. Even though he agreed to my request, I feel the sting of his dismissal like a slap. I don't have time to follow up on what Davis is doing, or why the FBI is poking around in Wilmington.

I have my own mystery to solve.

TWELVE

Kate

————

The room looks just like it does in the movies.

The walls are a dull beige and made of cinderblock. Partitions separating individual chairs that face a plexiglass window, a phone hanging on the wall. The setup is the same on the other side.

I take my seat, placing the notebook and folder on the narrow table, then stare at the list of rules on the poster hanging on the wall. I'd already been subjected to security searching my person, a fat metal wand ghosting over my body. I wanted to reassure the guards that I had no interest in doing anything wrong. I'm here for information.

Answers.

The loud buzzer shocks me from my thoughts and the door opens on the other side of the glass. A man I've never met before, never seen outside the mugshot in his file comes into view. His uniform is gray, the letters DOC stamped on his chest. His eyes are trained on me—curious. When he sits across from me and picks up the phone, I do the same.

"Mr. Hendricks," I say, taking in his skinny frame. He's pale, with weathered tattoos inking his forearms. "I'm Kate Stevenson, we spoke on the phone."

"I remember," he says, bushy eyebrows furrowing together. "You're younger than you sound."

I give him a tight smile. "I hear that sometimes, but I assure you, I'm old enough to have a degree in journalism and I'm just here to follow up on some questions from a case I'm investigating."

"You're going to have to be more specific, darlin'," he flashes a gold tooth, "because I've been involved in a lot of cases over the years."

Fair enough. I've seen his rap sheet. It's thick. One thing stuck out to me, the drug bust and arrest at Wilmington Inn the week before Olivia Davenport was murdered.

"According to your record, you were arrested a few times for selling drugs out of the Wilmington Inn."

"Sounds familiar," he says vaguely.

"Did you know Olivia Davenport?" I ask.

He shakes his head. "Doesn't sound familiar."

I hold a photo to the window. If he recognizes her, nothing about his expression says so, although he does raise an eyebrow and say, "Beautiful woman."

I nod. "The kind of person you don't forget."

"You're right about that," he chuckles. "I remember her. Came in a few times looking for painkillers."

"She's dead."

"I heard. It was all over the news." He tilts his head. "Rich white ladies always get a lot of attention."

"Did she get a lot of attention at the inn?"

He shrugs. "Some. She wasn't our usual customer."

"Right. I thought that, too," I say, tucking my hair behind my ear. "Why do you think she came to you?"

"Same reason anyone came to me." He grins again, this time knowingly as if he can see behind my questions. "Desperation."

I shift uncomfortably. I'm not desperate, not really, but I do want to solve this case and let the boys move on with their lives. "Your record says you're in prison for murder."

All lightheartedness vanishes from his face and demeanor. "The record is wrong."

"You didn't kill three employees at the mattress store during a robbery?"

"I'm a drug dealer," he snaps, shoulders stiffening. "Not a murderer."

I watch him carefully. It's common for a criminal to deny their crime, but it's different to admit to one while arguing another. "The court found you guilty."

"It was a setup."

"The police and prosecutors never found any evidence of a setup." I flip open the folder. "In fact, it says here your DNA was found on the scene."

"Bullshit," he mutters. "They wanted to take me down. To shut me up, and that's how I got tagged."

I frown. "Who wanted to take you down, Mr. Hendricks?"

His eyes narrow and he tightens his jaw. I think he's not going to say but he blurts, "A former business associate who wanted me out of the way."

"And you have evidence of this?"

"Not that I can prove, but I know who it was."

"The police found a knife at your house—the same knife used in the murders. It was hidden under the porch."

"That shit was planted."

I nod. "By your former business associate?"

"You don't have to believe me." His tone is defensive. Angry. "No one else does. That's what happens when men with power decide you're a threat. You become disposable."

Is that what Olivia became?

Disposable?

"Why were you set up?" I ask, feeling like this is the unanswered question. "Why did they want you out of the picture?" His expression goes from hard to suspicious. Like a switch flipped. I lean forward and ask again, "Who had the power to take you down?"

"Is this really why you came?" he asks, eyes narrowing to small slits. "Who sent you? Why are you asking these questions?"

"I'm just trying to solve a murder."

"No, you're trying to pin another one on me! I will not allow that to happen again!" He shoots out of his chair, dropping the phone with a clatter. "We're done."

My heart pounds because I feel like I'm close. So close to finding out what I need to know. I shout, hoping he can still hear me, "Who set you up, Mr. Hendrix? Who was it?"

He lunges for the receiver again, pulling to his ear. "I don't know who you are, Ms. Stevenson, but let me tell you one thing," his finger jabs at the window. "Digging around in this ancient history is only going to cause one thing. A whole lotta pain. Watch yourself."

This time he hangs up, the sound echoing in my ear.

"Guard!" I hear him shout, muffled through the plexiglass. "I'm done!"

The door buzzer echoes in the cement and metal room. Without another look back, he steps out of the room, leaving me clutching the phone in my shaking hand.

STILL RATTLED, I exit the visitation room and start down the hall. I few feet before the exit a corrections officer approaches and says, "Ma'am, I need you to come with me."

I pause. "Is something wrong?"

"Just follow me."

He's tall, heavy set. The kind of man that looks like he'd be able to handle a group of prisoners. There's a belt around his waist, filled with instruments to do his job—weapons. A can of pepper spray. Handcuffs. A thick baton. I do as I'm told, but not without wondering what's going on.

"Did I break a rule? Or cause a problem? I had all my paperwork filled out. Approved by the front desk—"

He opens a door that leads to a small square room. A holding room? Maybe an interrogation space? There's nothing in it but a small metal table and two chairs bolted to the floor.

Then I see him.

Davis.

He's standing in the corner of the room, the blinking light of a camera a few feet above his head. His muscular arms are crossed over his chest, his cold eyes trained on my face. My heart lunges in my throat.

"Thank you, Officer Jenkins."

"You're welcome, Detective."

The officer moves to close the door and I hear Davis clear his throat. "Officer?"

"Yes, sir."

"Please turn off the camera. Ms. Stevenson and I have something to discuss in private."

"Of course."

Before he gets too far, Davis adds, "Oh, and leave the baton."

My stomach drops, and I look to the officer for...something. If it helps, I'm out of luck. Officer Jenkins removes the baton from his belt and hands it over to Davis. The final gesture he makes before he walks out the door?

A wink.

Fuck.

A moment later the red light from the camera blinks off and we're alone.

"How did you know I was here?" I ask, standing on the opposite side of the table as if it will provide some kind of protection.

"I have eyes and ears everywhere, Katie. You should understand that now."

"I didn't do anything wrong," I say quietly. "Your assistant gave me the files and I found a few leads. One to Hendricks."

"I don't give a rat's ass about Hendricks." He thrusts his hand into his hair. "Coming to the office, showing your face there, and giving the impression we're familiar to one another—that was dangerous."

"I'm sorry."

"I've worked my whole goddamn life trying to get ahead. To remain credible so that me and the boys can do our real work. And what's more fucking credible than the FBI, Katie?" His head tilts, but I know he doesn't want a response. "*Nothing!*" He slams his fist on the metal table top. "There is nothing more credible than the FBI and they came to *me* for help. Me!"

He laughs darkly, voice echoing on the cinderblock walls.

"But here's the irony. They want help on murders I helped commit. Men I hunted. Bodies I hid. Evidence I buried. So yeah, I finally get the notice I deserve, and what? I have to spend it covering my ass and everyone else I care about."

"That has to be hard," I say, swallowing past the lump in my throat.

"No, bitch," he says, circling the table. I keep an eye on the baton in his hand. "What's hard is trying to justify why you came into the building making accusations about my loyalty to my friends—my family."

"I shouldn't have—" he lunges for me, and the room is so small, there's nowhere to hide. He grabs the front of my shirt, just under my throat, and presses me against the table. I swallow and try again in a steadier voice. "Davis, this is a misunderstanding."

"I don't think it is, Katie." He nods to my waist. "Remove your pants."

I don't argue. I know better. He's set this up so that no one will come. No one can help me. I let the fabric drop to the floor.

"Panties," he commands curtly.

They fall next to my pants.

"Get up on the table." I ease up, flinching from the shock of the cold metal table. "Spread your legs."

I stare at the baton in his hand. At least if he's fucking me with his cock, I know he can do only so much damage, but the baton...a tremor of fear runs through me.

"Please don't hurt me," I say, widening my legs.

His eyes drop down to my pussy and a smirk tugs at his lips. "God, I can smell you. You're hot for it aren't you, little whore?"

The embarrassing thing is that I am. They've trained me to be like this. Conditioned. All those sessions in Paul's office. Jack lurking in the dark corners of my room. Oliver's demands that I pleasure him in public. And Davis...the way he jumps out at me when I least expect it. Alleyways and parking garages. Jailhouse interrogation rooms.

Fear makes me horny, but that doesn't mean I want it—not like this.

"I hate you when you're like this," I tell him, knowing punishment is coming one way or the other. "Not when you're coming after me for your own guilt."

He moves quickly, violently, the tip of the baton slotting between my thighs, bearing down at my entrance.

"You don't know the sacrifices I'm making," he says, increasing the pressure. "The pressure. The questions. The looks I get from the other officers!"

My thighs snap close on instinct, but it's the wrong move because when he pushes the tip of the baton inside it sharp pain shoots up my body. "Davis! Stop!"

He doesn't, pushing the thick stick all the way in, tearing and ripping me wide. I scream out in pain, but his hand clamps over my mouth, silencing me. "Take your punishment like a good little slut, Katie. You'll think twice about questioning my loyalty."

He fucks me with relentlessness, while never actually losing control. That's the terrifying part of this, Davis is fully in control. He's acting with intent. Desperate or not, he's fully in charge of his movements.

Which the only reason, is that instead of blistering pain, I feel the build-up of want deep in my belly. I scratch at his face, slicing his skin with a sharp nail. He hisses and kisses me, biting down on my bottom lip.

"Fuck," I groan, wrapping my hand around his neck, and holding on as he drives the baton into me. His knuckle grazes my clit with every thrust. Our noses are inches apart and I hold his eye. "Why are you doing this? Why the lies and secrets?"

"I'm doing my fucking job," he growls.

"Well, I'm doing mine!" I cry out, hips rocking to meet his thrust. "I'm helping my family!"

"You think I'm not?"

Words are lost to me at that point, his eyes are focused on me. On the hitch of my breath, the rise and fall of my chest, the quivering between my legs.

"Come, you little bitch, show me how much you love it when I treat you like this."

But I don't. I hate my body for betraying me. I hate the confusing way pain and punishment make me feel. The twist of want deep in my core can no longer discern what's right and what's wrong—what's good and what's bad.

All it wants is release and when it comes, it rips through me like a storm, tearing through my limbs, running along my nerves, pulsing in my pussy as he clenches around the invading force between my legs.

My hand is still around his neck, nails digging into his flesh, and the two of us breathe heavily as I ride out the orgasm.

"Never question my loyalty again," he says, voice strained and exhausted. He pulls the baton out, leaving me aching and empty, then turns without saying another word. The door opens and closes quickly, as I sit stunned on the table, trying to process what just happened.

It's not until later, when my brain clears, that I realize something important. Davis brutally punished me, but there's one thing he didn't do.

He didn't come.

THIRTEEN

Jack

"Open your legs, Katie. I want to see what that bastard did to you."

"Jack, it's not a big deal."

I motion to the bed. "You've been shifting on your feet, and you've refused to sit all fucking day. I know you met up with him at the prison."

She'd told me that much, anxiously talking about some rabbit hole she'd gone down, as an attempt to distract me from her stilted movements. "You know how Davis can be." She fuzzes with imaginary lint on her shirt. "He's...temperamental."

"He's abusive." I know she can say the same about me, but there's a difference. What I do to Katie is out of love. Davis is about punishment. "This was more than rough sex, wasn't it?" She won't meet my gaze. Her cheeks blush before she looks away. I know at that moment it's worse than normal and I try to keep the edge from my tone. "*Bed.* Let me see."

She glances at the flat surface, then swallows and slowly sits, wincing as her ass hits the mattress.

"Lay back, knees up."

She does as she's told. I push her skirt upwards, instantly noticing the bruises in the shape of his fingers on the inside of her thighs. The darkened marks give me pause. I don't like that savage feeling that rises inside me. I keep a leash on it, knowing she's watching my every move. "Tell me again about the prison."

"Hendrix had no idea about any of it." I reach under her skirt and grip the waist of her panties, drawing them down her thighs. I can see how red her pussy is. Red, swollen...and not in a good way.

I tug her panties out from under her feet. "Do you believe him?"

I don't give a fuck about this guy, Hendrix. I'm too busy staring at her swollen pussy. There's bruising around her entrance. I gently brush my finger along her swollen lips, and she flinches. "How bad does it hurt?"

I didn't need to ask, her breath catches from pain. "Just a little."

Just a little my ass.

"Take a deep breath," I tell her right before I part her pussy. "Fucking Davis. What did he use, Katie? This isn't caused by his damn cock." She pales, closing her knees. But I won't let her pull away from me. I won't let her protect the son of a bitch.

"It's fine. Things just got a little rough."

"Tell me, Katie." She moves to roll out of bed. But I stop her, grabbing her arm, forcing her gaze to mine. "Tell me."

"A baton." Her cheeks redden with the confession.

"A *what?*"

She meets my stare. "A baton. He got it from the guard."

A *baton?* Jesus fucking Christ. First the gun and now this.

I rise from the bed, gently pushing her back down. "Lay down and don't move a fucking inch." I lift the back of her hand to my lips, pressing a kiss. "I'll be right back."

As much as I love inflicting pain and as much as I know our girl likes it, there's a line. A line Davis has crossed. I make my way downstairs to the kitchen and grab a plastic bag from the drawer.

Oliver enters the room as I open the freezer.

I grab a handful of ice and toss it into the bag. "Hey."

He gestures to the ice. "What's that for?"

"Our stepsister's bruised cunt."

"Oh?" He gives me a look, one filled with accusation. "Things get out of hand?"

"It wasn't me," I snarl and turn away. "Davis took to her with a baton."

I catch the way his shoulders stiffen in the corner of my eye. "He...*beat her?*"

"No." I force the word through clenched teeth. "He fucked her with it."

I'd like to say that the sound of a familiar engine on the drive announces that Paul is here, but my brother's gaping jaw tells me he's in shock. Unfortunately, things are about to get worse because the doctor is going to fucking lose it when he finds out.

"Jesus," Oliver mutters, "how bad is it?"

"Bruised. Torn. Swollen." I slam the freezer door just as the kitchen door opens and Paul enters, carrying a brown paper bag with handles.

"Sorry I'm late," he says. "Dad wanted me to bring Katherine some of the leftover biscuits he made for breakfast and—" He takes in the two of us. The bag of ice. My furious expression. Oliver's gaping, fucking, jaw. "What's going on?"

"Davis hurt Katie." Oliver says, swallowing back his own anger. "Fucking her with a goddamn baton."

Paul is silent, then, "Did she want it?"

"It doesn't matter," I say, knowing she likes things rough. "She belongs to all of us and she's not his to take his frustrations out on."

I know I sound like a fucking hypocrite, but things have shifted lately. I see Katie for what she is to us, who she is. She's special. Ours. She should be protected, not used, and abused and that's exactly what Davis has done. I may be a cruel bastard, but this? This is sadistic.

"I need to see her," Paul says. "Examine her."

"Good idea." I push past them and head for the stairs. "She's upstairs on my bed."

The guys follow me and when we get back to my room. She's exactly where I left her, knees together, her panties in the middle of the bed. I yank open my dresser and grab a soft cotton shirt and wrap the ice with it. "Open wide, little sister."

She glances at the others as they come in the room behind me. "You told them?"

I give her a look. "I'm pretty sure they're going to find out sooner rather than later. It's not like we don't take turns regularly." Heat fills her cheeks as I sit on the bed. "Open."

She does, reluctantly, revealing her abused pussy.

"Jesus," Ollie curses at the sight. He sits next to her, shifting her body so that her head is resting in his lap. "Are you okay, baby?"

"It's fine," she says but breathes a sigh of relief when the ice pack connects with her bruised flesh. "He's under a lot of pressure at work and I upset him when I showed up unannounced." She looks up at my brother. "You know how I get when I have a lead."

"Baby," Oliver says, smoothing her hair, "don't make excuses for him. *Nothing* you've done justifies this type of treatment."

Paul is quiet as he runs his hand gently down her thigh. "Let me take a look, Katherine, and examine you for injuries."

She drops her thighs and Oliver takes the bag of ice from her. Paul sits on the edge of the bed, and examines her, carefully. "Take a deep breath, sweetheart, I'm going to need to examine you inside."

"Wait," I say, opening the bedside drawer. I pull out a bottle of lube and hand it to him. "Use this."

Katie eyes meet mine, softening at the gesture. Yeah, I'm worried about my girl. I'm worried about there being irreparable damage to her perfect and glorious pussy. I will hunt Davis in the streets if he caused permanent damage.

"Good idea." Paul coats his fingers liberally and presses them at her entrance. "Take a deep breath." Oliver strokes her cheek, comforting her as Paul slides his fingers past the tender flesh and into her pussy. "That's a good girl, Katherine."

"Any damage?" I ask, heart pounding. Every second that passes I get more upset. More furious at the thought of Davis punishing our girl like this. "If there is I'll fucking k—"

"No," he says decisively. "No tearing inside, although it also feels a little swollen." He raises his eyebrows at Katie. "Do you feel any pain when I do this?"

She shakes her head. "No."

I exhale. "Thank god."

If he'd done something irreversible, there's no doubt in my mind I'd kill the bastard. As it is...

"He's gone too far," I announce. "It's one thing for him to be a dick, but it's a whole other thing for him to damage our property and punish you over his personal problems."

"Jack," she says, and I know before she says it, she's going to defend the bastard. "I think something is wrong. The pressure from the FBI. The scrutiny of the missing men cases is getting worse. He just snapped."

I don't bite back the icy tone when I say, "You mean other than he's hiding something from us? Avoiding us? Hurting you?"

There's a strength in her stare as she says, "I can't explain it, but he seemed almost...scared. Desperate, maybe?" She pushes up from Oliver's lap and grabs my forearm. "I think there's something wrong, something he isn't talking about to us."

"Katherine," Paul starts, "we've known Davis our entire lives. We don't keep secrets from one another. We work as a team. A well-oiled one at that. You of all people should know that."

"And yet you sense it," she replies, quieting the room with her intensity. "You feel it." She opens her legs wider, giving us all a view of her battered pussy. "And you *see* it. There's something he's keeping from us, and I think whatever it is, it's bad."

I don't want to believe her.

I sure as hell don't want to feel sympathy for the bastard.

What I do feel is dangerous as I stand over her. "I hope for his sake you're right, little sister." I glance at the others. "But there's only one way to find out."

My brother and best friend look at me.

Then they both nod in agreement.

"We find him." I cross the room and reach into my dresser, drawing out my gun, tucking it into the waistband of my trousers. "And we have it out once and for all."

FOURTEEN

Kate

It's the butter that makes them so good.

It has to be, because why else would I eat the entire bag of biscuits Paul brought me from his father while sprawled on Jack's bed in the middle of the afternoon?

Note to self: Find out what's in the homemade butter recipe from Derek the next time I see him.

Of course, I could be stress-eating. The guys have been gone for an hour and I've had no word from any of them. I checked their location on my phone app, but all three have been turned off. Unfortunately, they only do that for one thing: Hunting.

That's what sends a chill up my spine. What Davis did to me was wrong. Painfully wrong, but there have been other moments we've shared, like the night at Hades when I was overwhelmed by panic, or when he saved me from Christopher Watkins, that makes me know that under all that tough, dangerous, exterior is a man who cares.

Just in his own way.

Something about all of this is wrong.

I should do something other than eat my feelings away. Call Davis? Warn him? Call Jack and beg him to come back. Go get in my car, drive around to their hunting spots, and see if I can stop them from making a mistake. I ease my legs over the edge of the mattress, taking care not to move too fast. Yeah, I downplayed it to the guys. My pussy hurts like a mother—more now than when he actually inflicted the abuse.

Ice. Maybe I'll start with ice.

I'm still trying to talk myself into moving when my stomach gurgles loudly. "I know," I tell myself, "I get it. Six biscuits were one too many."

It rumbles again, this time followed by a lurch. Shit, no, really, something *is* wrong. With my stomach.

"Oh, man." A shiver runs along my nerves, followed by a thin coat of sweat popping up on my skin. I press my hand to my forehead, checking for a fever, but I just feel clammy.

And like I'm going to vomit.

Clutching my phone in my hand, I force myself off the bed, taking tiny shuffling steps toward the bathroom. My head spins. My stomach *churns*. I'm sick. Like really sick.

I sag against the door jamb and press the first number that pops up. It goes to voicemail.

"Paul, hey, I know you're busy—" bile rushes up the back of my throat and I hold it back. "Shit. I'm sick. Like the flu? Or something? Just...I need you."

I hang up, dropping the phone on the floor where it skitters across and under the bed. Perfect. The nausea fades, slightly, but my stomach cramps again and I fall like the phone, down to my knees. I press my forehead on the cool tile. "Oh god."

Somehow, with my head swimming and my limbs feeling like they weigh a million pounds, I crawl over to the toilet and hoist myself to the bowl.

Then, I heave up everything. I mean, everything. Biscuits. Butter. The coffee I had before I went to the prison. I vomit until there's nothing left—like my body is trying to wring itself out—trying to expel an evil force inside of me.

When it's all out and my stomach can do nothing but spasm angrily that there's nothing left, I slump to my back, the hard floor against my back. My eyelids feel heavy and now that my body has stopped revolting, sleep seems like an awesome idea. In fact, right here is fine. Who needs a bed? I roll to my side, pressing my cheek to the cool tile.

My eyes flutter shut and I drift off until...

Creak.

The hinges whine, drawing me back to consciousness. I look at the door and see legs. Shoes. Walking my way. A shadow crosses the bright lights over the sink and I blink at the face.

"Oh," I say, struggling to rise. "It's you. Thank God you're here. I'm—"

My head spins, stars bursting in front of my eyes. I rub my eyes but everything's too heavy. Too hard and without warning, I slump back, fading into the dark.

"WAKE UP." A hand presses against my forehead. "As much as I'd like to say we have all the time in the world, we don't."

I blink into a bright light, searching for the person talking to me, but the smallest movement sends my body into spams. My back seizes first, painfully aware of the unforgiving hard surface under my back. My guts feel hollow—wrung out and exhausted from vomiting. My mouth is dry, bitter, like I've been chewing on cotton. And my core is still sore, and the bruises from Davis' assault still angry and irritated.

My first instinct is that I'm still on the bathroom floor, but that doesn't feel right. My legs are heavy, as though they're bent at the knee and hanging down. My shoulders ache, and I move my fingers, they touch one another. They're bound at the wrist, over my head. I yank, but feel nothing but the burn of rope on my wrists. I'm restrained.

The familiar lick of panic tickles my spine.

Twisting my head I get a glimpse of the room—not the bathroom. The kitchen. The pale green cabinets—the shiny brass knobs. My stomach rolls when I realize my position—the vantage point. There's only one place in the room that allows for it.

"I didn't mean for you to get this sick," the other person in the room says, "but you really gave me no choice."

I jump at the voice, how even disoriented I am, I know it. I close my eyes and think back to my last coherent thoughts. Upstairs, sleeping on the floor, cool tile...someone came in. Someone I know. Someone I was happy to see.

Oh God.

Oh God.

Footsteps echo off the kitchen floor. I shut my eyes, willing this to go away. It's a nightmare. Too much trauma. Post-traumatic-stress. All the things we talked about in Paul's office, in between my training, all the things wrong with me.

Fuck. *Paul.*

"You weren't taking the pills regularly," he says, continuing as if we're having a conversation. "So, I had no other option but to adjust."

I gather the strength to jerk my limbs, pulling at the restraints but they're firm, only leaving burning pain along my skin. "Why are you doing this?"

"Ah, you *are* awake." Fingers trailed down my throat, gentle but terrifying. "It was always coming to this, Katherine, don't you realize that now?"

His head blocks the light, face coming into view. I wish so badly that it wasn't him. That this was just a fever dream, a hallucination from whatever sickness is kicking my ass. But Derek Sanders stands over me, his distinguished gray hair, his kind, intelligent face. His strong, handsome features. The eyes that are so much like his sons...

This house isn't kind to women.

He's the one that said that. But suddenly I realize with absolute certainty, it's not the house.

"If only you hadn't returned, Katherine. If you hadn't been so fucking nosy with your investigations." He rolls his eyes. "It's curious how you're so interested in solving crime unless it involves you and your brothers." This time when he touches me, I realize he's wearing latex gloves. It makes the feel of his finger trailing over my shoulder and down the 'V' of my shirt even more skin-crawling. "That's the irony, of course, that's why it had to come to this. You're just like her." His fingers graze my breast, lingering over the nipple. I feel it pebble and then he tweaks it *hard*. I gasp, but not loud enough that I don't hear him add, "*She* couldn't mind her business either."

She. Olivia Davenport. The last woman that was tied to this kitchen table.

"Dr. Sanders," I say, then shift tones, "*Derek*. Whatever is happening here, we can turn this around."

He grins. "Dear, I'm not one of those pussy whipped boys that will do anything for a moment sheathed in your warm cunt. I see you for what you are."

"What am I?"

"Trouble." His hands continue to travel across my body— methodical. Less seductive, more assessing. As if he's giving me a physical exam. "Like Olivia, although infinitely more capable. That's why I had to poison you."

Poison? Then it strikes me. "With the supplements."

"In theory, but you didn't take them like you should've." He grins. "Naughty patient."

"I tried, but they gave me bad dreams."

"Unfortunate side effect," he admits. "But then you came to my house, fucking Paul and Jack at the same time like a common whore, all while digging into my past, my *business*. I saw the way you devoured my homemade biscuits, and it was like a lightbulb. Mix it in your food."

"Mix what?"

"Tetrahydrozoline." When I stare at him blankly, he adds, "It's most commonly found in eyedrops. Almost impossible to trace. I couldn't give you enough to kill you," a slow grin spreads across his mouth, "because where's the fun in that? But I could incapacitate you. I did see what you did to that Watkins' boy. You aren't afraid to protect yourself."

"But she was, wasn't she?" I want to know why he killed Olivia. Me? It's obvious, now. I was getting too close. The trip to visit Hendrix was probably the final straw. I hadn't made the actual connection yet, but it was there. The drugs, the murder, the setup... Derek Sanders is not whom he seems. Never was. "She wouldn't fight back."

"Olivia?" His eyes glaze over for a moment. "She sacrificed herself for those boys. Gave them time to hide. Let me fuck her. Brutalize her. Butcher her." He comes back into focus, gaze meeting mine. "They'll be devastated when it happens to another woman they love."

"But why? Why did you kill her?"

"She was mine first," he says, facing the counter where I hear the soft sounds of him moving around objects. "I found her in that hellhole—the Wilmington Inn—working as a cocktail waitress in the bar. She was too pretty for that kind of place. Too smart. She deserved better, although I admit she was good at her job. Savvy. The dark streak in those boys comes from her. She knew how to handle a customer. How to barter with the dealers. The pimps." He glances over his shoulder. "I got her cleaned up, paid for her to move into a nice place, found her a legitimate job. I gave her social standing." He swallows. "I'm also the one that introduced her to my best friend, Montie." He looks around, at the high ceilings, the stained glass in the back window, and the fixtures. "She fell in love with this house—with his money. I was a doctor, but he was an exceedingly wealthy man."

"So, you were what? Jealous?"

"She was mine," he hisses. "And I wasn't about to let her go. I blackmailed her with her history. Montie and the women down at the club, the league, the school...they had no idea who she really was. Only I did. Forced her to move the product for me down at the Inn. Fucked her when I wanted to." He laughs. "It's not this house that isn't kind to women. It's me. I'm the one that ruins lives. Olivia. Your mother, and now you."

"What about my mother?" I ask, but I already know. I've seen the evidence. The pills. The glazed eyes from over medication.

"Sweetheart, I've been drugging her for ages. Ruining her for Montie the way he ruined Olivia for me." He licks his bottom lip. "But you...you slipped through my fingers. Sent away to boarding school. I knew then my son and your brothers had something to do with it, and I figured you'd never return. Thankfully, I was wrong about that."

I think of my vibrant mother, how strong and capable she was when we moved in and how over the years, she became more and more compliant. Absent. She spent her days irritable and angry. Dismissive, especially when it came to me.

"So what now? You murder me like you did Olivia? Leave me in pieces on the kitchen table?"

"Actually yes. Poetic right? Perfect for one of your little true crime stories you love so much." He turns fully away from the countertop. Something is in his hand, but he's holding it low, out of view.

"They'll find you."

There's no question who "they" are.

"I doubt it," he says, self-assured. The metal curve of a scalpel blade glints in the overhead light. Fear, along with the images of Olivia's crime scene, races through me. "There's a reason I've never been caught over all these years. Why your brothers, Paul, and Davis couldn't hunt me down like the other savages in this town? I cover my tracks."

He presses the tip of the blade against my T-shirt, slicing through the fabric with ease. Goosebumps, both from fear and the cool air in the room, rise across my flesh. Brow furrowed, his hands probe my lower belly. I suck in a breath, and he asks, "Sore from the vomiting?"

A nervous laugh bubbles out. "You actually care?"

"I'm a doctor," he says calmly. "I'm always curious about how my patients do with their medications."

No, he's *psychotic*, I realize. Deranged.

"While your 'hunters,'" he uses finger quotes, "have been busy chasing their tails, I've documented everything."

I blink. "You put the camera in Paul's office."

He nods, seemingly impressed. "Very good, Katherine. But yes, every time you fucked my son in his office—violating his ethical obligations—I have it on record." His blade goes to work again, this time cutting off my shorts. I'm not wearing panties, not after icing it earlier. He parts my thighs as far as they'll go since my ankles are bound to the legs of the table. "I have this on tape as well." He tsks at my sore swollen core. "He really brutalized you, didn't he?"

I heard Davis tell the guard to turn off the camera. I watched the light change. He's lying he has to be, but how else would he know?

Weakly, I defend him. "He was upset."

"Yes, those FBI agents have him in a tizzy, don't they?"

"You know about that?"

"Of course. I'm the one that tipped them off that there was a bigger case going on with the missing men in Wilmington. That Detective Higgins seemed to be indifferent about these cases and too willing to dismiss foul play. They took the bait." His hands hold me apart, drawing his gaze from my pussy to my eyes. "I know about everything. Every bruise on your body. The unreported gunshot wound. The violent abuse." His eyebrow lifts. "And if that isn't enough, I'll just direct them to the stacks and stacks of dead bodies buried in the woods."

"Why?" Dread rises along every nerve in my body. "Why are you doing this to me then?"

"Because you're the loose thread. You know too much, but the bigger issue is that you love them. You're as evil as they are, I saw it with my own eyes after you murdered that man in Jack's bedroom." He rises and holds up the scalpel. "But the real reason is that I'm going to kill you, Katherine, and then your lovers are going to take the fall."

FIFTEEN

Paul

"Let's just hear him out first." I step in Jack's way as he climbs out of the car, placing my hand in the middle of his chest. "We can't make a scene, not here."

The parking lot of the well-known cop bar is packed. Davis's four-wheel drive sits three cars away, drawing Jack's glare. I've been here a number of times. The last time was six months before. We were celebrating with the three lead investigators after they closed a five-year-old case. That has been by invitation only. You don't turn up uninvited and you sure as hell don't walk in looking for a fight.

Jack's lips curl, baring his teeth. I've seen him dangerous before—murderous. But this is a whole new level. He's unhinged and it was the sight of Katie's raw pussy that drove him toward the edge.

I don't like it either—hurting Katie like that? It's one step too far. But my concern at the moment is more about letting Jack walk into a bar full of cops looking for a fight.

With his best friend who is also a cop.

It's the fact that one wrong argument like this could ruin decades of friendship and I don't know if there would be any way to fix it. Not after what he did to our girl. I press my hand against his chest, forcing his gaze to mine. "You need to slow down. Let me do the talking."

He looks from the building, then over to me before he scowls.

"Jack," Ollie urges. "Listen to Paul."

It's the desperation in his brother's tone that breaks through his hard expression. Jack exhales and narrows in on me. "You'd better get to the bottom of this, doc. I won't have any loose ends here, and that includes anyone who is a threat to my sister."

His sister.

More like the woman who has his heart. Katie is going to be the death of us, quite literally. I give a nod and lower my hand. "Leave this to me."

With all the weight on my shoulders, I turn and head for the door. Music spills out and the deep throaty roar of male laughter follows. But I don't process any of it. Instead, I'm focused on the impatient heat of Jack's gaze on the back of my head and step through the door and into the smell of sweat and testosterone. The rancid tang blooms in my chest as I scan the gloom and find Davis sitting amongst a group of other detectives.

As if he senses me, his head snaps up. Dark, haunted eyes find us instantly. I see the change in him as he forces a smile, says something to his colleagues, and rises from his seat.

He makes no move toward us or even acknowledges us at all. Instead, he heads past the bar and toward a hallway that passes the dank bathrooms and leads to the storage room outside. Pallets of beer and untapped kegs sat alongside the wall. Davis disappears for a second as he rounds the corner. But when we follow, we find him standing there, his hands by his side and a stony look on his face.

Jack lunges before I have a chance to stop him. His fist cracks out, hitting Davis in the jaw. He stumbles sideways, his knee buckling for a second before he catches his fall. Then he straightens, standing motionless once more.

"That is for hurting my sister."

Crack!

Jack hit him again, this time the blow was brutal. Davis' knees give out, and this time he falls. He isn't so quick to rise. Heavy breaths consume him before he gathers his strength and heaves to his feet.

"And that one is for whatever the fuck you're hiding from us." Jack shoves him hard against the wall. "You wanted to do the talking, doc, so talk."

Blood trickles down from the corner of Davis' mouth, but he makes no move to wipe it away. When his eyes meet mine, I see someone unfamiliar to me. Someone lost and out of control.

"We need to know where your head is at," I start, dragging my fingers through my hair. "Talk to us. Why did you do that to Katie?"

I've never seen Davis like this. Red-faced, avoiding us. He's typically headstrong and demanding, but now he has the haunted look of the kind of man I'd spend months seeing professionally and barely scratch the surface.

"Where is my head?" he snarls, a little of that old fire flaring to life. He cuts me a glare. "Fuck if I know. Everything..." He glances at Jack who looks like he's one false move from murdering him right here. "I took it too far. I know that."

Jack and Oliver stand behind me, neither speaking. They want to know why as much as I do.

"I told her to back off. That she couldn't come to my office and ask so many fucking questions. They're watching my every move. You don't understand..." He exhales a shuddered breath. "But I took it too far. I know that. The pressure just got to me."

"The pressure of the FBI, you mean?" Jack takes a step closer, meeting him eye-to-eye. "Because that's what this is about, right? You're ready to move on, wanting to leave us behind. So, you pull a fucking stunt like you did today?"

Davis shakes his head. "No, you got it all wrong."

"Then why don't you set us straight?" Oliver says. "Or do you not have a baton handy?"

Davis flinches. "They have files on you, on me. On *all of us*. We need to be careful because I don't know how much they really know."

"What do you mean files?" I ask.

He meets my gaze. "They have all the documents on Jack's arrest for Ryan Watkins. They have stacks of files about the missing men—the men *we* hunted and killed. They know about your kinky-psychotherapy appointments with Katie. I don't know how, but they know we're all aligned, so I'm just trying to keep ahead of them. Figuring out where they're looking and how to cover our tracks."

"We didn't leave tracks," Jack growls. "Who's feeding this information if it isn't you?"

"I swear I'm not a narc. Everything I've done is to protect you."

"Bullshit," Oliver snorts from behind me. "That's bullshit. Jack's right. You want a promotion and this is how you get it."

"No," he says, thrusting a hand into his hair. "Fuck no. You know I'm not that guy."

But something he says triggers me and I'm the one that slams into Davis with aggression. "You let the fucking FBI record my sessions? Do you know how much trouble I'm going to be in for that? I broke Katherine down because we needed her strong. I did that for us!"

"Hey!" he shouts, fighting me off. "The FBI didn't record that. It was sent to us."

I blink, trying to process that.

"Someone else bugged my office?" I laugh darkly. "Now you sound like you're just scrambling."

My cell phone gives a buzz, but I don't reach for it. I watch Jack as a nerve twitches in the corner of his eye. He pushes me aside and steps in front of Davis. "Look me in the eye and tell me you're not planning on betraying us."

Davis scowls and shakes his head. "Of all the blows you've given me that one fucking hurts the most."

"Not as much as a baton up the cunt," Jack bites back. "Goddamn it, Davis, if you're in trouble you come to us!"

"I couldn't," he says quietly. "They're watching me. What were you going to do? Hunt and take down the fucking FBI?" He laughs. "I'm the only thing keeping them from you, and this is thanks I get."

There's something about the way he says it, the sound of defeat, the raw confession of barely keeping us alive, that makes me realize it's true. Davis isn't betraying us. He's protecting us. I glance at Oliver and he frowns, the truth evident to him as well.

"None of this makes up for what you did to Katherine," I say, hoping to make it clear.

"Paul's right," Jack cuts in. "You will make it up to her, do you hear me? You will fall on your fucking knees at her goddamn feet and you'll..."

"Kiss my whore's cunt better?" Davis snarls, his lips curling. "Because I'll do that. I'll—"

Jack unleashes a snarl, strides forward, and grabs Davis' by the shirt, staring him in the eyes. "You don't get it, do you? *I'd fucking gut you right here. I'd gut you and I wouldn't lose a goddamn moment of sleep over it.* But *she* would. It would break her."

I see the moment it hits Davis. Jack is as close to the point of no return as I'd ever seen. The case with his mom and his own emotional vulnerabilities when it comes to Katie have made him more dangerous than he's ever been.

And we all see that now. We *all* feel that. Because each one of us is the same. I see it in the way Davis searches Jack's gaze and the way his breaths deepen.

"You'll fucking do whatever she wants," Jack continues. "If she never wants you to touch her again, then that's what will happen. If she wants you on your fucking knees every goddamn day for her, *then that's what will happen.* For some sick fucking reason, Katie puts you above her own fucking pain. She's fucking worried about you and not the fucking beating you gave her. Let *that* sink in."

"Jesus," Davis whispers as his brow furrows.

Jack shoves him back. "Yeah. *Jesus.*"

We are all so fucking broken and damaged in our own terrifying way. Rejected. Abandoned. Betrayed. For the longest time, hunting and killing is what kept us together, but somewhere along the way that changed. Katherine's love is the glue that binds us. She's the one who keeps us from tearing each other apart. Davis sees that now, more clearly than ever before. In his own perverse way, it's why he went to her for relief and took his pain out on her.

And it's why she took it.

My phone vibrates in my back pocket–the subtle voicemail reminder. I reach into my pocket and pull it out.

"Who is it?" Oliver asks as I scroll down notifications.

"It's Kate." I hold out the phone and let the audio play. *"Paul, hey, I know you're busy—"* She pauses and there's a sound of gagging. *"Shit. I'm sick. Like the flu? Or something? Just...I need you."*

"Where is she?" Davis asks as I dial her number.

"At home, with an ice pack on her cunt." Jack's eyes darken. "Or she was. I swear to God if she's hurt worse than we thought..."

The call goes to voicemail and a chill races along my spine. I look up at my brothers. "I think something's wrong."

SIXTEEN

Kate

____

My mind spins.

Derek is the man my brothers and his friends have been hunting for years. He was right there the whole time. In this house. Caring for my mother. Caring for me.

Paul's father.

If I had anything left to vomit, I would, but the poison already emptied my stomach. Weakened me. And now there's nothing left for me to do but die.

A laugh bubbles out of me, abrupt and hysterical.

"You think this is funny?" Derek asks, forehead furrowed. "Or have you gone mad?"

I snort, trying to get it under control. I *must* look mad. Bound and tied to the kitchen table, clothes torn to shreds, yet laughing like an idiot. "I just...I always knew I would die in this house." I sniff, craning my neck to see him better. "I just didn't think I would be killed by you."

"Jack?" he muses. "I understand your fear, but he'd never kill you. He'd lose his plaything."

The frivolous way he calls me a plaything feels like a stab in the chest. It must show on my face.

"You think he really loves you?" He stands between my spread legs, fingers gliding up my thigh. Cold, paralyzing fear grips my spine. "He's incapable of love. You know that, right? He's a sociopath. Paul diagnosed him years ago."

"Because you made him one!" I shout, flailing futilely against my restraints. "Why? Why do you want to hurt them? Your own son?"

"Don't turn this away from who is truly at fault." He raises the knife, pointing it at me. "You came back. You started sniffing around in my business. They'd been bumbling around for years, Katherine. Too distracted by shiny new men to hunt to ever truly focus on their 'mission.'" He makes quotations, the blade glinting in the overhead light. "But you were exactly what they needed to find The Binder. The perfect bait. The perfect little investigator. The perfect cunt." He flips the knife clutching it by the blade. Blood drips from his palm, splattering on my inner thigh. He presses the handle against my core. "And I'm going to ruin you for them."

The bruising from Davis' attack is still tender, and even though he's not applying much pressure, it hurts. "You're right about Jack," I say, trying not to pass out from the pain. Desperation licks up my spin, and I talk. I say anything and everything—something to slow this down. "He doesn't love me. I am just a plaything. I always have been, but the best way to destroy my brother isn't by killing me."

"No?" His lips curve, patronizingly. "Tell me, Katherine, what do you think would destroy your brother more than coming home to your mutilated body."

"My betrayal." It comes out in a rush, and it hangs between us like a bomb of truth. It forces Derek to pause, leaving the handle of the knife between my legs in warning. "They think they have me right where they want me. They got me to come out of witness protection. I lied in court to free Jack. I ruined my reputation to keep their secret. They trained and conditioned me. Got me to kill a man. Showed me their hiding places. Taught me their kinks and secrets." Derek has stilled and I sense he's listening—really listening. I continue, "They *think* they created this person—this doll they can use and abuse—that will do anything and everything they want."

"But..." he says, prompting me to finish.

"But what if I've been in control this entire time? Getting them to do my bidding. Exposing them to my kinks. Wrapping them around my little finger." My range is limited, but I manage to spread my legs a bit wider, pressing my cunt against the handle of the blade. "They didn't convince me to allow them to hurt me. I convinced *them* to hurt *me*, Derek." I lick my lip. "Because I like it."

His gaze drags from the knife, up my body, to my face. Our eyes meet.

"Do you know how bad it'll hurt them to know I betrayed them? With you?" I laugh, thinking about it. "You don't have to kill me, doctor, but I'm okay if you want to hurt me a little bit, and then together, we can destroy the Davenports, once and for all."

Derek stands over me, his warm, bloody hand between my thighs, considering my offer. My belly flutters, and nervous energy coursing through my bloodstream. "If we did this," he says slowly, "and I mean *if*, you become mine."

"All yours to play with however you want."

"And we'll destroy the Davenports," he confirms.

Because that's what this is all about—getting back at Montie for taking Olivia from him all those years ago.

"I'm wet just thinking about it."

He pulls the handle of the knife back from my core and guides his hand to my face, running bloody fingertips down my cheek. "Fuck, you're a terror. A beautiful nightmare."

"And you're the handsome doctor. A real man. I'm tired of playing with boys." I lean into his palm. "But to do this, you're going to have to trust me, and let me off this table."

I've laid my case out for him, and told him everything that he needs to know to take me up on my offer. He rubs his bloody thumb over my lip and I give him what he wants, darting my tongue out to taste it. A smile teases at his lip, and his next movement is swift.

"God, you're good." And in a blink, I know I lost him. I pushed too far. The blade flashes to my left, moving with such speed that I wait for the impact. It never comes, although I do hear the *snick* of the blade cutting through my binds. "Such a good, good, girl."

I hold in the exhale, but he continues to undo my restraints. My wrists, my legs, he pulls me to a sitting position, my body weak from the poison. "Thank you."

"We're going to do such bad things together, Katherine." He grins. "You and I are going to destroy this family, one by one. Higgins will spend his life in the same prison as all the men he sent away, and my poor boy, Paul...well, he should've been smarter than to leave himself so exposed. I raised him better than that."

I tilt my face and I smile up at him. "I can't wait."

SEVENTEEN

Jack

"WE'RE GOING TO DO SUCH BAD THINGS TOGETHER, *Katherine," Derek says. "You and I are going to destroy this family, one by one."*

Betrayal.

That's all I think as I hear Paul's father speak to my stepsister.

Fucking betrayed.

I yank my gun out of the waistband of my jeans and step into the kitchen. "You fucking whore."

The two of them, the two lying, betraying, motherfucking assholes swing their eyes in my direction.

"Jack." Katie turns to face me. She's pale. Half-naked. Covered in blood. But that's not what rocks me. It's the scene. The tabletop. The binds dangling from the end. The knife in Derek's hand.

The familiarity is like a kick in the teeth.

"Katie?" Oliver steps into the room, his own pistol drawn. "What the hell is going on?"

"It was you," Paul says, entering the opposite door. Davis is with him, gun trained on Katie and Derek. But when he speaks again, it's to address his father. "You set me up."

I blink, trying to process the scene in front of me. The replicated murder scene. My stepsister's agreement to destroy the family. Paul's accusation. It's impossible to sort through. Not while my heart and soul are cracking in half.

"Son," Derek says, "you were sloppy. Too obsessed with Katherine's cunt to think about the consequences."

"You set me up!" Paul shouts, a different sort of rage coursing through him. It's deep-set and raw. He tilts his head to Katie. "And you were in on it?"

Katie doesn't speak. She looks like a deranged monster—hair matted, blood slicked. Her fingers coil around the edge of the table, as if she's trying to hold herself up. Finally, she says, "Your father's right. You shouldn't have been so sloppy." She touches Derek's chest and pouts. "Weak too. Like a little boy looking for approval, with the way he was obsessed with cleaning me up. Taking care of me. I wonder what's the psychology behind that. Oedipus complex?" Her eyes shift between me and Oliver. "Although that sounds more like you two." She laughs. "Don't think that every time we fucked, I didn't know you were imaging me as your mother."

Oliver's reaction is feral, unhinged. He throws himself at Katie, barreling into her so hard that she's knocked away from Derek and onto the floor in a hard pile. His hands wrap around her wrists, and his legs straddle her body, pinning her to the ground. "Shut your whore mouth!"

The rage I feel matches my brothers', but it builds differently. It's slow. White-hot. Controlled. I look back to the man standing in the middle of the room. The man I know understand is the killer I've been hunting my entire life. The man that killed my mother.

"It was you," I say, through clenched teeth. "You killed her."

"I did," he admits casually. "My greatest moment."

"And you came here to kill Katie?" Davis asks from the doorway. He hasn't moved an inch, although his eyes are calculating, assessing the room. He assured us he wasn't betraying us, but now?

I don't know who to trust.

"She was getting too close. But you know that, right, Davis? She was getting too close to all of us."

"Don't listen to him," Paul says. "He's trying to mess with your head."

"Me?" Derek says. "I'm just here to finish the job—if anything you should thank me. She was prepared to sell you out in a heartbeat."

He's still holding that knife, but I see that the blood dripping down his arm is his—not Katie's. Did she get the best of him? My eyes flick to my girl. Who's playing who?

Who's the hunter and who's the prey?

"She's right though," Derek says. "She's just like your mother. A liar. A whore. Conniving, using her pussy to control the men around her. She fooled me. Fooled your father. Just like Katherine when she walked back in the door. She's got you so twisted up; you can't see straight." He crosses over to Oliver and says, "Son, let her up. Let me finish what I started." He looks up at me. "If you play nice, I'll let you watch."

Oliver and Katie both glance back at me. Him for direction. Her to plead.

"Jack, please. I just told him what he needed to hear. Whatever I could do to buy some time."

Is she lying? I have no clue. I can't read these people anymore. Not my friends. Not my family. I'm lost in a sea of hurt and anger. So, I do the only thing I know that'll set us back on the right course.

"Ollie." I jerk my chin. "Give her to him."

"What?" Paul's voice is alarmed.

"Let him do what we couldn't," I say. "Because we should have killed her the first night she came back here when we caught her snooping upstairs."

"Jack's right," Davis says. "She's nothing but trouble."

My brother doesn't release her right off, leaning over her battered body to whisper something in her ear. A goodbye? An apology. He's always been too fucking compassionate, but he stands, lifting her off the floor by the throat.

"Take her," Ollie says, voice full of pained disgust. He shoves her forward and she stumbles toward Derek, hand out. He moves to catch her, but neither of us realizes that she's got something clutched in her other hand.

Not until it's too late.

The blade sinks deep in his belly.

He gasps, eyes wide, and she digs it in with a twist. "Fuck you, you murdering asshole. You think I'm going to betray my family? These people mean everything to me. They're my love and my light, the reason I get up in the morning." Blood gushes from the wound, coating her hand. "I'm a Davenport, through and through. We all are."

Derek blinks, gaze shifting to his son. "Paul—"

But his son doesn't go to his father's aid. Instead, he steps next to Katie, hand wrapping over hers. His long fingers curl around the hilt of the knife. He looks down at Katie, his eyes searching hers for a second before he murmurs, "I love you." And in one savage, swift move, yanks the blade up, just like we taught her, gutting Derek's insides.

She pushes up on her toes and kisses Paul's jaw. "I love you, too."

Together, they yank the knife out of his father and Derek collapses to the ground. Blood pools around him as he jerks and shudders. His wide eyes fixed on his son. Oliver approaches Katie, wrapping his arm around her waist. "Thanks for the knife, big brother. I was so scared he'd see me get it out of your boot."

Everything moves in slow motion like I'm trapped under water. I glance at Davis, and he looks the same; confused relief etched on his face, but he's in motion, taking off his jacket and wrapping it around Katie's body. My mind is a mash-up of images. Memories of finding my mother here. Then Katie. Then her betrayal? Derek's admission.

His body bleeds out on the floor.

I stare at it, trying to make sense of what just happened.

Katie looks over her shoulder and says, "Jack? Are you okay?"

I shake my head because that's the only thing I know how to do.

Am I, okay?

I don't fucking think I am.

I DON'T LOOK BACK as I walk upstairs, but I know she's there, following me. She makes no effort to skip the creaky step, and I make no effort to acknowledge her. She never should have come back here. I never should have let this woman in my heart. In my goddamn bed.

Fucking hell—at the landing I swing around and stare down at her. She's looks like a nightmare. Derek's blood splattered across her skin. She looks tiny with Davis' jacket hanging over her narrow shoulders. She looks like a terror.

She fucking gorgeous.

"You know the rule." I cross my arms over my chest. "Stay the fuck out of the top floor."

She looks at me, eyes wide with trauma and murder. "I don't think you mean that, big brother."

"I think I do." I take step down, hoping the move will intimidate her to leave. I want her gone. I want the sight of her. The smell of her. I want the *everything* of her to get out of my life, because she fucks with my head. My heart. My aching, deceiving balls. "I should have killed you the first night you came home."

"You could have," she says, licking her bottom lip. "Why didn't you?"

She's always like this: taunting and teasing. Playing games. How do I know what's real and what isn't? After what I just heard in the kitchen...one minute she was selling us out, setting us up with the doctor. The next...

Well, the blood on the bridge of her nose tells the rest of that story.

The problem is that I thought I was in charge. In that kitchen, I thought Derek had control. But neither of those things was true. We're all puppets. And this little wisp of a woman is our master.

Fucking hell.

"Why?" Katie asks, taking a step toward me. My heart hammers as she gets closer. "Why didn't you kill me that first night?"

"Oliver wouldn't let me."

Her eyebrow lifts at the same time she takes another step closer. "Is that so?"

We both know that's bullshit. I try again. "Dad...your mom, there would have been too many questions."

"Mmhmm." We're even on the step now. "There probably would have been, but still..."

I try not to absorb her. Not to look at her, to *smell* her. I fight it, but fail, inhaling her scent. It's a mix of sweat and blood and that sweet-smelling shampoo she wears. Her tits taunt me, the shadow of them just beneath the opening of Davis' jacket. Her pussy, still sore from Davis' brutality, is bare. My cock thickens from the assault on my senses. I shake my head. "Don't do this, Katie. Don't make me do something I'll regret."

"Our entire lives are built on regret, Jack." Her hand presses against my chest. "From the first moment I met you, I knew you would be the end of me—but I couldn't keep away. Not then. Not now. Not after everything we've been through."

I want to believe her—to fall for this fairytale—but she lies so easily. To the cops, to the judge, to Derek. She'll do anything to get her way. How do I know this isn't just more lies? That I won't wake up with a blade buried in my chest?

Fuck. Despite all my doubts, my cock is even harder than before.

She looks down, noticing the hard bulge of my erection. Her hand slips over it and she says, "You want me."

I shudder an exhale and admit, "Want and trust are two different things. I don't trust you."

Her neck tilts, eyes meeting mine. "See that's the thing, brother, I think you *can* trust me and that's what scares the shit out of you. You can trust me to have your back. To kill a man. To hide the evidence. To fight every goddamn time to come back home so you can fuck me any way you want."

"I'm not scared of anything."

She takes one more step, higher this time, forcing our eyes level. "You're scared of *us*. Loving me. Loving Oliver, Paul, and Davis." My hand moves on its own volition, sliding under the jacket, fingers trailing the sticky skin until I'm cupping her breast. "You're scared of happiness, Jack. The one thing you've been missing since your mother died. Since you started this mission." She's so close I feel the warmth of her breath on my cheek. "Well, mission accomplished. You're free. We're free."

Her words trigger something deep in my chest and my heart doesn't just pound, it cracks like an earthquake just rumbled through a fault line.

Happiness? Is that a thing? Something real? Something not made up by movies and children's books? Something that gets snatched away by a madman, leaving it bloody and discarded in the kitchen?

"I love you, Jackson Davenport, and I make it *my* mission to show you that for the rest of my life."

I run my hand behind her neck, pulling her face to mine. Foreheads touching, lips a breath apart, I ask, "And you'll never leave?"

Her lips brush against mine and she promises, "Never."

All the emotion I'm holding, the anger, the rage, the grief, surges out of me and I crash my mouth against Katie's. I fuck my tongue into her mouth. She takes it, takes me, the hard kiss, the hungry desire, moaning back.

I pull apart, breathless, and say, "I want to fuck you. I want to be inside you but..."

She's hurt. And I don't want to hurt her anymore. Not tonight.

"Just take me to bed, big brother. I'm sure we can figure something out."

My cock twitches. My heart thuds. Christ, this girl. This *woman.*

I lift her into my arms, kissing her the entire time, taking the path to my room by memory. At the door, she pulls away. "You sure this is okay? Because we can start this somewhere else—somewhere away from Davenport Manor." She searches my face. "There are so many ghosts here. Derek is the one that said it first, 'this house isn't kind to women.'"

"Babe," I say, cradling her in my arms, "I lost my heart in this house, but I also found it here again. These walls are steeped in blood, violence, and sex. This house made me who I am. It made *us.* I want you here. I want all of us here. In my room. In my bed. Fucking my brother and my best friends. Having our babies." Her jaw drops. "Yeah, I want Davenport babies. A fuck ton of them."

"Well," she says, linking her arms around my neck. "I guess we better get started."

EIGHTEEN

Kate

"YOU BETRAYED US." DAVIS STARES INTO MY EYES.

"You betrayed *us, too.*" I counter.

We're at a stalemate. Two deceivers. Two lovers. How could we ever tell the truth? Simple. We go back to who we are. The game we play. The emotions we toy with.

"Katie—" he starts.

Before he finishes, I lash out, my palm aimed for his cheek. But he catches my hand in an instant, his strong fingers close tight around my wrist. There's a savagery in his stare. A bottomless emptiness that calls to me. He is different from the others. He hits me in a way I can't comprehend and it's not just the degradation, not just the way my pulse races and I get wet when he handles me rough.

But it's this...this *fixation.*

As though nothing else exists. We're alone. The guys wanted to be here, and I sense Jack behind the walls, listening...waiting for Davis to step out of line. But I needed to talk to him in semi-privacy, to see if we can get on the same page and salvage this.

It's been twenty-four hours since I killed Derek in the kitchen. The house reeks of bleach and all the windows are open, letting it air out.

Another man is missing.

And the detective took care of it, of *me*, like he always does.

Davis's grip tightens around my waist and his dark stare bores into mine as he snarls, "Whore."

"Bastard." I counter back, feeling the warm heat pool between my legs. "No more batons."

Recognition flickers in his eyes and he nods slowly. "No more batons, not unless..."

"I want it," I supply. Because he's right. I like it when he manhandles me. Surprises me. "Also, I want..." I try to find the courage to say what comes next. "I want to go on dates."

Surprise brightens his stare even as his brow creases. "Dates?"

In the quickening of my pulse, I repeat, "Yeah, dates."

That frown deepens, before finally. "Okay. Dates."

"And flowers."

His lips curl as she shakes his head. "You trying to tame me, woman?"

"Being a bit more civilized never hurt anyone."

He grunts. "What kind of goddamn flowers?"

"I like daisies."

He yanks me closer until I slam against his hard chest. He's all brutality now, pushed to the edge of his comfort and this is where I intend to keep him. He can use me. He can degrade me. He can fuck me with so much ferocity that it takes me a day to sit properly. But I want pretty flowers after it and maybe one day for him to tell me he loves me.

"Fine," he answers, breath hot on my ear. "Anything else?"

"Maybe some choc—" I start, and his hand leaves my wrist to grip the back of my neck.

He jerks my head upwards. "Don't push it sweet, Katie."

And here is where I reach his limit...*for now.*

"There is one thing I need to do," he says, giving me a long, lingering stare for a heartbeat longer than necessary. I can't help but smile a little when he lets me go. I have him and he knows it.

"It's time to tell the FBI that I'm not interested in working with them."

"Are you sure?" Even though it's caused us problems, a job with the FBI is a big promotion. It's the kind of opportunity that changes a career. "I'm sure we can figure something out."

He shrugs. "I have figured it out. I want to be here. With you— with my boys. We're family and if I've learned anything the past few years it's that there are enough monsters close to home to keep me busy. I don't need to go anywhere else to do my work."

His eyes flick over my shoulder and I see that Jack has opened the panel, stepping out of the passageway.

I wrap my arms around my body, and in that moment, I feel peace. Safe. I feel us. We let too many people get between us. Our family. Killers. Police...but I see now that we're enough.

This connection that roars between us, drowning everything else out.

"Are we good?" Jack asks, keeping an eye on Davis. It's going to take him a while to trust him completely, especially when it comes to me.

"Yeah," I reply, "We're good."

And in this moment, we are...finally.

PTSD IS A BITCH.

"Hey." Oliver's blue eyes peer down at me. "You okay?"

"Yeah." My voice is groggy. The poison is out of my system now, but the side effects are lingering. I've been sleeping longer —deeper.

"Another nightmare?" he asks. There's a book in his hand. I glance across the living room at the television. I must've fallen asleep during the movie.

"I guess." I only remember flickers of the dreams. I just wake up feeling like I'm running for my life. Sometimes it's Derek. Other times Ryan or Christopher. I know we got the best of these assholes but still, the trauma they inflicted is real. I check the time. It's after midnight. "Are they back, yet?"

Jack and Davis are following up on a report Davis got at work about a guy they think is stalking an elementary school teacher. It's the first time they've gone out since everything happened with Derek. I wanted to go with them, but they suggested we take it slow for now. After all, it's an easy job, just some recon.

"They're fine." He strokes my hair. "I just texted Jack a minute ago. They should be home soon."

I fight off the shiver, but I can't get warm. I curl into him, inhaling his warm, clean, scent. Beneath my cheek I feel the hard press of his cock. My mouth waters and I look up at him again. I don't have to ask.

"You need me?"

I nod, already reaching for his button. "If that's okay?"

"Always, babe." His thumb brushes over my bottom lip, tugging my mouth open. "Whenever you need."

It's a relief when he's finally in my mouth, the salty, velvet tip, tucked between my lips. This ritual started as another one of Oliver's exhibitionist needs, and turned into our closest act of intimacy.

He no longer denies me the gift of sucking him off, but it's still not the point of these moments. I'm soothed by the feel of him in my mouth. I've finally settled down when I hear footsteps in the hall, followed by Paul's voice.

"Everything okay?"

"Another nightmare," Oliver says, running his hand over my back. His cock thickens in my mouth, the reaction to being caught. My tongue laps up the pool of pre-cum that oozes from the tip. "You know how it is when we're not all here at night."

"Poor thing," Paul says. He sits next to Oliver, pulling my legs in his lap. "Going to your brother for comfort is a good thing. It's a coping mechanism and I'm proud of you two for working something out." His hand glides over my hip. "Would it help relieve your stress if I stimulated you right now?"

I kiss the tip of Oliver's cock, before I rise to a partial sitting position. "I can't ask you to do that. I should be making you feel better."

He hasn't mentioned Derek's death more than a few times, but I know it's weighing on him.

"Taking care of you is what makes me feel better, Katherine. You know that."

I lean forward and kiss him, pushing my tongue against his. He kisses me back, sweet but strong. These men, they spoil me.

I curl back on their laps, taking Oliver back in my mouth. Paul pulls down my leggings, hand running over my backside, finger playing with my puckered ridge. I was wet enough before Paul got here, but the way he touches me—the way he coaxes my body—sends a new wave of heat between my legs. "Your pussy is the most beautiful thing I've ever seen," he says, pushes his finger inside.

The sensation is so good, so right, that I pant out, "Oh God," around Oliver's hard erection.

"That feel good, Katherine?" Oliver asks, fingers winding in my hair.

"So good." I'm no longer suckling Oliver's cock, but deep throating his length. I shift, getting up on my knees, wanting to taste him better. "Inside," I beg Paul. "Your cock, I need it."

He moves quickly, hiking my hips in the air, the rustle of his trousers as they drop. Oliver moves in front of me, knees bent, cock thrusting into my mouth. I gasp when Paul enters me, the feeling of fullness exactly what I crave. It chases the nightmares away, the darkness that lurks in the corners of my mind.

In this moment it's just us, our bodies, our lust and our love.

That feeling is what triggers my orgasm, my pussy clenching around Paul's cock at the same time Oliver groans, sending hot cum pouring into my mouth.

"Fuck," Paul grunts, his hips slamming against my backside, the final thrust so deep, it sends me into Oliver's arms. "Christ."

We fall into a pile of sticky warmth. Our chests rise and fall, a feeble attempt to catch our breaths.

"Better?" Oliver asks, pushing a strand of hair off my forehead.

"Yep." I kiss him. Then kiss Paul. An idea comes to mind—well to be fair, they're never far from my mind. Ever.

"Do you think we should go find them?" I ask, looking between them. "I mean, they may need our help."

Oliver's eyes dart to Paul, who is busy cleaning between my legs. "What do you think?"

"It's not a bad idea," he admits, balling up my panties. "They could probably use our help."

I hop off the couch, going for the door. I feel a surge of energy that only comes from one thing: hunting.

Paul raises his eyebrow and asks, "Where are you going?"

I grin back. "To get my knife."

Epilogue

KATE

"KATIE..." JACK STARTS.

"No." I watch the headlights flare behind us in the distance.

"If you just..."

I cut my stepbrother a glare. That dark, broody stare seizes mine as he climbs out of the driver's side. "I don't like this."

"I know." I close the passenger's door behind me. "But I have to do this. You know that."

There's a curl of his lips. A savage snarl. If Jack had his way, this would be a carjacking in the middle of nowhere. One that'd leave my target stabbed and bleeding out in a matter of seconds. But the cops would come and an investigation would be underway. The kind of investigation Davis wouldn't be able to control. No, we didn't want that. *I* didn't want that. That wasn't how I hunted.

It didn't *scratch the itch*.

I needed them to know, to understand...

To look into their eyes as it slowly dawned on them that they were never *ever* doing the vile things they craved again. Jack understood this, but that didn't mean he had to like it.

He gives a nod and headlights from Ollie's car flash from under the towering Ash trees at our right. "You need to go." I glance at the approaching car.

"I'll be right there," he says. "If anything happens."

I know he will be. But I won't need it. "Go." I urge and round to the back of the car, stab the button on Jack's keys, and pull the empty gas can from the back.

The holographic Baby on Board sign wobbles, but holds tight as I slam the trunk closed. Jack takes off at a slow jog, heading to where Ollie is hidden from view.

Orange hazard lights blink in the dead of the night as I step away from Jack's Audi parked on the edge of the road and start walking. The *click...click...click* from the signal muffles the sound of my heels crunching on the asphalt as I head for the service station in the distance.

This stretch of road is long...and isolated. But it's not long before the faint spill of headlights grows brighter behind me and my target nears.

I tug the leather jacket higher, still the satin dress barely warms me against the cold night breeze, sending a shiver along my spine. One careful glance toward the towering Ash trees and I find Jack as he climbs into Ollie's gray Mercedes and closes the door.

They are there, watching and waiting.

Making sure this doesn't get out of hand.

They don't like this...

Especially Jack.

He doesn't want me hunting alone. But alone is exactly what I need to appear. A young, helpless mother desperate to get back to her children. The faint growl of the Chrysler's engine grows louder. I know instantly the moment he sees the baby on board sticker placed in the back window of Jack's car.

Red brake lights flare as the Chrysler shoots past. My heart pounds as a rush hits me a little harder than ever before. The knife strapped to my inner thigh grazes with every step I take. But it's not the knife I care about, it's the small plastic syringe I narrow in on.

The scrape of the plunger is all I feel as the Chrysler comes to a stop on the shoulder of the road in front of me.. I glance nervously at the Chrysler as I near.

The number plates are government issue, letting me know exactly who I was dealing with. Senator Brandon Coleman wasn't like the other predators that we watch. No, this one is quiet and controlled. This one played the long game and right now that long game is Marisa Honeycut and her two young, unsuspecting children.

Children who will be safe after tonight.

Because I'd make sure of it.

The passenger side window rolls down as I approach. It's dark inside the car, but still, I find the outline of his face and catch the glint of those dark, beady eyes as Brandon calls out. "Can I help?"

I force myself to nervously glance inside. "No, thank you. So stupid of me to run out of gas in the middle of the night and tonight of all nights while the babysitter waits for me."

"Suit yourself," he mutters. Those hungry eyes take in my satin dress as the leather jacket slips.

I know what I look like. I look like her, his latest victim from a line of beaten women. I'm dark haired and sexy, just like Marisa Honeycut was on the first night he saw her. Young, free. A single mother on her first night out after her cheating husband left her. Only she didn't look like that anymore. Now she was careful and quiet...hiding the bruises on her face behind the oversized sunglasses she wore. She and her two children, Lilly and Tailor ages seven and eight, both stayed at home where no one could witness the sudden change from happy go-lucky children, to the thin, withdrawn ghosts they were now.

He beats them. That I knew.

I could still hear the screams. Still see their faces as I watched them the following days after the latest attack. I still saw the dark, empty stare moving into their eyes as I stopped and remarked what beautiful children they were in the middle of the aisle as they shopped. It was the same dark stare I saw in Jack.

A broken stare...

One that Paul assured would ease...*after tonight.*

"Wait..." I call out as the Chrysler inches forward. I give a wince of a smile. "The truth is...I'm broke. I spent the last money I had on the babysitter. I know it's stupid, but I just wanted to go out once, just feel...*alive.*"

The engine throbs.

His stare is heavy.

I glance toward the service station. "I was hoping they'd take pity on me and let me come back when I got paid."

"They won't," he answers, leaning across to push open the door once more. "But I will. Hop in and I'll drive you home."

Of course he'll drive me home.

He wants to see the kids, right?

I yank open the door and stop. "You're not a murderer or anything are you? You can't be too careful out here."

He laughs and that throaty sound carries. "No, I'm not a murderer. I'm a Senator, if that makes you feel better."

"Oh." I climb in and lift the gas can into the back. "I thought you looked familiar."

The door closes behind me with a thud. I risk a glance behind us to where Ollie's gray car waits and give the address to the Davenport house.

I lower my hand to the slip of my dress, watching for any sign of recognition. My pulse booms as he turns the wheel, swinging the car back around and heads for home.

Montie and mom are away and have been for the past month. The stress of what happened in the house by Paul's father finally tipped Mom over the edge. After a complete breakdown, Paul managed to get her into a treatment facility. Montie booked into an exclusive club not far from where she was just to be close to her.

She's getting the help she needs, which I'm thankful for. If the trauma over the last few months has shown me anything, it's that there's nothing more important than family.

It's family that drives me now. Mine—I glance toward the Senator—and Marisa Honeycut's.

Familiar houses come into view as I turn back. We turn into our street. My gaze instantly moves to the black Range Rover parked outside the house.

"Here we are," Brandon murmurs looking up at the towering house. His eyes widen when he looks down at me. "You live here?"

"For the time being. I'm housesitting for my parents." That part is the truth. "My partner kicked us out, so my kids and I have nowhere else to go and there's plenty of room."

"Of course." Brandon pulls up.

"They've been away for the last six months." I look from the house to him. "It's big and lonely."

"Apart from the children," he answers, those dark eyes glinting a little brighter.

"Apart from the children," I repeat, then quietly, "You're more than welcome to come in for a drink if you want."

He gives a strange smile. "It's late."

I nod, but inside I'm panicking. "Of course."

I reach for the handle.

"Maybe just one? Just to make sure you get inside okay."

I turn back to him, beaming. "I'd really like that."

I know once inside, he'll change. Out here he's careful, controlled. But behind closed doors...well, that's a whole new beast. I barely glance at the Range Rover as I climb out. I'm watching now, toying with him. "I can't thank you enough. I mean, the chances of me finding a nice guy in the middle of the night were slim."

He climbs out, then opens the rear door and grabs the empty fuel can before following me up the driveway to the front door. The heavy thud of his steps echoes behind me. I'm aware of everything. His focus, his breath, the distance between us as I fumble with the keys in the lock, rattling them before I step inside.

The house is filled with darkness. Floorboards creak from his weight until the rustle of plastic muffles the sound. The Senator looks down, concerned as he moves in. But he's too busy making plans to think about anything other than working out if me and my kids are the perfect replacement for the woman whose life he's almost destroyed.

He's too busy lifting his gaze higher to the floors above to notice me reaching under the slip of my dress to grasp the syringe. Shadows shift. I sense Davis before I see him. But he makes no move to step in, just watches intently as I lift the syringe to my mouth and bite down on the plastic sheath, drawing the needle free.

"Your kids must be asleep...as well as the babysitter." Brandon turns toward me.

I move fast, grab him, and pull him close. "Yes." I jab the needle into his neck and drive the plunger down, pushing the drug all the way into his bloodstream. "They must be."

The Senator's eyes widen. He slaps his hand against his neck and looks down to the needle as I step backwards.

Only now does Davis move. He hits the light switch for the living room and the space is illuminated in the soft white glow as he comes toward me with Paul close behind.

The thud of the front door sounds behind me. They are with me: Jack, Ollie, Davis, and Paul. Closing in like a pack of predators. Because that's what we are now. *We are the hunters and men like Brandon are the prey.*

"What...*what the fuck is g-g-going on-n-n.*" Senator Coleman slurs staring at the men behind me. "You can-n-n't do-o-o this-s-s-s...you can-n-n-n't."

"We aren't doing anything," Jack answers carefully as I reach under my dress once more and pull out my knife. "Our stepsister on the other hand...well, you know what they say. *What Katie wants...Katie gets.*"

The Senator's eyes widen as he turns back to me. His legs wobble, one knee collapses, sending him crashing to the ground. I shrug the leather jacket free, dropping it behind me, and reach for the thin straps of my dress.

"Wh-what the *fuck* are you d-d-doooing?"

"First rule," I murmur and clench the knife as my dress drops to the floor at my feet. "Never bloody anything you're not prepared to burn."

"Bloody?" He gasps, fighting to stay conscious now as I step forward, dragging the blade back in the air.

"You'll never hurt them again," I whisper. "Do you hear me? You'll *never* hurt anyone *ever* again."

I drive the blade down. The first blow glances off his collar bone, tearing open his skin. He opens his mouth to scream, but Jack is there in an instant, lunging forward, slamming his hand over his mouth as he steps around, holding him steady as I set to work.

Not once does he look away from me. Not once does he flinch as I swing my arm through the air and strike down again and again. Warmth splashes across my belly and dribbles down my thighs. I don't stop, not until his chest no longer rises and his glazed stare is fixed. Only then does Davis near and drop to the ground in front of him, pushing his hand into his pocket before taking out his keys.

"I'll take care of the car. You take care of the body."

Ollie nods as Davis rises. My breaths are fast and the pounding of my heart leaves little room to hear anything else. But I hear Davis as he comes closer, grips the back of my head and pulls me close. "You did well, Katie...*very, very well.* I'll be back as soon as I can. When I do, I plan on fucking you raw."

My pussy clenches with the words. I look down to the still body even as Ollie starts to undress. "Better hurry the fuck up, then." Ollie urges. "You know how our little sister can get."

Davis is gone in a heartbeat, leaving me to watch as one by one my men come for me.

"You did so well tonight," Jack whispers, reaching out to caress my breast. "So very, *very well.*"

Paul approaches, his electric blue eyes are neon bright in the gloom, "Such a good little hunter." His thumb pushes at the button of my pants, fingers forcing themselves inside. "Still gets you wet and horny, doesn't it?"

"Always," I confess, bucking into his hand.

"How do you want it?" Jack whispers as he reaches for the knife. "You want the doctor to eat you out or do you want me to fuck you with the knife?"

I smile. My men know me so well and I tell them the truth, "Both."

"Anything you want, little sister, you deserve it."

My heart beats a million miles an hour as I succumb to them. Giving myself over to the feeling. To the warmth, to the sensation as I draw in a hard gasp as they descend on me.

This is how it will be now.

Killing.

Fucking.

Them.

And me.

Always.

Afterword

Thanks for going on this journey with us! We wanted to test out the serialized writing format on Vella as well push ourselves with an over the top, serial killer romance! #goals

Don't forget to follow us on social media or check out our other books!

Both Angel & AK's other dark romances can be found on Amazon. If you'd like to follow them more closely for updates, new releases and news check out them out on social media!

Angel Lawson
Facebook
TikTok
Instagram

AK Rose
Website

Afterword

Facebook
TikTok
Instagram